A Baby to Die For

❖ ❖ ❖

Mike Slosberg

©2014
Nightengale Press
A Nightengale Media LLC Company

A Baby to Die For

For information about Nightengale Press please
visit our website at www.nightengalepublishing.com.
Email: publisher@nightengalepress.com

Library of Congress Cataloging-in-Publication Data

Slosberg, Mike,
A BABY TO DIE FOR/ Mike Slosberg
ISBN 13: 978-1-935993-64-3
Fiction

Copyright Registered: 2014
First Published by Nightengale Press in the USA

August 2014

10 9 8 7 6 5 4 3 2 1

Printed in the USA and the UK

*For Sam and Florence, who taught me all they knew about life,
then set me loose to make my own mistakes.*

OTHER WORKS BY THE AUTHOR

Mike Slosberg's other published works include:

THE AUGUST STRANGERS, a novel

THE HITLER ERROR, a novel

PIMP MY WALKER—
The Official Book of Old Age Haiku

SEVEN STORIES TO READ
BEFORE THEY BECOME MOVIES

KLANDESTINED, a cartoon book

A BABY TO DIE FOR is his third novel.

All six titles are available in print from the Author at
www.mikeslosbergbooks.com, on Amazon.com, BN.com
and many other websites around the world.

All three novels
are available as eBooks on
www.mikeslosbergbooks.com, on Amazon.com, BN.com
and many other websites around the world.

For larger or specialty print orders,
please contact the publisher at:
publisher@nightengalepress.com
for discount pricing

"*Twenty years ago, in an outbuilding of his Southern California estate, tycoon Robert K. Graham began a most remarkable project: the Repository for Germinal Choice, a sperm bank for Nobel Prize winners. Part altruism, part social engineering, part science experiment, the repository was supposed to help reverse the genetic decay Graham saw all around him by preserving and multiplying the best genes of his generation. By the time Graham's repository closed in 1999, his genius sperm had been responsible for more than 200 children.*"

—Chess Plotz, *Slate*, February 2001

"*Over 700,000 women are taken prisoner each year in the worldwide network of human trafficking. Approximately 50,000 of these women end up in the United States.*"

—Heather Leah, "America's Modern Day Slave Trade: Human Trafficking in the Sex Industry," *Yahoo! Voices*, August 2006

Chapter 1

Alamogordo, New Mexico, 1972

A lone, mud-spattered Mercedes 280SL sped south along a two-lane ribbon of blacktop, whipping up a rooster tail of sand as it traveled the scarred and cracked road stretching for miles in both directions. Across much of the road's surface tiny dust devils swirled in the strong winds blowing north from Mexico. The narrow road showed as a thin, red line on the map.

Inside the car, a brunette in her early forties groaned as her head slumped back against the soft leather headrest.

"I think I'm going to puke from reading this damned thing," Helen Kaufman said, tossing the unfolded road map to the carpeted floor of the car.

A forty-something, balding and slightly overweight Mark Kaufman momentarily took his eyes off the road to glance at his wife as he slowed down enough to pull off the road.

"Maybe I can figure out where the hell we are. Close

your eyes and breathe through your mouth and you'll feel better."

Helen, eyes shut, mumbled, "It's the right road. I'll be okay. Just keep driving."

"What if we missed it? I can't see shit with this damned sand blowing all over," he said, pushing down the irritated frustration he was feeling.

"Please, honey, don't stop. I'm sure we haven't passed it. The note said not to be late. Keep driving."

He ignored her and took his foot off the accelerator.

"I can see a crossroad up ahead. I'm stopping. It's no big goddamned deal if we're a couple minutes late. I'd like to see anyone make it all the way out here from New York and be exactly on time—fat chance. And this fucking sand isn't helping. I wouldn't be surprised if it eats the paint right off the car," Mark said, only half-joking.

As he spoke, Mark Kaufman steered onto the bumpy shoulder of the road and stopped. The wind swirled dust and sand around the filthy car, adding still another layer of grime to the already dirt-caked vehicle. Even the New York license plates were barely visible beneath a coating of the thick New Mexico dust.

Once stopped, Mark easily found their exact location on the map. His finger traced the fine red line from the crossroad where they were now parked, to the spot on the map circled with black magic marker.

Max Garfield left the map for the Kaufmans at the front desk of the Holiday Inn in Albuquerque. The adoption lawyer's phone call came over a week ago, just as they were preparing to leave for a long overdue Caribbean vacation. The call took them completely by surprise. Arranging a month off for a busy vascular surgeon is not a simple thing, and it took half a day to cancel their hotel reservations and airline tickets. They lost a few hundred dollars in hotel deposits, but it was worth it. They were finally getting the baby they'd wanted so desperately.

Rather than fly, they decided to drive and turn the trip into a vacation—not just to pick up their baby, but also driving to California and up the coast to San Francisco. They hadn't been in San Francisco since Mark's military tour at the Letterman Army Hospital, and it would be great to see old friends again and to show off their new baby.

"Oh, yeah, we're right on the money," Mark said with the same confident tone of voice he used with his patients before surgery. "Another few miles should do it. Are you feeling better, sweetheart? The sign will be on the right side. You feeling okay to keep an eye out for it?"

"No, really, I'm fine now. I'm so excited I can't believe it's finally happening," she said, kissing him hard. "Aren't you just so damned excited? We're having a baby—of our very own."

Mark kissed his wife—softly, gently, and on each eyelid, ending with another kiss on the tip of her nose. He could feel the curve of her full breast through his skintight driving glove.

Mark nosed the Mercedes back onto the scarred blacktop and picked up speed. The trail of dust rose once again behind them. He hunched over the steering wheel intent on the barely visible road. Helen rested her head against the right side window, peering through the dirty glass, looking for the landmark described in the note accompanying the map. '*Look for a sign depicting a charging red bull,*' it said.

During the long drive west from New York, they discussed Max Garfield's detailed orders—the place where they were to stay in Albuquerque, the map with directions, the note, the specifics about the money, and now the drive to God-only-knows-where, looking for a bull on a damned billboard.

Focusing on the road Mark said, "I have a theory about all of Garfield's mysterious crap."

"Which is?"

"I think he did it on purpose. You know, to make the whole adoption process seem—I don't know—more important. More 'value' for the money—a little theatrical fluff."

Helen thought for a moment. "You may be right, but you know what? I like it—the mystery, you know. Hey, why not? It makes it more fun, like an adventure. Think about the stories. Anybody can talk about the old '*middle of the night drive to the hospital*' chestnut—but *we'll* have a really unique story."

On the other hand, they both knew that what they were doing was a few degrees off the legal mark, and they would have to edit any tales they told about the adoption in the future.

"*There it is!*" Helen cried, like a child seeing Disneyland for the first time. "There's the bull!"

Sure enough, a faded and storm-battered old outdoor

sign appeared through the blowing dust. As Garfield's directions indicated, it showed a giant, red bull charging through the label of a huge package of Red Bull Chewing Tobacco, complete with painted smoke shooting from each angry nostril. The advertisement was old and broken and riddled with bullet holes, made no doubt, by locals using the sign for target practice. Ironically, if not for the holes, which vented the wind and sand, the large surface of painted sheet metal would have blown away long ago.

Fifty yards beyond the sign they saw their destination for the first time—an old, weathered gas station—no brand names or advertising posters touting oil or tires, no fuel prices posted. Just a small, broken down, single-story adobe building, with a lone gas pump standing guard a few yards from the front door. A layer of fine sand coated every visible surface of the place, making it as one with the surrounding desert.

As the Mercedes rolled slowly to a stop, an ageless and weathered woman shuffled out of the building, shielding her face from the relentless wind with the tattered sleeve of her cardigan. She, too, appeared devoid of color.

The old lady approached the car and squinted into the window, inspecting Mark and Helen Kaufman. Then she shuffled to the front of the car and with the edge of her long skirt, rubbed at a thick layer of dirt covering the license plate, just enough to read the numbers. She compared them with those on a small scrap of paper she took from her sweater pocket. With a single nod of her head, she indicated satisfaction and released the paper not bothering to watch as it fluttered out of sight like a little butterfly. She shuffled back to the shack, opened the door, turned, and smiled. Two or three jack-o-lantern-spaced teeth, yellow from age and nicotine, broke the otherwise emptiness of her smile as she beckoned for the Kaufmans to follow.

"Hello," Helen said as she approached, "I'm Mrs. Kaufman and this is my husband, Dr. Kaufman."

The old woman shrugged, saying, "*Yo no hablo Ingles*," in a rasping, smoker's voice.

Inside, the shack was clean, neat, and pleasantly warm. An old army cot sat in one corner covered with a patchwork quilt, faded with age but spotless. An iron stove burned a fragrant smelling wood and on top of the stove a large metal coffeepot was warming. The rich aroma of strong coffee filled the tiny room. A brand new chrome payphone on the wall looked ridiculously out of place. A door next to the phone was partially open and revealed a tiny bathroom with a shower.

The old woman pointed to the opposite side of the room and smiled. There, against the wall stood an old Coca-Cola cooler, its top ajar. Most of the red painted finish had long ago faded, chipped, and peeled from its sides. In the summer, when the cooler was used to keep soda chilled, it stood outside the shack next to the gas pump. Now, washed clean, it was serving quite another purpose.

Mark and Helen, confused at first, stared at the beat-up old cooler. Helen was the first to move, slowly walking to the cooler. Her hand reached out, haltingly, as if she might burn her fingers on the faded red lid. She lifted the top to its full open position so it rested back against the wall, then she reached down, bending from the waist, both arms going down and disappearing deep inside the cooler. When they came up again, they were filled with a soft, pink blanket. Two little arms, covered in tiny, clean, jersey sleeves waved in circles and ovals, and the gurgles of an awaking infant filled the shack. Mark leaned over to see the baby cradled in Helen's arms, but he couldn't see very well, as tears blurred his vision.

Helen cooed, "Hello, Amy. Amy Kaufman. Oh, my God, Mark, she's beautiful!" Helen said, her own tears streaming down her face.

Right now and for all time, the money they had spent for Amy suddenly seemed irrelevant, after all, it was only money and, thank God, they had it. And the baby, *their* baby, was so beautiful, with huge black eyes, clear skin, and thick blond hair already covering her well-formed head. She was everything they had wanted. She was everything Max Garfield had promised—maybe more.

Mark finally tore himself away from looking at the baby, and removed a thick package from inside Helen's shoulder bag and presented it to the old woman. With arthritic hands, she tore open the sealed package and removed the bills—$40,000 in the form of four hundred slightly used hundred-dollar bills—the final payment for their baby.

It took the old woman, mumbling to herself in barely audible Spanish, a long time to count the money. While she did, Mark went outside, filled his car's gas tank, and using a hose, washed road-grime off the windows, then got rid of the accumulated trash from inside the car.

When the old woman finally finished counting and was satisfied it was all as it should be, she placed the bills in a large plastic freezer bag, took it to the refrigerator on the far side of the room, and placed the cash inside.

Moving from the refrigerator, the old woman shuffled back to the cot, reached under, and pulled out a brand new zippered carryall. She opened it and proudly showed the Kaufmans that it was filled with diapers, wipes, baby formula—all the supplies they would need for their new baby, at least for a day or two—enough, at least, to last until they could buy more.

Helen thanked her, then pivoted so the old woman could see the cooing, gurgling child cradled in her arms, and the old woman nodded knowingly, for she had spent several days with the happy baby. Mark paid the woman for the gas, took the bag of supplies, and thanked her.

Mark helped Helen into the car with the baby. Once behind the wheel, he made a U-turn and headed back to the main road where they would eventually connect with the Interstate. The baby had cost the Kaufmans a lot—almost $7,000 a pound! First, there was the check for $10,000—a strictly above board payment up front to Max Garfield. Conversely, the $40,000 in cash, now sitting in a refrigerator not far from the Mexican border, would go where, or to whom, the Kaufmans had no idea, nor did they give a damn. They finally had their baby, and that was all that mattered. Helen held the child in her arms, kissing the top of her little head, talking to her, stroking her. Mark tried glancing over to see his new daughter but was too nervous—convinced a moment's distraction would result in a fiery car crash. He had to be extra careful. They were three now.

The old woman watched the Kaufmans' car disappear into the distance. A tear washed a path in the fine, dry film of dust on her wrinkled cheek. She would miss the baby. It was lonely living alone, tending the station. She hoped maybe the American with the black beard would bring another baby someday soon. It made her days less lonely.

In the car, Helen held the sleeping child safe in her arms while Mark squinted at the road ahead. An equally dirty Avis rental car passed, going in the other direction, its own plume of dust trailing behind it. Mark noticed the driver had a thick black beard.

Given where he was headed, the bearded man at the wheel of the car had to chuckle at the irony of the song playing on the radio, and he happily sang along with Paul Simon belting out *"Mother and Child Reunion,"* while at the same time keeping a sharp lookout for the Red Bull Chewing Tobacco sign. A few minutes later he spotted it and pulled into the ancient service station. His arrival was so close on the heels of the Kaufmans' departure that for a moment the old woman thought the new parents had come back.

Rick Shelby greeted the old woman, using the few words of Spanish he could remember from high school and headed for the refrigerator.

"Can't keep all that lettuce in the refrigerator too long, Mrs. Rodriguez—you'll pardon the pun—or it'll spoil," he continued in English, "besides, I got a plane to catch," he said, handing her a small fee for her baby sitting services. "It was only a few days but you did a great job. It was a pleasure meeting you. Thanks."

The old woman just stared at the bearded lawyer, unable to understand much of anything Rick Shelby was saying. She just missed having the baby to keep her company. It was hard to see Shelby's smile under his thick beard, but it was there nevertheless.

Meanwhile, the newly expanded Kaufman family proceeded happily on their long-overdue California vacation.

Chapter 2

New York City

Iron-cold air flowed off the choppy waters of the Hudson River gathering speed as it pushed through the streets of upper Manhattan. A thin scattering of pre-rush-hour vehicles labored this way and that, trailing white puffs of frosty condensation. Bunches of workers huddled around corner bus stops, some hunched sleepily around steaming take-away cups of hot coffee. Still others shuffled down steps into dim subways.

Two runners jogged across Seventy-second Street, the hoods of their faded sweatshirts drawn tight, exposing as little skin as possible to the frigid air. In that pewter-colored divide between dark and dawn, tiny silver flakes of snow danced around their feet, a frozen hint of more to come.

Ellen and Tuck Handler hadn't exchanged a word since leaving the warmth of their tiny West Side apartment. And even though more than four years of marriage had taught him that Ellen—at twenty-six a year his senior—would talk when she good and ready, Tuck still felt a faint hint of unease. For weeks his instincts had been telling him something was going on with his wife, and whatever it was started around the time he got his gold detective shield.

So Tuck simply mimicked Ellen, stride for stride and silence for silence. Anyway, it was too damn cold to talk.

They were almost home when, on an impulse Ellen spoke, her words puffing out in cadence with their steady running pace.

"Listen, Tuck we've gotta talk."

Tuck responded with a grunt.

"Really—it's important."

"Yeah, okay—so talk."

Ellen Handler stopped in her tracks. Her nose was running, and she wiped it with the back of her glove and bent at the waist, breathing hard, hands on her knees, eyeing her husband as he continued, unaware that he was running alone. Finally realizing, he stopped, turned and jogged back to Ellen, a half-grin plastered across his unshaven morning face.

"What is it sweetheart?"

"I want a baby."

"It's a little cold out here on the street, honey, but I'll sure give it the old college try," Tuck said.

"Tucker, I'm serious!" Ellen said, using his full given name, as she did whenever they were having a serious conversation, or when she was pissed off at him."

Tuck hated when she called him Tucker, and immediately understood that joke-time was over. "Come on, El, let's keep moving. We'll talk at home. We stand here much longer we'll catch pneumonia."

"Okay, but I'm serious."

"I know you are, I really do. So let's do it. We'll make a baby."

"Don't patronize me, Tucker, it isn't funny."

Tuck laughed and put his arm around Ellen's shoulder, "I'm not patronizing you. I mean it. We'll make a baby. We can start tonight. If I didn't have Nick picking me up in an hour, we could have started this morning."

Ellen pulled away from Tuck's arm and stood looking at him, at his stupid grinning face and burst out laughing. "You really mean it, Tuck, really?"

"Yes, I said so, didn't I?"

"Oh, God, I love you, Tuck Handler," Ellen said, throwing her arms around her husband and planting kisses all over his face.

They jogged home, or rather, Tuck jogged and Ellen skipped, while sing-songing, *"we're going to have a baby, we're going to have a baby.*

It was the first time Ellen had skipped since she was in grade school and she was surprised how easily skipping came back to her.

Chapter 3

A month later, Ellen Handler was pregnant.

Unfortunately, two months later Ellen suffered a miscarriage caused by an ectopic pregnancy—a very dangerous and uncommon condition that occurs when the fertilized egg remains in the fallopian tube instead of moving into the uterus. Her doctors were not in agreement about her future chances of having a full-term pregnancy.

Even so, less than a year later, she was pregnant for the second time.

Overall, life was good. Tuck loved his job, finding his days as a New York City detective to be as fulfilling and rewarding as he imagined they would be. His decision to go onto the police force after completing law school turned out to be an excellent move. In the back of his mind thoughts were beginning to stir that maybe, just maybe, politics might be something to consider. But for now he was enjoying his life just the way it was.

Ellen's second pregnancy was moving along quite normally and the doctors were cautiously encouraged.

And so, early one evening, as Tuck and his partner, Nick Brennan were having a drink after work at the Men's

A Baby To Die For

Bar in the Biltmore Hotel, all was right with the world. As they ordered a second round of bourbon, the little beeper on Tuck's belt sounded, signaling him to call his precinct. He quickly excused himself and made for the public phones.

A minute later he rushed back from making the call, his brow creased with concern.

"Christ, you okay?" Nick said, "You're white as a sheet."

"*No, damn it!* It's Ellen. She's in the ER at Roosevelt."

Tuck threw down a few bills and with that, both men hurried from the bar.

By the time they arrived, lights flashing, siren bleating, Ellen's condition had thankfully been stabilized.

But she had lost a great deal of blood and was lucky to be alive. And that was only because she had been able to somehow alert a neighbor, who called the fire department. Even after being briefed by the doctor about Ellen's brush with death, Tuck wasn't fully prepared for the look of strain and grief that contorted his wife's clay-pale face.

Tuck leaned over the side rail of the bed, avoiding the tubes that were inserted into both of Ellen's arms and kissed his wife. And they cried. Cried for the child who would never be, the second child who would never be. Two tiny human beings who, for the shortest of time, had been a part of their lives and were now gone.

Tuck and Ellen held each other, rocking slowly and sobbing.

Some days later, when Ellen was strong enough to be discharged, her doctor showed up. He was a squat and powerful-looking man with a face that hinted it had studied the canvas of a boxing ring close-up, and more than once. Ellen slowly shuffled around, packing a few things into a small duffel bag—a few magazines, her robe, and toiletries. Her blonde hair was brushed back and pulled into a ponytail. She was dressed in fresh clothing that Tuck had brought from home. Nevertheless, she looked distracted and slightly disoriented.

The doctor greeted Tuck who was standing next to the window, then addressed his patient.

"How are you feeling, Ellen?" he asked.

"Sore…stiff…tired…a little weak. But other than that, I guess I'm okay, Doctor," she said, shrugging.

Her eyes were red-rimmed from crying.

"And you? How do you feel, detective?" he asked Tuck.

Tuck cocked his head to the side, a bit puzzled.

"How do I feel? I don't know—I guess I feel sad—grateful for your—relieved. Why? How should I feel?"

"Well, for openers, you should feel lucky," the doctor said, sharply, "damned lucky that your wife has the opportunity to leave here through the lobby and not through our morgue down in the basement. We—no, you—you damned near lost her. You should know that and thank God she's alive. You're not Catholics, so birth control isn't a problem. So why did Ellen go through this ordeal for a second time? I told you both after the first miscarriage that I thought it would be dangerous to try again. How come you people feel you can play Russian roulette with your sex organs?"

"Hold on a minute, Doctor—"

"No, you hold on! I nearly lost my patient, almost had a dead body on my hands, and on my conscience. Damn near dead from something that you should never have let happen—and, I promise you, if Ellen gets pregnant again, there's a damned good chance it will kill her. Is that clear enough for you?"

Tuck and Ellen said nothing. They just looked at the man in the white coat. His pugilistic face was engorged, and a vein in his forehead pulsed.

With visible effort, the doctor continued, in a softer and slightly more sympathetic tone.

"Both of you—listen to me. To get pregnant again would be akin to suicide. In my professional opinion, Ellen, you will not likely ever carry a baby to full term. You've heard all this before. You just have to accept what I'm saying. It would be deadly to ever try to have a baby again."

"We know that, Doctor," Tuck said. "We've been through the lecture with Dr. Feder, our GP. We thought this time it might work out."

Tuck made no attempt to mask his sarcasm.

"Look, I won't lie to you, Detective Handler, I couldn't go into a court of law and take an oath that Ellen could never, under any circumstances, carry a child to full term, but—"

"Yes, doctor," Ellen said, cutting him off, "I know the details. We've heard all this before."

"Well, apparently you weren't listening. We're not exactly sure why, but for whatever reason, Ellen has these problem pregnancies. The end result, in the extreme, is bad—massive hemorrhaging and possible renal shutdown. In lay terms—you run the risk of bleeding to death, Ellen. And if and when it happens, it happens real fast. You were lucky this time. If you hadn't gotten the neighbor's attention when you did, it would have been the end. Consider yourself lucky to have survived, having ignored a second warning. Look, it's not the worst thing in the world," he continued. "You can always adopt a baby. Some of my patients—especially after a hard delivery—claim that adoption would have been a welcome alternative," the doctor said, smiling professionally.

Chapter 4

The Kitano Hotel, New York City

Max Garfield approached sex in much the same methodical way some men cleaned gutters and downspouts or chopped cord wood. It was simply a chore, a job to get done—not necessarily pleasant, but one that filled him with some stirrings of satisfaction when finished.

Right now, the only thing on his mind, was the rough surface of the straw Tatami mat cutting into his knees and elbows.

"Porter, this goddamn mat is slicing me to pieces!"

With a small grunt, Porter Gibbs, using her body, pushed Garfield roughly toward his side and using that momentum, completed the roll, ending up astride, looking down into Garfield's hard eyes.

"You're such a pussy, Max. Is this better, you big baby?" she asked, continuing to roll her hips.

Moments later, she threw her head back, shut her eyes, and allowed a low, well-bred, upper-crust groan to exit her throat and pass across a small fortune in cosmetic dentistry, as a powerful orgasm danced up like electricity through her well-toned body.

Max, noting her climax and being a world-class egomaniac, chalked up the afternoon as a smashing success.

Porter got to her feet and padded naked to the bathroom.

"You got a great ass, you know that?" Max said, rubbing his sore knees.

"You better believe it," she said, meaning it.

Max just grinned and lit a cigarette, enjoying for a moment the serenity of the well-appointed and very expensive Japanese suite of rooms he booked for their weekly trysts.

Minutes later, Porter was back, her oversized terry robe flapping open, a tiny residue of toothpaste clinging to a corner of her mouth. She lowered herself to the mat once again, this time near his feet, a short reach away from a small, lacquered table, which held a thermos carafe and several tiny porcelain teacups. She opened the thermos and filled a cup with steaming tea. She slowly sipped the tea, letting her mouth become warm from the liquid. Then, with her mouth filled with the warm tea, she straddled him, her face over his face, her legs astride his hips. Slowly, she crawled backward down the length of his naked body. She moved toward his feet, releasing a bit of the warm tea, first onto his chest and abdomen and finally, slowly, sensuously, across his stomach and pubis until the liquid was gone and all that was left was Porter's incredibly sensuous, warm mouth, into which she attempted to take Garfield.

He pushed her away, a cruel half-smile on his face, "Christ, Porter, you try too hard, you know that? You're like a two-bit hooker trying to make enough quick cash for a fur coat after she hears a snowstorm is on the way. You'd be better if you could relax and not push so much. I don't like to be conned. I don't particularly like to be taken like some pubescent boy. When I want you to go down on me, I'll ask you—so next time, don't push me."

Porter didn't respond. She just looked at Garfield. *You're nothing but a complete putz.*

She was accustomed to his cruelty, almost expecting it. She knew he would fall asleep soon. That was fine with her. She wanted time to think about a few things anyway. The whole Florida operation was in need of her personal involvement, and she had to figure out how to get the LaFrance lady into line. Sarah LaFrance was making too much money, and so was Toby Wine, the nut case she worked with in Washington. She wondered absently if there were any really sane people left in the world.

"Putz," she murmured, this time under her breath, as she looked down at Max and went into the bathroom. Garfield was already snoring, spread-eagle on the floor.

Max was far from being a *putz*. He was no petty jerk. If anything, Max Garfield was more like a Formica counter top—a strong veneer that covered a cheap piece of plywood. On the outside Max was sophisticated and smart, yet underneath, cruel and self-absorbed. Problem was—though blissfully unaware of it, he just didn't give a shit.

Porter Gibbs was a little like that, too—the major

difference being that she had her viciousness under control and knew when and how to unleash it.

Max Garfield had become a lawyer because—as one former classmate wryly observed—'there were no more concentration camps to run.' So, after a dismal undergraduate experience at the University of Connecticut—mostly while distracted by the growing needs of elderly parents in Westport, followed by three years at Harvard Law, he moved to New York. First, he tried corporate work but was bored to distraction. Then he dabbled in criminal defense work, tried his hand at personal injury, and even did some real estate deals, but none of those areas of the law satisfied him.

Almost by accident, Max Garfield got the chance to go it alone by taking over an old-line law firm, Finn & McGuire, by simply assuming the obligation of its leased office space. The small firm was closing because Finn had recently died in a nursing home at age ninety-three, and his "young" partner, McGuire—in his late seventies and not in the best of health—had only worked part-time in recent years in order to service a few of his old clients.

The firm was little more than a shell, which was perfect for Garfield because he wanted to build a new practice in a dark corner of the law where his kind of icy pragmatism translated into cold, hard cash—lots of it.

So, in he crawled and never looked back.

Working out of the offices of Finn & McGuire, Max Garfield became a baby lawyer—over time, the busiest, most successful baby lawyer in New York City, and therefore, by default, in the United States. He didn't work for babies, represent them, or defend them in court. He sold them like prime cuts of beef during a meat shortage.

It didn't happen overnight, but in a few short years, Garfield was able to pull together a loose network of lawyers who were delighted to sell babies to adoptive families. The larger the network grew, the more demand there was for their quality product—healthy, white newborns, sporting "impeccable" biological pedigrees. Sadly, the pedigrees were not always reported to prospective adoptive parents with much veracity.

His success became both the nucleus and the driving force behind a shadowy network in black market babies.

His influence pulsed and grew slowly, like a tumor, and was felt wherever babies were sold, bought, or produced for sale. Max Garfield profited, one way or another, from the majority of the transactions.

He commanded a vast, complicated, and highly lucrative machine.

Porter Gibbs was Max Garfield's first mate and right hand. However, that afternoon at the Japanese Kitano Hotel, Max's first mate made a major decision which she had been working on for some time.

Chapter 5

Dallas, Texas

The face staring back at Rick Shelby from the bathroom mirror looked the same as it did every day—a thick head of dark hair, graying at the sides, slightly drooping eyelids and a full beard. However, since his recent trip to New Mexico to pick up the Kaufmans' money, he might look the same, but hopefully his life would be quite different. He just smiled, knowing that the $40,000 sat secure inside the sturdy safe in his office. By next week, the cash will find its way to Max Garfield in New York.

Shelby's connection with a local rich Texan changed everything. If it weren't for that crazy bastard, the slave auction in Casablanca and the pregnant Polish girl, he'd never have met Max Garfield. Max Garfield was Rick's ticket into a world of opportunity. Just the thought of that brought to mind Humphrey Bogart's line in the movie *Casablanca*: *"I think this is the beginning of a beautiful friendship."*

Working with Max Garfield on the Kaufmann adoption had been an important first step for Shelby.

A Baby To Die For

His connection with the Texan had been most fortunate, albeit serendipitous, and represented a major turning point for him, as well. He had been doing adoptions for some time, and although they had proven to be profitable, getting babies and prospective buyers was a frustrating and mostly hit-and-miss proposition. But the more deeply he became involved in the business of selling babies, the more Shelby came across the name of Max Garfield. Without question, he was the go-to guy in the field, and hooking up with Garfield was akin to plugging into a high voltage power source—not unlike having a baby-selling franchise. If Garfield was pleased with Shelby's work on the Kaufman's adoption and the way he handled it, there was a good chance he could continue to work with the New York lawyer. In this last placement, Shelby made a deal to sell the baby supplied by the Texanwhich, in turn, gave him the excuse to contact Garfield. Garfield then found willing buyers—Doctor and Mrs. Kaufman.

Shelby felt confident that the future would hold more of that kind of profitable give-and-take. And of course, those profits would be split accordingly. Best case—Rick Shelby would become Max's "franchisee" for the entire Southwest—a potentially sweet deal all the way around.

Shelby had given a lot of thought to Max Garfield since his return from the trip to Morocco with the Texan. He felt he could learn a lot from the man. It had only taken Garfield a month to place the Polish girl's baby. This fact delighted Shelby and, in turn, the Texan—who was happy to get a quick return on his investment. Rick was particularly intrigued by the unusual circumstances surrounding the delivery of the Polish girl's baby. Garfield's idea of taking the baby to the old woman in New Mexico and then picking up the money from the Kaufmans had, at first, seemed like a stupid idea. The Kaufmans could have easily flown to Dallas, picked up the baby and given the cash directly to Shelby.

But the more he turned the idea over in his mind, looking at it from different angles, the more sense it made. For what they were paying, the adoptive couple deserved a little theater, a little excitement and mystery. Why not? He imagined how they'd relish telling the story of the long drive from New York, the sand-swept road, the Red Bull tobacco sign, the strange old lady, their precious infant in a beat-up Coke cooler. They'd tell it over and over—discretely, of course—to friends, and relatives, and with each telling, the details would be stretched ever so slightly. And the Kaufmans would repeat it endlessly. So, actually it was a damned brilliant word-of-mouth marketing scheme for Max Garfield's network. Without question, Shelby had a lot to learn, and Max Garfield was one smart son-of-a-bitch to learn from.

Rick Shelby was proud to be part of the operation. Prominent people would steer more lucrative adoptions his way. That's how the network operated—by word of mouth. Even in his small way, he was already making the kind of money that he'd always dreamed of. When all the smoke cleared on the Kaufman adoption, Shelby would have a fat little payday. Not a fortune, but then he didn't have to do very much to earn it—and the IRS would never know about the cash he got from his cut of the deal. He was finished with those stupid house closings and two-bit personal injury cases.

By the time it was over, everyone involved with the Kaufman adoption would have gotten a taste—the Texan, Shelby, and, of course, Max Garfield. Even the old lady in New Mexico would get a few extra crisp bills in the mail, anonymously, of course.

For Garfield, the best part was that Uncle Sam would be lucky to see a fraction of what the Kaufmans paid him for baby Amy. And even if he declared a few dollars for tax purposes, most of that would be offset by inflated deductions for his operating expenses.

Now, examining his reflection in the bathroom mirror, Rick suddenly had a crazy impulse. And so, without another thought, he grabbed a pair of scissors, a can of shaving cream, a razor, and—for the first time since entering college—he shaved. Slowly and carefully he eliminated his full beard from the entire right side of his face—every single strand—until his face, to the right of center and from nose to neck, was as clean as a baby's bottom.

He washed and dried his face and laughed at the half-and-half effect. He turned to the right, stood erect, shoulders back, and gazed at the new, successful lawyer. Then he turned to the left, slouched a bit, and was transformed back into his old, familiar down-at-the-heels ambulance chaser, which made him laugh even more.

The one dark cloud on Shelby's horizon was Pauline, his wife, and it looked like the kind of cloud that was sure to produce one hell of a thunderstorm. Rick instinctively knew that when she learned the direction he was taking his practice, she would throw a fit. And, without question, she *would* find out. Dallas was a small town. Gossip was the lingua franca of Pauline's circle of friends. The adoption part would not be her issue. Pauline had no negative feelings toward adoption *per se*. She had always said that when the time came, if conceiving was a problem, she would happily adopt.

Her objection would be the selling of babies. The thought that he was exchanging infants for large sums of cash would freak her out. He knew Pauline would have nothing to do with the black market aspects of Rick's adoption business. Pauline was that way. She grew up rich, so she could easily afford the price of moral indignation.

Wearing nothing but a towel around his middle, Rick Shelby stood silently in the open doorway of the bedroom waiting for Pauline to sense his presence. When she finally looked up from her book, it took a moment for her to realize what Rick had done. Then she laughed for a long time. He walked across the room to her side of their king-size bed. She put aside her book and studied the shaved half of her husband's face. She had never seen him clean-shaven before. Even when they first met, he wore a beard. It was like seeing a strange—yet somehow familiar—face.

"Amazing," Pauline said. "I certainly hope you're going to do the other side, as well." She reached up, running her hand slowly along the unfamiliar smoothness of his cleanly shaved cheek, and it excited him.

"That feels good, honey. Don't stop," he whispered,

instantly aroused, and reached down to embrace her. He'd forgotten how long it had been since they last made love.

Pauline tensed up, a subtle but clear rebuff to his intent.

"So tell me, Rick, this new look, what's it about? You're not having one of those mid-life things, are you?" she said, her voice slightly frosty.

Rick was puzzled, not sure why Pauline had reacted as she did. His mind raced trying to think of what he might have done, or not done, to cause this effect. Finally he shrugged and stepped back. Obviously sex was not in the cards, but he knew he was in for some sort of confrontation. He was feeling cheated, rejected.

"Nothing special. I just felt like a change. I got bored," he said with a shrug, matching her cool tone of voice.

Pauline studied her husband. There were some important issues she had to bring up with him. The gossip was keeping her awake nights, and even though there was a very good chance a confrontation about it would not end well, she quickly decided that now was as good a time as any to air her concerns. She felt her stomach tighten, hoping she was wrong and, at the same time, dreading being right. All she was certain about was the sure knowledge that things had to finally come out into the open. If correct, there was really no question it had to be dealt with. Didn't someone say sunlight is the best disinfectant?

"Since you brought up the issue of change, Rick— there's something I need to know: where have we been getting so much money all of a sudden?"

The question took Rick completely by surprise, and he didn't know quite how to respond.

"What are you talking about?"

"Please, Rick! Before you get defensive," Pauline said, holding up her hand like a crossing-guard. "Let me finish."

"Okay, go on," Rick said warily.

"Would you like to hazard a guess how long it's been since we had an argument about money?"

Rick looked at Pauline for a long minute with a puzzled expression on his face. "What in the fuck does that have to do with anything?" he finally shouted. "Are you trying to tell me that you're upset because we're *not* arguing about money?"

"In a way. Actually, yes!"

"Man, you are one sick puppy, you know that?"

"No, Rick, don't you understand? Our *not* fighting about money *is* the point. That's what we used to argue about all the time, Rick. But apparently we have enough now so we don't even need to talk about it, let alone argue anymore."

"I'm confused. What the fuck is your problem?"

"I want to know where's it coming from. Suddenly you have some new clothes, new shoes. The last few times we went for dinner, you paid with cash. What's going on, Rick? I do the checks every month, I see our bank and credit card statements when they come in—I haven't spotted any clothing charges, so either you're getting gifts or paying in cash. I'm guessing it's the latter, so where's the money coming from?"

A Baby To Die For

Rick, feeling blind-sided and vulnerable, hesitated a beat too long, then smiled a little too wide. His mind was scrambling and trying to come up with a plausible answer.

Finally: "Hey, no big deal. Work's been good, you know. I settled a couple of divorces, closed a few houses, and collected some receivables. You grew up in a businessman's family. You know how profits fluctuate. It's not like I was some fixed-salary schnook living on a weekly paycheck."

"Come on Rick, don't patronize me. I'm not a child," she said. Her jaw tightened. She met his eyes and held them. Rick looked away. He stood there in his towel looking stupid in his half-beard. Pauline listened as he wove some nonsense about how business and the law practice was growing and how he finally had cracked the good ol' boy tight-knit fraternity of Dallas lawyers.

Pauline noticed that for the first time since meeting her husband, she could—at least on the clean-shaven side of his face—see that he was lying. She realized with amazement that the beard masked a "tell" in the form of a cruel little upturn of his mouth. It said, *"I'm lying,"* as clearly as a six-year-old with chocolate smeared on his face, trying to hide the fact he stole a cookie. Maybe that's why Rick had always been such a good poker player. With the beard, the "tell" was impossible to spot.

Pauline grabbed a pack of cigarettes from the nightstand and lit one. She inhaled deeply. With as little emotion as she could muster, when she spoke smoke surrounded each word. "Rick, listen to me. You can bullshit as much as you like, but I think I know what's going on."

"Really? You think you know what's going on with me?" Rick bullied. "What's going on is you're having a shit fit over money or whatever the fuck it is you're talking about."

Pauline ignored Rick's outburst.

Pauline reached for the water glass on her nightstand and took a sip before responding. "A couple of months ago, I was at the hairdresser and I overheard some women talking. One of them said, 'You know, if she wants to adopt a baby without any hassle, there's a lawyer, I think his name is Selby or Shelby, who can get babies for a price.' Is that true, Rick? Are you the lawyer they were talking about? Are you selling babies?"

The newly shaved half of Rick's face suddenly took on an even lighter shade of pale. He didn't protest. He remained silent, just letting her continue—a trick he learned in law school, which gave him some time to think.

"I wasn't eavesdropping," Pauline added, filling the void. "The woman had a voice like a foghorn. You could hear her a block away. She was going on and on—that for the right price, this Shelby guy can get babies for couples who don't want to wait for an agency adoption. She said she knew about it because two women she was acquainted with had done it. She mentioned how much they had paid, and I almost fell over. It—made me sick, Rick. I've got to know if it's true, because if that's where our sudden financial windfall is coming from, if you're selling babies by the pound, and using the money to buy your clothes and fancy dinners for us and pay our mortgage—well, it stinks. Do you understand? I refuse to have anything to do with it."

A Baby To Die For

Rick was shaking inside. Every instinct in his body screamed for him to flee back into the bathroom until Pauline could calm down. But he knew she wouldn't calm down. He forced himself to walk to the bed. He say down on the edge near his wife. Years of experience had proven that Pauline was beyond stubborn and did not change her mind very often, especially over issues of conscience. Rick figured there were only two choices she would ever offer him: either stop selling babies or leave—*permanently.* Either way it would cost him plenty.

Pauline put her hand on Rick's arm.

"Please, do me a favor, Rick. Don't try to lie to me, because, in my heart I know the truth."

Then she reached up to touch the bare side of the face that she had been with so long and had never touched or even seen before. But Rick turned away before she could. Hefisheda cigarette from her pack, remembered he was trying to stop and threw it down. "Fuck it," he said. He took it up again and lit it. He was angry but he was, in a way, relieved. Pauline would have to know eventually, and this simply saved him the mess and trouble of telling her. At times, Pauline could be a pompous ass. He knew that—she with her fancy family and their holier-than-thou bullshit. What the hell did she know about what he was trying to build for himself?

"Pauline, look. I won't lie to you. I swear I was going to tell you. You're right, I am— have been for some time—doing some adoption work. But so what? I think you're over-reacting. It's not illegal. Lots of lawyers do adoptions."

"Adoption work? That's just a goddamned

41

euphemism. You mean you're selling babies! It's the black market, for crying out loud!"

"No, damn it—not selling babies—not in any illicit sense. It's adoption work—gray market stuff, okay? So it's not through an agency but perfectly acceptable and aboveboard. There's not a damned thing wrong with what I'm doing, Pauline."

"That's horseshit, Rick, and you know it. What you're doing has got to be over the line if you're making a pot full of money doing it. If it was just some ordinary, run-of-the-mill adoption work, the fees would be modest and probably not in cash—but for the longest time you've been giving me cash for the household expenses, instead of writing checks, as you always did before. Why suddenly cash? And I've never seen any bills for the clothes you got recently, which, like I said before, means you're paying cash for them, too."

"What's the big deal? So I have some cash. Why are you making such a big thing over cash?"

Rick knew he was on the defensive now. He hated arguing with Pauline. It always reminded him of litigating, and he knew he wasn't very good at that either.

"The lady in the beauty shop talked about a fee of $32,000, and she said most of it had to be in cash. Another woman, one from my tennis group, adopted and told me it cost them even more. And I happen to know it was money they didn't have. And you know where they got it? They had to mortgage their goddamned house, and he brings home a pretty decent salary. Christ, Rick, maybe you did their adoption? Are we running our household on the money those poor people raised when they mortgaged theirs?"

A Baby To Die For

Pauline took another cigarette out of the pack Rick had thrown on the bed. She lit it and inhaled deeply. Smoke came out her nose as she exhaled. Rick remembered the bullet-riddled Red Bull sign with the painted smoke shooting from the flared nostrils of the angry bull.

"I won't go along with you on this, Rick. It's not negotiable. Dallas is a small town, and this is not who I am, nor do I want my family or friends to think that it is."

Rick got up from the bed and walked into the bathroom. He got his robe. He felt naked without the whole beard. He wished he hadn't shaved it off. The irony was, he suspected one of the adoptions Pauline heard about in the beauty parlor was one he'd done almost two years ago. He made a $20,000 profit, all in cash, and the experience had given Rick his first taste for how lucrative it could be. It convinced him that selling babies was a way to make a bundle of money easily and very quickly.

Rick came back into the bedroom, tying his robe. "I don't think what I'm doing is wrong, and I'm not going to stop. And that's not negotiable for me either."

"But, Rick ... "

"Wait, damn it, now it's my turn, so let me finish! We've been living in Dallas for years, and I've been trying to make it work all that time. It was your idea to come back here It was your home, not mine. I could have done just fine in New York, but no, you had to live near your mother and father with all your rich friends around you. So I came along. It was useless, I wasn't going to make it doing all the ordinary, mundane, piss-ant legal crap that happened to come my way—or make it on the few crumbs that your father would occasionally sprinkle on me from his business. I'm a *failure* here, Pauline. Can't you understand that? I can't live with that. No, that's not entirely accurate. I *won't* live with that anymore."

Rick jammed another cigarette into his mouth and lit it.

"But, Rick, I never needed all the fancy stuff, the big house or the cars or … "

Rick stared at Pauline, head cocked slightly to the side. A look of pain flashed across the clean-shaven side of his face.

"I don't give a rat's ass about what you do or do not want to settle for. I know what I want. I'm the one who needs the big house, the fancy car, the money in the bank, and in my pocket. I need those things because I've never had them before, and you don't give a damn about them because you've always had everything—whatever you wanted—and for Christ's sake, you still do.

"You think I was happy about the credit cards and your charge accounts at Neiman Marcus and a half-dozen other places that get billed directly to your father? I've said nothing about them for years, and let me tell you, that hasn't exactly been the greatest thing for my ego. I've been chasing ambulances, Pauline. Do you know how low on the lawyer totem that is? So when I stumbled across another way—a specialty where I could make some big money and liked doing—sure, I grabbed at it. I'm going to keep grabbing at it. You think I'm doing some horrible thing? Okay, think whatever you damn please. But it's not a horrible thing. It makes people happy and, yes, it will make me a lot of money. Besides, there are lots of good, decent people out there who just want kids to raiseas their own. But they can't have kids. For whatever reason, they just can't have any. There's another bunch of people who are having kids. Some are little more than babies themselves—screwed up high school cheerleaders, bored young singles, or housewives having affairs, whatever. They can have them, but they can't afford them, or don't want them, So I put the parties together—the sellers and the buyers. Now what's so bad about that? It's just a matter of supply and demand."

"I never said anything was wrong with adoption. We're not talking about adoption. I'm talking about selling babies—human beings, flesh and blood—in exchange for huge amounts of money. Cash payments that are so high that only rich people can get kids. Tell me about that part. Tell me what the IRS would do if they knew about all that money you're collecting and, more than likely not declaring? They'll just slap your ass in jail!" Pauline said, looking her husband in the eye, the one on the shaved side.

Rick walked to the dresser and gazed in the large mirror. He stroked the bare side of his face and looked at Pauline reflected in the glass.

"You're a hypocrite, you know that Pauline? What about your father's business? Did you cry your fucking eyes out and call him a crook when he raised beef prices? People who didn't have the money couldn't put meat on their table. What about that? Can you tell me about that, Pauline? What about that?"

Pauline paused for a moment. She smiled.

"You've got a valid point, Rick. I can't fault your logic. It is impeccable as always. I never said anything to Dad about that. To tell the truth, when it happens I'm not even aware of it. But that really isn't the point, is it? Doesn't the fact that very few attorneys want to handle these adoptions give you some idea how rotten a business it is? My God, the things you read in the magazines and see on the news! No one respects what you and lawyers like you are doing. I didn't invent the name black market. I didn't decide to condemn it. There is a groundswell of revulsion over what you are doing that makes it morally wrong. Maybe legally wrong, even if you put aside the money aspect of it. If making a fortune in black market babies was as legit as prosecuting or defending clients or earning fees from house closings, don't you think there'd be more lawyers trying to get into it? And if there were more lawyers running after the same fees, don't you think they'd be lower?"

Pauline lit another cigarette and took a hard pull, sucking the smoke deep into her lungs.

"You're either naïve or kidding yourself, Rick. The game you're playing stinks. That's why so few others want to join in. If you had a choice of being an astronaut or a garbage collector, would you have to think about it?"

Rick just stared at his wife. It was twilight outside and the shadows in the bedroom turned a bluish purple—*a lot like the color of a bruise* "Someone said that our lives are the accumulation of the choices we make. At some point, you made a choice," Pauline said, her voice softer than before.

"You can choose to listen to what I'm saying and make another choice, this time the right one."

Rick shrugged his shoulders and turned his hands palms up and chest high.

"You want the truth? I like what I do. You and I, we've

been—I don't know—it's always been different here in Dallas. I don't belong here and you know it."

Pauline shook her head and looked at her husband. He seemed to shrink back from her gaze. He turned his beard side toward her, trying for some protection. She smoked in silence for a few moments.

Finally, in partial control of her emotions, she said, "That may be the major difference between us. You're trying to justify your actions with some red herring about my growing up rich, but I really don't believe that's a basis for this disagreement. This is about morality and values, not rich and poor. I've got to think about this a lot, Rick. I'm not joking. I've really got to think about it. It makes a lot of difference to me—to us. This is not making me happy."

Rick turned and walked out of the room and went to the kitchen. He returned with a cup of coffee for Pauline and one for himself.

"Do you remember the opening line of *Anna Karenina*? I was never much for Tolstoy but I never forgot that line. *'Happy families are all alike and every unhappy family is unhappy in its own way.'* So, yeah, you think about it, Pauline—you do that. Maybe we can find some acceptable way for us to be together as an unhappy family, maybe not. But remember one thing. I'm not changing my mind. Never. No more ambulance chasing or house closings— ever again."

Rick turned and went back into the bathroom.

Christ, I look like a jerk. He hated arguing with Pauline and he sensed this confrontation was quite different from all the others. His hand was shaking slightly as he realized how pissed off he was at himself for the fear he was feeling.

Everything was going so damned well. Why did she have to be such a self-righteous jerk? There was a fortune to be made.

He knew what he was doing. The decision was not negotiable, and Pauline would just have to deal with it or not, depending on how much she was willing to let go down the drain. Secretly, Rick suspected she was willing to let it all go, maybe even use the whole episode as an excuse to break up the marriage altogether. The last few years together had not been completely happy—too many arguments, too many lies and half-told truths.

Rick began carefully and painfully to remove the remains of his beard.

Actually, the bottom line was not as bad as it appeared. It just might be a damned sight better having a lot of money than having a lot of Pauline, Rick decided as the last of the hair came away from his face.

"I'll take $1 million collecting garbage any day, and fuck the moon!" he said into the mirror, clean-shaven for the first time in ages.

"Damn," he said out loud.

He had totally forgotten how weak his chin was.

Chapter 6

Ellen Handler had slowly developed two distinct personalities. By day, she demonstrated an almost manic level of enthusiasm over the idea of adopting a child. She bubbled and glowed with excitement as if willing herself to believe it would be the perfect solution.

After all, providing a child with a warm home, with loving parents, snatching a needy waif from the dark clutches of an unspeakable alternative, wasn't that a noble and righteous thing to do?

She said all this to Tuck one evening.

His only reaction was to look at her in disbelief and mumble, "For crying out loud, Ellen, we're adopting a baby, not rescuing Oliver Twist from the clutches of Fagin."

But in some parallel universe, Ellen's other persona—her dark self—crept up in the damp, tangled sheets of sleepless nights, appearing as prodding, nagging guilt. And even when sleep did come, it was disturbing and dream-filled. By three or four in the morning, Ellen was awake and prowling the apartment—cleaning out drawers, watching but not seeing old movies on television, sipping hot tea or warm milk, and the whole time, ripping herself apart and feeling that, as a woman, she was an abject failure.

She would sit, warming her hands around a mug of tea, tears running down her cheeks. She overflowed with regret that she'd never see herself or Tuck reflected in another human being, because after all the excuses and rationalizations, in the end it was her job to have the baby, and she had failed. She was unable to accomplish that one basic female obligation, never to experience a child growing inside her body. Rational or not, that was the acid that seeped into her soul, and it was eating her away from the inside.

"My God, Ellen, listen to yourself!" Tuck said, when the sound from the TV woke him, and she'd railed on about her feelings of failure. "You're not looking for a baby—you want to be cloned!"

Without a doubt, the idea of adopting scared him, too. And he was certainly sorry that they could not be biological parents. But he was incapable of understanding the depth of Ellen's mourning over her inability to perform the act of conception and childbirth.

He spoke freely of it to his friend, Nick, who was already getting the increasingly alarming, day-by-day reports about Ellen from his wife. But Tuck admitted he never could discuss it rationally with Ellen. She had lost her ability—or maybe it was her desire—to accept the reality of her situation.

"Nick, believe me, given a choice, there's no question, I would prefer our own baby—conceived, carried, and delivered. And yes, I know what everyone says—there is no difference with an adopted child. You love them the same—as soon as you pick them up, they're yours—and all the other platitudes people have spewed out, trying their best to reassure us."

Nick Brennan concentrated on his pipe and picked at the cold dottle in its bowl with a toothpick until it was loose and then whacked it out into the callused palm of his hand.

"Platitudes are usually the truth writ large. Take my sister, for example, you know she adopted a baby, and five years later, she got pregnant and had one of her own. I'll stand them in front of anyone and bet they couldn't tell me for sure which one is adopted. Truth be known, they're both pains in the ass right now. Natural or adopted, you get no guarantees, right? Two seconds after you adopt the kid, and Ellen gets a whiff of that old J&J powder—she'll go all soft in the center, just like every other mother does."

Tuck wanted desperately to believe his friend, wanted to be able to dismiss the issue of adoption as easily as Nick did. Had the roles been reversed, he could even hear himself dishing out the same lecture, using the same fortune-cookie philosophy. But inside, there was real fear and imbedded superstition that went way, way back to someplace, and it said: *We don't let strangers into the family. An aunt or an uncle, we take in. A brother, we give cash if we have it. But a total stranger? Never!*

And Tuck remembered something from a long time ago—his mother sitting at the kitchen table with Tuck's father, Roy, facing her. Nine-year-old Tuck was in his tiny bedroom, a paper-thin wall separating him from the conversation.

And Tuck could picture his mother sipping her tea. He saw he fingers of her hands, red and chapped, little black hairlines on the thumb pads and forefingers from where the paring knife pressed when she sliced vegetables for soup, which was often.

And Tuck could hear them through the wall as clearly as if they were in the room.

"You think something's wrong with Helen?" his mother said. "You want to know what's wrong with Helen? Stanley is what's wrong with her. I never trusted him, with his fancy car. If he were home more and not selling plumbing all over, he could give Helen a baby, and they wouldn't have to take a stranger's problem into their home."

Roy Handler kept his eyes leveled on the front page of his *New York Times*.

"So they can't have a baby," he said. "What's the big deal? You'll see, they'll adopt the baby, and everything will be fine, the baby will be just fine. In a hour it will be like she gave birth."

"*Fine?*"

His mother spit out the word like a baseball umpire calling a play at home plate, expelling the word with a lot of body English.

"What do you know about babies? You sell insurance. I'm the one who knows about babies. She adopts, she gets garbage! Take my word, she'll get nothing but garbage— garbage—garbage!"

Nick Brennan had been talking while Tuck was remembering, and now Tuck tried to pick up the thread of what the detective was saying.

"...It's just an accident, Tuck, no one's fault. Ellen can't carry a kid. Can't reproduce. It doesn't mean she's a bad person."

"But Nick, damn it, that's exactly what she *does* think. She's convinced she's a bad person. There's something inside her—in her genes—this overwhelming need, this compulsion of hers to carry a child."

"I know it must be a bitch to deal with. You have to help her take a long view—like the pictures the astronauts took of Earth—with perspective. What the hell's the difference? Your baby, their baby. It's totally irrelevant," Nick Brennan rested his case.

"That's terrific, Nick. I can't wait to get home and tell Ellen what you said. 'Don't worry, honey,'" Tuck mimicked sarcastically. "'Nick says not to worry, the fact you can't have the kid is totally irrelevant—at least as viewed from outer space.' Well, listen, I can assure you, viewed from the foot of the brass bed on the Upper West Side, it's a fucking tragedy, and the pun is absolutely intended."

Nick chuckled and signaled the waitress for another beer. Tuck placed his hand over his glass. He was going home. Tonight, they were finalizing their 'List,' a document to show the adoption agency, which had taken on all the importance of the Dead Sea Scrolls.

After dinner, Ellen and Tuck settled down, propped up on a bunch of cushions, in front of the fireplace to discuss the details of 'The List' one more time before their meeting the next day at the adoption agency.

Ellen consulted the notes she'd made.

"Do we have to tell them you changed your name?"

"I didn't change my name, it was my grandfather, for God's sake. At Ellis Island, when he came to America. The idiot at immigration couldn't pronounce his name and just put down something close. They don't need to know that."

"I'll cross that off. Okay, we agree, the baby has to be Jewish. That's right here on the top of the list," Ellen said.

"It's really not a big deal for me personally, but technically, as long as the mother is, then the kid will be—in Israel, anyway."

"And dark hair like yours," Ellen added, smiling.

"I think it should be blonde. I love blondes. Especially females," Tuck said seductively, as he leaned over and nuzzled Ellen's neck.

"Tuck, be serious, this is important!" Ellen said, brushing off his comically feigned advance. "Dark hair is dominant, and to be perfectly authentic we should insist on having a dark-haired child."

"Well, if dark hair is so dominant, why are you always bossing me around?"

Ellen ignored Tuck's attempted joke.

"And also, the backgrounds of the mother and father both need to be really impeccable. I've thought about that a lot, and it may be the most important thing. And no drugs in the mother's history. Or alcohol. And we can't have any serious family illnesses in their medical history, you know, like cancer or diabetes."

Tuck nodded his head in agreement. They had been over the ground so many times he was ready to scream— what the baby's physical characteristics needed to be—

the background of its parents—the physicality of the parents—not too short, not too tall—the medical history— the drug and alcohol issue. Endlessly they hashed and rehashed it all.

But Tuck could see that going through the process made Ellen happy, maybe even acted in some strange way as a replacement for the months of gestation she would never experience. So, no matter how frustrating it became, he always played the game as seriously as he could. Actually, he wanted the child to be perfect, too. The emotions were so complicated.

An hour later, they had the infamous list neatly typed, with demands that ranged from religion to the physical characteristics of the biological mother and father. As lists go, it was a damn fine 'List.'

"You know, El, to keep this adoption in the true spirit of authenticity, we should have a conception celebration," Tuck said, with a mock flourish, consulting his watch. "Tonight would be a good time, don't you think?"

Ellen, still absorbed in the list, said without looking up, "Honey, do you mind? Could I have a rain check?"

Chapter 7

Sipping a vodka at thirty-five thousand feet felt really good. This is exactly what he'd thought about—actually, fantasized about—for a long, long time.

Jake's trip to Dallas had been a milk run as far as work was concerned. He went to Rick Shelby's office, just like Max instructed, picked up the money, and caught the next flight back to New York.

This was a far cry from Vietnam. To be truthful, he had enjoyed playing war. Hell, he was stoned out of his mind most of the time so, hanging from a monkey harness out the side door of a B-25 or a chopper, popping three-ounce chunks of lead from his M60 into any slant-eyed gook that happened to be in his sightline, was a double rush. He got an intense, wild feeling of pleasure from seeing the carnage he could create with the powerful weapon he controlled—bodies cut in half, heads blown off—all from a safe distance, with the only sound coming from powerful engines and the chatter of his M60—an exhilarating abstraction, hundreds of feet removed from reality.

A Baby To Die For

But then one day, Jake's worst nightmare was realized. His chopper took a hit, a bad hit that destroyed the rotor. Lieutenant Lawson, the pilot, screaming like a baby with a diaper full of crap, somehow crash-landed the burning ship without killing anybody on board. That was a miracle—and given what happened next, not necessarily a blessing, not by a long shot. Even before the crash dust cleared or the bloodied crew could crawl out of the burning wreckage, a few dozen screaming Vietcong soldiers surrounded the ship.

Jake and the crew where kicked, pushed, and beaten through jungle so thick, Jake couldn't see more than the narrow path in front of him. Some hours later, they stumbled into a clearing where Jake, the pilot, co-pilot, and crew chief were thrown into a cramped bamboo cage. Over the next six days, the VC tortured them unmercifully. They beat Jake, but not on a regular basis, so he never knew when the next beating would take place. They had him kneel for hours in the communal cesspool, where the filthy muck reached to his chest and flies covered whatever else was exposed. They shot the pilot when, in the midst of a brutal beating, he suddenly broke free and ran screaming toward the jungle. Then one day before sunup, the co-pilot and crew chief were shackled and marched out of the clearing by several of the Vietcong. Jake never saw them again.

That left Jake to be the sole object of his tormentors. They fed him drugs for days at a time until time itself seemed to disappear. And after he was totally fucked up, they withheld the drugs and tormented him when he screamed and begged for more. Then one day, he was dragged into the center of a tiny, one-room building—the only permanent structure in the clearing. The rough cement walls were about ten inches thick. A door was cut into one wall. Another wall, the one in front of Jake, had a two-foot, ragged, square window cut into it about four feet off the ground. The roof was nothing more than a tangle of dry branches.

Jake was manhandled onto a low wooden chair, and his left hand was tied to one of the chair legs. His right arm was secured to his chest in a way that positioned his hand about eight inches under his chin, so it was impossible for him to move it in any direction. Then, as Jake watched in detached horror, they loaded an ancient-looking revolver, sliding six bullets into the six chambers. Laughing like a bunch of playground bullies, they forced the loaded piece into Jake's hand, the barrel pointing up, the muzzle jammed painfully into the soft flesh under his upraised chin, forcing his head as far back as it would go. Then they roughly forced his finger around the trigger. With both arms pinned, his finger was the only thing that Jake could move.

"You shoot! You shoot!" One of the soldiers screamed in broken English.

Then the soldiers went outside the concrete room and began a noisy card game, leaving Jake in the chair, his arms and the revolver immobile, only his finger able to move.

Intermittently, one or two of the men would come in and whip the bottoms of Jake's bare feet with a length of bamboo, while screaming, "You shoot, you shoot!"

At this point, Jake—never a stable person in the best of times—had been pushed to some strange new level of insane rationality. He was, for all intents and purposes, already dead.

Fuck it! If I'm going to die, I might as well do it myself.

A heavy rain ended the card game, and the soldiers came back into the room. Water poured through the makeshift roof, soaking Jake. They beat him and screamed in his face, "You shoot! You shoot!"

They gave him more drugs. Then Jake was crying, not from fear or anger but from pure, blind frustration.

Fuck it!

Screaming, he pulled the trigger.

All he heard was a hollow click, then the high-pitched laughter of the soldiers yelling, "No fire pin! No fire pin!"

It was at that moment that Jake's mind cracked, and any semblance of sanity he'd been hanging onto was gone.

Some time later—it might have been hours, days, or weeks—Jake woke to find the clearing empty of any Vietcong. His cage was still locked. He lay there for hours, not sure his captors were really gone. Then he set about escaping from the cage. It took him hours, but he finally succeeded by chewing through some of the heavy rope used to secure the pieces of bamboo. His mouth was bleeding, and he'd broken or lost several of his teeth in the process, but he made enough of an opening to squeeze through.

He limped barefoot for days through miles of tangled jungle until, finally, he crossed the path of a marine patrol.

A Baby To Die For

The government slapped Jake Garfield into a VA hospital in order to heal the physical wounds he suffered from his ordeal. They also weaned him away from the drugs he'd been fed and to which he'd become so deeply addicted.

After almost a year, and in the spirit of a pressing government austerity program, they popped Jake Garfield, like a ripe pimple, back into civilian life, along with a disability pension and about as much mental stability as a trailer park standing in the path of an approaching tornado.

Jake Garfield's older brother, Max, immediately brought him to New York. Max was always there when Jake needed help and always would be. They were actually quite alike, these two vastly different men—the successful, cold-hearted New York lawyer and the younger, never-been-completely-stable, former POW and ex–drug addict. Max tucked his madness away inside the body of a respected lawyer. Jake's insanity was much closer to the surface.

For as long as Jake could remember, it was Max who had taken care of him and their sister. Jake was what was called in those days "an accident child." So from the beginning, it was Max, forced by circumstances to mature beyond his years, who cared for him. The parents were just too old and ill prepared to care for an infant.

And then one day, their father was gone, killed in a stupid accident, when the driver of a taxi he was in had a massive stroke, lost control of the vehicle, and crashed. Max was in a nearby college at the time and living at home. Even before their father was killed, their mother was only marginally effective. After her husband died, she was totally useless. So Max took over the responsibility of raising Jake and his sister while also attending his classes. Max really didn't mind the extra work. In his own way, he loved his siblings very much and truly enjoyed the responsibility.

So when Jake Garfield was discharged from the VA hospital in Maryland, it was Max who was there to pick him up. He set Jake up in a one-bedroom apartment in Greenwich Village and gave him an allowance for running his errands and doing all the gofer work that his office and his kind of law practice required. And there was enough of it to keep Jake out of trouble.

So, for the moment, as the plane cleared the cloud cover, revealing the lights of Manhattan, Jake Garfield was happy and relatively stable—providing he took his medications.

Chapter 8

San Francisco, early 1970s

The phone call came without warning less than twenty-four hours earlier—as did the slim, black-leather briefcase. Both arrived at Dr. Kevin Tyler's San Francisco apartment within minutes of each other.

The caller inquired, with a European-sounding voice, "Am I speaking, please, with Dr. Kevin Tyler?"

Then, a pause for affirmation. Once satisfied it was Tyler who had answered, the voice continued.

"My employer, Mr. Edmond Calendar, would like to speak with you. You have heard of Mr. Calendar, yes?"

Tyler frowned. Of course he'd heard of Calendar. Who hadn't? It would be like asking if he'd heard of Joe Namath or Jane Fonda. His name was as recognizable as his vast, and sometimes predatory, business exploits. Conversely, few could claim—at least in the past dozen years—that they'd met him in person or, for that matter, even seen a recent photo of the reclusive billionaire. The man's vast wealth had allowed him to replace the reality of Edmond Calendar with a highly polished myth.

A Baby To Die For

"Of course. Yes, I've heard of him. But why on earth would he—" His voice trailed off.

"Good," the voice jumped in. "Mr. Calendar has a business proposition he would like you to hear and, hopefully, to consider. Naturally, if interested, you can expect to be compensated handsomely."

Compensated handsomely? Tyler had to stifle a laugh. He was a scientist in good standing, well known in his field. But in all his years, he had never even come close to being compensated handsomely.

"What sort of proposition?" Tyler asked, his curiosity, as well as his guard, now raised.

"In the next few minutes, someone will…"

At that moment, as if on cue, Tyler's loud front doorbell buzzed.

The caller continued, "Ah, yes, your doorbell—that would be my colleague. I'll hold, if you'd be kind enough to go to the door and accept a briefcase he will give you," the voice continued.

Tyler, as instructed, went to the door, and then stood trying to decide whether or not to open it.

Could this be some elaborate scam? A robbery, perhaps?

He looked back into the apartment. He saw his worn couch, a black-and-white TV, a secondhand stereo, a large rack of jazz and classical records.

Hell, if this is a heist, someone is going to be pretty damned disappointed.

He peered through the peephole and, sure enough, saw the lens-distorted image of a tall man in a dark suit, holding a briefcase. Only then did he open the door and take the wordlessly offered, thin black-leather briefcase from the nondescript young man.

Tyler watched as the man headed for the elevator. Then he hefted the expensively crafted case as he returned to the phone.

This damn thing probably costs a month's salary.

"Uh, hello, yes, I have it."

"Good. Mr. Calendar wishes to meet. At that time, he will explain everything. If you agree to proceed —well, as I said, there will be a suitable financial arrangement."

"And if I'm not interested in—how did you put it—proceeding? What then?"

"Then that will just be that."

"And what am I supposed to do with this—with the briefcase?"

"Take a look inside, Doctor, and consider it and its contents proof of Mr. Calendar's good faith. All is yours to keep regardless of the meeting's outcome."

"Yes, well there are locks on both latches."

"Sorry about that. Make sure you've got the lid of the case in the UP position. That makes the combination on the left side: '1,2,3…and the right lock: 3,2,1."

Tyler pressed the phone's receiver between his ear and shoulder, freeing his hands to key-in the simple combinations and snap open two thick brass latches. He lifted the lid and stared in amazement. The case was empty save for four packets of bills each banded and marked "$5,000." Unless fake, the bills worth $20,000 represented more money than Tyler could hope to save in several years.

A Baby To Die For

Tyler tried to take in the strange request being posited by the phone-voice. It was a preposterous idea. And claiming the request was being made on behalf of none other than *the* Edmund Calendar, one of the richest men on the globe? On the merits of the phone call alone, he'd have hung up, positive someone was trying to scam him. But here Tyler was, looking at a great deal of money. He picked up one of the packets and flipped through the bills—this was what he was seeing with own eyes, and suddenly 'crank phone' call took on a 'solid validity.'

Finally, trying to keep his voice as neutral as possible, Tyler said, "What could Mr. Calendar possibly want from me that could be worth this kind of money?"

"Very honestly, Dr. Tyler, only Mr. Calendar can answer that."

Well, if the man wants to see me that badly, the money's reason enough to find out what this is all about.

"Okay," Tyler said. "When does Mr. Calendar want to meet?"

"He would be pleased if you could meet with him during the afternoon, uh, for you, that would be the day after tomorrow."

"I don't think that would be a problem," Tyler said, warily, "but what do you mean, 'for me'?

"It's a long trip. The car is downstairs."

"You mean leave now?"

"As a matter of fact, yes. Is a half hour's time enough to pack a few things? Nothing fancy."

Tyler didn't know whether to be amused or really pissed off at this back and forth he had to go through.

A Baby To Die For

It was like the proverbial pulling of teeth. "So, where exactly is this meeting?"

"Switzerland. Just outside Zurich."

Chapter 9

An adoption agency, New York City

Harriet Flynn tried and failed to successfully stifle a short laugh. Then, she blushed beet red, and spent an awkward several minutes apologizing to Tuck and Ellen.

Flynn was a professional social worker who had worked with the indigent and the mentally confused for decades. One day she decided it was time to get into a more pleasant and less stressful area of social work, so, she took a job with an adoption agency. Harriet Flynn was good at it from the very beginning. In those days, plenty of babies were available for adoption, and adoption agencies had the luxury of applying experience, insight, and special vision to skillfully and effectively match adopters and adoptees. She prided herself on making good matches, finding the perfect key that opened the correct lock. For her, it was a calling.

The landscape looked quite different now. Still, it was most unprofessional, embarrassing, and completely out of character for her to laugh at prospective clients. But she couldn't help herself.

A Baby To Die For

It was their "List"—still another pathetic, little, typed-out list filled with impossible demands, which usually started out as being non-negotiable and then, one-by-painful-one, they fell away like leaves dying in the autumn. That's what had caused Harriet Flynn to laugh—laughter being one of the ways in which Harriet Flynn tended to deal with the deepening degrees of frustration she faced every day. It wasn't like she'd never seen a list like it before. Every couple that started the adoption process had one, if not on paper, then certainly stored carefully in their minds and expectations.

So Harriet Flynn wasn't laughing at Tuck and Ellen, as much as she was laughing simply because it hurt less than pulling her hair out from the total inability to accommodate any of their wishes.

I'm only a social worker, not God.

"Please, Mr. and Mrs. Handler, I'm really sorry about…well, it was just rude and unprofessional. It's just this list of yours—maybe it's better that you understand now, and not months from now, the reality of what's going on with adoption today. Because the sooner you find out what's been happening, the easier and less stressful it will be for you in the long run. The truth is, there are so few healthy Caucasian infants available, that it can take literally years for a family like yours to adopt."

Tuck looked at Ellen then back to the Flynn woman: "What does that mean? A family like yours?"

Harriet Flynn leaned back in her chair and waited a moment before responding. "A middle-class couple with very specific demands and a reluctance to wait, in order to meet them." Doing this, day after day, was making her sick. She felt her stomach rumble, and she wished she had an antacid or a glass of milk.

Tuck rose from his chair and, walking to the window, looked down on the traffic moving along lower Fifth Avenue. He glanced over at his wife and could see Ellen was near tears.

A wave of helplessness engulfed Ellen.

"So what's 'a family like ours' supposed to do? You're right, we don't want to wait for years. We want our baby now. I know of people who are getting babies, who have adopted babies. What do they do? What about other agencies—"

Ellen's voice trailed off. She now sat in silence, head down, eyes fixed on her lap. Tuck instinctively moved to her side, placing his hand on her shoulder.

"There are some things—" Harriet Flynn began, "— actually, three things that have totally changed the supply calculus for a certain category of babies. Remember, I'm talking only about healthy Caucasian infants. Plenty of minority babies are available—black, brown, yellow. And of course, there are all kinds of older children who need homes, as well as handicapped children. And there are some couples—not many—who have made the decision to adopt babies from foreign countries... and..."

Tuck injected, "We've discussed all those alternative options, Mrs. Flynn, and we're not interested in pursuing any of them," he said with a brusque finality.

It was clear to Harriet Flynn that nothing short of a healthy, white newborn would satisfy the Handlers.

"You mentioned three things?" Ellen said.

"Uh, yes, well, in a way the three are interrelated.

A Baby To Die For

There's the whole issue of birth control. I'm sure you're aware of how readily available it is now. The stigma of asking a doctor for the pill is, by and large, gone. More moms are getting pills for their daughters the way they used to buy them training bras. And condom use is out in the open—some being dispensed in vending machines like cigarettes or chewing gum. It's not uncommon these days for a young woman to carry some in her handbag.

And then there's the recent Supreme Court decision on *Roe v. Wade*. So now, even if a young girl does become pregnant, there's a legal alternative to a back-alley abortion.

"And the third? You said there were three reasons the supply was so low," Tuck said.

He was getting bored with what sounded like a lot of bullshit excuses.

Harriet Flynn arranged several pencils on her desktop. The hostility coming across her desk was palpable, and she never got used to it. No matter how many times a day she met with couples, it was the hostility that was eating her stomach lining away.

"Yes, that would be the shift in psychographics. By that, I mean it used to be that about twenty percent of pregnant girls kept their illegitimate babies and raised them as a single parent or allowed them to be raised by a close relative—a grandparent, for example. Conversely, about eighty percent surrendered their child for adoption. Now, with the easy availability of abortion, the ratio has almost exactly reversed. Though the number is much, much smaller, almost eight out of ten girls keep their babies. As a consequence," Harriet Flynn continued. "We're seeing girls not much more than babies themselves raising their babies. And you put those three things together—birth control, legal abortion, and a higher percentage keeping and raising their babies—those three things have resulted in the current and extreme shortage. It's not a good situation, I know, but it *is* the situation. And the chances of its changing any time in the near future are slim—very slim. We talk to couples like you every day, and we're not the only agency in New York City. And we're not the only city in the state, and you extrapolate out from there and quickly realize that adoption agencies all over the country have the same problem finding babies, and, well, it's a sad and discouraging scenario."

Tuck was mad but not with Harriet Flynn. He was just sick and tired of the problem. It was humiliating, embarrassing, and frustrating to want something and be told by some petty bureaucrat that what they wanted wasn't possible or, at least, close to being impossible.

He also knew that Ellen was feeling a grossly exaggerated sense of guilt over not being able to carry a child.

He moved his arm instinctively, protectively, across her shoulder and, trying to keep his voice under control said, "Look, we're reasonably intelligent people. I'm a lawyer and a police officer. Mrs. Handler is a professional, a CPA. We have a lot to offer a child. What the hell *are* we supposed to do? Where are we supposed to go? I know perfectly well that plenty of people in this city are adopting white babies. We personally know couples that have gotten healthy, Caucasian infants as recently as a few months ago. What do they know that we don't? How do they do it? Where do they go?"

The Flynn woman focused her gaze somewhere beyond Tuck's left shoulder, deliberately avoiding direct eye contact. She just couldn't look him in the eye.

"Well, you know that sometimes a doctor will have a pregnant patient who, for whatever reason, doesn't want to raise the child but doesn't want an abortion, and this doctor might have another patient who's trying to adopt —and he—well, he can get them together, you know, without using an agency like this."

An awkward silence settled on the room like a blanket.

"Are you trying to tell me that all these adoptions we see are the result of those neat little coincidences you're describing, convenient matchups made by benevolent family physicians? Come on, Mrs. Flynn, do you think we are naïve children? What about the black market? It's not a secret. It's in the papers all the time. What about that? How can we do that, go that route?"

Harriet Flynn continued the eye contact with the wall beyond Tuck's shoulder. Her face remained impassive, although it did turn slightly pale. She cleared her throat and answered in a stiff, formal tone.

"Mr. Handler, you must have some idea of how that works. However, the real question is not about the "how" of the black market, but rather, do you *want* to travel that path? We do not recommend any adoption outside a legal, licensed, and sanctioned agency. And that's not just our policy. The same will apply to any authorized adoption agency you go to. They will all tell you the same thing. There are issues of home studies and background checks. No matter how long you have to wait, an official agency placement is always preferable."

It's useless arguing with this woman.

Nothing he could say was going to change her position. He got up and Ellen followed, as did Harriet Flynn.

The three stood by the office door and Tuck said, "Thank you for your time, Mrs. Flynn. We understand, but futile as it may be, we intend to continue pursuing an agency adoption," he said wearily. "We want to see a few more agencies. Since we already have the appointments, we might as well learn as much as we can. Who knows? Maybe we'll get lucky. But honestly, if that pursuit fails, we intend to investigate whatever alternatives we can find, the black market included. If and when we decide to go down that road, Mrs. Flynn," Tuck continued, evenly, "do you think you would be able to help us at all? As you said, you have been doing this for a long time and must have lots of contacts in the world of adoption outside the limits of the agency. Would you help us at all—please?"

Still avoiding eye contact with either Tuck or Ellen Handler, Harriet Flynn answered his question as simply and honestly as she could.

"No, Mr. Handler, I cannot, and I will not."

Chapter 10

Jake's plane from Dallas touched down at JFK in the early afternoon. Max and Porter were at the Kitano Hotel for their weekly rendezvous. Max was sprawled naked and snoring on the Tatami mat, his carnal needs sated. Porter stood, studying him as one might gawk at a beached baby whale. Finishing her post-coital cigarette, she padded naked into the bathroom for a quick shower, then lowered herself gingerly into the giant wooden soaking tub, slowly letting the clear hot water suck at each pore of her body. Finally, all the way in, she sat relaxed, her body from her neck down fully submerged. With a freshly lit cigarette in her mouth and her long hair floating on the surface, she assessed her situation.

Porter Gibbs had always known she was a woman who needed money—big money, copious amounts of money. So, as her involvement in managing Max's adoption enterprises deepened, she realized he'd never pay her as much as she wanted, and since she found nothing else of his worth having, she decided to simply make up for the difference by stealing from the operation.

A Baby To Die For

Without question, she deserved it. After all, she was attractive, still had a figure that turned heads, firm tits and ass, and great hair. Inside she was tough. She had an excellent education and a solid, affluent upbringing. She also had the good luck to be raised by a glamorous and talented mother who had added much needed spice to her father's otherwise bland ancestral genes.

Family legend had it that Porter's father, Kirby Gibbs, handpicked her mother, Sally Kopecky—a Midwestern first-generation Czech—from a popular Broadway musical where she was high-kicking in the chorus. After a whirlwind courtship, consisting of a tsunami-like shower of champagne, flowers, and fancy chocolates, they married. Soon after, Sally—whom everyone now called Boop, for some long-forgotten reason—was stashed quite comfortably fifty miles north of the Great White Way in Southport, Connecticut.

Once there, Boop quickly produced a modest road show of her own, consisting of Porter and then twin boys who died within a week of delivery. That tragedy led to the tentative beginnings of a "nerve condition" which led to Boop's growing penchant for dry martinis. Suddenly, twenty years of her life had evaporated.

The nerve condition and gin finally combined in a tricky way so that when Kirby Gibbs found himself financially wiped out, due to some Canadian oil-drilling fiasco, Boop was just crazy enough to kill herself.

So, while Porter was in Germany studying the Schoenhut wooden doll exhibit as part of her postgraduate thesis, her father was breaking down the thick oak door of the master bath in the Gibbs's elegant and now heavily mortgaged Southport Tudor. There he found his wife firmly packed in a bathtub. Apparently, Boop had filled the tub with very hot water, added boxes and boxes of strawberry Jell-O, then polished off the best part of a fifth of Gilbey's while swallowing God-knows-how-many of her "nerve pills" and then settled in for the long sleep. It was in all the papers. FRUIT CAKE IN ASPIC ran the cruelest headline. Obviously, Boop didn't have all her laces tied.

So, Porter inherited a great deal—her mother's acting ability without, thank you very much, the woman's "soft center" that drove her to such a bizarre suicide, along with her father's good looks, minus his fortune, which, sadly, he never recovered before he died.

"What are you thinking about?" Max said.

And Porter, startled by his voice, would have jumped, except for the seventy-two gallons of hot water holding her in check.

"About you, asshole. Get in the tub, I'll scrub your back."

Max complied, and they laughed as the water spilled out over the sides and flowed into the drain. They did have fun together, in a weird sort of way, two happy scorpions playing in the sun.

"Today was very, how can I put it? Satisfying," Max said.

Porter was more than surprised. Max didn't usually toss compliments around. It rarely occurred to him to do so, and besides, for his taste, compliments didn't hurt enough when they hit someone.

"But I got to get going soon," Max said. "I got a desk full of work. And Jake's coming in with the Kaufmans' money he picked up from Shelby, that Dallas lawyer. I'll probably work late, so, at least I'll be there when he shows up with the cash."

Chapter 11

Jake Garfield was halfway through the Midtown Tunnel on his way in from the airport when he remembered his promise to meet Max at the office later. It was just as well. The cash he was carrying would be a lot better off in his brother's safe than in the pouch strapped around his waist under his shirt.

Jake checked his watch and saw he still had plenty of time before his meeting, so he opted for a quick drink and some relaxation at his favorite watering hole. And who knew? Maybe he'd meet an attractive young lady.

As he liked to say, "One never knows, do one?"

Twenty minutes later, his suitcase dropped off at his apartment, Jake entered Maxwell's Plum, in his opinion, the best singles' watering hole in Manhattan. God bless Warner LeRoy!

In the months since Jake Garfield first set foot in Maxwell's and bellied up to the bar, he'd spent enough in tips to be known as "a friend of the house." Ralph, the ex-marine bartender, spotted Jake as he elbowed up to the middle of the long and crowded bar and had a double scotch, neat with a twist, resting on the immaculate mahogany before Jake's thick hands ever touched the wood. Jake and Ralph had the Vietnam War in common. And that was good enough for both of them.

"*Gracias*, Ralph," Jake said, slapping a ten-dollar bill on the bar and making a little hand signal to Ralph that said, *the change is yours.*

Jake was in mid-sip when he spotted her coming in the door. She stopped, looked around, and clearly, was intimidated by the crowd. Jake made a quick assessment. Thick black hair pulled back in a ponytail, perfect tight little body, about nineteen, and very cute—in a working-in-the-typing-pool kind of way. He knew the type. They filled the bar at Maxwell's every night.

Jake left his drink, gave Ralph a *hold it for me* nod, and knifed his wiry, muscular five-foot-eleven through the crowd to the door, walked up, smiled broadly and said, "Hi."

The girl did a head-to-toe of Jake and, after a moment's hesitation, smiled back.

"Hi," she said.

Great teeth.

"Name is Jake. I once screwed a monkey," he said. "Let me buy you a drink and tell you all about it."

For some insane reason, the preposterous line worked to Jake's own count about sixty-five percent of the time—at least, for a drink. What happened after that, in most cases, proved to be highly successful.

Later that evening, the two of them left the bar and took a cab to his brother's office. Jake left the young woman, whose name was Sandi—"with an *i* not a *y*" she'd pointed out—in the temporary care of the main lobby security guard. She immediately became engrossed in watching the little television security monitors.

Coming off the elevator, Jake noticed the door to the outer reception area was open, and inside it was dark, unlike Max's inner office, which was lit by the green shade desk lamp that threw long shadows across the well-furnished room. One wall was filled with law books—dusted often but rarely touched—a holdover from the office's former occupants.

And then there was Max's baby rattle collection, started when one of his first adoptive families presented him with an early 19th century silver rattle as a thank you for getting them, according to the attached note, *"for getting us the baby of our dreams."* Along with the rattle, Max also received a thick stack of highly negotiable paper rectangles, each featuring the portrait of a dead president.

Many more rattles and portraits of presidents followed. The rattles were all over his office. Silver, pewter, plastic, wood, dozens of them, and no two were alike.

When Jake walked in, Max got up, and came around from behind his desk.

"Hey, little brother how was Dallas?" Max asked, warmly embracing Jake.

"Piece of cake, Max. Not a hitch," Jake said, unbuttoning his shirt to remove the nylon money pouch tied around his middle. It was khaki-colored and had a long, zippered pocket that Jake opened, withdrew bills, and handed them over to his brother.

"Good work," Max said. He gave the stack of money a cursory riffle. "Gotta love that Rick Shelby guy. He may turn out to be a real star. How is the good ol' boy?"

"I tell you, Max, I damned near didn't recognize him. He shaved off his fucking beard. And you know how he usually looks like some yahoo who picked his clothes out of a Salvation Army bin? Well, he got himself some classy threads. Not flashy, or anything like that, but tasty. A lot like the kind of stuff you wear, Max. Tasty."

"Maybe we're giving him too much of a cut?" Max

laughed, but not too seriously. He took five one-hundred-dollar bills out of the stack and handed them Jake. "For you, little brother. A bonus. You did a good job. I especially like that you were on time tonight. It shows responsibility. That's good. It's a very positive sign. Keep up the good work."

Jake was beaming from his brother's words as he entered the elevator. Sandi was still standing right where he'd left her, focused on the security monitors as if they were tuned to a game show.

Christ, this one's got the brains of a tire pump. If I don't score with her tonight, I might just as well give it up.

Chapter 12

A château near Zurich, Switzerland

Edmond Calendar's Dassault-Breguet Falcon 200 taxied to a private tarmac area of Kloten Airport. Tyler was quickly escorted to a nearby helicopter, past the bowser, which was already refueling the coal-black plane.

The copter was also pitch black—and Tyler, again, the only passenger. What followed was the most terrifying ride of his life—skimming, skirting, and traversing around, over, down, and through the Swiss Alps for a hundred kilometers before descending amid the twinkling lights of the fairy-tale village of Gstaad.

Following a greatly expedited check-in at the Palace Hotel, he was escorted to his accommodations, a tastefully furnished suite of rooms. A bellman took Tyler's breakfast order, and by the time he'd showered and shaved, the food was waiting, laid out on a table in the sitting room. An envelope, Tyler's name neatly typed on its face, was propped against the coffee carafe. Inside was a note of welcome, along with a politely worded request directing him to don the surgical scrubs which, the note indicated, would be found in a sealed plastic bag in the large, well-stocked bathroom.

Tyler, albeit puzzled by the strange instructions, did as the note directed. Later, as he sat—dressed from head to foot in sterilized, white surgical scrubs and booties—sleepily sipping the last of the coffee and waiting for something to happen, he had a chance to consider what little he knew about his host, Edmond Calendar.

Like most literate people on earth, Kevin Tyler had heard of Edmond Calendar but knew very little about the man. For years, the press had tried to unearth details, but Calendar—as only the superrich have the wherewithal to do—had erased out of existence just about every scrap of relevant public information about himself. As far as anyone knew, the man could have sprung full-grown from a pumpkin and gone on to amass a staggeringly huge fortune, which, it was said, generated more profit per day than most Americans made in a lifetime.

Fortune Magazine speculated that Calendar was as rich as Howard Hughes, maybe richer. Regardless, they both played in the same exclusive league, consisting of two powerful teams: Calendar and Hughes.

And play games they did. Big-money games like 'Swallow the Business' and 'Destroy the Competition.' And after each bout, whoever won got to rape, plunder, and pillage the particular objective. They were both clearly crazy as loons, which, given their vast power, allowed them to act pretty much as they pleased and still be perceived under the rubric of mysterious, rich, old eccentrics.

And that was about everything Kevin Tyler knew about Edmond Calendar.

He was beginning to nod off from jet lag when a member of what he'd begun to regard as Calendar's Army arrived to escort him to the meeting.

Tyler had expected to be taken to an office of some sort, but instead he was ushered into a large bedroom, not unlike his own. However, the windows here were completely covered with opaque sheets of black plastic, taped tightly all around so that no outside light could intrude. Obviously, the reports of Calendar's hermit-like nature were all true.

The room was dimly lit by the soft green glow from a half-dozen sunlamps arranged around the supine old man. As Tyler's eyes became accustomed to the room's strange light, the details of his surroundings came clear.

Tucked into the deep shadows, an attendant dressed in white scrubs—similar to those worn by Tyler—sat, arms folded, his unblinking eyes glued on Edmond Calendar. The stoic-looking man was obviously being paid to pay attention.

Calendar was stretched out full-length on a white sheet that was thrown across a large padded lounger. The old man lay totally nude, save for tiny white briefs, and encircled by a half-dozen sunlamps that bathed him in their greenish glow. Two round, opaque, white discs protected his eyes from the lamps. A fleeting image of Little Orphan Annie crossed Tyler's mind.

All of Edmond Calendar's body hair was gone— head, chest, and even his eyebrows. His artificially tanned skin was a color that reminded Tyler of an old catcher's mitt he had as a boy. The old man's knees, elbows, and shoulders were wrinkled and gnarled, like the knots of a weathered tree. Edmond Calendar reminded Tyler of a horribly shriveled, dark-skinned mummy.

Tyler, bone-weary, waited in the shadows just outside the circle of green light. After what seemed like an eternity, Edmond Calendar's strangely feminine high-pitched voice broke the silence, drifting out from the pool of green light.

"Dr. Tyler, you coming all this way to see me. It's much appreciated. Of course, you're dying to know why I sent for you."

"Yes, I would say so, sir."

"Curiosity. That's good. I wouldn't expect anything less from a distinguished scientist," Calendar said, with a touch of condescension in his reedy, high-pitched voice.

"So, why am I here, Mr. Calendar?"

"I need your help getting something that's very dear to my heart. Something I want very much. You probably find it hard to imagine a man like me wanting for anything. At least anything money can buy, right? You're a smart guy. Do you have any idea what it might be?"

Tyler had no idea what Calendar could possibly want that his immense fortune could not secure for him? Redemption? Immortality? Tyler's thoughts flashed on Citizen Kane, the Orson Welles film where a dying Charles Foster Kane obsessed for Rosebud, the fucking sled he'd had as a child! What on earth could be Edmond Calendar's Rosebud?

A Baby To Die For

So, figuring he didn't have much to lose, Kevin Tyler took a shot and answered the old man's question as best he could.

"To tell you the truth, all I can think of is that old saw that goes, 'What do you give someone who has everything?'"

"And the answer to that question would be?" Calendar asked, a faint smile playing at the edges of his thin lips.

"A box to put it in."

"Bingo, son! A damn good analogy! A box to put it in! You see I was always too busy and too damn selfish to have children. I've no intention of letting my fortune fall into the hands of my scum-sucking ex-wives, or support a bunch of dogs or cats, or, for that matter, make some bleeding-heart charity richer than shit. That's why you're here, Dr. Tyler—to help me get that 'box to put it in'—as you put it. In this case, it's to produce an heir. You're a geneticist and can do whatever is necessary to make that happen, 'cause that's exactly what I want, an heir. Yes, sir, a human box into which I can put everything I own."

Chapter 13

He clutched his heart as Ellen opened the front door. Then Saul "Twosie" Bootman staggered into the Handler's apartment.

"*Good Lawd!*" Saul shouted, in his lame imitation of a strangled British accent. "The climb up here puts me in mind of my failed attempt to conquer Mont Blanc's dreaded north face."

Ellen and Tuck, startled at first, burst out laughing. The Handler's Upper West Side, four-story, walk-up rental was the butt of endless jokes—and the occasional leg cramp. But it had a good sized living room, at least by New York standards, with two small skylights on the north side, plus a real working fireplace. Years before, back in the early thirties, it had served as an artist's garret. Now it was a warm, friendly home for the Handlers. They'd spent a year painstakingly stripping decades of paint, exposing two beautiful brick walls, and sanded and shellacked the hardwood floors.

A cozy blaze was now dancing in the small fireplace. A dozen squat candles placed around the room glowed and melted and filled the whole space with the aroma of musk. Well-worn, thrift shop oriental rugs softened the look of the gleaming floors. Several framed vintage posters were comfortably at home on the walls.

"Damn, Twosie, you're looking younger every time we see you," Tuck said.

Saul's own two children, as well as his nieces and nephews, always addressed him as Twosie. The nickname came from his longtime, unshakable habit of giving all of them gift money for birthdays, holidays, graduations, and sometimes just for the hell of it, but always in crisp, new two-dollar bills. When one of the kids did anything bad, Twosie would always admonish by saying, "If you don't behave, next time you're only getting Onesies."

The kids ate it up and gave him his nickname, and never forgot those two-dollar bills. He refused to reveal the source of the rarely seen bills, mostly joking that he printed them himself.

Saul Bootman earned his living as a lawyer but was, above all, and in his heart of hearts, a frustrated comic. He was a tall, skinny guy with a shock of unruly gray hair. An Ichabod Crane in a Brooks Brothers suit. He longed to play comedy clubs and dreamed of doing twenty minutes in a smoky room, stalking the stage in a tux with a microphone in one hand and a scotch-on-the-rocks in the other, "killing" the audience until they slapped the tabletops begging for a moment's mercy, and guys in silk sharkskin suits peed their pants.

"After the hike up to this joint, I'd be lucky to pass a life insurance physical. You could make a fortune renting

Sherpa guides to lead your guests up from the lobby-level base camp. I left my bag of pitons out in the hall with the rest of my climbing gear. Ach, but you kids are lucky, since the angel of death can't even fly this high. What's for dinner , beef jerky? Hey, that's not a bad name for a wrestler. And now, in the ring for the first time," he growled in his best ringside announcer's voice, "the pride of New York's Upper West Side, the one and only—Beef Jerky!"

Ellen finished laughing and then hugged and kissed her uncle.

"Twosie, you're funnier than ever."

It had been a wonderful evening, filled with good conversation, good food, and genuine laughter. Then, stuffed with tons of lasagna—some clearly in evidence on Saul's tie—the three lounged comfortably near the fireplace and sipped the brandy Saul had brought as a house gift. Tuck knew Saul had got the one-liners out of his system over dinner and could now be counted on to handle a more serious subject.

"Twosie," Tuck began, "Ellen and I have a bit of a problem we'd like to discuss."

For an instant, Saul formed words for a flip reply but sensed Tuck's level of seriousness, thought better of it, swallowed, nodded, and sipped silently from his brandy.

His silence was a signal for Tuck to continue.

"You know Ellen has had several miscarriages."

"Two," Ellen said, always the accountant.

"Yes, two, to be precise," Tuck agreed. "We were told it would not be wise to become pregnant again. Actually, very dangerous."

"Sounds like the right advice," Saul said. "I assume you're trying to adopt? And suddenly, I'm up here for Saturday night dinner. So that means you need some professional adoption chitchat?"

"Oh, come on, Saul, we wanted you here, just to be here," Ellen added, embarrassed by what her uncle Saul was saying, mostly because he was partially right.

"Sweetheart, please, don't worry. I'm the family consigliere, no? If not me, then who? Your husband's a cop now, ergo he knows zilch about the law."

Tuck smiled, "Sure as hell not much about adoption."

"So, let's see," Saul said, summarizing. "It's too risky for Ellen to have another pregnancy—two miscarriages were enough, right?"

"Yes, and so we decided to try and adopt a baby," Ellen said.

"Believe me, you're far from being alone. Every day, couples like you go through the crazy kabuki dance called adoption. You just want to give a kid a home, raise it like your own. The trouble is, you want it to be perfect, because if you had a child, it would be perfect, right? Gorgeous, white, and healthy. You fantasize maybe you can get one from a movie actress who happens to stray into a brief but tender affair with her wildly handsome director during the shooting of a deep and massively meaningful cinema epic. Or—possibly the offspring of a young, brilliant English Lit major at some hot-shot ivy league college. One day, over tea and cookies, her handsome, albeit older professor shows her a draft of his new novel, and she's gently seduced. Am I close?"

A Baby To Die For

Saul didn't wait for an answer. He knew what it was.

"And, of course, you probably had a list of all the details you were looking for, from the mother's religion to the father's hair color. And you were shocked to find out that there ain't no babies, regardless of hair color. So you went to another agency—and another —and another. No luck. 'Maybe a child in a few years,' they said. 'Be patient,' they said. But you don't want to be patient and wait a few years. And somewhere along the line in your digging and searching, you find out about the black market—the way to get a baby right now. No waiting. No number to take, like at the deli counter in Zabar's."

Tuck and Ellen looked at each other and then back at Saul, realizing he's correct on each and every point, but not quite understanding where the conversation is going.

"Saul, wait…" Tuck began.

"Tuck, look, I'm not trying to demean or be flippant about what you probably went through, I just want you to know that I understand, so please, let me finish," Saul said, then stood, walked to the parson's table that served as the bar, and poured himself another two fingers of brandy. He came back with the bottle and added similar amounts to both Tuck and Ellen's glasses. "So you called me. You figure, maybe Uncle Saul knows his way around the black market, has a few contacts in the network. And you know, you're right. I do have a few contacts. And, of course, I will do everything in my power to help you."

Saul ended to his monologue triumphantly with a smile, sat down, and waited for audience reaction.

"See, Tuck, I told you," Ellen said. "I knew Twosie would know what to do."

A Baby To Die For

Tuck was still looking a bit skeptical.

"Tell us about it, Saul. I know from working the street where some of the babies come from. Not a few of those women are pretty rough specimens—infected, booze and drug addicted. Certainly, not anyone whose baby I would want. They don't all get abortions, even with the recent legalization."

A shiver ran through Ellen, and she took a long swallow of brandy.

"You're right, Tuck," Saul said. "And some of those foolish, sad women go ahead and have their babies. Have them, then put them into plastic bags, and drop them in bus terminals or toss them into garbage cans, shove them into bus station lockers. And if one of those babies gets really lucky, maybe it ends up on the steps of a church or a police precinct."

"We don't want any part of that, Saul. Why would we want the offspring of a drug addict or drunk? Truthfully, if you were in our place, would you feel any differently?"

Saul shook his head.

"I agree with Tuck, Twosie," Ellen said. "And we need you to please help us make this happen. We've hit a brick wall at the adoption agencies. Every one of them has the same story. It's harder than ever to get a baby now, a minimum wait of close to two years. But I know there's an alternative to the adoption agencies."

"What do you know about the black market, Saul?" Tuck asked.

Chapter 14

Kevin Tyler studied the cadaver-thin body that was Edmond Calendar and struggled to digest the billionaire's crazy request in his overly tired brain.

An heir? So that's why this nut flew me halfway around the world. Just to have me put his semen into a test tube so the old bastard could breed.

The faster he got out of this place, the better. But then Tyler considered the briefcase filled with lovely, crisp, hundred-dollar bills sitting in his San Francisco apartment, and he commanded himself to slow down. Slow down and listen to what the old man had to say and maybe, just maybe, he'd hear an opportunity knocking—a sound he'd been waiting to hear for a long, long time.

Calendar raised his head no more than an inch or two, cleared his throat rather loudly, and said, "Dr. Tyler, did you hear what I said? I know everything about you, and I know you're the expert in doing this sort of thing. I've spent a shit load of money to get you here, so at least give me the courtesy of a response."

A Baby To Die For

Of course, Calendar knew about Tyler. Men like Calendar never moved into the unknown. Calendar knew the outcome of most situations many steps before he entered. So he knew Kevin Tyler was a respected expert in the rather obscure and undistinguished field of genetic engineering known as cryobiology—basically, freezing sperm for breeding cattle and racehorses, and more recently, storing sperm to solve infertility problems in humans—exactly what Edmond Calendar was looking for.

He also knew that, as far as his day-to-day existence went, Tyler had a crushing mortgage on his tiny apartment in San Francisco, an anemic balance in his savings account, and a money-hungry ex-wife—exactly the kind of person Calendar liked to negotiate with, one who, given enough cash incentives, could easily be manipulated.

But Tyler would not turn out to be the pushover Calendar expected. Like most research scientists, Tyler's work required funding, and the good doctor had become a connoisseur of wealthy donors, expending no small amount of energy studying the potential sources of funds—endowments, grants, and fellowships. Patrons were patrons and they all liked their butt's kissed. Even so, he was never more than a stack of bills away from shutting down the Bunsen burners and locking the doors.

And now, one of the richest men on earth, maybe *the* richest wanted Tyler to personally harvest his sperm, and use some of it for making a baby.

Chapter 15

"What do I know about the black market," Saul mused, hoping his short outburst about the state of adoption hadn't been too harsh.

The room was dim now, save for a single table lamp. He got up from his chair and, using the fireplace poker, jostled the smoldering logs back to life.

"Actually, I do know a bit about this business of selling babies—the black market, as you call it."

"See, I told you, Tuck! I just knew Twosie could help!" Ellen said emphatically.

"Please, Ellen," Twosie said, "don't get carried away. This adoption business that skirts the legal channels is complicated. It's a big business, and it's been around for a long, long time. Did you ever hear about orphan trains?"

Tuck and Ellen looked at each other, shrugged their lack of knowledge, and looked back at Saul.

Saul waved away his question with a flick of his hand.

"Of course not. Why would you?"

"What the hell are orphan trains, Saul?" Tuck asked.

"Back in the early 1800's, before the Civil War, the

orphan trains were like adoption agencies on steroids. The big East Coast cities—New York, Baltimore, Philadelphia—were beginning to overflow with immigrants and as a result were, of course, crawling with poor immigrant kids. Some of them were orphaned or homeless, but many were the human overflow from large families who just didn't have enough money to feed everybody. So, here in New York, the Children's Aid Society decided to round up these waifs and ship them out west, where, in their wisdom, they decided these kids could be placed with more stable, God fearing families. The whole concept turned 'children's aid' into an oxymoron. From the time it started right up until the Great Depression, about a quarter-million poor kids had been rounded up, packed into trains and shipped west. At each stop along the way, they would be herded onto the train platform and put on display. Any family who wanted or needed a child could check out the inventory and take one—or maybe two, and that was that. Few, if any, questions were ever asked, and no records were kept."

Ellen ran her hand nervously through her hair. "It's hard to believe there were so many people who couldn't have children of their own and had to get one off a train platform."

"No, no," Saul said. "Being able or not able to have children of their own had nothing to do with it. That wasn't the reason someone came to the station to take a child. Most had families already, some that were very large. These people were taking these kids to be farmhands, to help with chores, to become apprentices, to clerk in stores, or just to do all the crap work around the farm or house or wherever."

"Christ, that's practically slavery," Tuck said.

"You're damned right. For some of those poor kids, it was, but no one was around to ask any questions. Some of the lucky ones were taken into good homes, with loving families. Years after, in a few cases, some even found their way back to their original families. But more than a few were exposed to some pretty harsh treatment."

Ellen stared at Saul, eyes wide.

"That's—I don't know—so barbaric."

"Were they simply grabbed off the streets? Kidnapped?" Tuck asked.

"No, not at all. The theory behind the trains was a distorted notion that the children of poor Catholic and Jewish immigrants could be rescued from their so-called depraved urban surroundings and 'Americanized' if they could just be placed with upstanding Anglo-Protestant families in culturally worthy environments. The parents gave the kids freely, thinking they'd have a better life or simply because they didn't have enough money to feed them. Remember, life wasn't very pretty in the ethnic ghettos of New York City back then."

Tuck fetched the brandy and freshened Saul's glass with a generous splash.

"That's a chilling story, Saul."

"Yes, it is. The orphan trains are gone, thank God. But supplying children to families who want kids hasn't stopped. It's simply evolved, ever so slowly, into more formal and highly reliable adoption agencies. However, over the years, the supply of Caucasian infants has gotten smaller than the demand. And so, enter the black market, which has become a more sophisticated, more lucrative, and a damned dangerous business. If enough young couples want babies, you can bet the farm that somebody is going to find babies to sell to them. And like any other crop, the greater the drought, the higher the price."

Now it was Tuck's turn to take a poker to the fire, and he added a log before returning to sit next to Ellen.

"What kind of money are you talking about?" Ellen said.

"Think of the price in two parts. The basic cost is minimal," Saul shrugged. "About what you'd expect to pay for the pregnant girl's living expenses, transportation, doctor and hospital bills, that sort of stuff. Pretty much the same kind of costs you'd have to shell out with a pregnancy of your own, or what you'd pay for a baby through a legit adoption agency. But the network is in the business of selling babies for profit, so the basic cost is just the beginning. After that, the second price kicks in. The one that's paid in cash, under the table, and is never reported to the IRS."

"Saul, we understand that a black market baby costs more," Tuck said. "But the question is how much?"

"It's hard to say. When you move into the black market you're entering the Wild West, so to speak."

Tuck was sitting forward on his chair, the snifter of brandy in his left hand, his right hand nervously tracing the dark end of day stubble on his jaw.

"I understand. So take a fucking guess, Saul! What's

the price a good baby scalper gets nowadays?" Tuck said, with a tinge of aggression.

"Tuck, please," Ellen scolded, "Saul's trying to help. It's not his fault."

"I'm sorry, really, Saul. It's just so damned upsetting," Tuck apologized.

"Not to worry, I understand."

"We don't have much," Ellen added. "We're not rich."

"Honest to God," Saul said, "I don't know how much it would be. I have the contacts but I don't know the going rate. It could be five, ten, twenty grand. Maybe more."

"Are you serious?" Tuck asked, the shock evident on his face.

"These things depend a lot on timing, luck, and a little fast-talking. The timing and luck are up to the scalpers, but not too many can talk as fast as your old Uncle Saul."

Ellen wrapped her arms around Saul in a bear hug, "I know you'll do your best, Twosie. We're depending on you."

Twenty minutes later, the three of them stood at the front door of the apartment building, bundled against the evening blast of arctic air that had migrated from Canada and settled like a shroud over the Upper West Side of Manhattan.

Chapter 16

"Well, Dr. Tyler, will you or won't you help me?" the old man asked in his gruff, croaking voice. He rolled his head toward Tyler and, with a subtle lifting of both eyebrows, caused the white protective monocles to fall onto the sheet, revealing the old man's intense, hard eyes. Younger looking by decades than the face that framed them, his eyes jabbed into Kevin Tyler like the sharp prongs of a carving fork.

"I've no damn intention of wasting your time or mine, Tyler, so let's cut the crap. My doctors tell me my sperm count is weak. Like that's supposed to surprise me. Just between us, I'm amazed and slightly amused there's any of the little buggers left to count at all. It may be the sheep-gland concoction they've been shooting into my ass for the past ten years—who knows?—anyway, they tell me there's still some life down there. So while there is, I want to take advantage of the situation. So will you help me or not?"

Will I help him? Research scientists like Tyler lived off grants that came from wealthy strangers. Like all rich people, Edmond Calendar was a fish to be hooked. But Calendar wasn't any ordinary fish—oh, no—Calendar was the biggest goddamned catch in the ocean. A fucking Moby Dick. And Kevin Tyler was Captain Ahab. And all Tyler had to do was hook the old gent and then carefully—very, very carefully—reel him in. The key word was: *carefully*. Calendar had been listening to sob stories and deflecting open palms ever since he made his first million. He knew all the tricks, had heard all the spiels. Old lures, snapped leaders, and barbed hooks bristled all over him from as many failed attempts. He'd been approached with every con story on earth and been subjected to more ass-kissing sycophants than Kevin Tyler could ever imagine.

"What exactly do you expect from me, Mr. Calendar?"

"I'm prepared to outfit your clinic to the state of the art and pay to keep it that way. In addition to the equipment and upkeep for running the lab, I'm prepared to pay you $50,000 a year to do the work. That's $50,000 *after* tax dollars—net to you. But let's be clear, I expect you to work for me and me alone. No moonlighting, do you follow me? Whatever the price tag, the sole purpose—the *only* purpose—of the clinic will be to do whatever is necessary for me to end up with that 'box' you talked about, preferably a male box. If and when that happens, the lab and everything in it is yours to keep. In addition, I'll continue your salary for five years beyond my death. Does that idea interest you enough to proceed?"

Kevin Tyler bit his tongue and applied tremendous willpower just to keep from shouting with joy. It had actually happened. Some wonderful act of Providence was shining down on this old scientist.

A Baby To Die For

Don't blow it now. Don't blow it. Just keep your eye on the prize, and don't be nervous.

Kevin Tyler took a deep breath.

"Possibly it's my Scottish blood, Mr. Calendar, but although your offer is beyond generous, and most research scientists in my place would probably commit murder for a lot less, frankly, it's a waste of your money. There are several established labs who do what you want all the time. In fact, there's an excellent sperm bank—"

"I spoke with those yahoos out in Iowa. I don't wish to be one of their customers—or anyone's customer. I want my own lab, damn it! My own sperm bank."

Tyler couldn't help but realize he was witnessing an old billionaire stamping his foot—metaphorically speaking—and having a little shit fit.

Play it right, and there's a chance the old man will bankroll the library!

"I don't play well with others," Calendar continued. "And I sure as hell don't share worth a damn, and I'm prepared to pay whatever it takes for that idiosyncratic privilege."

Tyler squared his narrow shoulders, pulled himself to his full five feet eight inches, and gave Calendar what he hoped was a friendly, albeit hard, glare.

"I'm sorry, Mr. Calendar, I'm truly flattered, but not interested. It's overkill and a waste of your money."

"A refreshing answer, son. Not the right answer, but refreshing, nevertheless. I got to hand it to you, Doc, it takes balls to stay honest when offered a lot of moolah. Most of the jerks I deal with are reduced to whining ninnies just thinking about how much they might squeeze out of me. I could tell them shit was Shinola, and they'd scoop up a handful and rub it all over their fucking Gucci loafers."

Calendar paused, shook his head, and gave a short bark of a laugh.

"To tell you the truth, Tyler, it's a big pain in the ass. So, as far as my money is concerned, you don't have to be concerned. I *have* more than enough. I know it's not a big deal to freeze sperm. I also realize that wanting my own genetic laboratory working for me alone would seem to just about anyone else a waste of money—*overkill,* as you called it. They made the same bloody comments about Howard and that big fucking wooden airplane he kept in a hangar for so many years—the Spiced Grouse, or Spruced Goose, or whatever it was he called that seventy-yard-long pile of firewood. But people like us—Howard and me—we don't give a shit about what anybody thinks. You may be unlucky enough someday to have the kind of money one needs to understand what I'm talking about, enough so that everything can be exactly the way you want it. Every fucking thing! It's an important concept, and you got be real goddamn wealthy to understand it. So—do we have a deal, or not?"

Time to set the hook. Tyler moved toward the door, and as he grabbed the doorknob, he turned back, facing the old man.

"Would you consider a counteroffer, Mr. Calendar?"

"Counteroffer? Damn it, man, you think you can negotiate with me? I just put a small fortune on the table. Take it or leave it," Calendar growled, "You're starting to piss me off."

Tyler forced himself to stay calm and ignore Calendar's growing agitation.

"What would you say if I told you that what I have in mind has little to do with your generous offer?" Tyler said, one hand still holding the doorknob. "I'd like to propose something that will give you the heir you want—and a lot more—while also giving me something I want as well."

Calendar looked at Tyler for a long moment, pursed his lips, and said, "Okay, son, you got my attention. Explain."

Chapter 17

Tuck was standing in the kitchen working on his first cup of coffee and reading the editorials in the *New York Times* when the phone rang. It was almost two weeks after the dinner with Saul and his promise to dig up more information about a black market adoption.

"Tuck, it's me," Saul said, "I got news."

"El, get the phone, it's Saul," Tuck shouted to Ellen, who was in the bedroom.

She immediately picked up the extension.

"Is it good or bad, Twosie?"

"Well, actually, a little of both."

"Okay—give us the good and to hell with the bad," she said.

Saul forced a small, nervous laugh. "Phew, your apartment is so high I get winded just talking to you on the phone."

"Please, enough with the apartment jokes, Twosie!" Ellen demanded nervously, sensing what Saul was about to tell them would not be good.

"Right, okay. There is a baby available. Or, I should

say, almost available. The mother will give birth in about two weeks. And from what they told me, this could be the one."

"Oh, my God," Ellen screeched. "Details, details, please, Twosie," she said, trying to control her excitement. "Is it a boy or girl?"

There was a long silence on Saul's end of the line.

"Saul? Are you still there?" Ellen said.

"Look, before you get your hopes up, you better hear the bad news."

Saul took a deep breath, one that tries to suck courage from the air itself. "They're asking $18,000 for the baby," Saul said, softly and with a touch of resignation and a hint of bitter anger. "And to be perfectly frank," Saul continued, even before Tuck or Ellen could react, "the chances are more than good that there is another buyer, and they'll push the price up a lot higher, easily to $20,000. And that could quickly go up by another $5,000 or possibly more."

"There's another buyer?" Ellen said.

"That's what I was told. There's no way of knowing for sure. It could be a ploy to jack up the price. Like when you find an apartment, make a bid, and the real estate agent tells you there's another buyer, and ends up getting you to cough up a few more thousand for the place, using what is essentially a head-fake."

"Wait a second," Tuck barked. "We're not discussing an apartment or a used-car auction, for Christ's sake!"

Saul's soft, frustrated laugh was mostly to himself. "Tuck, I know you don't want to hear it, but it *is* like a used-car auction. Exactly like one. It's business: supply and demand. That's what this black market thing is all about. What they quoted me is the going price, and the going price is always going, but it only goes in one direction—up!"

"What about all your fucking contacts? The fast-talking you told us about?" Tuck shouted.

"Tucker, please!" Ellen injected, cutting him short. "Twosie isn't to blame. He warned us how it might be."

There was an embarrassed silence.

Finally, Tuck said, "You're right. Shit, I'm sorry, Saul. I didn't mean to take it out on you. But those numbers, eighteen, twenty—maybe more. It's way out of the question."

"Hey, it's okay, Tuck, I got thick skin."

"Who are these people you're dealing with?" Tuck asked.

"The guy I spoke with is a lawyer named Max Garfield. All he does is sell babies. Some people swear by him. Think he's doing a great service. At least, that's what his customers claim. They love him. Some families have gotten two and three babies through him."

"And they paid that much?"

"That much and, probably in some cases, a hell of a lot more. But Garfield gives them babies that meet their demands. Like you, they want infants with excellent backgrounds. Tall fathers, attractive mothers, certain religious backgrounds. Garfield supplies whatever the buyer desires. Made-to-order suits cost money, right, and so do custom-made babies," Saul said, with a touch of sarcasm.

107

A Baby To Die For

"Even if I had the money..." Tuck said, "...aw, fuck it! I just hate getting ripped off!"

"What if you tried another lawyer, Twosie?" Ellen said.

"Truth is, sweetie, most of the action in the baby market goes through one lawyer: Max Garfield. He somehow manages to get a piece of almost every adoption that takes place, and not just in New York. He has a network of lawyers all over the country feeding him leads on potential buyers and available babies. He's even got abortion clinics here and some in Canada."

"Why on earth would he have abortion clinics?" Ellen asked.

"Yeah, at first blush it does seem counterintuitive, but think about it: their clinics are a perfect resource for leads. Not all the girls who go to an abortion clinic are able to have an abortion. Some are easily talked out of it or change their minds. Some are too far into their pregnancy—that sort of thing. In some cases, when necessary, Garfield's people pay the girl to carry to full term."

Tuck refilled his coffee cup. He was furious. The muffled sound of an ambulance siren drifted up from the street.

"They actually bribe them to carry the baby? You know that for a fact?" Tuck asked.

"Probably couldn't prove it in court, Tuck, but they do bribe them with cash, college tuition, a car, or a trip around the world. Whatever they want. The extra cost is no problem—it's just passed on to the couple that wants the baby. And like I said, the customers are delighted. Do you think they really care if part of what they pay Garfield goes to send some teenage girl to spend a week in the Bahamas?"

"Would this Garfield character listen to some reason? After all, we can give a child a good home…" Ellen's voice trailed off.

She knew the answer to her rhetorical question even before she asked it.

"After what I told you, what do you think? Max Garfield is as cold as ice, Ellen. His whole network is like that. It's not personal with them, just business, and money talks. Babies are just another commodity, it's as simple as that. Even I was shocked," Saul said. "The prices have shot up since last I heard. The numbers I gave you had been right not too long ago. But the $18,000 they're asking is rock bottom. Next year, it will seem like a bargain. There's no haggling. Garfield made that clear. He claims he's got more than enough couples waiting, going crazy wanting a kid, all willing to throw in a few thousand extra for a healthy, white, adoptable baby. That's why the prices will keep going up."

Tuck let a low groan escape. "Christ, Saul, I never imagined. It's like a bad dream. This Garfield guy, does he work out of the city?"

"Yeah, right in midtown. Pan Am Building. As far as the black market in babies is concerned, he's the man."

"Well, Twosie, I guess we can forget the whole thing. We don't have that kind of money now, and by the time we saved it, the prices would be even higher. It's the old double bind. But thanks for trying. We certainly appreciate it," Tuck whispered, as he slowly placed the receiver back.

A Baby To Die For

That night, Tuck and Ellen lay in their darkened bedroom, each trying to sort out their individual thoughts. Saul's phone call had shattered and smashed their neat and naïve plans. The reality took their breath away like a bucket of ice water dashed across a sleeping sunbather.

Tuck felt sick. Maybe he should have taken the job at JD&E, then by now, he would have the money they needed. His decision to become a police officer instead of practicing law made this his fault. His selfishness. And the rage and guilt threatened to overwhelm him. Who the hell was this Max Garfield to decide who could and could not have a baby?

But Tuck also knew from his own study of the law that this man was doing nothing illegal, not by placing babies anyway. He might be dancing close to the edge with his taxes and hiding the income, but a smart lawyer could find ways to hide all that, even from the IRS. Basically, helping a couple get a baby hurt no one—just a "victimless crime"—unless, as in Tuck and Ellen's case, you happened to be the victim.

Meanwhile, mere inches away, Ellen was curled around her own darkness. She was still convinced that this failure was her fault. It was she, not Tuck, having the miscarriages. It was her job and she had failed. And now, they couldn't even afford to buy a child! It was humiliating. It brought tears to her eyes, it was so sad. Two professionals, a lawyer turned detective and an accountant with a good job, two bright, articulate people in need of a warm, cuddly baby, and they didn't have enough money. A rich bookie, a successful porno dealer, or a premier pimp could get one , or two, or a house full, but they couldn't.

A Baby To Die For

Goddamn it! Goddamn Max Garfield!

Ellen hated what it was doing to Tuck. He was a strong person, yet he seemed defenseless and frustrated, and she loved him so much. She couldn't let that happen. She would have to protect him. This was her problem. And, she was sick with misery.

They lay like that in the darkness for hours, each filled with anger, guilt, and self-recrimination.

Sometime before dawn, Ellen touched Tuck and he touched her, and the coolness of the sheets that had been empty between them felt good on their warm, naked bodies. They made love, not slowly, like gourmets, but aggressively, with an unfamiliar and desperate hunger.

And when they were finished and sharing a cigarette, Tuck asked Ellen, "The diaphragm, you did have it on? You know what the doctor said."

"Don't be such a worrywart. I came to bed with it," Ellen whispered, kissing Tuck on the tip of his nose.

It was the first time she had ever lied to her husband.

Chapter 18

"Like I said, son, you got my attention," Calendar barked.

By challenging Calendar with his counter offer, Tyler had crawled far out on a very thin limb. He had to somehow gather his talking points as rapidly as he could while he held the old man's attention and interest.

In a split second, a scene flashed into Tyler's memory. He was just a skinny nine- or ten-year-old, frozen on the quivering end of a diving board twenty feet above the water. A half-dozen of his friends had already jumped and were in the pool shouting for him to follow, calling him chicken, making clucking sounds and laughing. He was scared, his heart pounding. And that's exactly how Tyler felt now, facing the old man in the lounger—the one person who, if he could sell him on his idea, might become his benefactor. Finally, those many years ago, he had jumped and, of course, he was okay.

Fuck it! And he jumped again.

He began by walking to the window and pulled aside an edge of plastic covering one of the windows just far enough to see outside. Heavy snow was falling at a forty-five-degree angle, illuminated from the full moon reflecting off the frozen snow crystals. He saw an unreal quality to the scene, as if he were looking into a child's snow globe. He could easily imagine a giant hand shaking it hard—with him in it.

"Mr. Calendar," he began. "let's assume for now we go forward with your offer. Of course, I would do everything humanly possible to help you produce an heir. But using your money to have me do that alone, would be…well, let's say, it would only be a fraction of what we could really accomplish. We have the potential to do so much more—something that would immortalize your name. Something truly monumental."

"You talking about some sort of statue or building? Hell, I don't need none of that kind of crap," Calendar muttered, growing impatient.

"No, nothing like that. I want to build a sort of library."

"A library!" Edmond Calendar exploded. "What in fucking hell are you talking about? Are you out of your mind?"

"Please, hear me out, sir. I'm not talking about a library of books, I'm talking about a library of *people*."

"People?"

"Not actual people, no .Men's sperm—*your* sperm, for example—frozen. Not just yours. Yours and hundreds of others like you."

"Why on earth would you want to do that?" Calendar said, pushing himself up on an elbow and challenging Tyler.

"Evolution."

"What the hell's evolution got to do with collecting sperm?"

"As it turns out, quite a bit. Darwinian evolution is based on the strongest and smartest among us surviving," right?

"Right, although I've known a few bible-thumpers who'd argue the point."

Tyler's hand gesture pushed the comment aside. "Now, conversely, the weakest of the species simply die off. And that theory has worked really well for millions of years. But you see, we now have a problem. The smarter man has become, the better he's gotten at *stopping* the weakest from dying off. And that means that it's no longer just the fittest that survive. Thanks to the methodical advances in medicine, miracle drugs, better nutrition, and a bunch of other human interventions, the weakest among us are kept alive as well. The ones who are less healthy, with lower intelligence levels, and less earning power—they are not only surviving, they are thriving. And, ironically, they procreate in greater numbers than the stronger, smarter, and wealthier of us."

"So you're saying all the good stuff—the wonder drugs, the medical advances—all that stuff may actually be fucking up the works?"

"In a manner of speaking, yes. Add to the picture our modern-day exposure to radiation, hormones introduced into our food chain to increase production, chemical waste seeping into our water supply, the depletion of the ozone, et cetera—all these things are conspiring to alter the integrity of our basic gene pool. Human sperm and eggs are inevitably going to be genetically altered. It's happening to some degree already. So, we might be forced to counter those changes, not to improve our species but in a proactive act of biological self-defense, to keep the species from degrading. We need to put a genetic line in the sand *now*...a benchmark that we can come back to in the future and use as an accurate guide."

"And how exactly do you think this library of yours can tackle that?"

"We would choose the best and brightest men in the world and have their sperm frozen and safely stored, so that we have insurance against the gradual and alarming genetic changes we are sure to face in the future. Think of what that could mean, sir. A genetic library, a collection drawn from the greatest people alive today—scientists, mathematicians, philosophers, Nobel Prize winners, business leaders, Olympians, artists, writers—their sperm frozen and available, not for use now, but for future generations. It's not a question of *if* our species will degrade, but rather *when* and how rapidly. The contents of such a library would be the biological azimuth against which we can measure the degree of drift and adjust for it, as necessary. Imagine, sir, The Edmond Calendar Library of Life. That, sir, would be a legacy you could be proud of."

The old man didn't say a word. The room fell silent. The world outside no longer existed. The only sounds to be heard were the breathing of the two men and the barely perceptible tone of the air-purification system. Finally, without moving his piercing blue eyes from Kevin Tyler, the old man spoke.

"I think the doctor could use a glass of water," he said, and the attendant sprang to his feet.

Both men remained silent until the mineral water was served. Tyler was parched from talking and eagerly gulped at the cool, sweet-tasting water. His thoughts were prosaic, possibly a fleeting curiosity about the cost of the water and his feeling of utter exhaustion. He accepted a refill and finished that, as well.

"I'll be honest with you, Tyler, this is an area I never gave much thought to. This genetic drift thing—a sort of dumbing down of our species, huh?"

"Precisely. And this is the kind of legacy you can pass on to mankind—and, in the process, have what you wanted in the first place: an heir."

The two vastly different men faced one another. Tyler could feel—almost see—the intense level of concentration as Calendar digested what he'd heard, a process he was most familiar with. He did the same whether buying a company he coveted, or making a billion-dollar deal—he absorbed the facts, then rolled the dice based on his instincts—the "feel" of the deal, as he was fond of saying. And he usually came out on top.

Tyler felt the unbearable silence like a weight pressing his body down.

Finally, Calendar said, barely over a whisper, "Damn, son, you got yourself one brilliant fucking idea!"

Tyler resumed breathing.

And, when days later Tyler boarded the helicopter to

begin his journey home, Project Encore—the code name Tyler gave it—was about to be a fully funded reality. The Edmond Calendar Library of Life, at least on paper, was now a legal entity, and Dr. Kevin Tyler was its partial owner and managing director in perpetuity.

Chapter 19

Tuck and Ellen were walking and laughing. It was the kind of giddy laughter triggered by something that wouldn't be nearly as funny, absent the festive mood of the evening. They had just left a dinner party at the Algonquin Hotel, hosted by Ellen's firm, to celebrate a very profitable new client acquisition, and they were both sated by the excellent meal and also a little bit drunk.

Traffic was light as they turned into Fifth Avenue. The night was perfectly balmy, without even a hint of fall. The stores were closed for the day, but most of the large windows fronting the upscale Fifth Avenue stores were illuminated, and they stopped occasionally to examine the beautifully displayed merchandise.

Ellen looked particularly attractive in a thin crepe-de-chine dress that seemed to cling to all the right parts of her attractive figure, as a gentle, late-summer breeze stirred the fragile material. There was no doubt Tuck and Ellen made a handsome couple. Tuck, unlike most men, had no fear of strolling the streets of New York late at night. After all, he was a New York City detective and could take care of himself.

A Baby To Die For

Right now, his focus was on Ellen who, at this moment, was happy and smiling. It was rare, of late, to see her this way, and he was enjoying the change. The adoption issue was playing hell with their relationship. They found themselves at an impasse, spread across the horns of a dilemma. On one hand, Ellen had been unable to carry a baby past the inevitable miscarriage. On the other, they couldn't scrape up enough money to buy a baby on the black market. Well, at least one half of the dilemma was moot—there would be no more pregnancies. The doctors had finally made that point very clear. However, something permanent had to be done, so Tuck was scheduled for a vasectomy the following week. There was no longer any question, since another miscarriage could very easily be fatal.

They walked on like Siamese twins joined at the hip, close together, in step, and in silence. Tuck's jacket was around Ellen's shoulders, his arm around the jacket.

A few blocks later and completely out of the blue, Ellen asked, "Did you masturbate when you were a kid?"

Tuck paused, trying to decide if Ellen was serious or just drunk. "What brought that up?"

"I dunno, it just popped into my head."

"Well, yeah…hell, yeah. A lot, now that you mention it."

"How old…when you did it the first time?

Tuck thought for a moment.

"I have no idea about the first time, but I remember I did it a lot around the time I started smoking cigarettes after class with Porky Fishman. I was around twelve."

"Porky? He was fat?"

"No, he was actually a skinny kid. It was because every day his mom packed him the exact same lunch: bacon and peanut butter sandwiches. Every single day, without exception," Tuck laughed.

They walked a while more, maybe two blocks, without speaking, just enjoying the evening.

Finally, Ellen said, "I didn't do it until my first year in college. With boys, it was thought to be okay, you know... more acceptable for boys."

Tuck mulled that for a moment then nodded in agreement. "Yeah, I guess so. I really never gave it much thought," he said and started to laugh.

"What's so funny?" "Just remembering. We used to have these circle jerks," Tuck laughed. "Can you imagine that? Four or five little farts sitting around in some kid's bathroom when his parents were out...all smoking cigarettes and whacking off." Tuck laughed at the memory.

Ellen also started laughing, just picturing the bizarre scene. Tears rolled down her face, and she stopped to fish around for a Kleenex in her purse. It was infectious, and Tuck was laughing, as well.

A block later, they finally stopped laughing. The effects of the wine were softening, wearing off.

Tuck put his arm tighter, more possessively around Ellen's shoulder.

"Yeah, they were pretty funny. We'd each put a quarter into the pot, and the first kid to come won the money. The idea was to be really fast. A fast, oversexed kid could win four, five bucks a week."

"How did you do, tiger?" Ellen whispered in Tuck's ear.

"I lost. I *always* lost! I thought something was really wrong with me, an incurable disease of my thing or something like that. I recall there was a whole summer when I was really worried. Almost asked my father about it."

Ellen stepped back, then threw her arms around Tuck, and shouted to the empty Saturday-night buildings, "Thank God you lost!"

"At the time, we were enamored of speed," Tuck said.

"Hey, maybe that's the best way to pick men...a new criteria for selection. It could be a terrific article in *Cosmo*: Circle Jerks. For Real Happiness, Pick the Losers! They'd sell a million copies."

Tuck kissed Ellen's ear. "How did we get onto this subject anyway?"

"I was thinking about sex."

"Really? Oh, really? How pleasant of you, how wonderfully pleasant. Shall we grab a cab or hump right here in the doorway of Tiffany's?"

Ellen turned to Tuck. She wasn't smiling anymore.

"I'm pregnant again, Tuck."

It happened so quickly, so deftly that he never had time to sense—let alone see—it coming. It was as if he had been punched in the gut, like a mental mugging that took his breath away, along with the effects of the wine he'd consumed.

They had stopped and were standing in the circle of light spilling from one of Tiffany's small, front display windows. Ellen placed one palm on Tuck's chest and the other gently over his mouth.

"Please, before you yell, hear me out. *Please.*" Ellen pleaded, her words tumbling rapidly from her mouth, "I know it will work this time, I can feel it. I want to go through with it, and don't even mention an abortion."

Even as she spoke, she kept her hand over his mouth as if to stop his objections, like a child asking to go to a movie on a school night, while knowing and fearing the obvious answer.

Tuck just stared at Ellen, then inhaling deeply like a swimmer before a high dive, exhaled the words through her fingers, "Oh, dear God!"

"Please...please...please..."

Ellen circled Tuck with her arms, pinning his to his sides, as she tried to physically hold in his displeasure, certain it would explode.

"How could you let this happen to yourself? To us?"

"I wish I knew how to make you understand, Tuck," Ellen wailed.

Tuck felt the truth like a slap.

"This wasn't an accident, was it? You *let* yourself get pregnant, didn't you?"

"No...yes...but not really. It's so complicated."

"Complicated? You did it on purpose. How complicated is that? You said you took pills, you said you used a diaphragm. But it was all a lie, wasn't it? Goddamnit, Ellen, you lied to me!"

"Tuck, I really want this baby. I don't know why it's so very important to me. *But I've got to have this baby!*"

A Baby To Die For

"But damn it, Ellen, you said it didn't matter, you said it was going to be okay. We agreed we could adopt or just not have children. Is just the two of us so totally unacceptable to you? God, I feel like such an asshole. I should have seen this coming. You can't do this! You know that, and damn you, why did you tell me it didn't matter?"

"I'm sorry," Ellen said, her voice weary and childlike. "But it does matter. I didn't think it did, but it does. Something inside told me it mattered. I can't help it. It was like one of those little gears inside an expensive watch that only turns every four years to adjust for Leap Years. It just sits there, and you forget about it, and suddenly one day, a fraction after midnight, it wakes up and does its thing. That's what it was like for me, Tuck. As if a little gear suddenly turned, and I just knew I had to have a baby, *my* baby, not an adopted baby."

Tuck shrugged angrily away from Ellen's arms and walked to the curb. A lone cab slowed, thinking Tuck was going to flag him, and then seeing he wasn't, sped off. Tuck placed both his hands on the top of a parked car and leaned his weight like a thief about to be patted down. He stood that way for a minute, saying nothing, then banged his fist down hard on the roof.

"How could someone so smart do something so stupid and suicidal? Why would you risk your life? And then lie to me about it?" Tuck asked, his question coming out in a frustrated wail.

"I didn't lie to you," Ellen said, more like a revelation than a defense of what she'd done.

Tuck turned and looked at his wife.

"What are you talking about? You don't think you lied?" he asked.

"When I said it didn't matter, I really believed it. At the time, I believed it so much that, in a way, it was the truth. I lied to myself, and once I believed the lie, everything I told you became the truth. Can't you see that?"

Tuck came back and grabbed Ellen by the shoulders, "Fine. You can rationalize this thing until hell freezes over. But, bottom line, you're going to have an abortion. It would be suicide not to. End of story!"

"Never! Don't even say the words," Ellen said, angrily pulling away from Tuck, her position set in stone.

"You're getting rid of that baby, Ellen…that's final!"

Ellen recoiled away.

"If you force me to lose this baby, Tuck, I swear to God, you will lose me, as well."

Tuck didn't answer, just studied her face.

All he could see was a mask of determination. Finally, his voice soft and pleading, he said, "If you do this, the doctors all say you could die."

"And I say, I will carry this baby…*and* I will be a mother."

They were both quite sober now.

Chapter 20

One week later

Ellen knew she was pregnant. No assumptions. No speculation. Not even intuition. When Tuck heard that, he pressed for a more rational, less harebrained explanation. All she could say in her defense was that some primal change transmitted the news to her body as clearly as ancient jungle drums. She swore she knew the morning they made love, that Tuck's sperm fertilized her egg. She even claimed she felt a microscopic docking at the moment of impact. No one could tell her or convince her that she hadn't felt it. And then there was the tingling in her breasts. Unmistakable.

Hearing all this only fueled Tuck's anger and he insisted she be tested. He prayed she was wrong.

Murray Feder, Ellen's doctor, insisted she wait another week to make sure the test results would be accurate, and another two days for the results to be returned.

Now she was back in Dr. Feder's office waiting to hear the results, albeit knowing what the verdict would be.

"You know," Ellen said, smiling, "back in the old days when you guys used rabbits to test for a pregnancy, I would have killed quite a few—almost enough, my dear, to make a coat."

Murray Feder didn't laugh at Ellen's rabbit joke. Feder was the doctor who had known and taken care of Ellen ever since she arrived in New York to attend graduate school, and he was angry and sad and worried sick for her. Their long history gave him a proprietary interest.

"Ellen, look, this isn't fun-and-game time. You're right. The test is positive. I had them run it twice. I want to arrange for you to be aborted right away. It's the only sound medical advice I can give you. I spoke with your ob-gyn already, and he totally agrees. He's equally upset that you allowed yourself to become pregnant again."

"I told Tuck and I'm telling you, Murray, this is my decision and not, in all due respect, yours or his. I'm not killing my baby now on the outside chance it might die later on. I mean, for God's sake...the hard part is over: I'm pregnant. Why would I give up this chance to try again?"

"Damn it, Ellen! This is not about trying to have the baby, it's about the probability of your dying in the process," Murray said, agitated, his voice rising, as he tried to find his cigarettes and, failing, picked a decent-sized butt from the overflowing ashtray and lit it.

"That's sickening, Murray. Why don't you stop with the cigarettes? You're going to kill yourself," Ellen said.

"Don't you dare!" Murray said, harshly, peering over his half glasses at Ellen and exhaling smoke, which he fanned away with his hand. "...Don't you dare talk about

killing myself. You've got some nerve! What you don't have worth a shit—pardon my French—is an ounce of common sense. We're talking about your life, you idiot ...*your life*. Another episode like the last one and there's a damned good chance you can forget about the future. That's it, Ellen. Odds are, you'll be dead. Finished. No chance to live your life, no chance for you and Tuck to grow old together. You'll just be as dead as a herring nailed on a door in the hot sun, and that's that. How many times do you have to be told?"

Ellen couldn't stifle a laugh. "Murray, your herring analogy is beautifully graphic, but this time it's going to be okay. We're not giving up on this baby. It's going to be terrific this time. I can feel it's going to be okay. Didn't I know I was pregnant before any fancy tests? So, why would you question my instinct about carrying to full term? You know, Murray, women have that ability...it's a sixth sense."

"You mean a *sick* sense! For God's sake...Ellen, listen to yourself! You 'can *feel* it's going to be okay?' What a load of bullshit!"

Murray got up and stormed out from behind his desk, yanked open the door to his waiting room. "April, get me some cigarettes," Murray Feder shouted to his receptionist. "Ask in the waiting room. Or, go down to Dr. Stella's office. He's an orthodontist. Half the twelve-year-olds in there have cigarettes."

Murray Feder slammed the door and stormed back behind his desk, sat down, and rummaged unsuccessfully through the ashtray. Murray drummed his fingers on the desk and Ellen sat with her ankles crossed—unconsciously holding in her child? The two of them sat that way, in silence.

A small smile turned up the corners of Ellen's mouth. *This lovely man worries about me. I love him for that, but he worries too much..*

Just then Murray's receptionist popped in and laid an assortment of cigarettes on his cluttered desk—some with filters, some without.

"From who?" Murray asked.

"You were right. It's a collective gift from Dr. Stella's braces brigade. One from each."

Murray looked at the array in front of him, chose one, and lit it.

"I should have been an orthodontist. The bastard is making a fortune."

Ellen laughed. "You're wonderful, Murray. I love you."

"Terrific. That makes me very happy. You're going to commit suicide, and you love me. Listen, I'm not Romeo and your name isn't Juliet, so I want to talk to Tuck—and not on the phone. I want to see you both face-to-face. I want him to see my expression of fear. I want him to sense the ice in my stomach without any emotions being filtered through Ma Bell's equipment, understand? I insist on it."

"I don't want him upset," Ellen interjected. "He knows he can't force me to stop this."

"Tough shit. *I* want him upset. I want him to be as scared and frantic as I am. If you were my daughter...even if you were the wife of my most hated enemy, there is no way I would let you get away with this."

"All right, Murray. It won't make any difference, but come Friday for dinner. We'll talk."

"What are you having?"

"What would you like, darling?"

"Something earthy, traditional...something to celebrate the night before the Sabbath...how about Chinese?"

"You're on. Want to bring a date?"

"I've been to your place once and trust me, none of the women I go out with are young enough or strong enough to make it up the steps. I'll bring a cute bottle of Chablis instead."

Ellen came around his cluttered desk and kissed Murray on his cheek. She could feel the coarse stubble of beard on his face.

"You're a doll, and I'll see you Friday at about eight."

On Friday, Murray Feder and Tuck spent most of the evening trying, unsuccessfully, to convince Ellen to change her mind about the pregnancy. Although there was no doubt Tuck was his ally, Murray did most of the talking. Tuck was adamant about wanting Ellen to abort the baby, but knowing, that even if she could be talked into doing so, their relationship would be forever changed and not for the best. But even with both men making the argument, their combined powers of persuasion hit the immovable wall of Ellen's stubborn and absolute certainty that she could and would carry the baby to full term.

"It's *salto mortale!*" Murray Feder finally said, and banged the table with his fist for emphasis.

A Baby To Die For

"Salted what?" Ellen asked.

"No, damn it, *salto mortale* is a circus expression used to describe a somersault on a tightrope...that's the kind of chance you're taking. You've about as much chance of carrying full term as doing a somersault on a friggin' tightrope."

"What do you know from circuses, Murray?" Ellen said, laughing.

"From dealing with clowns like you, Ellen," he said, with a touch of disgust in his tone.

"Touché, darling, but be calm. This time, it's not going to be a problem," Ellen bubbled.

"I need a scotch," Murray said. "Make it a double."

Ellen went to the kitchen to get Murray's drink.

With Ellen out of the room, Murray was able to speak candidly to Tuck. "Look, it's obvious there isn't much you can do. She is being downright pathological about this pregnancy."

"Tell me about it," Tuck said sadly. "Honestly, Murray, I'm not sure our marriage could stand the pressure if Ellen were forced to abort."

Feder was surprised by Tuck's brutally frank assessment but decided to stick with the medical side of the problem. "Then given the circumstances, I think the only course of action would be a strict regimen of rest until either she gives birth or has a miscarriage. I doubt you'll ever see the former, and frankly, I'd pray like crazy that the latter comes as quickly as possible. The sooner she miscarries, the better and safer it will be for her."

Murray's advice was cut short by Ellen's return with his Scotch, along with one for Tuck, as well.

A Baby To Die For

With Ellen back in the room, his tone became softer. "Okay, kiddo, if this is the way it's going to be, then you must at least get the hell out of the city until the baby is born—God willing and the planets align."

"You want us to leave Manhattan?" Ellen said.

"Absolutely. The climb up and down from the apartment alone would be enough to abort a healthy elephant. You've got to cut out anything that isn't good for the pregnancy. You've one slim hope for carrying this baby to term, but it's a very fragile one," Murray said, accepting that no argument he could muster would have any effect on Ellen's decision.

Ellen glanced at Tuck, as she remembered that the pains preceding her second misscarriage had started after struggling up the four flights of steps to the apartment. Ellen nodded her head in agreement.

At last, sensing some small victory—if not for an abortion, at least for some modicum of common sense—the elderly doctor pressed on.

"I don't mean just getting out of this apartment. I mean you should leave the city altogether, get away from the pollution and the crowds."

The three sat in silence. Tuck and Ellen tried to wrap their heads around the idea of leaving Manhattan, while Murray's stomach rumbled in reaction to the Chinese food and alcohol he'd consumed.

After a few moments, Murray, addressed Ellen. "You're betting your life that this pregnancy will work out, and your odds are really terrible. So, any edge you can give yourself is good, any problem, no matter how small, has got to be eliminated. Your life could depend on it. I understand you may not see it exactly that way, but I do. So, taking off for a while isn't such a hardship. I've known some women who stayed in bed for eight months in order to carry to full term. Go somewhere, maybe to the country—fresh air, no steps, no cars, no subways, or pollution, just lots of rest. Believe me, Ellen, it's worth the disruption. It could tip the scales just a little bit in your favor. Tuck, please, take my advice. Either way, you won't be sorry. If you lose the baby..."

"We're not going to—lose our baby," Ellen quickly interjected.

"Okay, sorry, Ellen. Regardless, at least you'll know you did everything you could possibly do, right?"

It took them several weeks to make the arrangements to leave. Ellen was granted a medical leave of absence from her firm, which stopped her pay but kept her medical insurance in effect. Tuck applied for and was given an open-ended hardship leave from the police force, which worked out fine with his captain since departmental budgets were once again searching for ways to save money.

A six-month sublet of their walkup apartment was quickly snapped-up by a personable young couple, Ken and Mary Flower. The quirky little apartment, its comfortable furnishings, as well as its attractive rental price, delighted the Flowers and even provided a small but welcome monthly profit for Ellen and Tuck. The short length of the sublet was ideal for the Flowers, since Mary only had less than a year left on her residency at Roosevelt

Hospital, with no idea where she would be going next. Her husband, Ken, was a hardworking journalist. He freelanced for a large number of magazines and newspapers, and seemed to know everyone, while keeping up to date on everything. Fortunately, he could work from wherever his wife's career might take them next.

The two couples quickly took to one another and spent several social evenings chatting and getting better acquainted. Best of all, Ellen was looking good and feeling better than she had in ages.

Tuck and Ellen poured over maps and brochures and contacted half a dozen chambers of commerce, searching for an ideal and affordable place to spend the pregnancy. With the money previously earmarked for the adoption, plus a small monthly profit from the sublet of their apartment, it would still be financially tight. At one point, Aspen seemed ideal, but upon hearing of the plan, Ellen's doctor vetoed the idea based on the altitude of the picturesque Colorado town, a definite no-no for a problematic pregnancy.

They were still heavily into researching alternatives when Murray Feder called with a possible solution. A good friend, an anesthesiologist living in Virginia Beach, was leaving his practice for six months to join Doctors Without Borders, a recently created humanitarian organization. After some pointed interrogation on Murray's part, it turned out his friend was open to the idea of Tuck and Ellen moving into the departing doctor's house as temporary caretakers. It was a large home near the water and, more important, had an excellent hospital minutes away.

A week later, their red Volvo packed to overflowing, Tuck and Ellen crossed the George Washington Bridge. They planned to make the trip slowly, driving no more than three or four hours a day and getting in as much casual sightseeing as possible. Neither had been to Washington, D.C. since they were youngsters, and the prospect of seeing the capital together was very exciting.

Ellen had never been to Atlantic City, so when they saw the Route 30 cutoff that would take them to the coastal resort, they took it, like two kids on a new adventure.

They never made it.

Ellen died inside the restroom of a gas station twenty miles from the boardwalk.

It happened while Tuck stood watching the attendant filling the gas tank, oblivious to his wife hemorrhaging not more than twenty-five yards away. When he finally became worried and knocked on the bathroom door, he heard Ellen moaning. He tried breaking down the heavy metal door but was unable to do so. It took a crowbar from the service bay to finally break in. Tuck's work had exposed him to many homicide scenes, but he'd never seen one with so much blood. By the time an ambulance arrived, it was too late.

There would be no baby. Tuck had Ellen and what little remains there was of the child cremated in a town nearby. He called Uncle Saul, so the family would know. And Murray, so the house they were to watch over wouldn't be left abandoned for six months.

Days later Tuck drove off, the urn of ashes next to

him on the front seat of the Volvo. Where he was headed, he had no idea, nor did he much give a shit.

Chapter 21

Traveling into New York City, through the Lincoln Tunnel, there's an old mottled stain on a small section of wall, about midway from the New Jersey side. And every time Karen Boyd saw it—and she had, dozens of times—she was, for the moment it took to zip past, filled with unease.

In the beginning she thought it was the tunnel itself that did it. After all, anyone driving through a very old, 8,557-foot tube running under a zillion tons of filthy Hudson River water couldn't be blamed for feeling a little skittish. It didn't make for relaxing thoughts.

However, Karen finally concluded it was all about proximity. The stain was a sort of demarcation point, one that said she was getting closer to Max Garfield, and the closer she got to the lawyer, the worse she felt.

Karen Boyd hated Max Garfield and, looking down, she realized her knuckles were white from clutching the steering wheel. She flexed her fingers. A thin line of perspiration rimmed her forehead like moist lace. She shook her head to clear the thoughts, and her body relaxed somewhat. Karen's long auburn hair responded to the sudden movement and swept across her face. She pushed it back behind her ear.

She clearly understood it was unhealthy to dislike someone so deeply, to hold a grudge for so long, to yearn for revenge so passionately and completely.

You'll be an old broad and still messing up your head with thoughts of revenge.

Disliking Max Garfield had become her hobby.

Karen easily surrendered to the temptation to relive the events in her mind. After all, it was her obsession that kept the hatred alive, or maybe it was the other way around. It made no difference and, besides, in some masochistic way, she enjoyed it.

Ten years earlier, Sausalito, California

She must have walked around the phone booth a hundred times, a single Indian circling an empty wagon train. Her blood, she decided, felt like ball bearings moving through her body, and the light coming off the water hurt her eyes. People passing watched her, some with caution, some with pity. She was scarecrow thin and her hair was streaked with shades of color not seen in nature. She had to struggle just to remember why she was orbiting the phone booth. Then she recalled it was to "wind up" her courage. She'd decided the more revolutions she made the more courage she would have. So, she needed just a certain number of circles for enough courage to call her brother. If she could only remember how many that should be. She was afraid to call, but there was no one else. It was always that way. She would explain the problem, and then her big brother would fly into his predictable emotional tantrum, which spanned a range from pissed-off to tolerant concern. Unfortunately, she was having trouble at the moment visualizing just exactly who her brother was. She kept mentally mixing him up in her head with a drug dealer she lived with for a time in Toronto, or was it Seattle? But this time, her problem was serious. This time, she needed more than drug money.

Even armed with courage accumulated from her circling of the phone booth, she was still reluctant to enter. It was a machine after all, and she didn't relish the idea of walking into the mouth of a machine.

"My name is Moon," she whispered, over and over, just to nail it as fact. "My name is Moon. My name is Moon."

It seemed like everybody she knew had names like Moon or Sunburst or Oxygen. It was the way she and her friends identified one another in their roiling sea of denim, beads, headbands, and powerful drugs. Moon had been so full of drugs for so long she had difficulty determining if she was currently stoned or just in desperate need of another fix. Sometimes the creepy, crazy feelings came so close together it was hard for her to tell the difference.

A thick fog began to roll out of the Sausalito hills, where apparently it stacked every day, like planes over a crowded airport, just waiting for the right time to spill onto the town. It was a damp, chilling attack that emptied Sausalito of tourists, who would rush, shivering, to their rented cars or tour buses like oranges bursting from a torn paper bag. Men in white shoes, plaid slacks, and drip-dry shirts, women in shorts and summer dresses, their stiff lacquered hair piled on their heads like perfectly coiffed condominiums, hailing from places like Cleveland and Kansas City—places where, unlike Sausalito, summer meant heat and not cold, damp fog.

A beat up old VW Bug, painted like a hallucinogenic rainbow and stuffed with a tangle of hippies yelling and waving, drove past Moon, but she paid no attention. She decided she had to clear her head and padded up the street, feeling the texture of the cold cement through the crusted dirt on the bottoms of her callused feet. She bought a container of coffee, spiking it with a half-dozen tablespoons of sugar. Not even remembering where the money came from, she gave a handful of change to the pimple-faced kid who sat behind the cash register.

Back on the pier, near the dreaded phone booth, she huddled around herself and sipped the coffee and tried to be small, inside her old army jacket, her only protection from the cold and fog. The sugar and caffeine slowly began to melt the ball bearings in her blood. Sea gulls swooped out of the fog, confusing shadows in the water for food, and then, squawking irritably, did their business on whatever happened to be below.

Sometime later, Moon finally entered the phone booth. Using the number she had scrawled on the back of her hand with a ballpoint pen, she called—collect, of course—and his answering service, knowing who she was from a hundred collect calls in the past, immediately accepted the charges. They took the booth's phone number, repeated it twice for accuracy, and told Moon to wait, to remain within hearing distance of the phone. They did all this with the same tone of voice an experienced cop would use when speaking to someone ready to leap from the rail of the Golden Gate Bridge. Moon's brother had long ago put the fear of God into the answering service when it came to any calls from his sister, and since their business wasn't that good, and he was an excellent customer, they responded accordingly.

Ten minutes later, the phone in the booth rang. Moon ran the twenty yards from where she had been sitting on one of the pilings. She grabbed the receiver with a slightly trembling hand, on the sixth ring.

"Max? Is it you?"

"Of course, it's me, Karen…you're in a phone booth …who else would call you there? Christ, it's been six months, I've been worried sick…what the hell are you doing in California?"

He'd called her Karen. She'd almost forgotten that was her name. And that fucking tone of voice, the strident, staccato hammering didn't go well with what was left of Moon-Karen's fragile state of mind.

"How do you know I'm in California?" Moon-Karen asked, trying to orient herself, trying to focus.

"Jesus, Karen—the area code—the four-one-five. How smashed are you? You don't sound well. Are you okay? I've been crazy with worry. You can't keep doing this to me."

"Uh, I'm…sorry…I'm okay…no, I'm not okay…Max

...Max, listen, I'm in trouble. I'm going to have a baby. Shit, I don't know what to do, you know."

There was a long pause on Max Garfield's end of the phone. The faint sounds of electronic beeps and buzzes crackled on the line between the two coasts.

"*Fuck!*" Max breathed the word into the phone, barely audibly. "Oh, God—how many times have I told..."

Max started to toss the platitude across the three thousand miles, then thought better of it.

"Look," he finally continued, "give me your address, a phone number, someplace where I can reach you. I don't want you to move around, stay put where you are, okay? Don't leave town."

Max never waited for an answer. His mind was struggling to pull out of the dive Karen had sent him into. Like a fighter pilot, he fought with gravity and clawed for altitude.

"Listen, I'll send Jake out there to get you," Max said, and Karen could hear the gears shifting in his voice as he took command. "I'll get him on a plane right away. He'll have money for you—you need money? Why the hell am I asking you if you need money? When did you ever *not* need money?"

"Please, Max," Moon-Karen interrupted, "can't you come? I need *you*, not Jake. I don't...Jake doesn't..."

"I know, Karen," Max said in a slightly softer voice, "but I can't just pick up and leave my practice. For crying out loud, you don't call for six months, and then I'm supposed to leap out of my chair and hop a plane to California?"

"But I need you, Max…"

"You're just confused and scared—everything will be fine."

Max's voice took on an edge again.

"Jake will be fine and he'll bring you home. Hey, your brother Jake is as confused as you are," Max said with some humor. "Maybe you can help each other, you know? Just don't panic, okay? You'll be fine. What month are you in?"

"I'm not sure. I don't know."

"That figures."

"What, Max…I can't hear you."

"Nothing, nothing, honey. Look, Jake will take you to a doctor I know in San Francisco. He'll give you a checkup, and we'll know for sure where we stand, okay? Right now, you don't need to worry about a thing. I'll take care of everything. As soon as I hang up, I'll wire you some money to hold you over until Jake gets there. Go to a Western Union and pick it up, okay? Do you have an address? Where can Jake find you?"

Moon-Karen gave Max the name of a bookstore in North Beach where she knew a guy, hung up, and felt much better. Her brother, Max, her big brother, Max, always looked after her. She could depend on Max to make everything right. He was her family, along with Jake.

Max is right, Jake is a lot like me. He's strange—but then so am I.

Outside the phone booth and out of the orbit of her brother's voice, Karen became all Moon once again. She shuffled down the sidewalk away from the phone booth.

A Baby To Die For

The wide, tattered bottoms of her demolished jeans seemed to melt into the concrete. The late afternoon light shot through her tangled hair. She should stay off drugs. For the baby, she should stay clean. She would pick up the money Max was wiring then maybe find Billy-Pilly and score some weed. Until she knew what was going to happen for sure, she would only do grass, nothing hard. She dodged the cars and crossed Bridgeway to catch the traffic heading south toward the Golden Gate Bridge and San Francisco and then she raised her arm and stuck out her thumb.

Chapter 22

Possibly it was the disturbing thoughts of Max and the memories of that day in Sausalito, but whatever the motivation, as Karen exited the tunnel, she surrendered to an impulse to continue driving. It was a beautiful day and, besides, she wasn't expected anywhere in particular.

An hour or so later she tossed the correct change into the tollbooth basket at the Westport exit and steered onto the off ramp. Even though she hadn't been to her hometown for years, she easily found her way to the beach at Compo, parked, and strolled along the shoreline. It was hard to believe so many years had passed since she was last here. It was the same beach where she had played as a child, but on that last visit, she wasn't there to play but to scatter the ashes of her very young and very dead husband.

Poor Norman Boyd. The moralistic high school pal, who tracked her down and despite her pregnancy, loved her enough to propose marriage. Truth was she never loved Norman Boyd. He just happened to be crazy enough about Karen—and had been throughout high school—

to offer her a last name for the baby. Karen was scared, desperate, and selfish enough to accept his proposal. Soon after a tiny, nondenominational wedding, Norman was drafted, trundled off to basic training, and shipped to Vietnam where, before he had a chance to spend a full week in that pathetic excuse for a war, he was returned to her as a tightly folded flag.

Karen stood on the damp sand at the edge of the water gazing out toward the dark line on the horizon that was Long Island. For a fleeting moment, she wondered what happened to that damned flag she'd been given by the State Department.

God, I was fucked up back then.

But there was another place she wanted to see. She left the beach and drove slowly through town, her memories brought places to life—the playhouse, the movie theater, Main Street, and the little park beside the library where she and her high school buddies had smoked dope and swapped their parents' prescription meds like they were baseball cards.

Ten minutes later Karen parked on the grassy edge of Long Lots Road, across from the Hall-Brooke hospital. A stone wall ran along the edge of the broad, sloping lawn. She rolled down the car window and let the smell of the fall afternoon fill her senses.

After her brother Jake found her in San Francisco, he got her cleaned up as best he could and flew her back East where Max had her admitted to Hall-Brooke. It was a hospital and a sanitarium.

In the center of the big front lawn, there was a broad bench. It was the kind with two thick, cement, molded end pieces and slats of heavy wood running between them for the seat and back.

Karen, behind the wheel of her car, could picture herself so clearly, sitting on that very bench, looking small next to the huge house, the wide expanse of lawn, and the giant trees.

Back then, her body was waif thin from drugs, her eyes huge brown puddles, vacantly staring at the road at the bottom of the rolling lawn thirty yards away. She would sit very still, her hands folded on her belly, her legs together with feet planted flat on the grass. Her shoulders slumped slightly, fighting their trained inclination to be very erect. She was pretty—at least, at one time she had been—and she would be again, but now she was somehow in transition. Even her clothing, a faded housedress, designed—if you could call it that—for a woman three times her age, was borrowed, not hers, not permanent. Nothing in her life was permanent, except for her baby.

The breeze blew a bit harder, and Karen's hair moved with it, flowing out to the side as if she were moving fast in an open car. The sleeves of her faded dress fluttered and rose higher, revealing needle tracks lining the insides of both her arms. They were not fresh. Even the most recent ones—many months old—were fading. Karen's mind seemed to be focusing better every day, clearing somewhat. For years, her mind had seemed smeared, like a child's finger painting.

Pregnancy sobered Karen, pulling her out of her confusion. *And a child shall lead them.* God, how she wanted the baby! She knew it was her lifeline, a bright doorway to a new and better life.

A Baby To Die For

That's when Max took her out of Hall-Brooke and sent her to Florida, to stay with Miss LaFrance, where she joined a half-dozen other pregnant girls and was cared for until she gave birth. Her labor was easy compared to the grief and confusion of Norman's death. But she happily clung to her newborn baby, naming her Nina and experiencing such an overwhelming feeling of joy from the child growing inside her body that it was almost impossible to contain.

And then, only days after giving birth, the child was gone. Max had come and taken the baby away. Apparently, Karen had signed papers while at Hall-Brooke, while sedated and still emotionally unstable, granting permission to place the baby for adoption.

Max sold her baby! Sold Nina. Karen had begged him not to. She screamed and cried. They just gave her more sedatives. By the time she was able to pull herself together, she was out of the hospital and back in Hall-Brooke.

Months later, sitting again on the bench in the fresh air, a fraction of a smile bent her lips, she vowed she would get well and when she did, she would get her baby back. Somehow, Karen would find Nina and get her back.

But ironically, the stronger she got, the more rational her thinking became, the more she realized that her baby would never be back in her life. And in a way, it became an important sign that she was getting better. The baby was gone—taken and sold to the highest bidder. All she could hope for was that Nina had a good home with loving parents.

But she never had any doubts as to who was at fault. It was Max who took her baby, and she hated him for that, and her hatred became the motivation for her recovery.

Now, sitting in her car, looking at the empty bench in the middle of the lawn, it all looked so much smaller. Even the memory seemed smaller. Karen smiled. My baby.

Christ, she would be eleven years old by now. Maybe even living right here in Westport.

That was a pleasant fantasy, however a far more satisfying one was the thought of shoving a lit stick of dynamite up Max Garfield's ass.

Chapter 23

Washington, D.C.

Porter Gibbs had to laugh. Here she was, seated in the plush, first-class section of a jet, drink in hand, stacked over Washington National Airport, orbiting around America's seat of power like a monster moth circling a porch light. And all she could think about was being late for the appointment with Toby Wine, a crazy, self-professed psychic.

She tried, without success, to spot the Watergate complex every time the plane banked to the left on its northernmost turn. She would have loved to peek right into Toby's Watergate living room and maybe spot a crystal ball—if she had one. Porter figured Toby probably kept one, out of sight, of course, reserved for her more gullible, albeit famous, clientele. Many were bored-to-distraction wives of congressmen, several of the better-known judiciary, not to mention lobbyists, and a generous assortment of Washington's movers and shakers.

The long trip was almost over, and Porter was very glad her stop in the capital was the last one before heading back to Manhattan. She was even beginning to miss Max.

A Baby To Die For

She thought how pleasant it would be to spend a leisurely afternoon bedded down with him at the Kitano, having lots of cold sushi and hot sex. Porter chuckled at the image and smiled at an air force lieutenant seated across the aisle—looking to Porter's eye to be about twelve years old. He smiled back with a mixture of booze and not-too-far-out-of-his-teens lust.

Porter adjusted her seat, relaxed, and enjoyed the last of her scotch. It was pleasant looking out the window and watching Washington twinkling below in the early evening darkness. It gave Porter an expansive feeling as if she could actually visualize her organization from the lights below, as one sees constellation formations in the stars. There was Toby Wine twinkling to the left. And over there was The Sunshine Home, a national chain of abortion clinics. And of course, there were the scores of lawyers like Rick Shelby in Dallas—and others scattered over the country—like some judicial Milky Way. And, of course, there were the private suppliers like Sarah LaFrance down in Florida. The operation was growing. The budget for the Yellow Pages advertising for abortion clinics alone was costing a small fortune. Fingers doing the walking didn't come cheap, that was for sure. And Porter was controlling it all. It was a far cry from when she first started out as Max's secretary.

She controlled the network—the whole damned thing. Max Garfield could believe what he wanted to believe, but Porter Gibbs knew damned well it was she who pulled the strings. There were lots of other lawyers like Max around. But there was only one Porter Gibbs.

A Baby To Die For

The leverage Porter had was simple. Max charged her with building the network from the bottom up. Not only did she understand every piece, she understood how every piece fit with every other piece. So, when it came right down to it, she controlled the supply of babies, and a short supply was what the business was all about. Control the supply, and you control the price.

Porter manage the abortion clinics by making them into efficient suppliers of adoptable product.

The clinics are a regular mother lode. Porter smiled at the pun. *God, I'm beginning to think like a damned used-car salesman.*

Chapter 24

Once on the ground, Porter spent ten frustrating minutes in line waiting for a taxi. Forty-five minutes later she walked into the Watergate, Toby Wine's apartment building.

Toby Wine was a bit of a nutcase. She had to be, considering she spent her days doling out her psychic mumbo-jumbo to the great and near-great of Washington's power-hungry elite. But Porter also knew Toby Wine was a smart and crafty businesswoman, so she had to be cautious in her approach.

Porter exited the elevator on Toby's floor, and stood for a moment in front of the door before pressing the buzzer. Before she could, Toby Wine's smoke-graveled voice drifted out of a small speaker embedded in the door's frame.

"Porter, darling…I sensed you would be calling on me," the voice said, followed by a percussion of locks and bolts clicking, sliding, and banging. Finally, the door swung open to reveal Toby Wine, resplendent in a flowing concoction of multicolored fabrics, her thick, pure white hair cascading over her shoulders from under an ornate headband.

"I had such a strong feeling of your approaching presence. My antenna is so very sensitive lately. It's always like that around the time of my period. I'm accepting impressions through every pore, it seems," Toby sighed, an audible punctuation to her psychic burden.

"You're about as sensitive as a toilet seat, darling. It's probably menopause," Porter said and pushed past Toby into the living room. "You haven't had a period for a decade, and I happen to know you simply pay the doorman a few bucks every month to call and tell you exactly who's on their way up here."

"Really, Porter, my dear, why are you so harsh with Toby? Your hormones must be out of balance. I can see it in your aura."

Toby Wine was a singular-looking woman, with thick features and a pitted, almost oatmeal-textured face. Yet, a certain whiff of beauty, confidence, and sexuality hung about her like a light perfume haze. A heavy smell of incense filled the apartment, helping to round out the image.

Toby Wine landed in Washington from San Francisco where she had been reading tarot cards and creating astrological charts from a tiny storefront in North Beach. Upon arriving, she instinctively recognized how vast the opportunities were in the capital city, and for the next dozen years, she slowly wheedled her way up the D.C. power food chain. Toby Wine was now the respected psychic shoulder upon which the Washington elite wept.

Senators and congressmen, their wives, lobbyists, and highly placed bureaucrats, society matrons and foreign dignitaries, all ascended the same elevator, pressed the same buzzer, regurgitated the same insecurities, hopes, dreams, and complaints, and were soothed enough with what they heard to come back for more.

To Porter it always seemed strange to lead one's life based on that kind of mysticism, yet in Eastern cultures she understood it was rather common. The flag of South Korea, for example, had at its corners the hexagrams of the *I Ching*—the very *Book of Changes* that psychologist Carl Jung ascribed to, and by which he mysteriously and incongruously directed much of his life.

Toby Wine's methods were all embracing, a virtual psychic supermarket for her clients. She could provide what they wished or required, whether it be readings— palm, tarot, tea leaves, visions—or *I Ching*, astrology and, on occasion, for a few carefully chosen clients, a little marijuana to enhance their receptiveness.

Dear, pockmarked Toby Wine could take a congressman through a deck of tarot cards as easily as Julia Child could run through a recipe for carrot cake. She could also listen sympathetically to the complaints of everyday power and wealth that oozed out of their ethically ruptured seams like crude oil escaping from the hull of a rusted tanker.

Porter was well aware that Toby was a nonpartisan mystic, sucking up secrets and gossip like a human vacuum cleaner—a *Hoover*, of course, since, after all, this was Washington. And like that similarly named and legendary head of the FBI, Toby's secrets were carefully filed away in a secure spot, the location of which many, many people would give a great deal to know.

What a growing number of her clients did know was that Toby Wine had links to a baby-selling chain. Thanks to the intimate information she got from some of her "consultations," she was able to help a congressman or senator deal with, say, a pregnant mistress or solve the potentially embarrassing problem of a pregnant daughter and, at the same time, turn those much appreciated solutions into a tidy little profit. Hardly a week went by without Porter's being offered a prospect or two from Toby Wine.

Even if Porter personally disliked Toby, she had to admit the woman got the job done.

Porter sat on the couch waiting for Toby to fetch the foul-tasting tea she insisted on serving. Always in the God-awful painted porcelain pot with the paper tags hanging by their strings from under the cracked lid. Porter accepted the tea and added some lemon and four cubes of sugar, hoping to mask the taste. She was still feeling a little tense from the flight.

"Here's your money," Porter said, fishing an envelope from her handbag and handing it to the psychic, trying as best she could to soften the distaste she felt for the woman. "We need all the new names you can give us. Business is brisk, to say the least."

"I'm certain it is, darling. If you'd let me give you a quick reading, I could tell you how good it's going to get," Toby said, with a light smile and a slight edge.

It was an ongoing struggle between them. No love

lost, but Toby was one of those people who shed insults easily, as did Porter.

"Just tell me, how many names you have this time?" Porter was all business.

"*I Ching*, then . . . surely you have time for me to throw a few yarrow stalks and consult the oracle?"

"Just the damned names. Please?" Porter said, adding a frigid edge to her request. "How many?"

Toby Wine sighed. Actually, she enjoyed the badinage that invariably went on between them. It was a high point when Porter visited, infinitely more stimulating compared to the whining weaknesses of the rich and powerful she dealt with in her day-to-day practice. Toby placed her palms together in front of her as if in prayer, nodded once to indicate that from that moment she was going to be all business.

"Actually," she said, "I've quite a few. And from excellent breeding stock, I might add. But, darling, the amount you're paying for each name is simply no longer sufficient."

Porter hadn't needed any tarot cards or *I Ching* to have anticipated a shakedown was coming. It was inevitable. Toby Wine knew exactly what happened to the names she sold to Porter. Even if she did receive a hefty bonus for the successful adoption of a baby resulting from one of her leads, it was still small change compared to what healthy Caucasian babies were selling for. No psychic readings were necessary to know that. It was in the news on a regular basis. Porter even heard that the recent publicity had stirred rumblings up on the Hill to enact some sort of legislation to control the black market in babies, but she also knew it would be a long time in coming—if ever.

Too many powerful people needed its services.

Porter knew Toby would hit her up for more money. She'd mentioned it to Max several weeks before, while he was going over the books, and he reacted with a shrug of his shoulders and a mumbled, "So what?"

"So what?" Porter exclaimed, seated across from the lawyer. "So it's going to cost us more money for those damned names, that's what," Porter said. "It cuts into our profits!"

"Frankly, I really don't give a shit. Look, as long as we make money from the names Toby Wine gives us, I don't mind her getting a few more bucks. Let's not be greedy. It's not good for business, and besides," Max smiled, "the extra cost just gets passed on to the buyers. We lose nothing. No problem. Let's just keep her happy and get the names."

Porter knew their discussion was purely academic, but she needed to know the boundaries, needed to calculate how far she could push Max. After all, what Porter paid Toby Wine for names was usually half of what she told Max it was costing.

"What if our little stargazer starts to push us too far? Where the hell do we draw the line, Max?"

"The line, my dear, is drawn where I say to draw it. And when that time comes, she will go along."

"What makes you think so?" Porter asked, sensing the conversation was winding down.

"Porter, use your head. If she doesn't sell the names

to us, what else can she do with them? She sure as hell isn't going to go into the adoption business on her own. And she certainly can't sell them at a flea market. Look, Toby Wine needs us. She has babies, and we have buyers. It's a pure and simple symbiotic arrangement. She needs everything we have to offer, even more than we need her. Worse comes to worse, we'll get the names elsewhere. Believe me, Porter, you worry too much."

Porter remained silent. She had heard what she needed to hear.

Max just yawned and went back to studying the ledger.

Now, sitting with Toby in her Watergate apartment and sipping vile-tasting tea, Porter decided to ease up just a little, maybe even throw the psychic a bone or two.

Who knows, I may need a favor from her someday.

"How much more do you think your precious names are worth?" Porter asked with some contempt. The two women went back and forth for the next quarter hour.

Finally, Porter knew she had a deal.

Toby looked at Porter for a moment, trying to take the measure of this woman, but she saw nothing but a solid brick wall.

"Very well, darling, Toby will accept your terms. I'll send up the new list. It should be close to thirty names by the end of the month. I'm expecting one or two more from a certain senator who's trying to help two pregnant young women in his district. I don't know for sure, but I suspect he may have personally been responsible for one of the pregnancies. Randy politicos are turning out to be a rich source. In addition to any trouble they instigate themselves, they spread the word to their constituency back home and the names flow in," Toby continued, her voice gathering back its old confidence, healing quickly from the financial negotiations at the hands of Porter Gibbs.

Porter nodded her satisfaction.

Toby smiled. "I'm leaving for short trip to Switzerland tomorrow, but I'll have the list complete by the time I get back. I won't be gone long."

"I never thought of you as a skier," Porter said, frankly amazed.

"Skiing? Heavens no! I've a reading there, darling. A client flies me out every six months or so. You've doubtless heard of Edmond Calendar, I'm sure. A dear, dear man, very rich and crazy as a loon. I'm his personal astrologer."

Porter recognized Calendar's name as one of the richest and most eccentric men in the world. And, Porter's nod and pursed lips revealed that she was impressed.

"By the way, Porter, what *is* your sign again…I would love to do a chart for you. It would occupy my time on the flight to Switzerland. I'm sure it would turn out to be *very* interesting."

"I don't believe in signs, my dear. They're usually trying to get me to do things I don't want to do—like *stop* and *yield*.

Chapter 25

Tuck was impervious to time and space, feeling nothing, aware of little. His objective was to flee, to put as much distance as he could between him and the vile, disinfectant-smelling gas station restroom where his wife had died. Everything he cared about was gone—Ellen, the baby. He was a gutted house, empty to the walls, with nothing inside, absolutely nothing.

He drove, turning here or taking a back road there. He carried a can of gasoline in the trunk, for at times, service stations were few and far between. He drifted, wandered, and relived every minute of his and Ellen's life together, editing a million small details into a mental video of his past with the woman he loved so much.

Sometimes he had to stop, his eyes so filled with tears that he couldn't see the road ahead. He was miserable, the rock of grief in the pit of his stomach unbearable. Lines formed around his brows and in the corners of his eyes. One morning a patch of gray hair appeared on the left side of his head, looking as if he had brushed up against a bit of wet paint, and at first, he thought he had.

A Baby To Die For

Sometimes when night came, he simply kept driving, just thinking, right through until dawn. Other times, he would pull onto the side of the road and doze, fitfully, for an hour or two. Occasionally, he would check into a motel and shower and sleep between sheets. It was at those times that he would wake in the morning and, for that instant sliver of half sleep, before the reality of the dingy motel room came into focus, he would not remember. And for that one moment, there was a blessed absence of pain. Then, the crushing reality would break over him like a crashing wave. So, mostly, he slept by the side of the road. That way he could be miserable all the time, every instant, and never forget—his penance.

Tuck ate when he felt the stirrings of hunger. Whatever was at hand would do, a candy bar or a steak or a bag of fruit. It made no difference. Nothing seemed to have any taste.

Flashes of reality intruded now and then. He vaguely remembered standing, overlooking the Grand Canyon, aware of the sun coming up. Then, seemingly a moment later, Tuck found himself walking the length of the Golden Gate Bridge, hunched against the cold wind and thick fog. He just wandered like that, like some sad, lost soul.

Occasionally, he worked odd jobs, not that he needed the money. He didn't have enough to buy a baby, but he did have enough to stay on the road for a long, long time. So he took the jobs, staying at each just long enough to collect his wages in cash and then moved on. The interludes between were lost somewhere in his subconscious. Hollywood Boulevard somehow melted

161

into a small Arizona town. A hundred bars and greasy roadside diners were like watercolors on a wet paper, all running and mixing together.

And then one morning, almost six months after Ellen's death, Tuck woke up in a cheap motel room and knew he had to stop, had to somehow pull himself together or die—if not actually, certainly figuratively. It was the kind of decision made by a diver who's gone too deep and stayed too long. He had to come up out of his misery because to not surface was to perish. Grief has a half-life, even if memory does not. These thoughts came all at once as Tuck lay in a tangle of cheap bedding.

He got up, walked to the window, and pulled open the curtains. The filthy, road-weary Volvo was parked a few feet away facing the monastic room. Tuck pulled open the door and stood blinking, unsteady and still sleep-dazed, as the dry, hot desert air hit his face. The pathetically weak air conditioner's grinding sound announced its inability to change the room's temperature.

He slipped into a pair of stained Levis and a T-shirt and walked across the highway to an overly air-conditioned truck stop. He quickly realized he was very hungry. Five eggs and lots of bacon and potatoes and toast and coffee later, Tuck started feeling some life returning as his head cleared. He paid the cashier from a wad of crumpled bills he found in his pocket. He was surprised to discover some Mexican money mixed in with the American greenbacks. He had no clear memory of ever being in Mexico.

A thin, worn telephone book in the bug-splattered glass phone booth told him he was in a place called Luna, New Mexico.

A Baby To Die For

Tuck suddenly craved some human contact. For some reason, Rick and Pauline Shelby came to mind. They would be ideal. The funny lawyer and his delightful wife wouldn't let Tuck stay in the depths of depression for long. They never had before. As good friends in New York, they called themselves The Four Muscatels. Rick was already practicing law and Tuck studying law, so they had a great deal in common. Ellen and Pauline were close, too, so it made for a natural combination, right up until Rick and Pauline moved back to Dallas. After that, they lost touch.

Tuck felt certain that Rick's reaction to his choice of law enforcement would be jealousy, since, like Tuck, Rick was never quite happy with his chosen profession.

For the next hour, Tuck tried to make the Volvo more presentable. He washed off months of dirt and bugs, threw away a vast accumulation of paper garbage, food wrappings, empty bottles, things he barely remembered. Looking at the car's odometer, he was amazed at the number of miles he had accumulated. When he left the car as almost new.

God, I've been completely out of it.

Tuck sat on the fender of the freshly washed car and looked through his checkbook. By his entries of the checks written, he traced his travels. For Tuck, it was like looking at a work of fiction. Fortunately, although he had traveled far and wide, most of the nest egg he and Ellen had so carefully saved was still intact. A second account in New York held the $7,000 they had put away for the baby.

Using the phone in the motel's office, he dialed Texas information. A few minutes later, he had Rick and Pauline

A Baby To Die For

Shelby's number in Dallas. He checked the map and saw that Dallas was a straight shot east of his present location. The motel manager said it was about eight hundred miles, an easy two-day drive.

He ran his dirty laundry through the coin-operated machine at the back of the motel office. He borrowed an iron from the old man at the front desk and pressed each piece. He would have to stop along the way at a decent store and make a few purchases. The things he had were fine for the road but not suitable for Dallas. He carefully shaved off weeks of beard, leaving a thick, dark mustache. He showered and dressed in his freshly washed and ironed clothing.

Under the front seat of the car, he located the plastic bag and removed his service revolver. He carefully cleaned and oiled it, reloaded it, and placed it back in the bag. This time, he tucked it into the glove compartment of the Volvo.

By early evening, he was on his way to Dallas to find his friends. And for the first time since the funeral, watching the sunset did not make him weep.

Chapter 26

"She's fucking you over, Max, you know that," Jake said.

Jake was curled up in the corner of the sofa in Max's office, a bottle of San Francisco Anchor Steam beer in his right hand. In his left, a long Macanudo cigar curled smoke from its delicate white ash.

He would have liked to roll a joint, but his brother threw a fit if he even hinted at any drug use. Well, hell, Max was still the boss, even though he was his brother.

"Shit, Max, that cunt is probably pulling down bundles of dough right out of your underpants. She better be damned good in the sack for that kind of money."

Max looked up from the big desk and inspected his brother carefully.

"Every business has a certain amount of bottom-line tolerance when it comes to employee compensation," Max said finally, with a little laugh.

Max Garfield was not well known for his sense of humor. The laugh should have been a signal to Jake, a danger signal. Max was a cruel man, not a funny man. He was more Torquemada than Woody Allen.

But Jake stupidly pressed on, taunting his older brother.

"Yeah, she's good in the sack all right. Maybe you're even in love with the old broad. What say, my brother? Are you in love with Porter or just plowing her fields like a tenant farmer?"

Max rose slowly from behind his desk and walked casually to where Jake was reclining on the sofa.

"Listen to me, Jake, you may be my brother, but just remember, Porter is my right arm around here."

He was smiling when he said what he said, and as he spoke, he held his hand out to Jake.

"A sip," Max said, and accepted the bottle of beer from Jake's hand.

Max took several sips of the beer.

"Hmm, this beer is really very good. It's hard to find around here," he said, before continuing his remarks about Porter. "Look at it this way, Jake. If Porter wants to skim a little from me off the top—that's okay. As long as I know about it and control it, then, you see, it just becomes another piece of her compensation. And I *do* know she's doing it, and I *do* control it. So you see, Jake, it's like her bonus. Look at it like her bonus. Porter makes a great deal of money, but, unlike you, Jake, she earns a much larger amount of money for me, do you understand that concept? Porter represents income, and you, on the other hand, are an expense. Remember it that way, okay?"

Before Jake could answer, Max continued.

"And another thing I'd like you to remember," Max said in an even, sensible, almost tender tone.

And as he spoke, he took the Macanudo cigar from Jake's hand and dropped it down into the neck of the bottle of beer. The lit cigar hissed as the cold liquid extinguished it.

"Hey! What the fuck you do that for?" Jake shouted.

Max cut him off, saying, "That's the other thing I want you to remember, my brother. I have all the rights. You have no rights."

"I dragged that fucking beer all the way back from Frisco, and that was my last bottle," Jake pouted. "You didn't need to do that."

"I paid for the beer. I paid for your trip to San Francisco. I pay for your clothes and your apartment. I pay for the food that keeps you alive and the meds that keep you halfway sane. I give you everything, and I can take it all away, understand? Sound familiar? Giving and taking is usually attributed to God, and for you, Jake, I am God. And don't you ever fucking forget it."

With that, Max began to pour the beer slowly into Jake's lap.

Jake, to avoid the deluge of beer and wet cigar, leapt to his feet.

"Hey!"

"Stop," Max commanded sharply and stiff-armed Jake back down into the sofa. "Don't move. Don't move one fucking inch or I'll cut off your cash flow. Just let it all soak in, like when we were kids, and you pissed your fucking pants and I had to clean it up. Let it soak in, brother and remember Porter is my concern—*not yours*. Don't you ever tell me what I can or can't do. You're just a little speck of shit and have nothing to do with this operation other than to stay halfway sober and run my errands and not go crazy again, understand? I pay you for that, to be sane. But don't get smart. Don't try to think or reason. Don't do a damned fucking thing unless you're told to do it."

The last thing to come out of the bottle was the beer-soaked cigar. It plopped like a foul turd into Jake's lap.

"Now get the fuck out of here, Jake, and clean yourself up. I want you to pick up Porter at the airport. She's coming in at noon. So try to be pleasant. If I hear you got the slightest bit snotty with her, I'll come down on you."

Jake's face was crimson with rage. Thick veins stood out along his temples and down his neck, looking ripe and ready to burst. To say nothing took a monumental effort. Jake rose from the couch and walked silently from the room. It was a study in control that somehow kept him from killing Max. He would have surely killed anyone else had they done what Max just did. He prayed his mind wouldn't snap. Remembering this was his brother was the only thing that held him in check. He prayed he could stay lucid enough to remember it was Max he was dealing with. Because if it all became a blur—if for one instant Max became a blur, just a man, not precisely and specifically his brother, Max—then Jake would kill him. He would kill a blur, no doubt about that. His mind was flicking pictures—a montage of Max, the helicopter crash in Vietnam, the bamboo cage, the revolver taped to his hand. Jake shook his head hard trying to clear the pictures. He had to remember or he would snap. He had to remember who he was, who his brother was or he would snap. And God help Max, or anyone else, if he did.

The thick oak door closed softly and Max, slightly shaken but totally oblivious to how close he'd just been to death, returned to his place behind the large desk. He buzzed his secretary in the special way that meant he wanted coffee. He sat staring at the far wall or, at least, at the photograph on the far wall. His hand was shaking, but the picture soothed him. The large and expensive photograph showed a huge expanse of lawn, his lawn, at the back of the big house in Connecticut. On the lawn, in the foreground of the photo, between the rear of the house and a huge pond, was a giant steel sculpture.

It was a peaceful, graceful work of art, a ton of steel that had been worked so skillfully that it seemed to be at one with every flower, every tree, even with the house itself.

He and Porter had fucked one afternoon under the very shadow of that sculpture. They had brought a wicker basket from the house, filled with lunch, spread a blanket next to the monumental piece of art, and attacked the food. The cold white wine was made more potent by the hot sun, and halfway through the second bottle they began to undress. The wine finished, they sat naked as babies, with their clothing draped at random over the sculpture like a gaily-dressed scarecrow, and then fucked as the kinetic piece swung slowly from the movement of a gentle breeze, a delicate, giant steel blade of grass. It stood to reason that every time he looked at the photograph, he got a vague and at times rather active stirring in his loins.

Minutes later, sipping his coffee, Max had to admit he was a bit scared of Jake, one of the reasons he was always tough with him. It was like having a trained but vicious pit bull that you had to handle with an iron fist. That was how it was with Jake. An inch off center and he had to be slapped down, no ifs, ands, or buts. The beer thing on the pants may have been too much, Max mused, but hell, if the error was made, better to let it be on the side of discipline and not laxity.

No excuses, no regrets.

That was something one of the Fords might have said. If so, Max hoped it wasn't Edsel.

The last thing Max needed was his little brother lecturing him about Porter's sticky fingers. He knew to the penny what she was taking. He had been a thief too long to be conned by an amateur. Max double-checked every financial transaction Porter reported. He knew about her deals with Toby Wine and Sarah LaFrance. He kept intricate records of the discrepancies between what they were paid and what he was paying. Not only those two, but with all the other parts of Porter's operations as well. Max even knew that Porter was down in Florida to try and skim a little more of the profit off the LaFrance woman. As soon as Porter told him she was going to see the old hag, he knew. Porter was so damned predictable he could forecast her actions.

But, hell, in her place, I would have done the same damned thing—maybe more so.

But Porter was worth it. Ten times over, she was worth it and not just because she gave the greatest head in the world either, and he smiled at that thought. He was making a fortune, and it would have been almost impossible without the work Porter was doing. So what if Porter took a little off the top? It showed initiative.

The baby business was good. Prices were moving up faster than waterfront real estate, for Christ's sake. As long as he could keep a low profile and not make any stupidly illegal waves, he would be okay. No scandals. No dissatisfied customers to blab to some headline-hungry district attorney.

Keep the customers happy and everything appearing to be squeaky clean.

That was why Max ran such an antiseptic operation. Not out of pride or concern for ethics. It was insurance, pure and simple. Any problem—no question, he solved it. Even if the adoptive parents needed a little time to get up all the money, that could be worked out, too. When a couple adopted through Max Garfield, they got the best possible service. Every customer became a walking advertisement for his operation. He had couples coming back for seconds and they told their friends, and their friends passed the word on, as well.

And Max paid generous fees to his fellow lawyers. The network's strength came from sharing, not cheating. Each member had to be certain of the other. Certain about what they'd get and willing to give without hassle or questions asked. That's how it was. That's how it had to be.

A perfect example was Rick Shelby, the Texas lawyer who was beginning to produce for Max. He could have given less to Shelby, but why do it? There was enough to go around and greed could screw up everything. Max recalled being told once that back in the day, when a cowboy rode into town, even before he had a drink or got laid, he'd make sure his horse was fed, because it was his horse that got him where he was, and would take him where he wanted to go. That's how Max wanted the network to function and grow, and that's why it would keep working and keep growing. The network was the horse that carried Max, and he intended to keep it happy and well fed.

He looked at the photograph of his house on the wall across the room and it reminded him of Porter, and he realized he was looking forward to seeing her tonight, to being with her. She was always particularly good after a business trip. He reasoned that her feelings of guilt at taking money from behind his back acted as an aphrodisiac. Like oysters, maybe.

Chapter 27

Dallas, Texas

Tuck felt a cool breeze move across his naked body as he awoke from the deepest sleep he'd had since Ellen died. He carefully withdrew his arm from beneath Pauline Shelby, causing her to stir slightly, mumble, then roll onto her side and draw her knees up toward her chest.

His arm had fallen asleep, and he rubbed it while studying this woman whom he'd known as a friend for years—at least, until last night, she'd been nothing more than a friend. He pulled himself up to a sitting position then slowly and carefully did an inventory of his emotions, much as someone might check for cuts and broken bones after a bad fall. As far as he could tell, everything seemed intact. No remorse fractures, no dislocated guilt. He had slept with his old friend's wife—correction: soon-to-be-ex-wife. He had been disloyal, at least to the memory of Ellen, but he knew that was inevitable and felt surprisingly okay about it—actually, better than okay.

Maybe I'm making progress.

A Baby To Die For

Pauline and Tuck had come together without excuses or rationalizations. It was biological hunger, pure and simple, anointed by their mutual loneliness.

It had been late evening when he arrived in Dallas. He was tired and road weary. He tried booking a room at just about every decent hotel in the phone book. Several giant conventions had swollen the demand for rooms far beyond capacity, and the thought of staying another night in a shabby motel room or the backseat of the Volvo was out of the question. He really would have preferred to contact his friends after he had had a good night's sleep, could buy some decent clothing and visit a barber. But the knowledge that good friends were so close at hand was too much of a temptation to ignore. So he phoned.

Other than Pauline Shelby's overjoyed response to Tuck's surprise call, there had been no detailed conversation. An unspoken agreement relegated all details to a face-to-face, in-person exchange of questions and answers. She gave him clear directions, which he carefully noted. Tuck had no trouble finding the house, and before he could even knock, Pauline pulled open the door. She was prettier than Tuck remembered. Her blonde hair was darker and shorter than he recalled, her face a little fuller. And there were eye glasses. She had never worn glasses before. They examined each other for a moment, and then without speaking, embraced, a bit awkwardly.

Finally, Pauline pulled away and held Tuck by the shoulders at arm's length. She studied him, not speaking, just looking him up and down. Then, a deep breath and a guilty smile pulled at the corners of her mouth. "Rick isn't here anymore. We're getting a divorce," Pauline blurted out. "I was too cowardly to tell you on the phone. Saying it out loud still seems strange to me."

Before Tuck could reply, she was pulling him into the entry hall and fussing over taking his coat and small suitcase. Then, over her shoulder she said, "And Ellen? How is she? God, don't tell me you two have…split?"

Tuck cut her off. "Ellen is dead, Pauline."

Pauline recoiled with shock, but other than a sharp intake of breath, she made no sound, then, "Tuck, I honestly don't know what to say." She took him by the arm and led him into the living room and proceeded to pour them each two fingers of scotch from the group of liquor bottles sitting on a rolling cart. "Tell me, Tuck, what happened?"

They sipped the drinks, and Tuck told the story. He started from the very beginning—the attempt at adoption, the miscarriages, the ill-fated last pregnancy, the decision to leave New York for its duration, and finally, Ellen's death. As he spoke, Tuck realized it was the very first time anyone had heard the entire story, spoken out loud, all at once—even himself.

When he finished, Pauline just sat silently rolling the glass between her palms. Eventually, she put her drink down and walked around the coffee table to where Tuck was sitting. She had tears in her eyes, and she gently touched his face with her fingertips.

"I'm so sorry," she whispered, mouthing the words more than actually saying them. "So very sorry."

A Baby To Die For
===

Her arms went around him, and she held him close. He could feel her crying. She could smell the road on his coarse woolen jacket.

What happened next was so natural, so very predictable and spontaneous that it bordered on a cliché. They kissed. They could taste each other's tears, and for all kinds of complicated reasons, it excited them. Their lovemaking was not tender that night. They clamped onto each other, both desperately trying to grab strength, express anger, sate lust, and escape loneliness. And they each took from the other whatever was needed. Sometime before dawn, they padded into the kitchen, scrambled half a dozen eggs, made toast and hash brown potatoes, and drank lots of strong coffee. And when hunger, the final sense dealt with that evening, had been satisfied, they talked. Christ, how it flowed out of them. It exploded like a verbal orgasm.

For three days, Tuck Handler and Pauline Shelby talked, made love, and slept. Sometime during the second day, Pauline started telling Tuck about Rick's law career in Dallas. Naturally, the particulars about the baby-selling business came out, but even as the details unfolded, Tuck never suspected that his old friend was involved in any way with his own disastrous adoption experience, until she mentioned Max Garfield. Of course, it was a name Tuck immediately recognized from when Twosie, Ellen's uncle Saul, first mentioned the man. And Pauline had a lot to say about Rick working with the New York lawyer.

Saul had told Tuck that much of the black market adoption went through one lawyer, Max Garfield. The conversation now seemed like a lifetime ago.

A Baby To Die For

And suddenly it occurred to Tuck that here were important connections: Max Garfield and the network and the impossibly high cost for a baby. And for the first time since he lost Ellen and their child, Tuck realized that maybe there was someone besides himself he could blame for what had happened to Ellen.

On the afternoon before Tuck was to leave, Pauline took him through Neiman Marcus. They were like kids in an amusement park. Pauline styled her old friend, dressing him as if he were a wonderful, king-sized Ken doll. That night, they sat across from each other in the rich atmosphere of the Pyramid Restaurant and sipped an excellent 1965 Pommard and reflected in the warm glow of what they had been able to do for one another. They both acknowledged they'd been conspirators in a selfish, albeit healing, act of passion, and yet they agreed there were no regrets. The refreshing part was that they could discuss it so openly. They both also understood that Tuck had to leave, had to return to New York, and salvage the remaining pieces of his life.

The next morning Tuck packed the Volvo with his things. Finally, he was behind the wheel, ready to go. Pauline, the sadness of his leaving etched on her face, leaned on the car's window frame.

"*Shoot!* I almost forgot," Pauline suddenly said under her breath and dashed back into the house. She returned with a huge Tupperware box filled with fruit and sandwiches, a thermos of coffee, and a neatly typed note containing some names and phone numbers she had copied out of her husband's address book.

The engine already running, Tuck got out of the car and embraced Pauline. They stood that way for a long time, holding tightly and smelling each other's hair and perfume and aftershave.

And then, Tuck was on the highway, with windows open and radio playing, and feeling certain for the first time in a long while that his life would be okay.

Tuck now had confirmation that the network was real. It had touched his life in too many heartbreaking ways for it to remain a fantasy. The network and, by implication, Max Garfield were responsible for his wife and child's death. Tuck was sure of it now, and he felt relief just from knowing. The guilt—at least some of it—could be shifted from his own shoulders. Seeking revenge against oneself could be called suicide, but to seek revenge from the network was a mission, one that Tuck could throw himself into with all his energy and all his heart.

Pauline was able to give Tuck lots of information about the network. In Rick's attempts to convince Pauline that arranging adoptions was not so terrible, he had revealed a great deal more than he should have. Pauline also had names, phone numbers, and addresses that she simply copied out of her husband's address book. So now, Tuck knew about people like Jake Garfield, Max's brother, and Porter Gibbs…and some lady named LaFrance in Florida who ran a little baby farm. He even told her about the trip he'd taken to Casablanca, and the pregnant woman they had flown back. Rick had bragged about being instrumental in selling the woman's baby to a family named Kaufman. Mr. Kaufman was a surgeon living somewhere near New York City. Tuck thought the Kaufmans could help him a lot, and they shouldn't be too difficult to locate. The phone book would probably do the trick.

And then there was an attractive young woman—at least, according to Pauline, she was young and attractive—named Karen Boyd. Pauline had met her on her last trip to New York with Rick. She worked for Max Garfield, but wasn't sure in what capacity. The girl took Pauline to lunch while Max and Rick were holed up in a meeting, and they immediately liked one another.

Pauline told Tuck, "I got a distinct feeling that she wasn't a Garfield fan, and for reasons well beyond boss/employee issues. I sensed something complex and disturbing about Karen Boyd. I think if asked, she would help you, Tuck. If you want, call her. Frankly, from everything Rick told me about Garfield's operation, the chances of catching anyone doing anything illegal—at least, anything that would stand up in a court of law—is slim to none. He claimed that it was doubtful if anybody has ever gotten into very much trouble placing babies for adoption—lawyer, client, or supplier."

Originally, Tuck planned to drive from Dallas directly to see the LaFrance woman in Florida, but the more he thought about it, the more convinced he was that he needed a new plan. Somewhere near New Orleans, he nosed the Volvo north toward New York. He was anxious to get started, and the first people he thought he should speak with were the Kaufmans.

Chapter 28

Bronxville, New York

The brown Mercedes squatted in the Kaufmans' driveway. It was a lot cleaner than it had been a year earlier when Mark Kaufman was steering it through a sandstorm somewhere outside Alamogordo, New Mexico, picking his way along a narrow rutted road, searching for a sign picturing a raging red bull.

Visiting the Kaufmans seemed a logical first step for Tuck. They had the experience of dealing with Max Garfield, and he hoped to get as much information as he could about the process they went through, as well as details about the money involved.

Tuck maneuvered his red Volvo off to the side of the Kaufmans' car, being careful not to block the two massive garage doors.

The Kaufmans' home was impressive. Tuck stood for a moment letting his gaze wander across the property. It was an elegant stone Tudor with a wide drive that curled around to the back of the house, leading to a parking area and the two-car garage. Green lawns and ancient plantings surrounded the home, and a tennis court nestled in the cool shade of large evergreen trees. Thoughts of Ellen suddenly flooded Tuck's mind, knowing how much she would have loved this house.

Helen Kaufman answered the door on the third ring. She was a handsome woman who wore her affluence casually. Behind her, a red-haired young girl, dressed in jeans and a maroon Vassar sweatshirt, pushed a vacuum across the foyer carpet as vigorously as if the devil were a step behind.

Helen cocked her head slightly to one side and said, "You must be Tuck Handler? Sorry, but I didn't hear the bell right away. The vacuum was blasting. You're right on time. I'm Helen," she said, as she stepped back and gestured for him to enter. "Come in, please. Mark's in the den." Then she signaled for the young girl to shut off the noisy machine. "You can do that later, Kim...take care of the laundry now, please. The young lady is our neighbor's daughter, and when she comes home on weekends, she earns some extra spending money helping us out."

"You have quite an outstanding home, Mrs. Kaufman. These old Tudors are a particular favorite of mine."

"Oh, thanks, but please, call me Helen. It took us forever to find it. It was built in 1935. You should have seen it around here for the last year or so. We were in heavy construction. We started out needing some extra room in the kitchen for a new refrigerator and ended up scooping out most of the whole house. At least, it seemed that way."

Helen Kaufman laughed as she threw off the remark, but her face showed the incredible pride she obviously had in her home.

A Baby To Die For

Mark Kaufman was sitting in a black-leather Eames chair. A child about a year or so in age sprawled across his chest laughing and playing with her daddy's thick, dark hair and heavy horn-rimmed eyeglasses. She was a strikingly gorgeous little girl with thick, blonde curls and wide-set, coal black eyes. Her skin didn't reflect the fairness of her hair but rather was a medium shade of olive. Tuck could easily recognize the progeny of the Polish girl and the French legionnaire that Pauline had told him about.

"Honestly, I'd get up out of this chair if I could, but she's holding me hostage, and I can't escape," Mark said, laughing. "Please grab a seat."

"Frankly, Doctor, I don't think you want to escape from that child at all."

"Mark. Call me Mark. You're right. I don't mind this kind of attention, especially on my day off."

"She's beautiful. Looks a lot like your wife. I'd never guess she was adopted," Tuck said, which was not much of a lie since there did seem to be a resemblance.

"Yeah, she does look a little like Helen. We've heard it from others, especially before they know she's adopted. I think it may simply be a matter of people seeing what they choose to see. They see Helen—a mother holding her child, assume it's biological, and put together what they believe is two-plus-two. And four is a socially acceptable answer. But that's just my theory. Now, for some coffee. How do you like it?"

Minutes later, Tuck and the Kaufmans sipped coffee and exchanged pleasantries until finally the child—Amy—settled among some trucks and colored blocks near the fireplace, her attention now seriously riveted on the toys.

"She's a real girl. She loves trucks." Helen smiled, gazing at her daughter.

Tuck set down his coffee cup and prepared to lie to the Kaufmans.

"First off, I want to thank you for taking time from your weekend to see me. As I mentioned to Helen on the phone, my wife and I are trying to adopt a baby. She would be here, too, but she's in retailing and Saturdays...well, you can imagine. We've tried going through agencies—about a half dozen, as a matter of fact—and I'm sure you know what that's all about. There are so few babies and to pin our hopes on one of those waiting lists, well, from what they said—it could take anywhere from two years to possibly never. We're really not young enough to waste time with that kind of uncertainty. Nor do we have the patience for it."

The Kaufmans exchanged knowing glances. Tuck could see that they had obviously gone through the same process, come to the same conclusions, and tried to avoid the same frustrations Tuck had just voiced.

"We just didn't know where to turn. So, when we decided to find another solution, my wife's uncle—he's a lawyer—made some calls for us and got a few names of couples in the area who had circumvented the regular agencies and adopted in a more—let's say—private way."

"How on earth did he ever get our name?" Mark Kaufman asked, expressing curiosity, not suspicion.

"As I alluded to on the phone, it was just one of several names Ellen's uncle gave us." Tuck shrugged. "You know how closemouthed lawyers can be. You were the first couple I called, and thankfully, you were good enough to agree to see me. I'm just trying to network and gather as much information as I can. I'll tell you, it's the most frustrating thing in the world. We're not wealthy people, you know, but I make out okay, and my wife works, but we were really amazed at the numbers we were quoted when we looked into a private adoption—the black market thing."

"We never thought of it as the black market, Mr. Handler. Private adoptions are quite common. But you're right, it sure isn't cheap," Mark said, keeping his eyes fixed on his child playing in the corner. "But without question, worth every penny."

Helen cleared her throat. "What can we do to help you?"

"Well, our uncle told us about a lawyer in the city who specializes in this kind of adoption, who doesn't go through what you might call 'normal' channels. Apparently, this guy has access to babies from all around the country. But I'm really reluctant to contact him until I can get a little more information about him, you know, how his operation works. I'm not even sure he would help us. We were told that he was the lawyer who handled your adoption. His name is Max Garfield."

Helen glanced at her husband before answering, and Tuck noted the almost imperceptible nod.

"Yes, that's correct. Mr. Garfield was the lawyer who handled the adoption. What is it you wish to know?" Helen said, her voice rock steady.

"Well, uh, I was interested in the procedure, how it

worked—sort of, the where and how of the process, you know. I'm really—*we're* really very nervous about this. You can understand."

For several minutes, Mark and Helen Kaufman took Tuck through what he could only imagine was a carefully laundered version of how they acquired Amy. Basically, all they said was that they'd gone to Garfield, picked out a baby that was due to be delivered soon, closed the deal, and got the baby. And even though Tuck, using his interrogation skills as gently as possible, tried to nudge and probe the narrative, the best he could learn were the sort of details that were obviously too pat, too textbook, and too rehearsed.

It was a rough approximation of the truth but far from the *whole* truth. Tuck was certain it had all been carefully scripted, along with very strong legal advice.

When they finished, silence followed. Finally, Tuck waded in.

"I know this is terribly personal, but could you give me some idea of the cost? The prices we've heard are really wild. Our uncle claims it might cost $10,000 to $12,000. Does that sound right?"

It was as if hoods came down over the Kaufmans' eyes like a camel's second eyelid that provides protection from sandstorms. The hoods came down, and Tuck could almost hear them lock into place.

Quick glances—silent communication—exchanged between husband and wife and finally, "I think we know where you're coming from, Mr. Handler. God knows Helen and I were just as uncertain. Actually, it turned out to be exactly $10,000, including the travel costs," Mark lied. "I've got all the canceled checks."

Tuck's jaw clenched, and his face hardened. If the Kaufmans had known him better, they would have noticed and been alerted by the change.

"Was that *all* you paid?" Tuck asked, incredulously.

"I don't think I follow you."

"Isn't it almost standard practice to pay more, sometimes a *lot more*—under the table—in cash? Isn't that what the black market is all about?"

Silence. Helen Kaufman glanced at her husband, and Tuck caught a slight frown, a wrinkling of her brow.

"As I said, we didn't use any black market. Amy's was a private adoption, and that was all we paid, Mr. Handler," Mark Kaufman smiled coldly, laying a hand on his wife's arm. "Hell, that was steep enough."

Tuck's eyes swept around the room, past the twenty-six-inch, color Bang & Olufsen TV, the stereo, and shelves stacked with the latest best sellers, past the oil paintings and the other obvious signs of wealth.

"Was it really just $10,000, Mr. Kaufman? Are you sure there wasn't any other money you paid out?"

"Really, Handler, that's about enough—"

"Wasn't there cash?" Tuck pressed. "Didn't you have to pay a large sum of cash when you picked up Amy?"

Tuck had decided to climb out on a limb. He hoped it wouldn't snap off.

The Kaufmans sat stunned by what Tuck was saying and by the tone of his questioning. Amy toddled over and scaled her father's leg, inching her way up onto his chest again. She laid her head under his chin and jammed her thumb into her mouth and almost instantly fell asleep.

Mark Kaufman took several seconds to regain his composure, and before he spoke, he handed the sleeping child to his wife, a move akin to removing eyeglasses before a fight.

"I don't know what you're talking about, Handler. We've been open enough with you to explain the financial arrangements we went through to get our baby. What you're suggesting is simply not the case. Garfield contacted a lawyer named Shelby who arranged for the baby, which we picked up out of state. There was no cash paid to anyone. No cash, just the total of $10,000 paid to him by check, and that was it. What part of that don't you understand?"

Tuck wiped his hand across his eyes in frustration.

"Mark, look, you can't tell me that someone with the reputation of Max Garfield is doing adoptions as a not-for-profit operation. By the time he gets his money, the mother's expenses are paid for, and the other lawyer you mentioned, Shelby, he gets his money, too. And you expect me to believe that's all it cost you—$10,000?"

"That's what I said. Now, I think you'd better leave."

Tuck hunched forward in the wing chair and, leaning toward the Kaufmans, his voice dropped in tone, became more intimate.

"Look, Mark…Helen, please, listen…"

Mark Kaufman stood and gently took Tuck by the arm.

"You have to leave now. I don't want to call the police,

but I will. Please leave us alone. There's not a damned thing here that can help you. Just leave us alone."

Tuck left and Mark Kaufman stood framed by the front door, watching him until he disappeared around the side of the house where the Volvo was parked near the garage. He started the engine and sat thinking of what he might do now.

With a sudden ratcheting sound, one of the automatic garage doors rolled up, slowly revealing Helen Kaufman standing in the opening. She didn't move, just stood holding Amy on her left hip. And then, hesitating slightly, she slowly raised her right fist to the side of her head, extended her thumb to her ear, and her little finger to her lips—the universal "call me" sign. Then, with a shrug that seemed to say, "If you wish," she turned and was gone, as the automatic door rolled closed.

Chapter 29

"Listen, Jake, there's a problem with one of the girls in L.A.," Max barked into the phone. "I want you to fly out and take care of it."

And on the other end of the call, Max's little brother knew that his weekend plans had just been shot to shit.

Twenty-four hours later, Jake Garfield sat on a cheap, threadbare couch in the "problem's" shabby Los Angeles apartment. And even though the tiny place was spotless, Jake felt he was somehow being contaminated and felt physically uncomfortable.

Ever since he started working for his brother, he took great pride in his appearance and chose his wardrobe carefully and wore the clothing well. His brown tweed jacket was soft as silk and, although purchased off the rack, well-tailored nevertheless. The tan shirt fit perfectly and the knit tie was a tricky shade of gray that went well with brown. Highly polished tan Gucci loafers poked out from the cuffs of his twill slacks.

So what the fuck am I doing in a cesspool like this when I could have been spending the weekend getting laid in Southampton?

A Baby To Die For

The second-floor space felt cramped and airless, a depressing little cliff dwelling stacked like a plastic block on top of another one just like it, not far from the Los Angeles International Airport. For an area as lush and lovely as Southern California, it had more than its share of crummy neighborhoods.

The young pregnant girl sat on an aluminum kitchen chair hugging her middle to keep the chenille robe closed around her large stomach. Her boyfriend straddled another chair next to her. She'd been a cute and perky high school sophomore, but now a weary look filled her eyes and the rough texture of her hair belied her sixteen years. Purple blotches showed where acne was healing on her chin and forehead, with several new eruptions as well. The shifting hormones of pregnancy were not doing her any favors.

The girl started to speak but her sentence was relegated to meaningless mouth movements, drowned out by the screaming sound of an arriving jet passing overhead as it crab-walked through the smog, its landing apparatus groping for solid runway.

"Like I told the man in your office, we—me and Burt—uh, like, we decided we want to keep our baby," the girl repeated, in a high, singsong whine. "Besides, we didn't sign no papers or nothing. Like you can't make me give you my baby if I don't want to."

She glanced over to the other chair. Burt was a bulky-looking eighteen-year-old, and Jake guessed from the look of his bulging arms that the kid was strong. The boy's hair was long and pulled back in a ponytail. The rough beginnings of a full beard sprouted all over his face. If he kept going the way he was, someday he would look like Kris Kristofferson.

Burt avoided Jake's gaze and kept his mouth shut. The faint smell of vomit assaulted Jake. Apparently, the girl was still having morning sickness.

"Can't you just get out of here and leave us alone, Mr. Jake?" Candy, whined.

"Yeah," the big kid added, "she told you we want to keep the baby, you know, so leave us alone."

Burt also had a whine to his voice that grated on Jake, and he hated the sound of it. Just being here was bad enough without having to listen to the big kid.

Jake remained silent. He just smiled a vicious smile, shook his head a little, and ran his hand through his thick hair. God, he hated complications. Why the hell did Max give him all the shit jobs while that bitch, Porter Gibbs, ran all over the place raking in the money, sleeping in fancy hotels, eating in great restaurants, while Max's own flesh-and-blood brother was relegated to cleaning up the dog shit again? A human, walking, well-dressed pooper-scooper, that's what he was. Well, clearly, he had to clean up this mess and do it quickly. The red-eye flight back to New York waited for no one, but he intended to be on it.

The girl, obviously nervous, felt compelled to break the silence.

"Yeah, Burt is right. We changed our mind, you know?"

Candy looked down. She always looked down, never made eye contact. She was like a paper-shy dog that's been smacked too many times and reflexively cowers in anticipation of the next attack.

Jake thought about Vietnam. He killed shapes there, not people. Here it wasn't much different. These were really not people to him, just shapes to be manipulated and moved about. The girl meant cash for Max—nothing personal, just business.

The big kid nervously cleared his throat. He worked in a gas station. Grease stained his coveralls. His hands, scrubbed almost raw, stubbornly held the grease traces that would be embedded there forever—like tattoos. A sprinkle of blackheads ran along the sides of his nose. Nonetheless, he was handsome, still young and not beat up or soured yet by life. That would come soon enough.

Jake remembered a story a stewardess once told him. It was her theory of why Southern California was populated by so many good-looking people.

"Apparently," she told Jake, "way back in the twenties and thirties, moving-picture-crazed kids from all over the country flocked to Southern California, each with the dream of becoming a movie star. In the hope of being "discovered," they'd hang out at the places they read about in screen magazines—the corner of Hollywood and Vine, Schwab's drug store, and Musso & Frank. Or they congregated outside the various movie studios' front gates with their pathetic picture portfolios, hoping to get a little work as an extra at the next casting call—you know, carry a spear or stand in a crowd—but the closest most of them got to a movie was by paying a dime to watch one. So, after what little money they had ran out, those good-looking would-be movie stars, ashamed to return home as failures, had to pump gas or wait on tables or work in a factory to make a living. It didn't take too long for the day-to-day grind of putting food on the table to win out, and the movie dreams simply died of necessity. So they settled down to an ordinary life and, because they were friends from hanging around the studios, they dated each other. Good-looking guys dating good-looking girls. Hell, the first big production any of them ever starred in was making a baby, and more times than not, a very pretty baby. And the pretty babies grew up and had more pretty babies and, well, that's why all those California kids look so damned luscious. It's breeding, honey—simple as that—good-looking failures, all fucking each other and making a lot of pretty babies and very little money," the stewardess concluded.

It was a good story, and at the time, Jake had had a good laugh. But he had to admit there could be some truth to it. Southern California had some of the most spectacular-looking, ordinary, middle-class people he had ever seen. And the streets and their cars were all clean, too. God, he hated Southern California.

Jake snapped out of the memory as the big kid took a move to rise out of his chair, muscles tensed. Jake could kill the boy, just like that. But he had no need to. Not that he would mind killing the big kid, it just wasn't the right time or place or even very smart. That's all Max would have to hear—that he had killed someone. But the kid was simply moving toward the door, responding to a scratching sound. He opened the door a crack, and a white cat shouldered its way in, squeezing its body to accommodate the narrowness of the opening.

"Look, a deal's a deal," Jake said evenly. "When we met two months ago, you agreed you wanted to give up the baby for adoption. Since then, we've invested a lot of money in you."

Candy looked helplessly over at Burt, then back to Jake.

"Well, back then, you know, I couldn't get the abortion. It ain't my fault. I was just too far gone, you know. The lady at the clinic gave me a lawyer's name. I called him, you know, but now I changed my mind. We want to keep the baby—it's our baby!"

"Uh huh. I can understand," Jake said, nodding. "I can certainly understand that point of view."

Jake uncrossed his legs and hunched forward in the couch, his forearms resting on his knees like an insurance salesman who is really getting down to a serious sales pitch. He absently fingered the cloth bag on the table next to him that held Candy's knitting paraphernalia. In it was a tiny, half-finished, pink-and-blue sweater appropriate for the coming baby, regardless of what its sex might be. Right now, it was one little sleeve and the back, all held together with two long, metal knitting needles.

"You know, this is really lovely work, Candy," Jake said, patting the sweater. "Look, you guys, I can understand how you might *think* you want to keep the baby. I'm sure you feel guilty and all that, right? It would only be natural."

Candy was silent, looking down toward the frayed

rug. It was Burt who spoke up. *Damned kid. If it weren't for him, I'd be back in New York instead of this asshole dump.*

"It's final, Mister. We ain't giving up the baby, and there's no law says we got to."

"That's fine and good, kid, but we went to a lot of trouble these past three months. You said the baby was up for adoption so we went ahead with some very complicated plans. We paid for all of Candy's medical bills and tests and sent you guys some money every two weeks for living expenses, isn't that so?"

Jake didn't wait for an answer but kept talking and hammering the facts home. "We busted ass to find a terrific couple to adopt the baby, and they're great people."

In reality Jake had no idea who would get the baby, nor did Max—not yet. They have money—really loaded—and they can take care of the kid, and give it all the things you want for your baby, right? Clothes, toys, good schools—all the stuff I'm sure you want it to have. You guys are in no position to do that for a baby now. Hey, you're both young, you need to look after yourselves first and foremost, so someday you can have a baby, lots of babies, and by then, you'll be in a position to take care of them properly."

Burt began to speak, but Jake held up his hand, palm out, like a traffic cop.

"Wait. Think of what I just said. We got lots of money invested here—the checks, the doctors, the plane fare when we fly out here, the phone calls—hey, and the cost of finding the couple to take the baby, don't forget that," Jake said, slowly, ticking each salient point off on a thick finger. "Why, it's *thousands* of dollars. Can you pay me—now, in cash? If you can, I'll go right now and leave you both alone."

Jake said this wide-eyed and innocent, knowing damned well there wasn't a chance in hell that the offer could ever be taken.

The white cat smoothed sensuously against Jake's leg, its tail pointed high in the air, the black button of its anus contrasting against its white fur.

The kid rose up slowly out of his chair.

"We can pay you back. I got a few hundred I can give you now, in cash, and we can send you the rest, a little each month. You'll have the whole thing in a year or so, I swear it," the kid said, and meant it.

Jake could tell he was one of those weird kids who wouldn't lie, who would pay back every dime plus interest and be putting a down payment on a gas station of his own at the same time. As bad as it looked now, this was a decent enough couple. It would just take them a few years of struggle to get started, like a cold engine that needs to grind and sputter a bit before it roars to life.

He also knew that he had better come back to New York with this matter settled or Max would have his balls in a vise.

Jake decided to try another tack.

"Come on, face it, you guys are committed to this thing. You just got a case of the guilts. You know I'm right. It's going be okay, it's the right choice, believe me. Someday, you'll look back on this and thank God you made the right choice."

A Baby To Die For

Burt was still standing but looked flushed in the face, like he was going to make a move on Jake. He was really pissed. Jake hoped he wouldn't be stupid enough to try anything.

"Fuck you!" the boy said loudly. "What if we refuse? What if we just plain refuse to do it—to listen to you and all your bullshit? We could go to the cops. There ain't a damned thing you could do. So—just get the fuck out of here! Leave us alone! Here's the cash I have now. The rest will come in payments every month, I swear to that," he said, as he slapped a fistful of crumpled bills onto the little dinette table.

"Burt, my man, let's just say it's a matter of honor. You really ought to honor your commitments—you should— it's just a matter of honor," Jake said softly, and as he spoke, he reached out to the cardboard box and picked up Candy's knitting. He slowly withdrew the needles and the stitches fell away as the work unraveled.

Burt leapt to stop him, yelling his objections, but Jake's foot came up to meet him, and the hard toe of his Gucci loafer caught the kid viciously in the crotch. He folded back moaning in pain.

In another slower motion, Jake scooped the small white cat from the floor and held it in his lap. It purred and rubbed up against the soft tweed of his jacket, its tail still high in the air.

Now Jake's voice hissed out cruelly at the young couple sitting terrified, Candy holding onto Burt, watching this madman.

"That baby is ours—bought and paid for—and so, no more bullshit about changing your minds. Don't forget, you came to us. You, Candy, and you, Burt. You knew back then, giving the baby up was the right thing to do, and it still is. And now, we got our plans all set, and you are not fucking them up, do you hear me? We paid good money, and we'll keep paying just like we promised—maybe even a little more for good measure. You can have lots of kids someday, but right now, the extra money we give you will do wonders for building a future. Think about that."

Burt glanced over at Candy, and in that instant, Jake saw it would be okay. He saw it in their eyes—the defeat, the resignation, and the reality that the madman was making sense. At least Jake hoped he saw all those things. But he had to be sure. He had no desire to be back here going through this whole thing again. He needed to seal the deal, once and for all. He stroked the cat, running the end of the knitting needle like a fingernail along its spine. The cat purred in pure enjoyment and satisfaction.

Jake's voice now turned soft.

"Look, Candy, it's going to be okay. Believe me, you and your boyfriend are too young to get tied down with a baby. You got a lifetime to make babies. Not to speak of all the practicing you can do, right?" Jake laughed. "Meanwhile, you stay healthy, keep up the doctor visits, take your vitamins, and we'll be here in a couple months for the delivery—okay? Come on, kids, let me hear you say we got a deal."

The boy and girl looked at each other.

Jake smiled, but his voice was a bit harder.

"What do you say? We got a deal?"

More glances. More silence.

A Baby To Die For

Jake waited.

Silence.

The cat screamed so loud it even startled Jake who, holding the cat by a fist full of neck fur, had driven the knitting needle fast and deep into the cat's anus. The skewered animal's legs desperately clawed the air in every direction as it flew from the couch and leapt through the open window, dots of blood trailing across the shabby carpet and over the windowsill. It landed on the cement two floors below where it twisted and jerked and tried, it seemed, to die as quickly as possible.

Candy screamed and rushed to the window, sobbing in horror. Burt, never taking his eyes off Jake, led her back to the couch, then ran to the bathroom and threw up.

"Why?" the girl finally sobbed.

Jake replied calmly, "Just in case you don't think we're serious—or think about changing your mind again. You're right, we may not have the right, but we do have a deal. That's what life is about, Candy, meeting your commitments, keeping your word. Honoring your obligations and agreements. Don't let me down, or you'll have more fucking trouble than you know what to do with. I'm not talking legal or illegal. I'm talking fact. *Reality*. It's life, honey, so you better get used to it."

On the way to the rental car, Jake stepped over the dead cat, its white fur contrasting with the pool of blood surrounding it. The tip of the needle protruded slightly out of its mouth; the tiny pink tongue next to it.

Jake looked up, squinting in the sun. The couple was standing at the window. The boy had his arm around

Candy's shoulder, holding her tightly. She was still crying. Jake nodded his head once up and down, then waited. A moment later the couple nodded, too.

At least now, he could tell his brother the trip was a success.

Chapter 30

The climb up the four flights of stairs to his old apartment tortured Tuck. Not the physical climb, but rather, the flood of memories. He had accepted Ellen's death. The logical left side of his brain told him it was so. But, good God, how she dominated his thoughts! He tried hard not to think about her, but in the process could think of little else. He pictured her waiting for him in the apartment, still in her office clothes or wrapped in a giant towel, having just climbed out of the bath. They would have a drink and talk about the day, go out for pasta and red wine—or order in Chinese and watch an old movie on television. It was an emotional bitch climbing those steps—his palms damp by the time he rang the bell.

A New Yorker knows not to open a front door without knowing who the hell's on the other side. So, in responding to the bell, Mary Flower only opened the door as far as the thick, short guard chain would allow. Cautiously, she peeked out, gasped, then slammed the door shut, fumbled the heavy brass chain off its track, and this time, yanked it wide open and threw her arms around Tuck's neck. She yelled to her husband, "Hey, Ken, come quick! You'll never guess who's here!"

Thankfully, Saul Bootman had already told the young couple about Ellen's death. So, Tuck didn't have to go through the ordeal of telling them. Ever since Tuck and Ellen had left New York, Saul had been acting, on their behalf, as a sort of quasi landlord for any problems that might crop up at their apartment. In the process, he and the Flowers had become phone-friendly and kept in touch on a fairly regular basis. When Tuck did finally surface in Dallas, he called Saul, who immediately informed Ken and Mary Flower.

So, now they knew that sooner or later, he would show up at their door. The apartment brimmed with a treasure-trove of emotional valuables. He couldn't stay away for very long.

"We knew it was just a matter of time," Ken said, grabbing Tuck in a man-hug.

"I can't tell you how many times we sent out for pizza or ordered in Chinese and hoped you'd show up. But you were always a no-show, until tonight," Mary said.

Tuck, smiling, said, "Well, I'm starved. So which is it? Pizza or Chinese?"

Mary laughed, "Actually, tonight I've got a huge hunk of steak in the broiler. Sorry to disappoint you."

Through dinner, Ellen's absence created a certain degree of tension in their conversation—a sort of forced formality. Everything they said filtered through that reality. But as the evening passed and more wine poured, the stiffness and self-conscious tenor of the reunion softened. They had started like strangers who knew *about* each other but did not *know* each other. As the awkwardness wore off, they began to relate more like good friends.

After dinner Ken fetched a bottle of cognac and three snifters.

"A gift from one of my grateful editors. I know it cost more than he paid me for the piece I wrote, and I'd bet a byline he received it as a gift and passed it off on me," Ken said, as he poured an inch of the amber liquid into each glass.

Ken proposed a toast to Ellen, they clinked glasses and downed their drinks, and he immediately supplied refills.

"So—what are your plans? Back to the job, or what?" Ken asked Tuck.

Tuck answered with a shrug. He had asked himself the same question more than once.

"I honestly don't know. My leave of absence doesn't have any specific end date. From what I hear, the way the city budget stands, they'd likely be happy if I stayed away for as long as possible. Truth is, I'm not even sure I want to go back to the job. I thought I'd just hang around for a while, not work right away. When Ellen…when she died, everything…I don't know, everything changed."

Tuck stared at the fireplace. He could still see a tiny spot of red enamel on one of the bricks. They'd had a fight about something, which at the time seemed to be of great importance. Ellen had thrown a bottle of nail polish, and when Tuck ducked, it smashed against the fireplace. It took hours to clean up the mess, and they left the small spot as a reminder of the stupid the argument.

"I've got enough money in the bank to last for a while. And Ellen's life insurance policy from her company wasn't much, but it's better than nothing. I'm just not sure I want to live in New York anymore—not even sure I have the stomach for it—too much to remember around here."

"What about this adoption network that Saul told us about?" Ken asked. "What's the story on that? It sounds intriguing."

"Honestly, it's still a bit sketchy. As you know, I spent time with an old friend in Dallas, Pauline Shelby. Her husband, Rick, and I met when I was in law school. He was in a couple classes ahead of me. We were both married, and until they left New York, the four of us were pretty tight. Not long after Rick graduated, they moved back to Dallas, where Pauline's from. Rick opened a small practice, but he never could quite overcome that good ol' boy thing down there, and he struggled for a while. Then, somehow he made contact with Max Garfield. When Ellen and I were trying to adopt, Garfield was the lawyer Saul thought could get us a baby. As it turned out, he was the one who basically priced us out of the market. From what Pauline said, he is the lynchpin of the adoption network in this country. He's got his fingers in much of the black market adoptions. Pauline told me some eye-opening stories about the network. Apparently, hundreds of babies and millions of dollars change hands every year. Maybe it's crazy and irrational, but the more information I got from Pauline, the more I was convinced that Max Garfield, as much as anyone else, was responsible for Ellen's death."

"Come on, Tuck, isn't that a bit of a stretch?" Mary said, and then felt sorry she'd spoken so bluntly.

Tuck nodded, thought for a moment, then said, "No, not really. Okay, so maybe he's not directly responsible, but there is a direct link. It may sound stupid, but frankly, for me to maintain some semblance of sanity about Ellen's death, I want—no, actually—I *need* to be able to place the blame on someone besides myself."

"Tuck, listen to me," Mary said, "In some way that only she could understand, Ellen knew the chance she was taking. It was wrong but it was her choice."

"But I should have stopped her, should have yelled and screamed and dragged her by the hair to have the abortion, but she was beyond reason. It was almost as if she couldn't help but react to some powerful biological imperative to be pregnant, to carry a child. Had I forced her to end the pregnancy, I hate to think of what it would have done to our marriage. It really was a kind of sickness, which I will never understand. I can forgive her for that, but I can't forgive Garfield for his role in what happened. He's just a greedy bastard. I can blame him with a clear conscience."

The three of them sat without talking for a time, thinking and sipping cognac.

"Do you honestly believe there's anything you can do to stop him?" Ken asked, with an edge of challenge to his voice.

"Truthfully? I'd like to see him dead," Tuck said.

"Come on, Tuck, that's just nonsense."

"Don't get me wrong, I don't mean physically dead. If I could have a wish, it would be to kill him professionally—make sure he, along with the network, went out of business. End of story."

"I'm sure that's easier said than done," Mary said.

Tuck rose from the couch and, carrying his drink, nervously paced back and forth.

"After hearing some of the stuff Pauline told me, I did have one thought. What do you think would happen, Ken, if Garfield's operations were uncovered and publicly exposed? The whole thing blown wide open for all to see— all the slimy, rotten details. All the lies about backgrounds. The phony competitive bidding that jack up the prices until they're out of sight. The cash payments hidden from the IRS—and not just Garfield, but all the other lawyers he works with. What if, somehow, we could expose the whole sordid mess? Don't you think that would put an end to the bastard? You do this kind of reporting, Ken. Isn't it the sort of story that can bring down Garfield and the network?"

Ken thought about the idea for a moment.

"Well, I'd certainly need more information and specific details, but yeah, from what you've told us so far, I'd say it might make a hell of a story, Tuck. But this Garfield guy must cover his ass really well. Every couple years someone does a story about the adoption business but not much ever comes of it. It's so hard to prove criminality when all the parties involved seem to be so satisfied with the outcome. Without more information I wouldn't know where to start. His whole operation sounds very sophisticated."

"No, you're right. Generally speaking, his type of crime is really hard to pin down, but I learned a lot of details from Pauline."

Ken leaned forward, "Like what?"

"She told me about one couple, people named Kaufman. They bought their baby from Garfield, but it was Rick Shelby who supplied Max with the infant, which he got rather circuitously from—believe it or not—North Africa."

"A black baby?" Mary whispered in surprise.

"As white as you or I. But I'll get to that in a minute. I really wanted to talk with the Kaufmans, so I contacted my old precinct and found out where they lived and called them. On my way back to New York, I went to Bronxville and spent time with them. Naturally, I wanted to learn more about the process they went through with Garfield. I knew from Pauline what they had paid for the baby, but I was interested to see if they would admit that to me."

"And they told you?" Ken said.

"Hell, no. They almost had a collective heart attack when I brought up the subject of money. I knew they had paid $50,000 for the baby, most of it under the table. They claim they only paid Garfield $10,000—and, they made a point of telling me that it was paid by certified check. I sensed you could shove bamboo shoots under their fingernails and never get them to admit to paying a penny more. And you know damned well the cash they paid to Garfield will never come close to any tax collector."

"$50,000! You've got to be joking." Mary couldn't mask her amazement. "One of the docs at work just bought a house in Greenwich, and he didn't pay much more than that. Talk about insane."

"Apparently, not to the Kaufmans it isn't. Like I said,

they'd only admit to giving Garfield a small portion of that amount, and they are sticking tightly to that story."

"How can you be sure the numbers Pauline quoted are true?" Ken asked.

"Because Rick collected the $40,000 in cash, which he then gave to Garfield.

"That's amazing. Clearly, Garfield would do just about anything to keep the IRS from looking too closely into what he's doing—or the bar association, for that matter. So he must cover his tracks pretty damned well," Ken added.

"Absolutely. You can see how pulling Garfield's little empire apart would make quite an interesting story."

"If we could really do it, it would be dynamite— enough to blow him and the rest of his buddies out of the water. And publishers eat this shit up, and the public, as well. But keep in mind, this sort of exposé about adoption has been tried before, and even though some of the details are pretty much similar to what you're describing, nobody ever went to jail or got disbarred over it. Even so, I'll tell you what. Let me give it some thought, Tuck. Perhaps I can come up with a spin or two on this thing that will flesh it out a bit more. But, do me a favor, don't get too optimistic. If the Kaufmans are any indication of the reception we'd probably run into with other adoptive families, it might be impossible to prove anything."

"But, Ken, think about it—can you really blame those people?" Mary Flower scolded her husband. "They must be scared to death. What if anything shady ever came to light? It could mean losing their baby."

"I don't think that would ever happen," Tuck said, but without much conviction. "Worrying about that sort of thing isn't very rational."

"For heaven's sake, Tuck, who's talking rational? Having a baby, adopted or not, isn't rational. It's all about emotion. The Kaufmans got the baby they had their hearts set on. Why should they make any unnecessary waves? They had the money. No one was hurt."

"You don't think anyone was hurt?" Tuck said, trying to contain his anger, since, after all, Mary was simply expressing her opinion. "What about the couple the Kaufmans outbid? You don't think they were hurt? Remember, Ellen and I were in that same position and we were devastated. The baby we couldn't afford went to someone who could pay the going rate. You can't take the attitude that the black market doesn't hurt anyone, that it's some sort of no-fault loophole that childless couples use, that the laws broken are no more serious than ripping little Do not remove under penalty of law tags off your pillows.

"Garfield's clients believe he is God's gift to the childless, and he's making a fortune from people just like the Kaufmans. For every baby he sells, the people who can't pay his price suffer."

"You said their baby came from Africa," Ken said. "How did that work?"

Tuck poured a splash more cognac and downed it before continuing. "Pauline told me the truth about the Kaufmans' baby."

"I'm afraid to ask," Mary said.

"Her mother was Polish, a girl who was sold to a rich Texan at a slave auction in Casablanca. She happened to be pregnant at the time and claimed the father was white, a French Foreign Legionnaire. Rick Shelby was there with the Texan when it happened, and they flew her back to Texas in the man's private jet."

"Come on, Tuck, a slave? That woman in Dallas must be pulling your leg," Mary said, stunned by Tuck's revelation.

"Yeah, it does sound like a joke, but unfortunately, it's not. Pauline didn't make this stuff up."

Ken Flower had pulled a fresh reporter's notebook from a shelf near his chair and jotted a few notes, then he settled back to listen to Tuck as he continued.

"Whether we want to believe it or not, the trading in slaves is apparently alive and well. And every year or so, this nut case flies to places like Casablanca and buys a young girl and brings her back to live and work on his ranch."

"How did your lawyer friend in Dallas get involved?"

"His ranch foreman's son had a fling with one of the girls and she got pregnant. The boy didn't want to get married and the girl didn't want a baby. But she was Catholic and refused to have an abortion. So, the Texan asked around and somehow got to Rick Shelby who was just starting to do some adoption work in Dallas. Rick arranged for the baby to be adopted. That's how the two met. Then one weekend about a year and a half ago, the Texan took Rick along on one of his trips to attend an auction."

A Baby To Die For

Ken Flower looked up from his note pad. "You're telling me that this Texan just jumps on his plane, flies to some place where they're having a slave auction, and buys another human being?"

Tuck just looked at Ken and said, "Yes. That's exactly what I am saying. On the trip with Rick, the Texan bought the Polish girl who—in a sort of two-for-one bonus—just happened to be pregnant."

"Wait a minute, Tuck," Mary said, "When you say he *bought* her, exactly what do you mean?"

"Bought. Purchased. Exchanged greenbacks for flesh."

Ken and Mary just stared at Tuck, barely able to comprehend what he had just told them.

"According to Pauline, Rick told her it was as if the Texan were bidding on a steer or a quarter horse. He paid U.S. dollars and took her back to the Lone Star State, the way some people bring back a Picasso print from Paris or a lovely teapot from London."

"And Rick got the baby to sell?" Ken said.

"Yes. Rick agreed to take the baby on the condition it was born healthy and white. Then he would sell the baby and give the Texan an agreed upon percentage of the net profit of the sale."

"And the Kaufmans would never know about the mother or father of their baby," Ken said.

"What about that poor girl?" Mary asked.

"As far as the Kaufmans are concerned, they got a baby tailored to their specifications. And, as far as its background, Garfield just lied, made up a story that came as close as possible to their specifications. As far as any of his clients are concerned, none of his babies come from biological parents who have health problems, or were rape victims or dope addicts or prostitutes. He 'launders' them like the Mafia launders money."

"He just lies to them?" Mary said.

"Yes, when necessary he lies. It's often total bullshit, complete fabrications. The Kaufmans were sold a fantasy, which they were as delighted to hear as they were anxious to believe."

"As for the girl, I'm not condoning the situation but, she's happy. Hell, she's eating three meals a day, has her own room, new clothes, and is living about a thousand percent better life than she would be hustling on the streets of Warsaw or Prague. In return, she has some light domestic chores and every so often is called on to entertain the troops, so to speak. And if she happens to get pregnant again, that baby will get sold, too, and the Texan will get another fee. Hell, she's doing better than most of the illegal aliens that Americans bring across the border to pick fruit or mow lawns."

"So, Rick Shelby got the Polish girl's child, then made up the whole background story and fed it to the Kaufmans who swallowed it raw," Ken said, half to himself.

"Actually, in this case Rick Shelby didn't try to do it on his own. He'd already done a bit of business with Max Garfield and wanted very much to play on his team—but on a more permanent basis. So, he told Garfield about the girl, even before her baby was born. Garfield, or his people, then went to work making up a strong story and lining up several buyers with deep pockets. The more couples they could get interested in a baby, the better, since Garfield's method is to create his own auction."

"What if he doesn't have a buyer at a given moment in time?" Mary said.

"The chances are that somewhere in his network one of the lawyers he works with can find a buyer. And even if there's only one couple interested, Garfield fabricates another buyer or two and manipulates the price upward."

"So, some poor couple ends up bidding against a shill," Ken said.

"Exactly. As for the Polish girl's baby, it was healthy, and Caucasian, and one white baby looks like the next, right? And like any commodity, it's only worth what someone is willing to pay for it. The Kaufmans were willing to believe strongly and then pay dearly for that belief."

"But surely," Mary said, not unkindly, "you can understand that, can't you? After all, what if Saul had been able to get you a baby, and you'd been able to scrape up the cash? You'd be like the Kaufmans right now. You'd have your baby, and you'd want to be damned sure that nobody took it away. And would you really give a damn if you got your baby by outbidding another family? Come on Tuck, you can't blame the Kaufmans. You know you can't."

Tuck hated to admit Mary was right, but he knew she was. What if it had been Helen Kaufman who'd died, not Ellen? And what if Mark Kaufman had come to him for help? Would Tuck have really given a shit? Would he be so anxious to cooperate, knowing it just *might*, expose them to legal action? Would he have done anything that might open the door to their baby being taken back to its biological mother? Mary's logic threw bright light but little heat on how Tuck answered those thorny questions. Somehow, he had to believe that his situation was different.

"Intellectually, I can't disagree with you. The Kaufmans aren't to blame, any more than we would be had we gotten a baby by outbidding another couple. But in my gut, it's another story. Someone once said that the difference between comedy and tragedy is: tragedy is when *I* have a headache, and comedy is when *you* fall down a manhole."

It was clear that Tuck's position was stubborn and arbitrary. "I guess it just depends on whose ox is being gored, right?" she said.

"Okay, yes, I'm a hypocrite and wouldn't give a rat's ass about the financial problem another couple was having. But that doesn't justify what Garfield does. The real issue is whether or not this network can—or *should*—be allowed to function at all. To even be in a position to put people in that kind of a double bind whether—"

"No, Tuck," Ken interrupted, "There's more to this than you're willing to admit. I interview people all the time, that's my business. I'm trained to hear reality, to try to pry innuendo out of hyperbole. Your real issue, as I see it, is *revenge.* You want some sort of emotional restitution for Ellen's death. You've put the network in your sights as the big, fat target, the institution that must be made to pay, and Max Garfield is its face and its name. Someone to hurt and force into making amends for what's happened. He's the center of the target you want to focus your crosshairs on, isn't that true?"

Tuck's eyes locked onto Ken Flower's. As much as it hurt, he knew Ken had cut to the heart of the matter.

Ken smiled, reached out, and touched Tuck's shoulder.

"Hey, there's nothing wrong with a little revenge, my friend. Great leaps for mankind have been made in the name of revenge. It's a hell of a motivator. Just don't lie to yourself about what it's all about."

"Revenge," Tuck said the word, then looked at it as it hung in the air between the two men. "Yeah, I guess, in a way, you're right. I really need to believe that Max Garfield killed Ellen. I have to keep that thought right on top. Because if he isn't to blame, then I must be—so yes, you're damned right. I *do* want revenge!"

Chapter 31

Tuck and Ken Flower rarely stopped their quest to create a workable scenario that would destroy Max Garfield's black market operation, bring him down, and send him to jail. But no matter how many angles they considered, none of their ideas seemed powerful enough to fool a person as smart and cautious as Max Garfield.

Tuck had returned to New York so full of purpose, but now his resolve was slowly fading and becoming less sharp around the edges. What the hell could really be done about Max Garfield? If the government was helpless or, at least, unwilling to do a damned thing about it, what could he be expected to do? The more he thought about it, the more discouraged he became.

Tuck, more out of frustration than motivation, even toyed with the idea of going back to work on the force. He had lunch with his old boss, but at the end of an hour, they had mutually agreed to continue Tuck's compassionate leave of absence a while longer. The captain was inwardly relieved. There was something strange he'd sensed, nothing concrete, nothing spoken, but it was clear that Tuck wasn't his old self. He appeared unfocused, more tense, enough to give the officer pause. So, using the excuse that budgets were tight and that there were family men who needed the work more, Tuck's leave was extended—indefinitely.

It was just as well, because when all was said and done, Tuck didn't have the heart or passion to go back onto the streets again, and the idea of a desk job was repulsive. Fortunately, he had enough money to last for a while. His needs were simple, and the tiny studio apartment he rented was affordable. Nevertheless, Tuck occasionally took jobs working security. It was easy money and gave him time to think. He decided that if he wanted, he could survive doing pretty much next to nothing.

It was early evening, a beautiful fall day, and Tuck had spent the afternoon riding back and forth on the Staten Island ferry, reading *The Day of the Jackal*, a new popular novel by Frederick Forsyth. He found the ten-cent round trip to be New York City's best-kept-secret bargain, and a soothing way to while away an afternoon. So, every few weeks he would spend a few hours on the East River. On this day, when he left the boat, he decided to grab dinner in Chinatown, at a small dim sum restaurant he and Ellen had always enjoyed.

He left the Whitehall ferry terminal and strolled north. It was the end of the workday, and he had to maneuver his way through the financial district crowds spilling out of hundreds of doorways, all frantically rushing to parking garages, bus stops, and subway entrances. A half-hour later, he was in Chinatown outside the restaurant. It was still a bit early to eat, so, Tuck stood outside, studying the menu displayed in a frame mounted on the wall next to the entrance. He peered through the front window past a rack of fat-dripping roasted ducks. Seeing the neat rows of mostly empty white cloth-covered tables, he was suddenly awash in a flood of loneliness. It was a panicky, terrifying feeling. His thoughts shot back to Pauline in Dallas, and he fumbled in his back pocket for his wallet, and the slip of paper with a list of names she had given him.

Karen Boyd's phone number was on the deep crease of the folded paper and Tuck found it impossible to make out the last digit of her number. He checked information, but there was no listing under her name. So, starting with a zero, he got as far as the sixth variation of the last digit before a woman named Karen Boyd finally answered.

A typical New York woman, she was suspicious as hell, and reacted to Tuck's call as just some crank with the old *"you don't know me, and I'm not sure you're the right Karen Boyd, but"* routine. She wasn't buying a word of it.

"Look, I'll tell you what," Tuck finally said, "do me a favor, Karen. I'll give you the number where I'm calling from—it's a phone booth—and I'll also give you my AT&T credit card number. Call Dallas and check me out with Pauline Shelby. I swear she'll vouch for my sincerity, honesty, and high level of dental hygiene. It's only two hours difference. Call her, please," Tuck pleaded. Then he added, "But if she's not home, do call me back so I don't spend the whole night waiting in this phone booth. It's a little cramped and, frankly, smells funky."

There was a pause, and all Tuck could hear was Karen Boyd breathing. Finally, "You know you're nuts, Tuck Handler, you know that, right? Look, where are you now?"

A Baby To Die For

"Outside a dim sum restaurant in Chinatown."

"Oh, great," she said sarcastically. "I'm uptown, Westside. I'll split the difference and meet you at Shun Lee Palace. It's on Fifty-Fifth, right between Lexington and Third. I need to shower and get into some decent clothes, so meet me there in about an hour."

They liked what they saw from the moment they found each other at the small bar inside the restaurant. It was a physical liking. A *"Wow! That's nice"* reaction, one Tuck might have when spotting a great-looking car in the window of an automobile showroom, or she might have upon seeing a drop-dead outfit in the window of Lord & Taylor.

By the time they were seated for dinner, they found talking came easily and flowed smoothly. The conversation was good, and the silences were not awkward. The subjects ranged the spectrum from movies—both liked watching them—to sports—neither enjoyed watching them. As for politics, both were Democrats and totally confounded by Richard Nixon.

They were halfway through the second part of the Peking duck course when Karen said, "I've got a confession."

"You really hate Chinese food?"

"No, not that. I actually did call Pauline. She does think very highly of you. And she told me that you lost your wife. No details, just that she had passed away. I'm really sorry."

Tuck pushed some rice around on his plate with one chopstick, thought about telling Karen the story, but decided not to and didn't say anything. Without words being spoken, the conversation had silently crossed an invisible line, and a blind date suddenly gained some vision. The small talk continued but grew larger. The generic morphed into the specific. Little secrets were cautiously traded. Here were two people who hours before could have passed on the street without the slightest recognition. Now, suddenly, their lives had intersected.

After dinner, without making any comment about it, Tuck hailed a taxi and they proceeded to Karen's apartment. She opened a bottle of wine, and they talked—and talked some more. And when they couldn't keep their eyes open any longer—from alcohol, as well as the hour—they slept—she in her bed and Tuck, fully clothed, on her living room couch. In the morning, Tuck awoke early and went to get coffee and bagels. The decision to spend the day together materialized quite naturally. Karen called her office and told them she would not be in, clearing the deck for a day in Central Park.

They were happy to have met but still slightly wary of each other. They were sharing a soft pretzel smeared with spicy mustard at the park's zoo when the conversation revealed a very surprising common interest—The Network. After that Tuck let it all come out—their attempt to adopt a child, the ill-fated final pregnancy, the miscarriages, Ellen's death, and, of course, Max Garfield.

Karen listened with little comment, just letting Tuck talk. Occasionally, she asked a question, more to keep him going than to gain additional information. She already knew far too much.

A Baby To Die For

When he finally finished, she remained silent. There was nothing to say, nothing to add. She took Tuck's hand, and they walked in silence for some time. At the boat pond, they watched a half-dozen little boys and girls race their popsicle-stick yachts, Dixie-cup battleships, and anything else that would float.

Finally, Karen turned to Tuck. "Of course, you know I work for Max Garfield," she said, rhetorically.

"Yes, Pauline mentioned it. She also said it seemed obvious there was little love lost between the two of you. She wondered why you stay there, why you don't just leave."

"Trust me, it's a bit more complicated than that," Karen said, with no small amount of irony.

It didn't take Tuck more than a moment to ask, warily, "Don't tell me...are you having...are you involved with him?"

"Oh, God no, it's nothing like that," Karen said, making a sour face. "It's a long and not very pretty story. Still want to hear it?"

Tuck looked puzzled, but nodded in agreement.

Karen took a deep breath.

"When I was a kid back in high school, I was into lots of—you know, *stuff*—booze, smoking a little dope, some prescription pills, stuff like that. But, even so, I still had fairly good grades and ended up getting into the University of California out in Berkeley. Looking back, it was clearly not the best choice for me at the time. Berkeley wasn't high school. Out there, the drugs were all over the place. My casual use turned into a lot more and soon it really kicked in. I flunked out my second year, and rather than go home to Connecticut, I just stayed, mainly around San Francisco. God, it was wild in those days. Everybody was a flower child, and every flower child was smashed most of the time. I was high on anything I could lay my hands on. When I think about it, it's a wonder I'm still alive. Suddenly, through the haze, I found myself pregnant. Of course, I turned to my brother for help. Max was all the family I had."

"Max Garfield is your brother?" Tuck said, stunned.

Karen nodded.

"Yeah, my big brother, Max Garfield. He got me out of California and slapped me into a fancy sanitarium in Connecticut for as long as it took for me to clean up a bit, then shipped me off to a place he operates down in Florida, where I was taken care of until I had the baby."

"Where was the father?"

"I'm embarrassed to say, I don't know."

"But your last name, Boyd—not Garfield?"

"Ah, yes, dear Norman Boyd. He was a boy who had a crush on me when we were in high school. We spent lots of time in the back of his father's car—a little kissing but mostly smoking dope. Nothing serious. But in his mind, our relationship was much, much more, and he fell passionately in love with me, as only a teenage boy can. I had no idea at the time how much he loved me, but as I said, I was weird back then. I'm sure I hurt him very deeply at the time. But he always was my friend, always seemed to be around when I needed him. I just never gave him back very much.

A Baby To Die For

"So, there I was, waiting to have a baby, living in this place where Max put me, not married and just a kid myself. Norman had been drafted and was on leave after his basic training. He wanted to see me before he shipped out. I'm not sure how, but he somehow tracked me down, came to Florida, and begged me to marry him. Imagine! He hadn't even seen me for almost three years, I was pregnant, and he was begging to make me an honest woman.

"I was so screwed up, and it seemed like the only right thing to do, you know, for the baby's sake. Christ, I was sick and depressed, and he was so sweet and caring at a time in my life when sweet and caring was almost as powerful as a drug. So, we found a justice of the peace and got married. He left almost immediately for Vietnam. At that point, I was excited and looking forward to having the baby. I was clinging to the idea that I would have someone who I'd be responsible for, and I was convinced the baby was my road to lasting and permanent rehabilitation. Suddenly, I had a life—the baby, and a husband. When Norman came home we would be a family. For a change, my life was good.

"But the good days didn't last. Norman was killed soon after he got to Vietnam, blown to hell by a land mine.

"Then the ultimate nightmare. I found that while I was still in the sanitarium in Connecticut, my brother had me sign some papers. I can hardly remember when it happened. I could barely hold the pen, let alone know what the hell I was signing. It wasn't until right after I gave birth, that I found out what I had signed. The documents allowed Max to put my baby up for adoption."

"That never would have stood up in court, Karen. The mother has very powerful rights," Tuck said.

"I know that now, but it happened so fast. And back then, I was in no condition to...frankly, Norman's death...the baby being taken...I think I was in the middle of a nervous breakdown. I went nuts, ran off, and immediately got high again. Max tracked me down using a private detective and put me back into the sanitarium in Connecticut."

Karen paused for a moment.

"She'd be ten now," Karen said, her eyes moist with tears, as she stared wistfully at the children playing at the boat pond. "It's hard to believe my *own* brother sold my baby. It damn near killed me. I've *never* forgiven him for that, Tuck—and I *never* will. Ever since then, I've dreamt of getting back at him somehow."

Revenge. Tuck recalled Ken Flower's admonition.

Just don't lie to yourself about what this thing is about. It's revenge, pure and simple.

"Revenge," Tuck said.

"Yes, I guess that's the word."

"But, Karen," Tuck said softly, "as horrible as it was, he probably did what he thought was best for you at the time. You even admitted you were really in pretty bad shape. How could you have taken care of a child? It was probably—"

"Tuck, you didn't hear me. He *sold* her. He does that. That's his business."

"Yes, I know."

And the son of a bitch is responsible for my wife's death.

Chapter 32

San Francisco, California

Sam's Grill has one of the shortest bars in San Francisco, but it's the food that attracts the customers, the bar being little more than a pleasantly active holding area.

Silvia Wilson sat at one end of the tiny bar, giving her a clear view of the front door. Silvia was an attractive woman, not quite a head-turner, but with a full figure and excellent hair, the color of chestnuts, streaked with gray. She was a "seasoned" journalist, meaning she was one of the older ones writing for the Associated Press. Right now, her date was beyond being socially late. Given her recent run of luck, the schmuck probably wouldn't show up at all. She was hoping it would be a great night. She deserved a great night, and Sam's was one of her all-time favorite eateries.

Silvia was famished, and the thought of digging into a delicious grilled abalone made her smile. Whether her date showed or not, she was going to have one more martini and then eat—alone if need be. She was in too good a mood to let something as trivial as being stood up get in the way of a pleasant evening. In her purse was the bonus check she'd gotten from the AP for a very long, two-part piece she'd written on the death of Edmond Calendar, one of the richest men in the world. And last but certainly not least, her date, if he ever materialized, was the morning jock from KISS radio: Van Brock—the baby's-ass-smooth voice that vibrated in a way that never failed to make Silvia feel slightly horny. Based on the voice alone, she was able to overlook the less-than-authentic-looking hairpiece he wore, which to her resembled a dollop of butterscotch perched on a ball of vanilla ice cream.

What the hell, it's not as if he is on TV where people could actually see him.

If he ever got tapped to anchor KGO's evening news or one of the other big TV jobs he lusted for, she vowed to present him with a gift certificate for a more-credible-looking rug.

The ever-attentive bartender, spotting her empty glass, and getting an affirmative nod from Silvia, constructed and presented her with a fresh vodka martini, frosty cold, bone dry, with one olive and one onion. He pushed a plate of fried zucchini within easy reach and brought two leather dice cups from under the bar and placed them next to Silvia's drink. Silvia laughed. When she first moved to San Francisco, she'd marveled at some of their local traditions. The bars, it seemed, all served fried zucchini and supplied leather cups so the patrons could play various versions of Liar's Dice. She even wrote a story about it that she sold to *Playboy* about how and where to drink and play traditional bar games in "Bagdad by the Bay."

A Baby To Die For

She and the bartender, using the dice cups, were up to *R* in a hot game of Horse when a little guy walked in, settled on the stool next to Silvia, and gave the barman his order. He downed the first martini rather quickly, asked for another, and continued to mumble to no one in particular.

Silvia and the barman continued playing. She rolled the dice while half listening to the man, the ingrained habit of a seasoned reporter. She suddenly recognized a mumbled name, Edmond Calendar, which popped out of the man's babble the way a familiar face grabs one's attention in a room filled with strangers.

Silvia, now bored with the dice and fast becoming pissed at Van Brock, who, it seemed certain, was standing her up, swiveled her stool and spoke to the little man.

"Excuse me, I didn't mean to eavesdrop, but I couldn't help hearing you mention Edmond Calendar. Did you by any chance know him?" Silvia asked.

The guy never even flinched in her direction, just sipped his martini, and continued the running dialogue with himself.

"Hey, chum," she tried again, and touched his shoulder. "You knew Edmond Calendar?

The man turned toward Silvia, looking a little like a slightly tipsy Adolphe Menjou in a 1930s film. "I'm sorry? Were you talking to me?"

"Yeah, I happened to hear you mention Edmond Calendar. It so happens I recently wrote about him— made page one in a lot of the newspapers—about a month ago. You might have seen it."

"I'm sorry, ma'am, could you repeat that, I'm a bit distracted."

Silvia tried not to laugh at the little guy. Actually, he was sort of cute.

"Edmond Calendar, you mentioned his name. I just did a news story on him. I'm a reporter with the Associated Press. He died, you know."

"Oh, my ! Was I disturbing you? Please forgive me…I must…I must have been thinking out loud. It's a bad habit of mine."

The man seemed to sober quickly.

"No, it's okay, I was just curious."

Silvia toyed with her drink, ate the olive and onion at the same time, which was her favorite way, then continued.

"Do you know Calendar? I mean, did you know him? Before—you know?"

The little man thought for a moment. In his condition, his reaction time wasn't all that quick. "I worked for him. In fact, I still do."

Silvia cocked her head to one side in a question mark. "I don't understand."

She was beginning to slur her words slightly. She was already ahead of the guy with her own alcohol consumption.

"Yes, well, you see, it's in my contract. My contract runs for many more years and, well, his estate provides for my salary and expenses."

"Really?"

"Oh, yes, that's correct."

"Now, that's what I would call a good deal. I heard about some of Calendar's strange arrangements when

A Baby To Die For

I was researching the piece I wrote. Rumor has it that dozens of people all over the world were on his payroll. Obviously, from what you say, there still are, doing all sorts of strange things. But I never actually ran across any of them."

Silvia leaned close and in a half whisper said, "I heard he still has chauffeurs with limousines waiting at airports every day in cities all over the world, just on the odd chance that he might show up at one of them. Weird— really weird, no?"

"Beyond weird, yes," the little man said, nodding his head solemnly and motioning the bartender to refill their glasses. "He had enough money to do things like that."

Silvia was getting smashed but, hell, that jerk Van Brock was now a definite no-show. At least if this clown wasn't joking, she could interview him, and if he didn't pick up the check, she'd submit an expense voucher or at least write it off her taxes as a non-reimbursed expense. She giggled at the thought of this cute little guy being a non-reimbursed expense.

The bartender filled the fresh, iced martini glass in front of her.

"Thanks," Silvia said to the bartender, then to the man, "I'm Silvia Wilson," and extended her hand. "And you are?"

"My name is Tyler, Dr. Kevin Tyler," he said, taking her hand. "Not a medical doctor, just a Ph.D. Actually, a geneticist."

"And you still work for the old bastard?" she asked with warmth and some admiration. "But you're the first person I've met who would actually admit it. Apparently,

Edmond Calendar was a demon when it came to privacy. He would fire most people just for admitting they worked for him. And once fired, he was terrified they would blab secrets to the press, so half the time he would keep them on payroll just so they wouldn't talk."

Silvia pulled the olive and onion off the toothpick and popped them into her mouth. "Yup, you got yourself a sweet deal working for a dead man. The best kind of boss," she said, chewing.

Kevin Tyler slid his arm around the back of Silvia Wilson's bar stool and ran his hand down her arm, in the process lightly brushing the side of her ample left breast, and said, "But, you see, Miss Wilson, in my line of work, Edmond Calendar is still very much with us."

Silvia laughed from deep in her stomach. She couldn't help it. Here she was, stood up by a bald-headed, sexy-voiced newscaster, sitting next to a spaced-out fruitcake, feeling her up and claiming to work for a dead man. And to make things worse, without even thinking about it, she had just knocked off another plate of greasy fucking zucchini, and her hands were slick with oil again.

"Okay, Doc Tyler. Please tell me all about it. I'm dying to hear your story, I really am. But, please, if we don't sit down at a table and have some food, I will pass out."

Early the next morning, Silvia Wilson quietly left Kevin Tyler's Russian Hill apartment. Her head ached, and she was hoping the four Excedrin she'd taken would soon kick in. All things considered, she felt pretty darn good. She'd found Tyler to be a delightful guy, she decided, once she got past her initial reaction to the man. He had a very good sense of humor, was compassionate in bed, and was in a very interesting line of work. She would definitely see him again. In fact, she seemed to recall in her post-drunken haze, that they'd made plans for dinner that night. He was no Prince Charming but, hell, neither was Van Brock, the no-show SOB.

Later that morning, she filed a short piece with her news service on the strange story Tyler told her about Edmond Calendar. She sensed something major in what he had related, but they had both been smashed, so she kept the piece she filed rather simple. She would look into the story further when she got to know Tyler better. For now, she filed her copy more out of habit than anything else.

It appeared, without a byline, in a bunch of papers. The Sunday edition of the *New York Times* ran theirs—one column by four inches—on page six of the business section.

Chapter 33

New York City

The Sunday *New York Times* is the journalistic tsunami that Manhattanites struggle through every seven days—a rite of passage for the week that follows.

For Tuck and Karen, it was more about spending the morning lounging in bed with a thermos of hot coffee, a few onion bagels, and plenty of cream cheese. They were happily propped up on pillows and the sun was spilling brightly through the bedroom window.

Tuck dropped the sports section, yawned, stretched, and then with a sly chuckle, slid his hand under the down quilt to explore the warmth of Karen's body.

"What's so funny, mister?" Karen asked, while removing the half-glasses she used for reading and snuggled closer to Tuck.

"Hmm, well, touching you reminded me of a story I heard. Seems there was this very elderly English butler, you know, the *veddy, veddy* proper type that you always see in those Brit movies. Anyway, he was being interviewed for a newspaper article because he was retiring after like a hundred years of working for some lord or viscount or some dignitary like that, and after a bunch of questions about his day-to-day work, the reporter asked the old guy what single memory stood out most vividly from his extraordinarily long marriage. Well, the old guy thought about it for a moment, and he finally said, "Lying in bed on a summer morning, with the windows open, listening to the church bells, and eating buttered toast with cunty fingers."

Karen laughed, threw her arms around Tuck, and kissed his stubbly morning face.

"Okay, hot lips, do you want me to make some toast?" Karen laughed, "or would you rather just cut to the chase?"

Tuck chose the latter and, sometime later, returned to his newspaper. A short article in the business section about the recently deceased billionaire recluse, Edmond Calendar, momentarily caught his attention. The man who had, only a short time ago, been front cover material for *Time*, *Newsweek*, and *People* was now relegated to a few column inches buried deep in the business section of the Sunday *Times*. The frantic interest in Edmond Calendar, instigated by his death, had quickly tapered off like the diminishing tail of a comet.

Tuck skimmed the short article, turned the page, and was halfway into another story when he paused, thought for a moment, and turned back to the Edmond Calendar story.

He read the short piece carefully several times and then let the newspaper slip through his fingers, where it joined the rest of the pile on the cluttered bed. He reached over and absently picked up his coffee and sipped the last drops of the now cold liquid.

"Oh, my God," Tuck finally muttered, "*this* could be it!"

Karen looked up from the crossword puzzle and said, "Seven letters, a butterfly—"

"Holy shit!" Tuck said, louder now.

"Stop joking, that's eight letters," Karen said, and poured hot coffee into Tuck's cup.

Tuck reached over and grabbed the telephone. If he called the *New York Times* office, he might be able to find out the name of the reporter who filed the little story on page six of the business section.

He needed to talk to that reporter.

"What are you doing?" Karen asked, as Tuck started to dial Information.

Tuck handed Karen the paper and pointed to the short article.

"Read that, and just keep your fingers crossed, honey. I think we might have found a Wile E. Coyote Acme Lawyer-Catching Kit," Tuck said, as he dialed information.

It was much easier to track down the writer of the article than Tuck expected. His call to the *Times* was passed from the Foreign desk to the National desk and, finally, to the General desk. A youthful, incredibly bored voice answered. Tuck inquired about the article's author, and in response, the voice said, "Read me the dateline, mister."

Tuck leaned over Karen's shoulder and read, "Uh— San Francisco, California, October 6—AP."

"Oh, yeah, well, listen, that's a wire service story, mister. It gets filed, and we just pick it up, you know.

A Baby To Die For

There may not be any writer at all, just a general news release that was picked up. Your best bet is to call the correspondency in Frisco. So now, I guess you want the number?"

Tuck placed the long distance call to the Associated Press office in San Francisco, and the person on the other end told him, without hesitation that one of their reporters, Silvia Wilson, had filed the story and would be in her office the next morning.

It was as simple as that.

Later that evening, while having a late dinner in a small Chinese restaurant on Forty-fourth Street, Tuck and Karen discussed the article.

"You know, sweetheart, I think you should try to contact that doctor, directly. Why even wait to talk with the reporter? Anyway, she might refuse to give out any information—protecting sources, and all that nonsense. The article was datelined San Francisco, so why not give it a shot, call information and see if the Tyler guy's listed? With the time difference and on a Sunday night, we might get lucky and catch him home."

Karen was right, and Tuck quickly nodded his agreement. With the napkin still tucked in his shirtfront, Tuck went to the pay phone outside the men's bathroom and dialed San Francisco information.

Moments later, he had Kevin Tyler's home and office numbers.

Chapter 34

Tyler stood by the large picture window and admired the dramatic view. Lights below Russian Hill and along the Golden Gate, the Bay Bridge and around Alcatraz Island glowed yellow through a scrim of heavy, moist fog. It was a romantic scene, made all the more intriguing by the guttural moan of boat horns, just loud enough to reach his apartment.

The apartment Tyler *now* owned was a far cry from the dump he lived in, BC—*Before Calendar.*

The dining table was positioned in front of the large window and was set with a starched white cloth and tall, tapered candles. A properly chilled bottle of a Ruffino Chianti Classico—a particular favorite of his—sat in an ice bucket waiting to be opened. A large, mushroom-and-cheese pizza, delivered minutes before from a famous North Beach pizzeria, was maintaining its proper temperature in the kitchen's oven.

The ringing phone surprised Tyler, since he rarely got calls at his apartment. He'd been sipping two fingers of an excellent single malt scotch while waiting for Silvia

Wilson to arrive for what they had, over the past week of their sexual activity, begun to refer to as P&P—pizza and pussy. One of the many things he liked about the reporter was her perversely sexual sense of humor, and he'd discovered he possessed a similar one, as well. He hoped the caller wasn't Sylvia cancelling their date.

"Hello?" Kevin Tyler said tentatively, answering the call on the fourth ring.

"Hi, I'm calling from New York. Is this Dr. Tyler?"

"Yes, this is he—who's calling?"

"Dr. Tyler, my name is Tuck Handler. I hope this isn't a bad time."

"That depends. What is it you're calling about?"

"Well, to begin, I'm assuming you're the Dr. Tyler mentioned in the article that appeared in this morning's *New York Times*—the person who runs the Edmond Calendar Library of Life?"

Tyler thought the publicity caused by Edmond Calendar's death had wound down, so he was surprised by the caller's claim. "Are you certain? I'm certainly not aware of any article," he said.

"It wasn't a big feature article, or anything like that. It was just a short piece in the business section of today's *Times*, mentioning your association with the library and a reference to its purpose."

Kevin Tyler was immediately alarmed. From the very beginning, the Library had successfully avoided all publicity. Even when the old billionaire died, and the story was a hot news topic, the library was able to avoid the frenzied reportage.

"How did you get my phone number," Tyler said while trying to keep his voice calm.

"I called the *Times* and they referred me to the Associated Press, where I was told a journalist named Silvia Wilson had filed the story."

"Are you saying Miss Wilson gave you my number?" Tyler said, somewhat annoyed.

"No, I've never spoken with her. I got your number from San Francisco information."

"I see, of course. I forget I'm in the book. Well, the article didn't lie. I am that Tyler, and I am the president of the late Mr. Calendar's Library of Life. Are you a salesman, because if—"

"No, no. Nothing like that."

"Then what do you want? I really don't have to . . . I'm expecting a dinner guest any moment now," he said, quickly deciding not to reveal that the guest was Silvia Wilson.

"I'm sorry, I'll make this fast. You see, I'd like very much to meet with you. I might be on the West Coast soon, but it would be ideal if you happen to have any plans to be in New York anytime soon—"

"No, New York is out of the question. And as for here, I am leaving tomorrow for a three-day convention in Miami Beach, and, frankly, I don't understand what your interest might be. Are you a physician?"

Tuck paused for a moment, thinking, and then said, "No, I'm not, but I do think I have some information concerning your work with Edmond Calendar that will be of great interest to you. If I were to go to Miami, is it possible we could meet for dinner? I could explain then. I think you'll be most intrigued by what I have to say, and I'm very anxious to learn more about your work." Tuck waited, holding his breath. "You've nothing to lose, Doctor," he added, filling the silence.

"Are you a reporter—a journalist? I really don't want any publicity. Silvia never should have—"

"No, no, it's nothing like that. And if you have any qualms about me personally, I'm a New York City police officer, a detective, but this is nothing official and I happen to be on a leave of absence. Please feel free to call the 9th Precinct in Manhattan and check me out. Just ask for Captain Seymour. He'll vouch that I am who I say I am."

There was a long pause.

Tuck could hear Tyler's breathing, then, "Uh, well, if you're willing to take the effort to come to Florida, I guess I could make time to meet with you. I'll be staying at the Eden Roc hotel. It's on Collins Avenue. Do you know where that is?"

"Don't worry, I'll find it. I'll be there the day after tomorrow, Tuesday. Let's say Tuesday evening at the Eden Roc for an early dinner. I'll look for you in the lobby at six."

"Wait—Mr. Handler, could you tell me a bit more about this thing, whatever it might be?"

Tuck deftly ignored Kevin Tyler's question and said, simply, "Thanks, Doctor. I really appreciate this and look forward to meeting you in Miami on Tuesday at six," and hung up.

Tyler stood, holding the dead receiver, thinking about the article the caller mentioned and remembering the good fortune that resulted from the last mysterious phone call he'd gotten.

Maybe lightning can strike twice.

As for Silvia Wilson, he was getting a sinking feeling that he might mean nothing more to her than a source for a story. He was starting to feel cheated, and his ego began to ache. He really thought that Silvia and he had a lot more going on between them than a little, soon-to-be-forgotten news article.

In fact, he was greatly underestimating Silvia Wilson's motivations. True, she had a great nose for a story, but that ability was nothing compared with her nose for an eligible bachelor—the more financially comfortable the better. And at this point in her life, it was the latter she was hard at work on, not the former.

Chapter 35

Tuck hung up and walked back to the table. Karen was sipping tea, just poured from a fresh pot the waiter had delivered, along with fortune cookies and the check.

"So?" Karen asked, while breaking open one of the cookies.

"Believe it or not, we're having dinner with Kevin Tyler on Tuesday night."

"Is he coming to New York? Let's go somewhere fancy."

"How's Miami Beach? Fancy enough for you?"

"Hell, yes!" Karen cried. "I'd like to finally see Florida. I was practically imprisoned there and never got more than a few blocks from the dump where Max put me while I was pregnant. I want to take a look at that place again, too. And I know that woman, Sarah LaFrance, is still there and working for Max."

"LaFrance! Of course! Pauline mentioned that name. In fact, when I left Dallas, I was headed to Florida to see her, but at the last minute, I changed my mind and drove to New York to see the Kaufmans instead," Tuck said.

A Baby To Die For

"You didn't miss anything. Trust me, seeing that old broad would have been a waste of time. I doubt she'd even talk to you. She runs that little operation of hers like a prison, euphemistically referred to as a "baby farm" by Max. She's the only cow on that farm. Been at it for years. Max keeps her supplied with young girls while they sit out their pregnancies. God only knows how many Max has sent to live there over the years. It was a horrible place. I hated it."

"So why on earth would you want to go back?" Tuck asked. "It sounds positively dreadful."

Even as he spoke, he could see the expression on Karen's face change, and he guessed she was thinking about her baby.

Karen absently crumbled the fortune cookie she was holding into a little mound of tiny pieces while she decided how to answer.

"It is strange, isn't it? But it's a lot like wanting to go back to your old grade school to see it again. In this case, to see if—with the perspective of time—it's as bad and threatening as I once thought. It was part of an important chunk of my life, and I can't forget it, Tuck. As bad as it was living down there, it was also five glorious, drug-free months of having my child inside me, and it really changed my life. That's what my memory is all about, and that's why I'd like to see it again. It was just me and my baby. Nina. That's what I called her. We were together. She growing inside me and I was growing up along with her. I don't expect you to understand, but we had this incredible bond. I would think it happens to all women during pregnancy. I talked to her constantly. She was all mine. I finally had something—of my own. And then, suddenly, she was gone. Part of what I detest so about Max is that he took that feeling of having someone away from me. I can't ever forgive him for that."

Tuck reached out and took Karen's hand, gently brushing the cookie crumbs from her fingers and palms.

"I love you—you know that, right? After Ellen died, I didn't think I'd be able to say that again. This meeting could give us the ammunition we need to destroy Max and his whole operation. I've the beginning of an idea that might work, if we can just get this Tyler guy to cooperate. But truthfully, if he doesn't, if it turns out to be a dead end, I'd just as soon forget Max Garfield and move on with our lives. I don't know about you, but I just don't hurt as much anymore. If you want, we can even leave New York. Maybe go out West and start all over."

Karen, lips pursed in thought, nodded.

"I'll never stop hating Max for what he did, but I agree, it's beginning to lose the edge for me, too. But I still want to go to Miami. There's a very definite reason, and since the opportunity has presented itself, I would very much want to see Sarah LaFrance and the house on Rainbow Drive one more time. It's exactly the right time to do it."

"Why so important now?" Tuck asked.

"I'll tell you when we get there. But right now, let's find a bar. I could use a drink, and you can tell me your fantastic idea for nailing Max to the wall."

Chapter 36

Dania Beach, Florida

The picket line of protesters started marching in front of the abortion clinic well before 9 a.m., when the facility officially opened. Over the next few hours, their numbers grew. Porter stood well away on the periphery, taking in the scene. A dozen women of varying ages, shapes, and sizes slowly circled the sidewalk holding aloft signs expressing various sentiments, all of which, in one way or another, damned abortions, abortionists, and all who trafficked with them. Each picketer marched with the proud certainty that God approved of her message. Near the clinic's front entrance, another half dozen of the faithful were on their knees in a circle, some holding hands, some holding bibles and all praying hard. Porter tried to calculate how the hell she could cross the damned picket line without getting into a fist fight or starting a riot.

Ironically, Porter used abortion clinics to maintain a steady flow of saleable babies, and the clinics did just that. It had been Porter's brainstorm that created the idea years ago.

A Baby To Die For

Porter watched the picketers marching and thought back on those early days.

It was before Max.

A time when Porter was going through one of her, *'what can I do with the rest of my life'* periods, bored with traveling, socializing, and basically, doing nothing. One evening at a friend's dinner party, she was seated next to Max Garfield. In the course of conversation, he mentioned needing a secretary, and on a whim, she said she'd like the job. Max, never one to spurn a pretty face, took her up on the offer. It quickly became clear that she was grossly overqualified for the menial duties the job called for. Max happily broadened the scope of the position to include much more responsibility. She took to all the new challenges with typical Gibbs' dispatch. It wasn't long after when Max added servicing his sexual appetite to her job description.

A round the time, Max's adoption practice was starting to expand at an accelerated rate. The adoption business was excellent, and profits were beginning to flow in, more and more in cash payments. The demand for babies seemed always to exceed the local supply, so Max, with Porter's help, started reaching out to lawyers in other cities in order to supply his needs. Those who were interested responded. Before long, Max and the lawyers were tossing the names of those wanting to adopt and babies ready to be adopted back and forth like kids playing catch. This was a whole new and highly lucrative source of income for all concerned. The number of lawyers Max dealt with and the number of adoptions grew quickly, and over a relatively short period of time, without ever planning it or even envisioning it, a network of sorts came into being.

Some states resisted independent adoptions, but only for a while. One by one, they caved in, as pressure from families who wanted children increased and ambitious lawyers looked for and discovered the necessary legal loopholes to squeeze their transactions through the system.

It was an exciting time for Max and for Porter, too. She quickly became as significant to his burgeoning practice as he was. She had been there almost from the beginning, so it became natural for her to know as much about the operation as Max—in many cases, more.

A great deal of the success of Garfield's baby business stood firmly on several beneficial conditions. First, and most importantly, abortion was illegal—and thanks to a general loosening of moral standards, the number of unwanted pregnancies was rising. As for the abortions that did take place, they were cloaked in a heavy social stigma, and not helped by the all-too-often fatal results of dangerously amateur procedures.

Then in 1973, the Supreme Court decided the case of *Roe v. Wade* and voted seven to two to legalize abortion in the United States.

Max was crushed by the Supreme Court's decision.

But Porter didn't crush that easily. She saw it merely as a problem to solve and kept examining the situation from every angle possible. The solution came to her in the middle of her morning shower—a tantalizing notion so simple, yet bordering on brilliance. The only problem, Porter knew, would be Max's ego. He tended to dislike ideas that didn't spring full-blown from his own head and could get rather testy about ideas served up by others. So she'd have to pick her shots, broach her brainstorm at the very best psychological moment, and help Max convince himself that her idea was really *his* brainstorm.

And so, it was during one of their afternoons at the Kitano Hotel that Porter found the perfect moment. Max was always at his most receptive after one of their sexual flights, and Porter had quickly learned to use that weakness as a marksman calculates and uses windage to hit a moving target.

They were both up to their necks in the soaking tub after a highly satisfying romp on the room's Tatami mat. Max was not in a good mood, still boiling over the court's decision.

"My father," Max lamented softly, "owned a gasoline station on the Boston Post Road, you know. He did really well, made a good living. Then, dammit, one day he comes home and reads in the newspaper that the Interstate Highway is going to be built just a mile away. And just like that, he was ruined. Well, that damned Supreme Court decision is my fucking Interstate Highway! It will ruin me."

Porter stroked his hair and kissed his ear and said, "Max, honey, it'll be okay. You said something once that gave me a wonderful idea…it was actually *your* idea…"

Max, irritated, brushed her hand away.

"Face it, the supply of babies is going to dry out like a grape on its way to becoming a raisin. Mark my words, the goddamned baby business, as we know it is finished. Kaput!"

"But like I said, you gave me an idea…"

"Yeah, I got an idea," moaned Max. "Why don't I just use my gun and shoot myself?"

Porter looked at him and shook her head. She half smiled. Max became almost human when he was feeling sorry for himself. His usual condition was that of a cruel robot. She liked him more this way. Like many women, she perceived a man's vulnerability as strength and was attracted to it. She reached down into the water and started to stroke him, and he responded in spite of himself.

"Damn, Porter! Be serious for once!" Max yelled, while pulling her hand away. "This Roe Wade crap is going to fuck us up. It may be terminal. I don't think you understand the full impact it's going to have. Now every broad who gets knocked up can just walk right into one of these new abortion clinics and poof! That's all there is to it. She walks in with a problem and walks out with a simple and safe solution. They'll probably have the clinics in shopping malls, like dry cleaners or shoe repair. It's basic math: fewer pregnancies mean fewer births, which equals fewer adoptions. And without a steady supply of babies, we don't have a business. Look what's happening to the adoption agencies already. They can't get babies, and they're damned near out of business. People could be waiting in line for years to get a kid from one of those agencies. Throw in vending machines filled with condoms, plus the birth control pill, and you've got the perfect formula for a bankruptcy—mine."

A Baby To Die For

Max struggled up and out of the soaking tub and retrieved a terry cloth bathrobe that hung on a wooden peg next to the door. He shrugged into it and perched on a low wooden stool facing Porter who was still in the soaking tub.

"Over the next two years—" Max continued, wistfully, "given our current national setup, we would have placed, on average, a baby a day. Do you realize how much we would have made? And damn it, most of it tax free!"

Now it was Porter who exited the tub, wrapped herself in a bathrobe, and going to the sideboard, poured hot Saki into two tiny porcelain cups, handing one to Max. She took her own and sipped from it. The hot liquid felt good and soothed her throat.

"Max, you're absolutely right. The *Roe v. Wade* decision could knock the crap out of the whole operation. But what would you say if I promised you that next year and the year after that—what if I could actually give you a *guarantee* that business would not just be good, but will be even better than it's ever been? What would you say to that?"

Max looked at Porter, trying to detect the joke if there were one, but all he saw was a beautiful woman standing in front of him—large, green eyes set far apart, long, thick, auburn hair still wet from the soaking, plus an incredible body mostly visible beneath her partially open robe. Max also saw a woman who lived, it seemed, for little else than pleasing him. He shrugged once and exclaimed, "I'd say you were either ingesting a lot more than Saki or you were just plain off your fucking rocker."

A Baby To Die For

"Max, sweetheart, trust me. If we play it right, this abortion decision can work in our favor, be a bonanza for us. Trust me, business will be better than it ever has been. Much better."

Max twisted his mouth into a sour-looking expression.

"Okay, tell me, what's your bright idea?" he asked, taking a sip of Saki.

He knew damned well that Porter didn't often makes jokes. Her ideas weren't always great, but they were always smart, and rarely, if ever, made in jest.

"Okay, hear me out," Porter said, and paused for effect. "We open a chain of abortion clinics."

Max exploded in a booming laugh that sprayed a mouthful of warm Saki into the air.

"A chain—of abortion—clinics?" Max managed to choke out. "That's got to be the dumbest fucking idea . . . shit, that's like a diabetic opening a candy store. Hell, Porter, I'd be better off buying a Kentucky Fried Chicken franchise. We might not make money, but at least, we wouldn't starve to death," Max said, sarcastically.

"Max, I know it sounds nuts, but please, just let me explain. The clinics would be a front, a way of creating traffic. Don't you see, darling? They'd give us access to a constant supply of pregnant women. And the reality is that a huge number of women who come for abortions will probably be past the point where they can safely qualify for one. Also, a certain number could be talked out of going through with it for any number of reasons— religious, moral, whatever. Don't you see? Instead of going after the girls, the girls would come to us."

A Baby To Die For

Garfield tried to interrupt, but Porter raised her hand, and the words continued to tumble from her mouth.

"We'd run a legitimate, money-making operation. And who knows? The government may even give subsidy money for clinics to get started. And the procedure will doubtless be covered by insurance. What could be better than that? And even if legal abortions mean fewer babies, that can only mean prices will go sky high. Admit it Max, you know I'm right. You've said as much yourself. 'The old supply-and-demand thing,' you always said, right? And that's only the half of it. We would also distribute abortion information and provide a real public service. That would be our cover. But in the process, we'd get the girls' names, addresses, and phone numbers and then have our people outside the clinic—those lawyers we've been working with around the country—have them follow up, contact the girls and gently pitch them on the idea of carrying to full term. We'd give them a few extra bucks for their trouble and put their baby up for adoption. In other words, we'd play both sides of the street. We'd become abortion experts, and we'd also play on the immorality of killing the fetus. It's a natural. Fewer babies, higher prices, we make more money," Porter concluded, breathless from her fevered sales pitch.

Max Garfield looked at Porter, then looked *through* Porter. His eyes narrowed in concentration as he circled the idea, looking at it from various angles. He poked it, prodded it, tried to break it down, and find its weaknesses. Finally, his mouth curved into a broad grin.

"Son of a bitch! Porter, that's absolutely fucking brilliant! I can't believe I didn't think of the idea myself.

It's positively genius," Max said, grabbing Porter in a big hug.

"You did, you really—Max—"

Max cut her off.

"Don't bullshit me, Porter, this was your idea. I'm cutting you in. You're in charge of this one. This will save my life. I'll never forget that."

Porter felt intoxicated, what with the combination of Saki, sex, and Max's honest concession that the idea had been all hers. It was a rare gesture on Max's part, and Porter would probably never see that side of him again. That he was willing to give her full credit without thought to his own ego only showed the seriousness of the problem she had solved. It was her first big score with Max Garfield, and now she was going to be running her very own part of the business. Maybe someday she'd run all of it.

Standing in the hot Florida sun, Porter thought back to those events so long ago and smiled at the memory of that afternoon in the Kitano Hotel in New York. Max and Porter were in the throes of discovering so many things, their mutual needs and ambitions, not to mention their instinctive wariness toward each other. They were two deadly snakes that had chosen to live in the same basket.

The noise from the chanting demonstrators rippled through the thick, muggy air. Under the hot Florida sun, Porter's clothes felt damp and uncomfortable. She stood across the street from the clinic, beneath a palm tree that was diseased and turning brown. She watched the reporters hovering with their television crews. The

A Baby To Die For

Sunshine Clinic—their thirteenth—was special. She remembered when they had opened it in Dania Beach, just outside Fort Lauderdale. It was their first in the Sunshine State, ergo the name, and Max had opened a bottle of Dom Perignon to celebrate.

She watched the picketing activity and the news crews.

Hell, we certainly can use the publicity, but why does it have to happen when I'm in town?

A red VW bus, faded by the sun to a sickening puce, pulled up, and a half dozen more women spilled out, joining the others and waving their signs high. Two were in tennis whites and had babies in sling carriers hanging on their fronts like kangaroos—marsupials for motherhood. RIGHT TO LIVE, one sign read. DON'T KILL THE NEXT SAVIOR, exclaimed another.

Yeah, or the next bank robber.

But the sign Porter liked best was lettered crudely on the back of a large piece of brown cardboard and exclaimed: TO A FETUS, YOU'RE HITLER.

Then, slowly, the chanting started. "Hey, hey, what do you say? How many fetuses die today? Hey, hey, what do you say? How many fetuses die today?"

The crowd quickly picked it up. Porter suspected the chant originated with two of the television reporters. If there were no news, the media would just have to create some. After all, it was just entertainment and, as everyone knows, the show must go on.

Only in America.

The chanting, spotty and awkward at first, began to

take root and grow. "Hey, hey, what do you say? How many fetuses die today?"

Soon everyone had picked it up, and the cameras were clicking and video was rolling. Porter marveled at this act of media incest. An event was coming to life, sired by the media itself. Sometimes, she wanted to run up and hug these protesters and tell them it was only an illusion—these clinics, they were on the same side, albeit for totally different reasons—so *please*, do not march back and forth and stop the girls. Don't these nutcases realize that a good number of the women going into the clinic were going to be gently pressured by experts *not* to have abortions?

She wondered how the Right to Lifers would feel if they learned there were growing numbers of such clinics designed and dedicated to the polar opposite of abortion. A whole network balanced precariously on the idea that women *should* carry their babies for a full nine months. Oh yes, Porter and Max wanted the little ones to be delivered every bit as much as the fanatics who were marching around the clinic's driveway, chanting their barren slogans. But the difference between them was stark. Porter and Max wanted the babies to place in good homes, albeit for profit. The antiabortion people just wanted the children to be born. After that, they really couldn't be bothered with things like education, nutrition, or medical care. Life for them began at conception and ended at birth.

Porter's brow creased with irritation. *Damn! Why today?*

She had come all the way to Florida to check out their Dania Beach branch, and now she was practically in the middle of a quickly growing riot. She could hear the far-off, high-to-low shriek of police sirens. Abortion clinics in the State of Florida—an irony that could be expressed by the subtle observation that the Sunshine State was shaped like a flaccid penis. With that phallic thought, Porter gave up on her visit, got back into her rental car, slammed the door very hard and drove away.

She burned a little rubber even though she knew license plate numbers were being taken in wholesale lots by the Right to Life organizers. These people were kooks, all right. So, this time they would trace the number and call a Hertz office.

Antiabortionists are fanatics, and they never tire, damn it.

That simple fact made things harder for Porter than she wished.

Porter had to make a physical effort to stay within the speed limit as she picked her way east on Dania Boulevard to Route 1A where she turned south, heading along the coast to Miami. The highway was a notorious hangout for cops, who spent their days hiding in the shadows behind billboards. They only came out to find a free lunch or to give tickets to half-blind octogenarians and blue-haired old ladies. "A cataract in every Cadillac," as Florida's highway patrol cops were fond of saying.

The smell of salt and seaweed raised Porter's spirits somewhat as she cruised slowly past Hollywood, Hallandale, Bal Harbor, and Surfside. Over the past few years, she had watched as numerous condominiums sprouted along the beach like expensive sandcastles, and she marveled at the bargains she'd missed by ignoring the obvious. Porter passed the John F. Kennedy Causeway and drove directly down Collins Avenue into Miami Beach. She loved the honky-tonk of it, the pastel colors and horrible architecture. She parked on Lincoln Road and had lunch at Wolfie's. The abortion clinic demonstrations had messed up her schedule and she had the afternoon and evening to kill. Porter's plane didn't leave until morning, and during the season, flights were full and it became almost impossible to change reservations. She tried anyway, but Eastern Airlines wasn't even answering phones, and all the call did was push Porter into the oblivion of elevator music.

Sated by the delicious lunch, she took the Venetian Causeway into Miami and checked into one of the better-looking motels near the airport, which was far enough away from the Miami Beach area to have a vacancy.

Porter showered and called Max in New York. He was out, so, rather than waste the day, she decided to pay a visit to Sarah LaFrance. Sarah's operation was pure overhead. And Porter felt she was making a little too much profit, especially since she generated no income. It was a lot like the situation in Washington with Toby Wine, except that Sarah LaFrance's function in Porter's operation was not to generate leads. Sarah's job was more akin to caretaking. Porter had close to two-dozen baby farms of various sizes spotted throughout the country. These places, both large and small, were similar to the one run by Sarah LaFrance—where many of the girls were sent to wait out their pregnancies, at least the ones who needed a place to stay.

A Baby To Die For

Sarah LaFrance was nothing more than a cost of doing business—like staples, stationery, and toilet paper. More for Sarah meant less for Porter and Max—even though, to be realistic, most of the expenses were passed on to the adoptive parents.

Porter called Sarah and arranged to meet after dinner. Then she removed the neatly folded paper she kept tucked inside her Filofax notebook detailing the directions to Rainbow Drive and placed it into her handbag.

This meeting could be fun.

Chapter 37

It was an ugly, two-story house. Its stucco-over-cinder-block exterior, painted pink many years before, was now faded and peeling. A pair of scraggly palm trees tried hard to keep a grip in the depleted soil of the small, sandy, brown-spotted lawn. The pink house wasn't much different from the rest of the houses on the optimistically named, Rainbow Drive—just one more unimpressive pile in the middle of an unimpressive block.

It was dinner time, so there wasn't much outside activity on the street. The men and women in the other houses, mostly working folks, were now home, their cars parked in driveways—older cars, one, its trunk lid tied down with an old jump rope, its one remaining red-plastic handle broken. A rusted-out pickup truck, the original color indiscernible, its cargo a jumble of paint-splattered ladders, cans, and drop cloths, had misspelled hand-lettering on the door reading, A. GARCIA PAINTING & PEPERING. Several worn, rusted bikes sprawled at rest on the mean-looking lawns. A few brightly colored plastic toys, scattered here and there, lay ready for any after-dinner action. It was that kind of a street.

A Baby To Die For

The evening was warm, so front doors were wide open, nothing blocking entry but aluminum screen doors, most puffed out from repeated pushing, looking like rusty mesh spinnakers. Radio, television, and people sounds drifted out along with a pleasant miasma of cooking odors.

Sarah LaFrance had owned the big pink house since 1969 and, ever since, had used it for her business, which supported her comfortably. Earlier in the day, she had been surprised, but not disturbed by the call from Porter Gibbs. Sarah was determined not to let the woman's unscheduled visit affect her usual routine or upset her delicate stomach. So, as was her ritual, at exactly 7:30 p.m., according to her Timex, Sarah emerged through the front door of the pink house, smiling and using a toothpick to clear the dinner debris from the spaces between her nicotine-stained teeth. Sarah was fifty-five years old, a singularly unattractive woman with stringy hair, narrow shoulders, an indifferent bust, and a monumental rear end, which produced the effect of a perfectly shaped pear.

She stood planted on the porch for several minutes, just thinking and looking smugly up and down the street.

A few more years and I'll be able to leave this dump forever, and buy a condominium on Miami Beach. At the rate the money is coming in lately, I just might be able to buy two—one for rental income.

She sucked some air between her teeth and flipped the used toothpick in an arc onto the infected-looking lawn. The screen door behind Sarah squeaked open and a pretty young blonde came out. Tall and gangly, she seemed younger than her seventeen years and was unusually enormous, even for someone in her third trimester. The door began to close behind her but a second hand stabbed at the screen, stopping it to allow a second girl to come onto the porch. She was shorter, older by two years, with dark hair, terrible acne, and less than a month away from giving birth to twins.

In a few minutes, there were six young girls clustered on the porch, talking and giggling. Most of them were smoking, cupping the cigarettes in their hands.

Sarah, smiling, strutted down the steps and along the cement walk that parted the sick-looking lawn down the middle. She carried herself in the exaggerated manner of a drum majorette leading a half-time march. The girls followed, some mimicking her slow, pompous walk, among lots of muffled whispers and giggles. After all, even pregnant, they were still just a bunch of kids goofing around.

At the sidewalk, Sarah hesitated for a moment, and then, with a firm directional nod of her head, turned smartly to the right, the girls strung out behind her—a goose waddling across a road, its goslings following behind, struggling to keep up.

The sun was practically gone now from Rainbow Drive. At the street crossing, she guided the half-dozen girls across, as a policeman does at a school intersection. Sarah LaFrance was as protective of her brood as any other farmer would be of a freshly planted acre. If she lost any part of her crop, she lost some of her income, and no income meant no condominium in Miami Beach, a sobering and terrifying thought, at best.

A Baby To Die For

Sarah received a weekly sum for each of the girls in her care. The amount was far more than Sarah ever actually spent to run her exceptionally frugal household. Additionally, at the end of each girl's stay, if all went well—which it almost always did—and after there had been a successful birth, LaFrance collected a cash bonus, double for twins. Given that Sarah usually had, on average, about a half-dozen young ladies staying with her, she was pretty much assured of a generous monthly income. It was clear Sarah LaFrance had one hell of a deal going for herself. And it was all cash money. Even though she kept meticulous business records and paid taxes on selected portions of her operation, in the end, the IRS ended up with a very small slice of Sarah's financial pie.

Now that Miss Porter was coming for a visit, Sarah decided it might be a good time to try to increase her financial arrangement a bit more. It had become almost a game between the two women. Sarah was convinced Porter would be disappointed if she didn't push for more money during her infrequent visits. But she would have to do it carefully. Why kill a good thing with excessive greed? She thought maybe she would ask for a little bump up on her weekly expense money or possibly suggest a raise in the "birth bonus" she got.

After all, don't I take wonderful care of these little snotty-nosed tarts? Don't I get them through the worst of their mistakes? If I play it right, miss-y Porter might be very generous to me on this trip.

LaFrance stopped at the edge of a small park. She stood watching the girls as they shuffled and waddled past her to move excitedly toward the swings and teeter-totters. Not one of her half-dozen charges was over nineteen years old, and three of them were little more than children themselves. And although they were all pregnant, none were married, and rarely did anyone claiming to be a father ever show up to visit. Children having children—it was some state of affairs.

Sarah scolded after them to be careful and then smiled as she remembered that Anne, the brunette with acne, was having twins and would be worth a double birth bonus. If both babies were adopted out, there would be two placement bonuses. Unfortunately for her bank account, all the others were only expecting a single child.

Thirty minutes later, Sarah, followed by her brood, made their way back to the house. She decided to put water on to boil. She and Porter would have tea, and hopefully, Sarah would be a little richer from the visit.

Like many people, Sarah LaFrance had a tendency to misjudge many things in her life.

Chapter 38

Karen and Tuck landed right on time at Miami International Airport, picked up their rental car, and headed out for Rainbow Drive. Even after all these years, Karen was certain Sarah LaFrance would be at the park airing out her charges, precisely on schedule. If nothing else, the woman was a creature of habit.

The sun was setting as they drove past the pink house and, following Karen's directions, continued on for several more blocks, parking across the street from the small playground. Tuck watched, fascinated, as the heavyset, matronly Sarah LaFrance hovered and fussed over her brood of giggling incubators playing on the swings and teeter-totters. Pregnant children gamboling like children. Karen found the scene almost comical until she remembered that she had been one of them not that many years ago. She vividly recalled how her brother, Jake, had delivered her, like a package, to LaFrance's doorstep, he carrying the suitcase, she carrying the baby growing inside her. The memory was so clear, albeit abstract to some degree, as if it happening to someone else or as if she'd read about it in a book or seen it in a film.

A Baby To Die For

About twenty minutes later, Sarah LaFrance checked her watch, rounded up her girls, and exited the small park. After she was out of sight, Karen and Tuck left the car, stretched, and drifted over to the play area. Karen could still detect the remaining residue of Sarah LaFrance's cheap, strong perfume. She felt strange sitting on one of the swings again, legs dangling down touching the sandy soil. The sun was very low and casting refreshingly cool shadows, but the swing's chain running along either side of her body was still warm to the touch, not hot, as they had been when the sun was high. Karen squinted in the half-light and watched Tuck chinning himself on the monkey bars. She smiled and felt good.

Karen glanced down at her stomach, remembering, and almost expecting to see the swelling under her dress that had been her baby. But it was flat.

"Okay," Tuck, coming up behind her suddenly, whispered in her ear, causing her to jump. "I've been patient as a saint. Now, what was the other reason you wanted to go through this little reunion? You saw the house, watched the old lady, and I even humored you with this little romp in the kiddy park. Tell all or I'll start pushing this swing very high."

Karen twisted her head and looked up at Tuck. His olive complexion seemed even darker and more handsome in the fading light. She leaned her face against the warm iron chain of the swing.

"We're pregnant," she said, smiling.

264

A Baby To Die For

It was dusk when Tuck steered the rental car away from the playground and headed toward the motel they had booked in Miami, once again passing the house on Rainbow Drive. This time there was a white sedan parked outside by the curb, and a woman was just getting out. It all happened in a flash. Karen instantly recognized Porter Gibbs and quickly slumped far down in her seat as Porter turned toward their car. They passed no more than five feet apart, and Porter's gaze as Tuck passed by was an open and frank appreciation of his good looks. Tuck, having no idea who Porter was, returned the stare and smiled.

Chapter 39

Karen and Tuck had no trouble finding Kevin Tyler in the crowded lobby of the Eden Roc hotel. It was about as difficult as spotting the guy wearing a clown suit in a nudist camp. In the sea of pastel-colored, casual resort wear, the diminutive scientist was dressed in a somber, gray, three-piece number, complete with a paisley bowtie.

After quick introductions, the three proceeded to the large, ornate dining room. There they were escorted to a table next to a wall of glass that revealed a coveted Miami Beach trifecta—a pool, a beach, and an ocean view.

Initially, Tyler was polite but understandably cautious. However, helped along by a second martini, he began to loosen up and soon became quite chatty. After some gentle prodding from Tuck, he slowly and with the loving detail of a proud parent, unfolded the story surrounding his background, as well as the Library of Life, which Silvia Wilson had touched on briefly in the *New York Times.*

Unlike the journalist's short piece, the scientist's telling of the tale was rich with detail and started with his general background and how, when in medical school, he had developed a surprisingly keen interest in the field of genetics. From there, he jumped right up to the phone call from the recluse billionaire, Edmond Calendar, and the sudden and mysterious flight to Switzerland. The part of the story where Edmond Calendar died came just as coffee arrived, as if the thermos carafe and cups were punctuating the end of his story. Tyler's discourse had obviously been polished to a high sheen, having been repeated many, many times in the past pursuit of his work.

Karen and Tuck had listened transfixed and now fussed with their coffee while silently digesting what they'd just heard.

"I must say, Dr. Tyler, that's one hell of a story," Tuck finally said. "And pretty damned bizarre, at that. A crazy old billionaire contacts you out of the blue and asks for your help to produce an heir and then ends up creating the amazing Library of Life?"

"The Edmond Calendar Library of Life to be precise, and yes, that about sums it up," Tyler agreed, sipping his coffee. "Pretty damned amazing, I'd agree."

"I'm curious," Tuck said, "In this, uh, library, how many 'human…books'—or whatever you call them—how many do you actually have?"

"We call them donor specimens—DS, for short—and we do have quite a few," Tyler said. "Before the old man died, I spent almost a whole year in a frenzy of activity collecting as many as I could. Edmond Calendar's name alone gave me access to just about anyone I wanted to include—and I mean, *anyone.* His persona, incredible wealth, and power were like magic and gave me unprecedented accessibility. It was extremely rare for anyone to refuse a call from me once I dropped the old man's name. And not too many of those I met with turned down my request for a donation. It wasn't as if I were asking them for money, which might have been a totally different situation. Some of the most impressive donors were not wealthy men, especially the academics."

"So why do you think so many of them were willing to make a donation? I mean, after all, why would a famous person want it known that their sperm was—please pardon the expression—floating around?" Karen asked.

"Excellent question," Tyler chuckled, amused by the pun. "Firstly, I was able to guarantee them total anonymity. But there was among the donors a more compelling and mostly mutual reason. You know how real estate people say success is all about three things—location, location, and location? Well, most of these men donated for three reasons—ego, ego, and ego. So, most of the gentlemen I approached were flattered to be singled out. Then, of course, there's the real practical issue we will eventually face. We must lay down a genetic benchmark for our species. Scientists are seeing early indications that all the bad things we're doing to ourselves—the hormones we pump into our food, the pollution of the environment—all those things will eventually cause some genetic drift. We need to have a stake in the ground if for no other reason than to be able to someday measure how bad things have gotten. In reality, it's impossible to tell how far one has traveled without knowing the starting point. Frankly,

I was surprised and heartened by the number of men I approached who were moved, by that fact alone, to make their donation."

"I understand, but to Karen's point, in the short run, what if the public somehow discovered the identity of all your famous donors?" Tuck asked.

"Not possible," Tyler responded emphatically. "You see, even though the freezers contain a veritable who's who in every field—science, academics, athletics, as well as the humanities—the specimens are not identified by the donor's name. The library is totally anonymous, cataloged only by a code that I created, which details each depositor's personal, medical, academic, and professional history. And naturally, the specimen itself contains the DNA of the donor but without identifying the subject by name. Basically, we want to know everything about the donor, except for his identity. Someday, when it's possible to do so, the sperm itself will become an easily 'readable' book and will give us the individual's complex genetic road map."

"But," Tuck objected, "someone—you, for instance—must know who each of these people are, correct?"

"Of course, I know who the donors are—after all, I alone collected the samples—but other than my own fragile memory, no record exists anywhere that could reveal their names. So, when I'm gone, that will be that. And frankly, for our purposes, the creation of a genetic benchmark renders the names quite irrelevant. Just imagine, for example, if a frozen prehistoric body was discovered somewhere—would anyone really care what the poor devil's name was?

A Baby To Die For

The benefit of this library is not much different from any library of books. It's not about the book covers, it's about their contents. Similarly, we don't care about the names, but rather each donor's characteristics. As for people finding out that the library exists, in actual fact, the whole project, so generously underwritten by Mr. Calendar, has had very little publicity. If it weren't for Silvia Wilson's short and inappropriate article in the *Times*, I doubt you'd have ever heard of the project. It will be unfortunate if her article stirs up a lot of additional inquiries."

Tuck poured more coffee from the large silver carafe the waiter had left. A silence hung over the group for the first time since they had arrived.

Kevin Tyler sipped his coffee. Then said, "So, tell me, why did you want to meet with me, Mr. Handler? Remember, you phoned, so it's your nickel. I'm going to order a decadent hunk of pastry from that cart over there and enjoy it while you talk."

Tyler signaled the waiter who arrived with a large cart heavily laden with a lovely selection of all things fattening. After careful consideration, Tyler chose a bulging éclair the size of a small throw pillow and settled back to enjoy the sweet and listen.

Tuck had to think for a minute to try to organize the many thoughts that were spinning around inside his head.

"It's a long story," Tuck said, haltingly.

Twilight had turned to darkness by the time Tuck finished.

"Look, Mr. Handler," Tyler finally said, "I can

certainly sympathize with what you've gone through. Losing a loved one is never easy, and the unfortunate circumstances surrounding your wife's death must make her loss even more difficult to bear, but honestly, maybe I'm missing something, but I'm not sure where you believe I fit in."

"Our goal," Tuck said, nodding toward Karen, "our primary objective is to expose Max Garfield's network in a way that puts an end to his operations and puts him in jail. The *New York Times* article about you and Edmond Calendar's Library of Life triggered an idea that could possibly do just that.

"Garfield's success relies on two things: a constant supply of infants to sell and the buyers willing to pay for them."

"So, for this Garfield person, the babies are just a commodity," Tyler mused.

"Sort of, but not exactly," Tuck said. "A commodity implies similarity. Garfield deals—at least he *claims* to deal with a product that rises above commodity status, a more exclusive kind of baby, one that commands a higher price. And, the more special a baby is, the higher the price he can get. The collection of sperm in your Library of Life represents the potential to produce very, very special babies…and…"

"Whoa!" Kevin Tyler interrupted, rearing back, his hands raised shoulder high, palms out. "Hold on, just a minute. If you're suggesting we use sperm from the library, that's just never going to happen. It's totally out of the question. I would never allow that. It would be completely unethical."

"Believe me, Dr. Tyler, I understand. That's not what I'm talking about. What I'm suggesting avoids that issue completely."

"I fail to see how," Tyler said, rather brusquely.

Tuck glanced at Karen and got no comfort from the defeat he saw in her eyes. "Look, Dr. Tyler, at best, our odds of stopping Garfield lie somewhere between slim and none. The plain fact is adoption's legal, at least on the surface. Garfield run his business pretty much aboveboard and within the law. But in actual fact, what he's doing is criminal and way outside the law. Certainly outside the laws of morality."

"But I can't see how," Tyler said, with a dismissive hand flip, while slurring words slightly from the effect of his liquor consumption. "You say that on one hand he's within the law, but also breaking the law. It sounds like a difference without a distinction."

Tuck was feeling a headache settling in as he continued. "I know it's hard to understand. There's such a narrow line between a baby being adopted and one being sold. The difference is the amount of money changing hands, and what happens to the money. Where paying for a baby becomes illegal is when the amount of money being exchanged rises beyond a reasonable level, so far beyond, that it must be kept secret. Costs so high that, if they were ever disclosed, no judge would allow the adoption to go forward. It would fall into the category of "baby selling." It's clearly why Garfield insists the major portion of his payments be in cash. And that's where he is vulnerable to exposure."

A Baby To Die For

The scientist's lips pursed with concentration, then, "Oh, I see. So taking the bulk of his fees in cash means he never has to report it to the IRS?"

"Exactly. Garfield keeps as much as possible in cash and bypasses the IRS. But in order to pull that off, everybody involved has to commit perjury. You see the last step in an adoption involves appearing in front of a judge who gets to hear all the details of the transaction. At that point most of it is pro-forma stuff. It's a happy time for all concerned. The new parents are, of course, delighted and, as for the judge, it's probably one of the more pleasant duties she can perform. But if the court learned someone was receiving an unusually hefty bundle of cash in exchange for the baby—say $40,000 or $50,000—it would stop the whole process dead in its tracks. And that's the dilemma, because neither Garfield nor the adoptive parents can tell the truth about the amount of money that changed hands, so they have to lie to the judge and claim to have paid only a modest amount, about what an adoption would cost through an adoption agency. There's also another place where Garfield crosses the line—not necessarily a legal one but certainly an ethical one. Where necessary, he partially or completely fabricates the backgrounds of the biological parents. Say, for example, the adoptees are set on having a baby of a certain religion. If the child Garfield has to sell doesn't fit that particular request, he just—*lies*. You want a baby with a specific religious background, he says 'of course, the mother of this baby was—and he just fills in the religion of choice. Was the father athletic? Was the mother an intellectual? If you want it, Garfield will deliver a baby that's as close to perfect as possible—anything you want, for a price, of course.

"Garfield and his cronies are all about greed. And greedy people, no matter how cautious or suspicious they are, can be made careless when the potential profits are high enough. It's a matter of risk versus reward. If we can feed that greedy side of Max Garfield, show him a big, fat rainbow, and then convince him that there's a gigantic pot of gold at its end, well..."

Tuck stopped and waited for Tyler's reaction.

"As a scientist, I look at facts then see where they lead me. I'm a geneticist with a laboratory full of frozen sperm from lots of famous men who I was able to convince—for the good of mankind—to ejaculate into a test tube. But I'm not sure how this adds up to a way of bringing down Mr. Garfield."

Tuck tried to think of the best way to answer Tyler's question, even as he watched through the window as an attractive woman lowered herself into the shallow end of the outdoor swimming pool.

"I think we can catch Garfield with a monkey trap."

"I don't know what you're talking about," Tyler said, looking confused. "What is a monkey trap?"

"It's more of a metaphor than a real trap. Visualize a box that has a banana inside and a hole on one side. The hole is big enough for the monkey to get his hand through and clutch the banana. But the only way the monkey can escape is—"

"To let go of the banana," Tyler said, finishing Tuck's sentence.

A Baby To Die For

"Exactly! What I want to offer Garfield is a baby to sell—a very, very special baby. A baby fathered by a person so damned famous, someone so perfect that a child conceived from his sperm would be worth a fortune. I want to give Garfield that kind of temptation. Not just one baby, a chain of top-quality babies, each with an illustrious father. And once he grabs onto that baby—like the monkey—he'll never want to let go."

"But I told you, I've no intention of ever letting you use any of the sperm!" Tyler said.

"We don't need to. All we require is the illusion that we have that kind of a baby. If we get Garfield to believe it's what we have to offer, we can make a deal with him based on that idea. The fact that there really is an Edmond Calendar Library of Life, and a lab filled with Nobel-level sperm, it all supports our story and gives it the legitimacy we need. This isn't a pie in the sky story. If you're willing, we could show him your laboratory. Let him see the setup for himself. At that point, the story becomes a reality."

Tuck could see Tyler's expression changing, his doubts falling away and his interest peaked.

"That's quite a plan, Mr. Handler, but I've a question. Iif you don't use our stored sperm, where would you get the so-called banana you need to trap Garfield?"

Tuck sat back into his chair, relaxed, and reached out to take Karen's hand.

"We're pregnant, and I'm suggesting we offer him Karen's baby to sell. Not just Karen's baby, but a baby she will claim was conceived with sperm from a very special father, a father recruited from the illustrious ranks of

Edmond Calendar's Library of Life sperm bank."

Slowly, a smile broke across Tyler's face.

"Why, Mr. Handler, that's downright devious of you. And of course, he'll have no practical way to prove your claim is not true. But wait. If Garfield is so—how can I put it?—deceitful—what would keep him from just making that sort of claim anyway? You said he often fabricated the backgrounds of babies, so why not just *make up* a Nobel Prize-winning background?"

"You're the difference, Dr. Tyler. Only *you* can provide the legitimacy that supports the lie. But we can't do it without your help."

"Who would you claim was the father?"

Tuck laughed.

"Well, Doc, that depends on who you have in stock!"

Chapter 40

New York City

"That is one friggin' bizarre idea," Ken said, while using chopsticks to grab an eggroll. "I'm amazed this Tyler guy is willing to go along with it."

The four of them were in Ken and Mary Flower's living room, hunched around the coffee table, enjoying the foods from a half-dozen Chinese take-out containers. Tuck and Karen had just finished relating their meeting with Kevin Tyler.

"It did take a bit of convincing, but in the end, he caved in to Karen's overwhelming charm."

"I admit I flirted shamelessly with him. I also pointed out that he wouldn't be doing anything more than letting us allude to his library as the source of the sperm. Even if Garfield wants to go out to California to see the lab, Tyler agreed to take him through and explain how it all works. He wouldn't need to do any more than that."

"And what did you have to offer in return?"

"That's the best part: Nothing. Frankly, I think the man is just bored out of his mind. He has a job for which he's paid to do nothing. He doesn't intend to expand the number of donors, and the day-to-day operations consist mostly of making sure none of his "books" defrost. Besides, he likes the thought of being part of a sting, without any fear of repercussions."

Ken sat back and sipped his wine. "Well, it could be a great exposé—a real news magnet—maybe even a book. A lot depends on Garfield's being convinced that you really have access to the 'celebrity' sperm. If you can do that, all you'll need is a credible couple to be on the buying side—folks with enough wherewithal to whet Garfield's appetite."

"Interesting you should say that. We gave it a lot of thought and believe we have the perfect couple," Karen said, while Tuck nodded in agreement.

"Great, who are they?"

"You guys," Tuck said, and before they could respond, he continued, "Don't say anything until you hear me out. You're a perfect couple. As the writer, you would be getting the story firsthand, from the horse's mouth, so to speak. As for the illusion of money, we'd need to fabricate a story, but that shouldn't be too difficult. Mary's being a doctor works perfectly. As for Ken, you would be exactly what you are, a journalist. All we'd need to add is a wee bit of a lie about a small fortune you inherited that allows you to follow the journalism career you always wanted without any concern about money. Because, as everyone knows, journalists don't make squat, right?" Tuck laughed.

Ken gave it about a half second before replying, "Hey, I could get on board with that. I just want to do the story, and it won't be the first time I went undercover. It's really up to Mary. She's the one working on a schedule, and a rough one, at that."

"It really depends on how much time is required. Like Ken said, my schedule is really tight and my first duty is to the hospital."

"Absolutely. We understand. Based on what Ellen and I experienced, the actual amount of time you'd need to spend will be minimal: a few appointments with some adoption agencies to get a basic feel for the process and then one—maybe two—with Garfield. He'll understand Mary's situation at the hospital, so it wouldn't be anything out of the ordinary should she not show up at all the meetings. Ken could cover most, without Garfield thinking anything was wrong. It should actually be pretty cut-and-dried."

"Clear something up for me," Mary said. "You need to get Garfield to take cash payment for a baby, then commit perjury, and eventually evade paying his taxes, right? So how will all that work? It sounds pretty damned confusing and complex to me."

"You're right, it is, but I think we have the solution. We would have to go through with the entire adoption process. Every single part of it," Tuck emphasized.

"You mean we would actually take the baby?"

"Yes, but for a very short time. Then the birth mother would take it back."

"Wow, now I'm really confused. Where do you intend to find a pregnant woman who is willing to go through all this? I know if you ever came to me with a request like that I'd tell you where you could shove it."

"That's the best part. We already have the pregnant woman, and she's ready, able and willing to do it."

"Who?" Ken asked.

Tuck looked at Karen, "Why don't you tell them?"

Sheepishly, with a broad grin, Karen raised her hand. "That would be *me*."

Chapter 41

It had been a long time since Karen Boyd had taken dinner with her brother. They sat in the small, darkened bar area of Rossini's and sipped their drinks, ate bar pretzels, and waited for their table to be prepared.

Max Garfield signaled for another drink, and the alert barman quickly returned with vodka on the rocks, while Karen toyed with her glass of white wine.

"You're not drinking?" Max said.

"Trying to lose a few pounds. The older I get, the harder it is."

"Tell me about it. I think I've been on a diet all my life."

Clearly, their being together, alone, was not something either of them was accustomed to. Finally Max reached out and patted Karen's hand, "You know, it's a shame we don't do this more often," Max said, a bit nervously, while stirring his drink a half turn with his right index finger. "Do you realize, Karen, this is the first time we've had... that we've been together just talking for, I don't know how long? I always knew what to say to you when you were in trouble: drunk, or stoned. The kind of trouble I could always solve. But this…" Max had to laugh at what he was saying, "this normalcy! It's a bitch to deal with."

Karen couldn't help but respond with genuine laughter. Her SOB of a brother had made a joke, and of course, she was the brunt of it. No self-deprecating for Max. No way. As for the getting together more often part, she didn't find any humor in that. He was certainly right, they didn't very often, and it was for a simple reason. Karen would have preferred elective root canal to what she was doing at the moment. Every time she looked at Max, all she could see was her baby. The last image she had of the infant was indelibly imprinted on her memory. She was only here for one reason—to destroy him. Thanks to Tuck, they had a plan, and tonight she would introduce the first phase of it. She would go through with this charade of rapprochement with Max. She had waited for a long time— always smiling and being civil to her brother—doing so for a little longer would make no difference. Tonight, Max would only hear what he wanted to hear. If everything went as planned, that was how it would be.

Karen sighed, "Being here, with you like this, reminds me of the old days. We had some fun times back then. But Jake and I, we must have been a handful. God knows I gave you lots of crap starting way back in high school, right? It couldn't have been easy for you, Max. It had to have cut into your life a lot, being both mother and father to two shits like us."

Karen smiled at her brother and he smiled back.

Contrition. His reaction to what she was saying was as clear to Karen as if clown-white suddenly appeared all over his face. *That's* what Max yearned to hear. To know that, after all those years, Karen was able to acknowledge the sacrifices made by her long-suffering and martyred brother, Max.

So Karen programmed "contrite" into her brain and continued.

"It's funny, Max, maybe it's age or maybe just the stars lining up, but I'm seeing what you did in a different light. I can even understand now about my baby. Do you realize she'll be eleven years old next month?"

"Christ, eleven already. That is hard to believe," Max said.

Karen was surprised to see moisture rimming Max's eyes and she was having trouble keeping a straight face.

"I have to be honest," Max said. "I'm really impressed with your attitude. It makes me very happy. I've no idea who the baby went to, she was placed through another lawyer, but I do know it was to a very solid young couple. I'm certain she's getting lots of love and the best of everything."

"Yes, Max, I agree. Given the condition I was in, I know she's better off for having been adopted. I never could have raised her alone. I was such a mess back then. It only would have hurt her. I know that now."

Max took a deep swallow from his drink in an effort to fight back the tears that he felt building up just behind his eyes. He had waited so long to hear his sister say these things, to admit that what he had done had been in her best interest. Maybe he was getting his little sister back again. That would make him so happy. He missed her.

As for Jake, he was another story. He was so volatile. His insanity was always so dangerously close to the surface, one never knew when it would break through. And that would probably never change. But Karen, she was bright and beautiful, a woman who could help him more at the office, maybe even take some of the weight off his shoulders. He knew damned well that Porter was robbing him blind with her skimming and side deals. He could envision having Karen trained by Porter, becoming her assistant, and learning the business from the bottom up. At least, Karen could be trusted. After all, she was family.

"I'm not looking for any tickertape parade, Karen. When Dad died, Mom was just too old to take care of you kids. I did what I had to do."

Karen smiled up at Max and thought calmly and clearly about smashing her drink on the bar, then driving the shards of glass into her brother's face.

Just then Josef, Rossini's owner, appeared, clutching several large menus to his chest, and led them from the bar to the spacious two-level room that made up the restaurant's dining area.

Karen was hungry from tension as much as appetite and ordered accordingly. They had salad, and then each had a generous portion of *Paglia e Fieno*, delicate pasta that is commonly called *Hay and Straw*. A bottle of chilled Pouilly-Fumé helped it all disappear and went perfectly with the whole striped bass, which they shared. Karen, of course, shouldn't be drinking but felt Max might be suspicious, so she sipped sparingly, enjoying the meal, and chatting easily about the past. They even laughed a bit and, despite Karen's misgivings, had a pleasant time playing with their memories.

It was over espresso that Karen turned the conversation to business.

"It was a wonderful dinner, Max. I really enjoyed it," she said and paused for a moment. "There is something serious I'd like to discuss," she began, launching into her pitch.

When Karen said "something serious to discuss," Max reflexively tensed.

"Okay," Max said, slowly, in a skeptical tone of voice filled with caution.

"I want to become more involved in the business. Believe me, I appreciate the salary you pay me, but I need more than that and, to be honest, I want to really earn it. Doing odds and ends around the office is not how I envision building a future for myself."

Max began breathing again.

Karen knew she had her brother's undivided attention and continued. "As you know, some months ago I went away for a long weekend. However, I didn't go to Bermuda."

"Really?" Max asked in genuine surprise. "You told me you were going there with your friend—"

"Actually, I went to California, to San Francisco, to see a doctor there."

"You're not sick?" Max asked, with genuine alarm.

"No, no, I'm fine. He's a man I met some time ago here in New York. His name is Tyler, Kevin Tyler."

"You met a doctor? Should I be overjoyed for you?" Max joked.

"It's not that sort of thing, Max," Karen said, staying serious. "I read an article about him in *The New York Times* and it intrigued me, so I flew out to San Francisco to discuss a business idea," Karen said, bending the truth slightly, but dramatically. "Our conversations were very productive. As a result, Dr. Tyler and I have become partners in an interesting venture."

"What sort of venture, Karen?"

"We want to become supplier—to you."

Max frowned and signaled a nearby waiter for some more wine. As the waiter replenished his glass, he asked, "Supplying what, exactly?"

"Babies."

"Babies?" Max repeated, a warning light starting to flash in the recesses of his mind. "I think you had better begin at the beginning."

"I'd rather have Tyler tell you himself. He had to be in New York to deliver a lecture this evening at the Columbia Medical School. He should be showing up—" Karen consulted her watch, "any minute now."

She leaned across the table toward him and lowered her voice. "What Tyler has done is nothing short of amazing. And, when you hear what he has to say, you'll understand what a wonderful opportunity it is for all of us. I swear, you'll be wild about Tyler and as excited as we are about what we can offer, so please hear him out."

As she was saying this, Josef led Kevin Tyler to the table.

"Ms. Boyd, your guest has arrived," the restaurant's owner said with a flourish, and then to Tyler, "May I bring you something to drink, sir?"

A Baby To Die For

"Just coffee, please—American, black," Kevin said, as he shook Max's hand. "Mr. Garfield, I'm delighted to meet you. Sorry I'm late. I had a bit of trouble getting a cab."

Fifteen minutes later, Kevin Tyler had finished an abbreviated version of his story. He leaned back and waited for Max Garfield's reaction.

Garfield's mind was spinning like a worn tire on an ice patch. Kevin Tyler's story was outrageous to the point of fantasy, and yet when Max thought about it, he had to admit, *why not?* The technology was there. He'd read about sperm banks and artificial insemination. Even the possibility of test-tube babies seemed to be just around the corner. He also had heard of the late Edmond Calendar. Everyone living in America knew about the crazy old billionaire.

No, the question was not one of possibility but rather believability. The whole thing was possible, but should Max believe it? Maybe *trust* would be a better word. Could he *trust* this man who called himself Kevin Tyler? His credentials would be easy enough to validate—a call to the American Medical Association would confirm or deny. But Edmond Calendar was dead. Who could he speak to in order to verify the authenticity of what Kevin Tyler was telling him? And would he want to have anything at all to do with something associated, however remotely, with Edmond Calendar? From what he read in the papers and law journals, Calendar's estate was even more ensnarled than that of his purported old buddy Howard Hughes. At least, the Mormons who were picking over Hughes's financial cadaver seemed to be playing by some of the rules. Calendar, if you could believe the newspapers, had been strongly linked to underworld interests around the globe. With that kind of money involved, the last thing Max Garfield wanted was to have Mafia types sniffing around *his* profits from *his* world of adoption.

And what about Karen? She was family, and he had no reason not to trust her. But he also had to face that Tyler might be taking advantage of her.

But damn it! If what Tyler said was true, the possibilities boggled the mind. Babies made to order— at that level of pedigree—could make what he currently charged seem like a small down payment. The couples that came to see him now were overjoyed just to have a baby whose parents went to college. He could only imagine how wild they would be to buy the offspring of an Oscar-winning movie star, a Nobel Prize winner, or an MVP shortstop.

Yes, a $100,000 baby could suddenly become more than just a pipe dream. But what if.... What if what? What am I so afraid of? How could I get hurt in this? It seems foolproof. So why am I picking up a barely audible siren in the back of my mind? What is Tyler's angle? There has to be a catch. What does Dr. Kevin Tyler have to gain? What harmful leverage could he exert?

If nothing else, Max Garfield was a survivor of the first order. His legally trained brain flipped the facts, looking for the traps, double blinds, snares, any possible ambush points. Max was almost dizzy trying to contemplate the pros and cons.

A Baby To Die For

Could it be true? Or did it all really come down to just taking a leap of faith. He would have to if he wanted in. It was an important calculation. He would have to be very discreet. If the story ever got out, it could mean big trouble. Max wondered what recourse a person would have against him or Kevin Tyler for dipping into his frozen sperm bank to make a baby to sell? On the other hand, what adoptive parent would complain? Sperm banks were perfectly legal, after all. And as Tyler pointed out, no donor names could officially be used. Although a wink and a whisper would, without question, do the trick quite adequately.

Even if someone complained, what exactly would they have to complain about? Obviously, this is not an idea that I can stay with for too many years. But God, what incredibly lucrative years they could be.

And Karen—could he depend on her? She had lots of street smarts, and he doubted she'd be involved if there was anything fishy about the idea.

But why was she being so damned pleasant all of a sudden?

She had been like butter the past few weeks, and Max wasn't a fool. He wanted his sister to love him, to be repentant, and to try to make up for the crap she had put him through for so many years. But he was also a pragmatist. She had blamed him for the loss of her daughter, and he knew it.

Is she now really prepared to push that aside and move forward? Does she have the same drive for success that I do? She could be doing it for the money. That would make sense.

His sister still had to live, and he wasn't paying her all that much for what she did in the office. If she had half the greed Max was born with, Karen could simply be taking advantage of an opportunity. That reason made the most sense.

"Well, Max, what do you think?" Karen's voice sliced rudely into his thoughts. "It's mind-blowing, isn't it?"

Her face flushed with excitement, and she leaned back and pushed her thick hair away from her pretty face.

"Isn't it exciting? We could make a fortune—all of us."

Just then Josef stepped to the table, and their conversation went on hold as the restaurateur placed a tiny snifter in front of each of them. From behind him a waiter materialized carrying a bottle of Amaretto.

"With my compliments," Josef said, and watched as the waiter filled each snifter with the sweet liqueur.

Max thanked Josef and slowly sipped the viscous liquid, felt the rope of heat it created in his throat, and took the extra time to continue his thoughts.

I love the idea. If it's legit, it could make a fortune. The potential is almost incalculable. But I don't want to sound too optimistic.

So Max shrugged and picked up the conversation in his negotiating mode.

"You're right, Karen, it certainly is an interesting idea, but we're getting plenty of money for babies right now. If we make much more, people could talk and the courts might get wind of it and start asking embarrassing questions. Actually, it's not that big of a deal. How do I even know it will work?" Max said, trying for a little more thinking time and a lot more leverage.

A Baby To Die For

"Don't know if it will work?" Kevin Tyler repeated, frankly amazed by the question. "That's like asking if planes can fly. It's just not a valid question, Mr. Garfield," Kevin Tyler said casually. "This method of impregnating a woman works. It's done routinely all the time. It is no longer a valid question. I'm sure you realize that—even as a layperson."

The reprimand was not lost on Max, but he had been a lawyer too long to let a little aggressive pushback bother him.

"Come on, Max," Karen said. "I know you. You're as excited as I am."

"Truthfully, Karen—I'm skeptical. But you're right. I'd be lying if I didn't admit to being slightly interested. One of these days, I might ask you to arrange for such a baby, but right now, I'm not sure I have any couples in my files who could afford the price we'd have to ask for a situation like that," Max said, as he mentally reviewed his files knowing damned well that several of his recent placements would have jumped at the chance to have such a baby—and had the bucks to pay for it.

"First of all," Karen countered, leaning in toward her brother, "you don't have that kind of customer because you haven't had this kind of product. It's a case of which comes first, the chicken or the egg. When word gets out that you have access to that caliber of baby, you'll have to stand back so as not to be trampled by wealthy couples. It would be like a half-price sale at Tiffany's," Karen said.

Karen's tone was gentle but cutting as she whispered, "And besides, Max, you know damn well that even when you don't have other couples bidding, you just make them up. Isn't that right?"

Max didn't reply. He just gave his sister a furious look. Karen had seen that look many times before and, realizing her comment had overstepped her bounds, quickly pushed past her blunder.

"The exciting thing is, we've already started. We're not here with some pie-in-the-sky idea. We have a real situation—right now," Karen said, as she placed a reassuring hand on Max's arm.

Max felt his pulse pumping at his temples. He leaned in toward his sister, lowering his voice, "Are you telling me you've already used the sperm bank? You've actually created a pregnancy?"

"That's right, Max, we have. And we want you to place the baby," Karen said.

Max pushed back in his chair and expelled air, as if punched in the gut.

"Amazing! Who is it? The sperm, I mean," he asked, suddenly filled with burning curiosity.

Karen breathed an internal sigh of relief. She knew the hook had been set and glanced at Tyler, then back at Max.

As agreed beforehand, Tyler would never be asked to commit to anything specific. His role was simply to explain the Library of Life, not to lay claim to having used any of its contents to make a baby.

"Whose baby?" Karen repeated. "Actually, it was one of the early specimens Dr. Tyler collected. It's logged into the library as EC-9. The EC standing, of course, for the library's benefactor, Edmond Calendar, and the number signifying the ninth specimen donated. As I mentioned, there is no cataloguing or record of any sort to identify the donor by name. It so happens specimen EC-9 comes from a very successful and very wealthy man. All his natural progeny are extremely bright and brilliantly successful. Any child from this man would be beyond special."

For a moment Tyler's ego got the best of him and he couldn't help but add, "It was a very exciting acquisition, and Edmond had to personally arrange for it to happen, but only after months of negotiations. Mr. Calendar was without a doubt the only person on earth who could have gotten this man to see me, let along donate a specimen. It was just a stroke of lucky timing that I was able to secure it while—let's just say, while he could still be an effective donor. Fortunately, he was an astoundingly virile man— very much so."

"For God's sake, Tyler ! Who is it? Don't play games with me."

Max Garfield's voice was dry and raspy with tension.

Kevin Tyler leaned across the table toward Max.

"I'm only going to make an exception this on time."

He held his napkin like a shield between his mouth and the rest of the room. He whispered a name.

"Who? I couldn't make out what you said."

Kevin Tyler whispered the name again—a bit louder.

Max fell back in his chair.

"You can't be serious!"

A Baby To Die For

Max Garfield's mouth opened in a perfect circle, and then he roared with an explosive shot of laughter, causing half the patrons in the room to turn, startled, utensils and glasses in midair, mouths in mid-chew.

"This is really true?" Max managed to choke out in a whisper, "*He* is actually the father of this child?"

"Yes, completely true," Karen said, jumping in, not wanting Tyler to be the one to confirm the identity.

Max just kept laughing, shaking his head from side to side in utter amazement and enjoyment. Finally, wiping tears from his eyes with his napkin, he managed to speak.

"Tyler, this is beautiful—just fucking beautiful. How in the name of hell did you ever…get *him*? Oh, my God! Just amazing!"

Max had finished his drink, so he took Karen's, untouched, and finished it off in one swallow. Karen and Tyler looked at each other and smiled.

Karen knew Max well enough to know for certain that her brother was hooked, but getting him into a judicial net would be another thing.

"You can imagine, Max, we needed to have a very special person to carry this baby. Someone we could trust implicitly not to change her mind at the last minute—that sort of thing. It took us a while to find the absolutely perfect surrogate."

Max nodded agreement at each point his sister was making.

"Oh, yes, wise, very wise. If this placement generates as much as I think it can, any hint of a last minute change of heart by the birth mother would be a total disaster. A deal this sensitive can't afford to be screwed up by some teenage kid who decides that she wants to keep her baby. So who is she?"

Karen, picking up her glass of water, made a toasting gesture to Max, and whispered just loud enough, "Me, Max. I'm the one carrying the baby."

Chapter 42

Upper West Side, New York City

It was early Saturday morning. Karen was still euphoric over the successful outcome of her previous night's dinner with Max. Having Kevin Tyler show up was the thing that really clinched the deal for her brother. Now she and Tuck were anxious to brief Ken and Mary Flower.

By mid-morning they simply couldn't wait any longer, jumped in a cab and ten minutes later were tearing up the stairs to the Flower's apartment. Even before they could catch their breath from the climb, they were blurting out the details of the dinner.

Ken Flower was overjoyed. His journalist's ability to swallow complex ideas in a single gulp had kicked in when he first heard the idea. Now that the plan was under way, he excitedly paced back and forth across the small living room like a ricocheting bullet.

"There have been loads of stories published about adoption, but it's such a universal issue there's always room for a new one—especially one with *this* sort of spin. Adoption is only part of this story. It's really about greed—and a network that smells a lot like infant white slavery. Nothing I've seen published even comes close to this, and I can only imagine the potential it has to uncover some real criminality.

"Ever since you got back, Tuck, I've been collecting a file on adoption stories. They're mostly run-of-the-mill— one or two attempts to go undercover, mainly trying to unearth information on prices being charged for black market babies. But here we have a story with all the twists and angles of an Escher drawing. I always felt there was a good story to tell, and now we've got a sensational one. Let me go grab the file," Ken said, as he hurried out of the room.

Mary went to the kitchen and put on more coffee. Moments later, Ken was back carrying a thick folder.

"Here's everything I've dug up," Ken said. "Remember, I mentioned before how some reporters go undercover? One of the stories I found—uh, yeah—here it is. This reporter and her boyfriend posed as adoptive parents. They made an appointment with a lawyer who was rumored to sell black market babies. They arranged for an interview, marched into the guy's office, and with a totally made-up cover story and a tape recorder stuffed inside the reporter's handbag, proceeded to ask about adopting a baby.

"On top of that, they arranged to have a doctor call the lawyer a few days before their appointment, claiming to have a young patient, pregnant and wanting to place the baby for adoption."

"He didn't really have a pregnant patient, right?" Karen said.

"No, no. The supposedly pregnant girl was a young actress they hired. The lawyer, obviously on his guard, agreed to meet her but insisted she bring a urine sample, which she did—actually someone else's—her sister-in-law's pregnant next-door neighbor."

"Jesus, I remember reading about that," said Tuck. "It was right around the time Ellen and I, you know, when we were going through it. In those days, anything about adoption grabbed our attention. It sounded to me like a damn good plan. But as I recall, didn't the lawyer get suspicious for some reason and just shut it down?"

"Exactly. He even had the gall to sue the reporter and anyone else he could find. He didn't get anywhere with the lawsuits, and as it turned out, the New York State Bar slapped him on the wrist with a mild reprimand, and the IRS made a feckless pass at his income taxes, but never could prove that there had ever been any undeclared money. As far as I know, the guy may still be selling babies," Ken said, as he sat down on the arm of the brown sofa. "He may even be working with Garfield, for all we know."

Mary Flower emerged from the kitchen carrying a tray with bagels, several kinds of cream cheese, and a fresh pot of strong coffee.

"I'm the world's foremost skeptic—and even *I* think the idea is fantastic," she said.

"Mary's right," Ken said. "This setup is perfect—it's a classic sting. Stories that have been done before about adoption, like these," Ken said, pointing to the press clips that were now scattered on the coffee table, "the problem with all of them is more about what they don't say. None of them go far enough. The reporters, or their subjects, pulled the plug before the action really got started. About the only thing exposed was the obvious fact that selling babies is something that happens—and the black market makes a lot of money from it. But, hell, that's not news. But *we* have the opportunity to go all the way—not just stating the obvious—that big money is changing hands— but to take the entire journey, and follow the money right to the end.

"Not only do we supply Garfield with a unique and irresistible item to sell, we also give him a perfect buyer. That's the beauty of it—unlike these other stories, we're in control of both sides of the transaction! I love it," Ken said, with the enthusiasm of a kid who just got a new bike. "I've got to hand it to you, this will be one hell of a story— Pulitzer material, if we're lucky and do it right."

Tuck sat silently for a moment. "Personally, Ken, I go back and forth. One minute I think we've built a better mousetrap. Then the next minute, I can't believe he'd be dumb enough to fall for it. You really think he'll bite? The guy is greedy, but he sure as hell isn't dumb."

"Karen, you were there last night. You said he was head over heels for the story, and if he swallowed it then, he'll go for it all the way. I know he will. On Wall Street, they call it the greater fool theory. In this case, it's Max Garfield who will be the greater fool."

"If you'd seen it," Karen said, "he was over the

moon. I've never seen him display that kind of unbridled enthusiasm over anything."

"I hope for all our sakes that you're right," Tuck said. "We do need to make him go through with the entire adoption, all the way—the selling, the delivery, the paperwork, and the final decree with the judge, even to his hiding of the cash—everything. And we'd have to document it very, very carefully, every step of the way. Nothing less will insure the end of Garfield."

"Max is now firmly convinced that a very famous celebrity is the source of my pregnancy. And after all, who could ever prove that it's not. The key to our story's power is that Edmond Calendar's Library of Life actually does exist. Sperm from a bank can, in fact, produce pregnancy. No part of our story is disputable. That's the beauty of the plan. Kevin Tyler may be a little strange, but he's an experienced and highly respected professional in his field. Edmond Calendar really did fund him, and Tyler has enough documentation, as well as an impressive laboratory, to prove it."

Now it was Tuck's turn to pace the small living room. It was nerves—maybe even a bit of healthy paranoia. The scheme was starting to take on a life of its own.

"Here's how I see this thing unfolding," Tuck said. "Ken, you and Mary are the buyers, so we need to have your stories down pat. Ken, you have to get audio on all of it, every meeting, every phone conversation—the whole nine yards, just like the article you talked about. The difference in our case is you guys will have to string along the process beyond the point where Max can pull out. Then it will work. I'm sure of it."

"And we need to go all the way," Mary said.

"Right through to standing up in court. That's the most important part. We need to get Max to formally declare, in front of a judge, his version of how much money he's charging to handle the adoption, which—if the past is prologue—consists of a small portion of his fee. The cover up will be the part he doesn't dare mention, the part about the cash. At that point, he commits perjury. Then it's just a matter of waiting. Once he files his taxes, we take the evidence to the IRS and they nail him for everything from illegally selling babies, to tax evasion and committing perjury."

"What are the legal issues involved when we actually adopt your baby?" Mary said, a look of concern creasing her brow.

"As far as the courts or Max is concerned, the baby will, in fact, be adopted—simply passed from Karen to the two of you. Of course, after taking the baby from Max, it will be with us. In a few months, you'll go through the court appearance and the final decree. At that point, we've pretty much nailed Garfield. When the story comes out, I don't think we'll have any trouble untangling the adoption issue. Unless there's some issue of abuse or question of parental fitness, the birth mother is, with rare exception, the one who gets the baby," Tuck replied, although even he couldn't be certain about the truth in what he was saying.

"That may well be, but what if he decides to haul us into court?"

"I don't think there's a chance in hell that he'd be that crazy. Besides, if he did sue, he'd be taking a chance that all his past transactions—all those fees he conveniently neglected to declare, would be uncovered. I think he would do anything to avoid that. Also, if I remember my law school lessons, there's a long-standing legal doctrine called *in pari delicto*, which could possibly apply—it's a long shot, but just might shield us from any legal retribution."

"What the hell does that mean?" Mary said.

"Simply put, it means that thieves can't sue thieves."

"Oh, that's just great," said Mary, the sour look of skepticism on her face, "very reassuring, really."

"Oh, boy," Ken exclaimed with delight, "this thing just keeps getting better and better. It's the *perfect* sting. The media will eat this story alive. How much do you think Max will try to get for the baby?"

"I don't know," Tuck said. "I've given it a lot of thought and feel confident he'll try for more than the $50,000 he got from the Kaufmans. Who knows? I mean, how many chances does one have to raise a celebrity baby?"

"Ideally, it will be a headline amount," Ken said.

"What is that?"

"Certain numbers make better headlines than others. A '$1 million something or other' sounds better than a '$900,000 something or other,' for instance. It's the kind of number that looks good on magazine covers. This kind of story will make every damned magazine cover and talk show in America. The twists are wild. It will get more space than if that peanut farmer down in Georgia were to end up in the White House."

Chapter 43

Rockefeller Center, New York City

The myth about Prometheus stealing fire from heaven is the subject of a huge golden statue overlooking the ice-skating rink at Rockefeller Center. At rink level, and separated by a wall of glass, is the Promenade Café.

Inside the café, crowded around a small table sat Tuck, Karen, Ken and Mary Flower, and Mark and Helen Kaufman. Their beautiful daughter, Amy Kaufman energetically wriggled and strained, trying to escape from her father's arms, attempting to grab the colorful skaters flashing past just beyond the glass. A popular holiday tune drifted over the diners, and the music combined with the sounds of laughter and scraping ice-skates fused together and filled the café.

Getting the Kaufmans to agree to meet was no small victory. Actually, it was Tuck's call to Helen Kaufman that finally sealed the confab. Tuck's first encounter with the Kaufmans had not gone well. As Tuck was leaving their home, Helen Kaufman had subtly indicated an interest in speaking further, and Tuck had waited for the right time to follow up on her willingness to do so.

A Baby To Die For

A bored, sour-faced waitress served hot chocolate all around. Mark Kaufman started to speak but stopped as Amy's tiny fist jabbed into his mouth, and he laughingly handed the squirming child over to his wife.

"What exactly do you think we can do, Mr. Handler?" Mark asked. "What you're suggesting—trying to stop what you're calling the black market—well, frankly, it sounds farfetched—possibly a bit paranoid, I would think. When we adopted Amy, we just wanted a baby," he shrugged. "There were none to be had through adoption agencies—at least in any reasonable time frame. You know that. You said so yourself that you came up against the same problem. So we asked around and somehow got to Max Garfield. Frankly, if and when we want another baby, we'd go to him again in a heartbeat."

"Amy is bright and beautiful and wonderful," Helen Kaufman added, proudly. "We couldn't love her more under any circumstances. She's ours in all the ways that mean anything. She's part of us. She comes from people much like us, decent, honest people, who could, if our roles were reversed, take and raise a child we might birth. A baby like Amy, parents like us, and the couple who biologically created Amy, we're like interchangeable parts, if you know what I mean."

Tuck forced himself to say nothing. He had told the Kaufmans in very vague terms about their desire to put Max Garfield out of the baby-selling business. He had, however, not mentioned Kevin Tyler, the library, the celebrity-sperm donors, or Karen's pregnancy.

All Tuck had told the Kaufmans was the plan to have Ken and Mary Flower going undercover to do a story about the black market in babies—including Max Garfield's role in the process. There was no benefit in burdening them with any additional information—the plan was simply too crazy, too hard to believe. Hell, Tuck could hardly believe it himself.

Mark Kaufman, taking Tuck's silence to mean he'd surrendered the argument, continued. "This nonsensical idea that you're going to uncover some financial shenanigans by Garfield is the stuff of bad movies. Besides, have you considered it might be you breaking the law by digging into his business and end up with a lawsuit on your hands? Have you thought about that?"

Tuck, digested what Kaufman was saying while watching skaters moving past—a kaleidoscope of colors and a mélange of flashing legs, teetering youngsters, graceful couples, and even a pirouetting Santa Claus. Ken and Mary Flower sat silently, as did Karen. Amy babbled through her limited vocabulary, fascinated by the spectacle of the ice rink. They all waited for Tuck to respond to Kaufman's negative assessment.

Tuck took a sip of hot chocolate, then said, "Look, Mark, for the sake of this conversation, let's assume everything about your adoption through Garfield was on the up and up. Okay? So think of it this way. We are simply trying to blow the whistle on a very pervasive practice that needs to be stopped. You know it exists and the evidence is overwhelming. Maybe what we're trying to do is crazy, but make no mistake, we intend to put a stop to the network, to put an end to the lies told to unsuspecting couples, to put an end to selling babies by the pound to the highest bidder, to put an end to families being forced to lie about how they pay for their babies and then to go to court and perjure themselves when asked about those payments," Tuck said. "If, in the process, we have to cross some legal lines, we're willing to take some chances."

I wonder how the Kaufmans would react to the truth about their baby. About Amy's birth parents.

Everything Pauline had told him in Dallas about the Kaufman baby flooded into his mind and he was torn over what to do—how far to go with the truth.

Will they even believe me?

The Texan, the slave girl, the French Legionnaire, not to mention the lies that led the Kaufmans to believe they were getting some sort of homogenized, Wonder Bread baby. The price for baby Amy had been jacked up to match the laundered story and the Kaufmans had naively swallowed it in the same way a hungry fish grabs at a phony fly. In the same way, ironically, he wanted Garfield to swallow the story about the celebrity baby.

Tuck went back and forth with himself trying to decide whether to tell them the truth.

What is the truth? What the hell difference does it make anyway? Is a nubile blonde college cheerleader guaranteed to produce a more superior human being than a Polish slave girl? Genes and chromosomes are strange and wonderful things. Sometimes whole generations leap over each other like children frog-jumping fire hydrants. Suddenly, a baby from solid, middle class parents could inherit the persona of a long-forgotten horse thief or the moral strengths of a great grandmother or the brilliance of a paternal uncle. Who can say? Who can or even want to speculate?

Before Tuck traveled that road, he wanted to take one more run at convincing the Kaufmans to help.

"Look," Tuck pleaded to Mark and Helen, "We swear no one will ever know you helped. Ken is a reputable journalist. Clearly, the materials he gave you with some of his investigative pieces demonstrate that in spades. When he writes the story he is honor bound and legally protected from ever revealing his sources. We're really not asking you to do very much. All we need is for you both to brief Ken and Mary about what you went through when you adopted Amy. They need to know the details so they can anticipate the questions Max Garfield might ask and avoid any problems, especially the financial details that took place. Like, if he claimed there were other bidders for Amy, and if so, how many did he claim were bidding? That's all we need. It's not a lot to ask. No one will ever know you spoke with us."

"That's all well and good," Helen Kaufman said, her tone now shifting from defensive to probative. "But a few minutes ago, you mentioned something in passing about adoptive families committing perjury. Please explain what you meant."

Tuck sensed this was his chance to cut through the Kaufmans' resistance. Once they realized that they themselves had breached an important legal boundary, they might be fearful enough to cooperate. "You and Mark went to court for the final decree, right?"

"Yes. Just a week ago, as a matter of fact."

"And the judge asked for the financial details of Amy's adoption, right?"

A Baby To Die For

Helen nodded her agreement.

"At that point, did Garfield tell the judge the truth—about all the money you'd given him?"

"Of course he did," Mark said, interrupting, as he placed a hand on his wife's arm.

The gesture spoke a language of its own, telling Helen to say nothing more.

"Come on, Mark," Ken said. "Did Garfield really declare the entire amount? Didn't he leave out the part about the cash you paid?"

At the mention of cash, Helen Kaufman pictured the dusty gas station in New Mexico and the old woman taking the packets of hundred-dollar bills and placing them in the refrigerator. She flushed, and her face answered the journalist's question as clearly as any words could.

Encouraged by her reaction, Tuck pressed further, "The point is, Max Garfield is a crook. He commits perjury as easily as you tell Amy her bedtime stories. And the cash never shows up on his income tax forms either. As for the adoptive families—people just like you—they go along with his lie or risk losing their baby. We really need to stop this man."

"I'm no lawyer, Handler, but this whole thing you're planning doesn't sound kosher to me," Mark said defensively. "It's like entrapment, or something. Garfield has been placing babies for a long time. If he were doing the things you're suggesting, he'd likely be in jail by now, but I don't think what you're claiming would stand up for a minute in court. Besides, I don't feel the same way about Garfield as you do. I've no axe to grind with the man.

What he did for us—getting us Amy—was a blessing."

Tuck decided to ignore Mark Kaufman's feelings about Max Garfield. He'd deal with those later. Instead, he addressed himself to the legal question.

"Whether we can get him hauled into a court of law is really not the point. The idea here is to drape Garfield with a bright red flag, so to speak. Scare off his following, break his grip on the network and, in effect, destroy it for good. Bring the issue to the cover of *Time* and *Newsweek* and *TV Guide*. Splash it all over the TV networks. That'll do more to dismantle his business than any possible courtroom histrionics. With coverage like that, you can bet the politicians won't be far behind with some tough tightening of the adoption laws.

"And worse case, even if we don't succeed in breaking up the network, the publicity sure as hell won't do it any good."

Ken Flower finally broke the silence. Gone was the initial excitement of the meeting. All that remained for Ken was the sure, dispassionate hand of the professional journalist. He spoke firmly, with authority.

"Look, bottom line, we need your help. I've done stories like this before. From the outside, these human-interest things seem so, so delicate, so easy to dismiss as not being worth the candle. I did one on cosmetic surgery, another on rent controls in Manhattan. You know the kind of thing, a reporter pokes around into some seemingly harmless issue that in most cases doesn't harm many people. Yet, in many instances, it's highly beneficial. Well, believe me, Mark, once I start poking around, it can get pretty vicious. I've been threatened and, in one case, damn near killed, over what many call a victimless crime.

"Have you heard that expression? Well, if you want to know how victimless they really are, attack the money. People with rackets like Garfield's can suddenly become very dangerous. You can bet your next surgical fee that Max Garfield will not take to this lightly. If he thought anyone was poking around in his private patch, he would be totally committed to stopping it, regardless of who's doing the poking. He can be a dangerous man. Garfield has millions of dollars at stake. He will not mess around or laugh off any attempt to break him. He can't know or even suspect what's happening. That's why we have to find out as much as possible about what we're getting into. You can help us a lot. You've been through it. All we want you to do is sketch it out for us. Just take it from the beginning. We'll never get you involved other than to explain to Garfield that when my wife, Mary, met you at the hospital, and in the course of conversation mentioned to you that we were having trouble adopting a baby, you referred us to him. You would have no other involvement, no mention in the story—nothing. It will be perfectly harmless, and he'll be a lot less likely to suspect any problem if we come to him through a referral from a satisfied customer."

Again the silence. Tuck had to concentrate to suppress his anger. He put down the water glass he was holding a bit too hard, and everything on the small table rattled a little. Fortunately, the baby was now sleeping soundly.

"Look, we're going to do this with or without you. Even if you don't help, we're going to do it."

A Baby To Die For

Mark Kaufman rose, and Helen followed, gathering up Amy and her accompanying paraphernalia.

"Look, I only agreed to meet because of Helen. She felt sorry for you, but there is no way that we will be involved with this project of yours. I can't tell you any more than what I've said already. It was all very cut-and-dry. Regardless of what you think, we gave no extra cash. For all I know, you're doing a story about us, and all this bullshit is just some sort of smoke screen. I'm sorry—more for you than anyone else. You're sick, Handler. Max Garfield played it straight with us. Maybe we don't owe him a lot, but I think we at least owe him our confidence. He promised us something, and he delivered, fair and square. Goodbye."

Mark Kaufman was a step away from the table when Tuck decided to speak.

"You picked up Amy in New Mexico, right? She was in a Coke cooler, wasn't she?"

The Kaufmans stood frozen.

Mark's voice was barely a whisper: "How the hell could you know about that?"

"It was right outside of Alamogordo, and you gave an old woman the package of cash. She counted it and put it into a refrigerator before you left—$40,000 in hundred-dollar bills. Am I right with the facts, Mark?"

The Kaufmans returned to the table and sat, almost in a trance.

"Go on," Mark said hoarsely, a note of fear in his voice.

Helen Kaufman held Amy more tightly to her chest. She was now sleepily playing with her mother's fur-trimmed coat collar. The wail of an ambulance siren came in, then out, of hearing.

"What else do you know?"

Tuck took a deep breath. It needed to be done.

What the Kaufmans could tell us would help immeasurably. The success of our plan depends on being prepared, knowing the territory. No surprises, those are the watchwords. And in the long run, the Kaufmans are better off knowing the truth. I'd want to know.

"Amy's mother wasn't a college student," Tuck said, his voice barely audible, his face turned down toward the empty cup in front of him.

"What?" Mark asked. "I can't hear you."

"The mother—Amy's mother—she wasn't a student. And her father wasn't a student either."

The Kaufmans sat silently, color draining from their faces.

"Please believe me, it's not that they were anything bad or sick or anything else that would harm Amy, in any way. What I know for certain is that you were lied to and manipulated by Max Garfield. You were used and overcharged. Garfield told you that you were bidding against another couple, right?"

Tuck saw Mark glance quickly at his wife.

"There was no other couple. He became his own shill just to push up the price, the price you would pay, push it to the very outer limits, and then beyond. That's how the network does business. And Garfield is the personification of that stinking system. Do you hear what I am saying? Is this is the person you wish to give your confidence, your loyalty?"

312

A Baby To Die For

Mark cleared his throat, then sipped from a glass of water that was in front of Helen.

"Tell us about her biological parents. The money means nothing now. Believe me, Mr. Handler, Amy was and is worth every penny we spent. No matter what we learn here today, we would do it over again. I just want to know. Closed doors have always bothered me. Who were they?"

Tuck looked around the table, from one face to the next. They were all looking at him. The tension was thick in the air. The sounds of Bing Crosby singing his classic "White Christmas" started and mixed well with the laughter of the skaters. A tall man glided past their window, his young son happily perched on his shoulders, his little hands cupped tightly under his father's chin.

"Amy's father is French. A soldier. A professional."

Mark Kaufman's face tensed.

"An officer," Tuck lied.

At the word *officer*, Mark's face relaxed slightly, and Tuck could read approval in his eyes.

Christ, is this how the lies begin? It was so easy to bend the facts, not for the money but for the parents. I can never tell the Kaufmans the whole truth. What good would it do? Tell them their child's mother was a slave? What would that accomplish? Nothing. Clearly, adoption is based largely on self-fulfilling prophecies. Tell adoptive parents something, and it becomes gospel. Tell them the father was an outstanding baseball player, and they will have a brand-new mitt in the kid's bassinette on day one. Tell them the mom was a ballerina, and as soon as the child can get up on two feet, the tutu arrives and the lessons begin.

313

A Baby To Die For

Tuck looked out at the statue of Prometheus. Bright sunshine burst in all directions off its angled gold surface. A far off pulsing car alarm shrieked in the distance.

"And the mother?" Helen Kaufman asked warily.

Of course, a mother would want to know about the mother.

"He said the mother was Jewish, was she really?"

Tuck felt Karen's hand tense on his leg. The meaning of her gesture was clear. He reached out and stroked the sleeping child's hair.

"Yes, Pauline told me Amy's birth mother was Jewish. Apparently, she's an artist. Polish descent. You can begin to see the bone structure and those wide-set blue eyes. She will be a heart-breaker," Tuck smiled.

It was so easy to make this stuff up—what my mother used to call little white lies.

"A lot richer background than two college kids, don't you think? You can be proud of that."

"We are," Mark Kaufman said, as he shrugged out of his coat, draped it across the back of his chair, and sat down again. "How do you know all this, Handler? You could be the one blowing all the smoke. How would we know?"

"You could be right, but think about it, what do I gain by lying to you? The only reason I know is because a friend confided in me. If you recall, when we had the meeting at your house, I told you I know this lawyer in Dallas—Rick Shelby. Garfield got Amy from Shelby. You could have picked her up in Dallas but Garfield wanted to add a bit of theater to your adoption process. I know Rick Shelby from when he and his wife lived here. We were all close friends. Rick is deeply involved in Garfield's network, and he told his wife everything about Amy's adoption. And about many other adoptions, as well as details about how he and Garfield worked together.

"Pauline—that's Rick's soon to be ex-wife—when she learned about the kind of law he was practicing, she gave him an ultimatum: either stop, or leave. Rick decided he wanted the practice and, most important—at least, to him—the fruits of the practice, more than he wanted to be married to Pauline, so they split up. I was in Dallas, and Pauline told me everything. That's how I learned about Amy's adoption.

"Of course, it was very indiscreet and stupid of Rick to tell his wife all these things. Max Garfield would never make a mistake like that. He's far too cautious and way too smart. That's why we need your help, Mark, especially because Garfield *is* so smart and cautious, and we can't afford to make any mistakes. Your input will be invaluable."

Mark thought for a moment. He looked at Amy and Helen. She held the now sleeping child close, her lips absently brushing Amy's soft, flushed cheek.

"We didn't start out going to Max Garfield," Mark began, "That only happened after we'd been blown off by all those adoption agencies. Once we heard how long we'd have to wait for a baby that met our list of—I guess you'd call them, requirements—we had a choice. It was wait for years or lower our standards, the latter being something we weren't willing to do. At one of the last agencies we met with, there was a very compassionate and sympathetic social worker. She's the one who surreptitiously slipped us Max Garfield's name and phone number. After that ..."

For the next half hour, Mark and Helen Kaufman told their story, leaving nothing out. Lots of questions flew back and forth. Most were answered. Ken Flower took detailed notes. And through it all, Amy Kaufman slept peacefully in her mother's arms.

Chapter 44

It was one day shy of three weeks since their meeting with the Kaufmans when Ken and Mary entered Garfield's outer office. They gave their names to the secretary and moments later were warmly greeted by the lawyer and shown into his office.

The appointment with the Garfield was easily arranged and after the initial call, they were sent a short form asking basic demographic questions, which they completed and returned to lawyer's office.

Preparation for the meeting had taken quite a bit of time and effort. In addition to the detailed planning sessions, Ken and Mary posed as prospective adoptive parents, and went through interviews with several adoption agencies around the city. As the Kaufmans had warned, and Tuck experienced firsthand, the Flowers quickly learned that it could be years before they could expect to get a Caucasian baby because, as they were told again and again, "there is a dearth of those particular infants."

Finally, when they felt sufficiently prepared, they arranged their appointment with Max Garfield.

A Baby To Die For

Both were a bit anxious, but confident. Their parts had been meticulously planned and, thanks to some extravagant shopping, they presented the perfect picture of an affluent, well-turned-out couple.

Mary Flower allowed herself a few moments to study Garfield's large office. What she saw was a comfortable, professional, and tastefully furnished space——more like a wood-paneled, book-filled den, arranged in three distinct areas. Garfield sat behind a huge, highly polished desk. The Flowers sat opposite on two side chairs. In the far corner of the office was a more formal meeting space, with six chairs surrounding an oval conference table. At the opposite end of the room a couch and two overstuffed chairs were arranged around a stone-top coffee table. A hint of Scott's Liquid Gold hung in the air. Mary was impressed and certain that any couple coming to Garfield would feel the same.

What was the old saying—there's never a second chance to make a first impression?

But what totally fascinated and intrigued her was Garfield's collection of baby rattles. There were dozens of them.

Max Garfield examined the young couple sitting across from him, and like a seasoned salesman sizing up a prospect, he was pleased with what he saw.

Without doubt, this is an attractive couple. Conservative, yet expensive clothing. No overt ostentation. Watches—both *Rolexes*—tastefully understated in *stainless steel not gold. And good haircuts, always a reliable sign of affluence. Yes, this couple is just my of tea. If I'm right, the Flowers will result in a very profitable placement.*

"I'm very happy to meet you both," Max said, enthusiastically. "When I spoke to Dr. Kaufman, he was most complimentary."

"Well, either he has great taste, or bad judgment," Ken said, "We're here today so that you can find out for yourself, Mr. Garfield."

"Touché. Good point, but, please, call me Max," he said, as his hands absently made subtle adjustments to the very few items on his pristine desk top, then came to rest, clasped in front of him. "Well now, before we start our journey, which let's hope will lead to your successfully adopting a baby, I always like to learn as much as I can about the folks who come to me—sort of a view of Ken and Mary Flowers from 30,000 feet, so to speak. But please, no pressure. This is not a test, nothing like that. Whatever you tell me—which, by the way, is in total confidence—just helps me to better understand who you are and what kind of baby you might be interested in. So, feel free to, you know, just ramble on, stream of consciousness, so to speak," Max concluded, flashing a broad smile. "I'm an excellent listener."

"Okay, but before we bare our souls, Mr. Garfield—Max—I am dying to know the story behind all these rattles?" Mary said, looking around the room.

"Ah, yes," Garfield laughed, "my collection. I may be the only man in America with a baby rattle collection. And, I might add, I'm real proud of each and every one. Years ago, back when I first started doing adoption work,

A Baby To Die For

a couple I helped get their baby gave me this one," Max said, picking up what was obviously an antique—the only one that he kept on his desk. "It's silver and, you see, it's engraved: 'Baby Nathaniel, 29 August, 1834,'" Max said and handed Mary the Rattle. "Soon a second couple gave me one, and, as any avid collector will tell you, a second of anything starts a new collection. It's turned into a tradition."

"Well, Max, I hope we will have the chance to add to your collection," Mary said.

Max just smiled an uncommitted smile.

For the next fifteen minutes, the Flowers did as Max requested, sticking to the script as planned, staying as close to their real-life backgrounds as possible, knowing there was always the real risk that Garfield would have them checked out. The only area where they bent the truth was about their fertility and their finances. They started with a phony story about how Ken was unable to have children, the result of a bad bout of chicken pox suffered while in college, which left him sterile. Then Ken described how he had graduated from Northwestern hoping to be a novelist —true—and then added the details of his father's sudden death—also true—and how, as a result, he and his sister now enjoyed a very large inheritance—a very big lie—which he now managed, along with the help of financial advisors, leaving him free to feed his appetite for creativity and personal fulfillment by working as a freelance journalist—true).

"Thank God, we don't need to live off what I earn from my writing," Ken said, trying mightily to sound self-depreciating while keeping a straight face.

A Baby To Die For

Then Mary related her background, substituting a scenario more fanciful than truthful. In reality, she had worked like a dog to get through pre-med and medical school, doing everything from waiting tables to temp office work and house cleaning.

By the time they finished, Max Garfield was noticeably impressed. As the interview progressed, Max became more and more convinced that this couple could easily afford an above-average placement, and certainly they'd be as lucrative for him as their friends the Kaufmans had been.

"And as I said before," Ken continued, "Mary will finish her residency early next year. Thankfully, her hours will be a lot less hectic, and she'll be in a much better position to have more regular work hours. Of course, we'd have a live-in nanny caring for the baby, as well."

"Frankly, Ken, concerns like that are less valid than they were years ago," Max said. "If you know what I mean. So many women are professionals these days that the traditional concept of the hausfrau has gone out the window. I wouldn't worry about how much Mary is working. The quality of the time spent with a child counts the most, not the quantity."

Ken and Mary smiled in agreement.

"You said you were investing full-time, is that right?" Max asked.

"That's a bit of an exaggeration since we have a small firm of excellent financial advisors doing most of the work. I meet fairly regularly with them, but most of the time I let those guys take care of the money thing. The bulk of my time is spent writing. That's the job I really love. The setup I have offers me the opportunity to pick my journalistic assignments carefully and only take those that interest me."

"Picking and choosing, that's a real gift. I think it was Confucius who said, if you have a job you love, you won't have to work a day in your life."

"Sounds right to me," Ken said. "Mary and I inherited some real estate, as well. In Arizona and California. I need to travel occasionally to keep an eye on that but have been able to work it into one or two of my assignments. Actually, Mary and I have a rather easy time of it."

"You're a fortunate young couple, indeed," Max said, smiling.

"Yes, we're well aware of that. Thanks to my dad working his butt off for almost a half century, we've been left very independent and very comfortable."

"You said you had been to several adoption agencies. No luck, I gather?"

"That would be an understatement," Ken said with disgust. "Luck doesn't seem to have anything to do with the reception we got. It was more about getting a painful lesson in supply and demand. The waiting list for a Caucasian baby is outrageous. We were told again and again, and in no uncertain terms, that it could be years before we got a baby. Frankly, we're not accustomed to waiting. So, if that sounds a bit elitist—I guess it is."

Max rose and walked to the window. With a finger, he pushed aside the sheer fabric of the drape a few inches and looked south, down Park Avenue, then returned behind his desk. He didn't sit again, just stood leaning forward with his fists planted on the polished surface, facing Ken and Mary.

"Yes, it is elitist, Ken. And you've every right to feel that way. You've heard the expression, 'beyond the pale'?"

The Flowers shrugged.

"Well, in Old English, a pale meant a stick. A bunch of them formed a fence or palisade. Pales were put up to create an enclosure to confine animals and sometimes even people. Those permitted outside, or who had escaped, were considered to be 'beyond the pale.'

"Adoption is a lot like that. Inside the pale, people can wait years for a baby. Beyond the pale, they don't. It's that simple. If wanting to be outside that reality is being an elitist, then so be it. What you heard from the agencies is correct. The supply is very thin. Nevertheless, I've had some luck helping people get the wonderful babies they want, without the inordinate amount of waiting time."

"And that's exactly why we're here, Max, in this case we'd like to be beyond the pale," Ken said.

Garfield flipped open a file on his desk. "Now, let's see—you were referred by the Kaufmans, correct?"

"Yes, that's right. I know Mark, Dr. Kaufman, from the hospital. As you know, Mark is a surgeon and I did a rotation through his unit. The four of us are friendly and get together socially every so often. We've seen their baby. Amy is quite special. Absolutely beautiful."

"Yes, I recall the Kaufmans," Max said, reflecting. He closed his eyes and leaned his head against the leather chair back and said, "Let's see, they went all the way out west for the baby. I remember that now. Lovely child. Good blood lines. Jet-black hair. "

"Blonde with black eyes. You must have her confused with another child."

Max wasn't confused. He was just making sure. A few phone calls would not be out of place. After all, one could never be too safe.

"Of course, blonde. I remember now. I do a fair number of placements, and it does get confusing at times."

Ken cleared his throat and looked at Garfield full on, "I imagine everyone says what I'm about to say, but we don't want an ordinary child. I know that sounds conceited—and you probably hear it all the time—but it's true. We honestly feel we can handle one that's well above average, and we're willing to pay the price. As I said, money is really not the issue, within reason, of course. It's time we're more concerned about. We are not willing to wait. We're both highly educated and talented, and we don't want a baby that's anything less."

"Do you feel guilty about those feelings?" Max asked.

Ken and Mary paused, looked at each other, and then Ken spoke.

"Maybe a little bit. Not much. Come to think of it, hardly at all," he said, laughing.

"Good, good. Believe me, it's a normal, healthy attitude. I handle a lot of situations and most of the clients I get in here are—let's just say, they're not run-of-mill people. They have to be just to afford my prices," Max smiled, but his eyes looked as dead as those of a shark.

Ken and Mary Flower had trouble maintaining a serious face while Max delivered his little speech then, holding back a smile, Ken answered, matching Max's serious tone, "I can see you understand us completely, Max. We are definitely singing from the same hymnbook. But let's get down to some specifics. Given what we are looking for, how long will it take to get a baby, and how much might we expect to pay?"

Before Max could answer, Mary interrupted.

"When we spoke to the Kaufmans, they were very circumspect about what they paid for Amy, but if I had to hazard a pure guess, I'd say it ran somewhere between $30,000 and $40,000. Would I be too far wrong?"

"I must stress right up front, any details from my other clients' adoptions are strictly confidential. I'm sure you can understand. As to the timing, it depends on what is available. Fortunately, we work with a broad network of sources. But you can imagine, a lot depends on the child you pick and where its mother is on her gestation path. I'd say the average time is—give or take a few months— ironically about nine months," Max smiled.

Ken and Mary laughed on cue.

"As for the Kaufmans' financial arrangements, I'm really not at liberty to reveal those details. As a doctor you can understand, Mary. It's a lot like doctor/patient confidentiality. The financial information is off-limits. Besides, every adoption is completely different. Each has its own set of financial circumstances. Let's just say, generally speaking and given what you've told me, it will not be prohibitively expensive. Of course, the very gifted babies are more rare and, you can understand, very popular. The prices are arrived at by simple supply and demand. The American way, right?" Max once again curled his mouth into his shark smile. "And also, with a better class of baby, the birth mother expects more for what she is going through. Her tastes are more expensive. She demands better medical care, better housing—things like that. I am simply the middleman. All I can hope to do is make both parties happy. There is no price list for happiness. What the Kaufmans paid—or any of my other clients, for that matter—will have little or no bearing on what you will have to pay for your baby. I will, as your lawyer, do my best to keep that amount to a minimum. You can trust me on that, but there is a price and value relationship that will come into play."

Ken and Mary sat silently for a moment, contemplating what Max had said. The tape recorder made a tiny growling sound, a gentle reminder to Ken that he was on assignment.

He coughed, cleared his throat, and then quickly asked, "Talk a little more about how long you think we'd have to wait for a baby?"

Max was just about to launch into a discussion about EC-9 when he suddenly changed his mind and allowed the words to die, unspoken. The timing wasn't quite right and, regardless of his first impression, he needed to be absolutely positive the couple sitting across from him really had the wherewithal to pay the kind of price he felt EC-9 would command. Worst case, the Flowers would be good for a very profitable placement.

So, instead of bringing up the subject of EC-9, Max said, "Well, as you can understand, we don't have a stock of babies sitting on a shelf," he said, hand gesturing toward an imaginary shelf. "But luckily, we've quite a number of women who at the moment are in various stages of their pregnancies, having anywhere from three to eight months to go. And, of course, they're all committed to releasing their babies for adoption. One of the situations just might work out fine for you. Just give me a minute to get my files and you can take a look through them and see if any strike your fancy. Meanwhile, how about some refreshments? Some coffee? A soft drink? Anything stronger?"

A half hour went by, with Max watching carefully the whole time while his new clients took a test drive with the merchandise. The coffee carafe on Garfield's conference table was almost empty. The assortment of cookies remained untouched. A number of manila file folders were stacked between Mary and Ken on the table's mahogany surface. Each file held information about the biological parents of a soon-to-be-available baby. There were numerous pictures of the birth mother and sometimes—but rarely— of the father. Also included were their familial, social, religious and medical history, plus any other relevant information. What the files did not contain was any information about the identity or location of the biological parents.

Mary and Ken carefully studied each file. Garfield sat at the end of the conference table, sipped coffee and watched—always the alert salesman. Meanwhile, in the outer office, his secretary had almost completed verifying all the information sent to her by the Flowers. One more call and she would have all the information her boss needed to decide whether or not to expose this particular couple to Karen's special baby, EC-9, or to simply treat them as any other client and just get them a baby. And the answer to that question would depend on his instincts and, to a great extent, the outcome of those phone calls.

In fact, the files the Flowers were so carefully reviewing were 'placebos.' In other words, they were all closed files that originally had come from any number of Garfield's sources—lawyers from around the country, like Rick Shelby, a few choice prospects from Toby Wine in Washington, and still others from his abortion clinics. In every case the mothers had already given birth and theirs babies had been adopted. The purpose of these placebo files was to see how the Flowers would react. It was simply a way to test their judgment. He'd incorporated this technique after a shopping experience he had with Porter at a Seventh Avenue furrier. At first, the salesman brought out some very attractive coats—not his best but good, certainly good enough to test the waters, a way to "calibrate" his customer. But when Porter rejected the coats, displaying a surprisingly sophisticated knowledge of furs, the man quickly went to his vaults and produced his finest coats, each with exquisitely matched and thinly cut pelts. Porter left the store with one of the most expensive garments the man had in stock.

The coat cost Max plenty, but the lesson he learned was priceless and did not go to waste. He knew this situation wasn't very different from his fur-coat experience. He was showing the couple reasonable candidates, but certainly not the best he had, nor anywhere close to the quality of EC-9. He smiled, sipping his coffee, watching Ken and

A Baby To Die For

Mary Flowers examining the files, and waited to hear from Isabel, his secretary, about the outcome of several calls she was making. He had to keep reminding himself that this adoption was just like any another. Regardless of how special EC-9 was, when you boiled it all down, it was just another baby. Even so, Max was feeling a level of excitement he'd never experienced before. He hoped the inquiry Isabel was making would produce the answers he wanted to hear.

Ken Flower didn't have the slightest notion of what he was looking at or looking for. Nevertheless, knowing Max was watching, he knitted his brow in a simulation of concentration as he read through the information contained in each folder. Most were fairly similar and, of course, without pictures of the not-yet-born babies. The background details in each folder all started to look alike.

What the fuck's the difference? After all, wildly successful people can climb out of parental gutters, and real dirt-bags can emerge from the most privileged upbringing. But this was Garfield's game, and we have to play it moving through the process at the lawyer's pace.

So he read on. Occasionally, he pointed out an item or two to Mary, acting excited or skeptical or cynical but trying as much as possible to verbalize his thoughts and reactions in order to feed their conversation into his concealed recorder.

Ken had no doubt that Max would eventually present them with Karen's baby. As a prospective couple, they had fashioned themselves into a target simply too tasty for the greedy lawyer to ignore. But Ken calculated that Max was too smart to ever reduce potentially explosive details of EC-9 into a folder. It would be too risky. Ken was convinced that Max would make that offer verbally.

Before today's meeting, Mary had expressed some concern that the baby might have been offered to someone already. But Karen assured her that none of Max's clients had had any detailed exposure to EC-9. The only exception had been a heavily veiled discussion with one couple, but it was quickly determined that they had zero ability to ever come up with the kind of cash needed to buy such a baby.

With a dramatic sigh, Mary Flower threw down the last folder from her pile, freshened her coffee, and nibbled at a butter cookie. Ken stared at his final folder for a minute more—just for effect—then followed suit.

Just as Max saw the Flowers were finished and started to speak, his office intercom interrupted. Leaving the couch, he walked to his desk phone. "Yes, Isabel?"

Max maintained a neutral expression as his secretary reported on the results of several phone inquiries Max had instructed her to make.

"*I spoke with the hospital, Mr. Garfield, and was told that Dr. Flower was out on a personal matter. As you instructed, I said I wasn't sure if I had the right Dr. Flower and described her. They confirmed it was indeed her, and assured me she was the only Dr. Flower working at the hospital. The Flowers are listed with the phone company at the address given. Oh, yes, yesterday I reached Dr. Kaufman at his office, and he confirmed referring the Flowers to us and—uh, let's see—Northwestern University finally got back to me, and Mr. Flower is listed as an alumnus* and graduated the year he indicated. Dr. Flower attended undergraduate and medical school exactly as she indicated. I reached Mr. Bootman, the Flowers' financial advisor and he would not give me any specific information but did note that if the Flowers want to buy a Jet that we should feel comfortable taking a check. He was actually very funny. Is there anyone else you wish me to check with, Mr. Garfield?"

"No, that'll be just fine, Isabel. Thank you. Thank you very much. And please, hold all my calls."

Max returned to the sofa and sat down. He was now an extremely happy and very confident man.

Before the lawyer could speak, Ken said, "Look, Max, there are some interesting choices here but to be blunt about it, I don't know. Maybe this will sound foolish, but while these files describe perfectly acceptable young birth parents, they all seem kind of . . . bush league, if you know what I mean. We're looking for more than some high school kid who got knocked up by the captain of the football team. Please, Max, some class, that's what we're looking for."

"Ken is right," Mary added strongly. "He's a journalist and I'm a doctor. After all, Max—any child of ours is going to have to keep intellectual pace with both of us, like it or not. That's just the way it is. If the child can't do that—doesn't have the potential to do that—it's going to be an uncomfortable situation for all concerned. I think you understand what I mean, Max—don't you?"

Max answered wordlessly, with pursed lips, nodding head, and grim expression.

God, I would have been a wonderful actor.

A Baby To Die For

Mary Flower felt as though she were going to throw up as each word left her mouth. She wondered how Max Garfield could swallow the pretentious slop she and Ken were chumming with. But he was completely attentive and seemed to take in every word. Clearly, Max was as susceptible to believing what he wanted to hear, as were the young couples that swallowed the lies he dished out.

Max got up from the conference table. He looked serious as he walked slowly to the broad expanse of drape-covered windows and pressed the button on a wall-mounted plate. The drapes slid open with a barely perceptible hum, revealing Park Avenue, looking south. It was a clear day, and the view was breathtaking. The southern tip of Manhattan pointed like a finger, and the crush of buildings that was the financial district bunched up around the twin towers of the new World Trade Center. Sun reflected like bright confetti off the bridges, turning the river into a carpet of shimmering silver. An L-1011 TriStar banked slowly, moving north up the side of the island, using the East River as a guideline, then banked east, for its final approach into LaGuardia.

Max just stood quietly, eyes squinting against the glare, lips pursed in thought, his thumbs hooked into the pockets of his vest.

This is the difficult part.

He struggled with the question of how to tell them about EC-9 without sounding insane. He tried to keep in mind that it was really just another situation. True, it was a little better, a little more lucrative, and a little more risky, but the Flowers seemed okay, better than okay—perfect.

And no matter how picky and sophisticated they tried to sound, the bottom line was they wanted a baby, and they wanted one that could meet their wildly unreasonable expectations. The wanted a solid platinum, diamond-encrusted Rolex baby! A Mercedes stretch-limo baby! A Tiffany diamond-necklace baby!

Max remained at the window, gazing into the distance, looking a bit like a ship's figurehead or a fancy hood ornament. Ken and Mary Flower exchanged quick, nervous glances back and forth. Each silently hoped that Garfield's next gambit would expose them to Karen's baby. They had set themselves up to be taken by Max. So why not? Hell, the man was in the business of selling babies, and they were there to buy one.

Garfield's mind was calculating wildly, and he had to force himself to pull away from the mesmerizing view.

Okay, they want special? They want expensive? Well, by God, Max Garfield will give them special and give them expensive. So special and so expensive it will knock their damned socks off. So fuck it! Here goes nothing!

Max went to the conference table, sat across from Ken and Mary, and said, in a voice barely above a whisper, "There is one possibility. Something so very, very special that I hesitate to even mention it—at least, not without certain ground rules regarding confidentiality."

"Look, Max, if you want, we'll sign one of those nondisclosure things," Ken said, attempting to match Max's serious demeanor.

"That won't be necessary, but you must promise that what I am going to tell you will never leave this room—under any circumstances. Is that agreed?"

A Baby To Die For

"Of course, agreed," Ken lied.

Mary nodded, also lying.

Max took a deep breath.

"Are you familiar with the name Edmond Calendar?"

Chapter 45

Hotel Kitano, New York City

"Max, how could you fucking do this to me? I'm not some little snot-nosed secretary. I run this goddamned operation! How the fuck can I trust you? Do you understand how far out of fucking line you are on this?"

Porter was fairly shaking with rage and was near hyperventilating from her furious tirade. She was standing in the doorway of the small bath area, just off the shower room of the Japanese-style suite. Max, in water up to his shoulders in the steaming teak soaking tub, looked at Porter as if she were some sort of insect.

He'd seen her angry before but never quite so upset as this.

The bitch! It served her right.

A little payback for secretly skimming cash, and now, when he's about to negotiate the major score of his career, she's right there ready to blow up the entire deal. Max closed his eyes and let his head lean back on the wooden rim of the round tub. The hot water was draining the tension out of his body, and he felt good. Maybe he no longer even needed Porter. If the deal with the Flowers came off, plus the prospect of future placements of similar quality, he could end up making more damned cash than he ever did. Three or four deals a year using sperm from the Edmond Calendar's Library of Life, and he'd have more than enough to live very well indeed. He might eventually be in a financial position to walk away from all the support arrangements he was dealing with like the abortion clinics and referral payments he was now supporting. Kevin Tyler's lab was all he needed to maintain a small but very high quality supply of valuable product. When the sale of EC-9 proved the viability of the arrangement, he would dump the expensive overhead and Porter could take a flying fuck.

The idea that Max was not reacting—but was casually soaking in the hot water and not arguing or defending himself from Porter's wild fulminations—only served to further infuriate her.

"Listen to me, damn it, Max!" Porter screamed, her face crimson and spotted from anger.

Max hated to be pressed and Porter was pressing very hard. Max rose up out of the tub very slowly, grabbed the thick, terry cloth robe, and pulled it around his body. The softness of it felt good against his wet skin. He leaned toward Porter, still with a half-smile on his lips, and bringing his open hand up from his side, slapped her hard across the face. Porter's eyes went round in shock and a tiny bulb of blood formed on her lip where the sharp edge of a tooth had punctured the skin. Max's hand only stopped for an instant before it swept back the other way, catching Porter full on the other side of her face. More blood sprang from her nose, and her right eye would doubtless soon sport a wicked hematoma.

He brushed past her even as she began to wail. He went to the bathroom and ran hot water on a washcloth. Then he picked up the small teacup and filled it from the pot that rested on a hot plate and took it back to Porter. She was on the floor and her face was a mess. She was crying and choking on her own fury, almost convulsing. Blood and mucus ran out of her nose, and the blood from her lip had been smeared over half her face. The area around her right eye had already started to go dark as blood from tiny broken vessels collected under the skin. By some miracle of self-preservation, Porter resisted fighting back. She knew to do so would bring an end to her relationship with Max—and an end to the money.

So she forced herself to allow Max to put his arm around her shoulder as he dropped down on the straw mat next to her. He tenderly wiped the blood from her face, then pushed the porcelain cup of hot tea past her objecting hands until she reluctantly sipped it. It seemed to calm her slightly. Max spoke slowly and softly, in a tone that was soothing, almost hypnotic, and gradually Porter's sobbing subsided somewhat, her breathing moderating.

"Porter, listen to me. Can you hear me? Nod, so I know."

He waited for her head to move.

"Good. I want to tell you something, so listen to me very carefully, okay? I don't work for you. Do you understand what I'm saying? You work for *me*. Is that clear? You work for *me*. Don't ever contradict what I do or say. This deal I'm doing is a good thing. You were not around when I was negotiating, and even if you were, there are decisions I make on my own. You've not been a good girl, Porter. You've not conducted yourself in a trustworthy fashion, so why should I worry about consulting with you? Do you understand what I'm saying? Do you understand what I mean?"

Again, Max waited for the head to move with an answer. Finally, it did, this time shaking from side to side.

"You don't know what I'm referring to? Really?"

Again, Porter's head shook.

"Okay, let me try a few things out on you. You're stealing from me, Porter."

Porter's eyes went wide with fear.

"Yes, darling, I know all about your little deals with Ms. LaFrance and Toby Wine, the psychic nutcase down in Washington. I know about those things. I know also that you've got little kickback arrangements set up with half the lawyers in the network, not to mention what you grab out of the abortion clinics. I have to give you credit. You have yourself a tidy little deal."

Porter started to object, but Max stopped her by putting his finger to her bruised lips.

"Please, don't take me for a fool. Don't insult my intelligence by clinging to the lies, Porter. I've known about it all along, but I never stopped you. I could have, anytime I wanted, I could have stopped you. So why didn't I? Because I liked how you pulled this operation together for me. It was worth it, you know. You made some extra bucks, so I figured that was okay because you were incentivized and worked harder, and I made more money in the process, get it? I could deal with that."

Max took Porter's bruised jaw in his strong hand and began to squeeze as he spoke.

"But now, you're doing something besides stealing, You're trying to run my business." He squeezed a little harder. "And believe me, darling, you have it all ass backward, because *I* run the show, not you." Porter could feel his fingernails embedding into her flesh. "Just because I put you on third base, don't kid yourself into thinking you hit a triple. I chose to make this arrangement with my little sister and Dr. Tyler, and you don't have a damned thing to say about it, one way or the other." The pressure increased. "Am I clear?"

Porter's eyes were watering with the excruciating pain from his tight grip on her jaw, but she knew she dared not strike back. She knew Max too well for that. She knew that he could hurt her physically and even more so financially. She had to play it very carefully. This would pass and when it did, she would figure out how to wedge herself into Max's new arrangement to make even more money.

"Do you understand what I'm saying, Porter? If you do, darling, just make a sign. You don't even have to open your bruised little lips."

Max's face reflected the joy he felt in this little episode—this demonstration of his power over another human being.

"A sign, darling. Let Max know that you'll keep your

fucking nose out of his business except when and where he tells you it's okay to put it?"

Max wants a sign. I'll give him a sign all right—a big fat sign, along with an unspoken guarantee that this black eye and my bleeding lip will cost him more than he will ever know. If he wants a sign of who is in charge, I'll give him one in flashing neon.

And with that decision, Porter reached down slowly, pushed Max's robe open with her hand, and continued until his penis was gently circled. Her fingers were still warm from the teacup, and she stroked him slowly and gently until he began to respond and swell. Without taking her eyes from his, she let herself roll back and under him, and his weight parted her legs. She poured what was left of the warm tea between her legs, and his hard penis slid easily inside. She could feel he was excited and on the edge of his orgasm, and she took her index finger and licked it, letting her spittle and blood make it very wet, then she reached up behind him, and gently and deeply, inserted her finger.

Max exploded in violent orgasm and Porter quickly followed. And then, she knew for certain that she was still in charge and that everything would be just fine.

Chapter 46

"I thought I was prepared to hear the actual number, but I was wrong. I wasn't ready at all and, truthfully, it shocked the crap out of me!" Mary said.

The four of them were seated around a small table in a quiet dark corner of a bar on upper Broadway. Ken and Mary were briefing Tuck and Karen on their morning meeting with Max.

"I think I was more nervous than you were. Last week when I overheard Isabel arranging your appointment, I found an excuse to be out of the office today. I was afraid I'd blow the whole deal if I was around when you guys came in," Karen said.

Ken sipped the last of his drink and signaled the waitress for another round.

"Mary's right, it was damned hard to keep a straight face when he started talking money. I mean the $75,000 just tripped off his tongue as sweet as honey. Has he mentioned any of this to you?" Ken asked, addressing Karen.

"No, not a word. He said he didn't want me involved in the negotiations in any way, shape, or form. I'm just the pot of gold, and Max is the rainbow."

"And a cute little pot, at that," Tuck said, giving Karen a kiss. "Getting back to the money, all this was my idea so it's only right that I assume the financial risk. I have the money we put away for the adoption, plus the life insurance from the policy Ellen's company gives all their executives. But that total isn't quite enough to cover what he's asking. We'll still be short."

The drinks arrived and no one said anything until they were served and the waitress had retreated.

Ken spoke up, "Mary and I have some savings," he said, looking to Mary for her reaction, which was an affirmative nod.

"I appreciate that, Ken—I really do, but I can't ask you to put any money into this. It's just too risky," Tuck said, shaking his head, "it's enough you guys are putting the sweat equity."

"Okay, so what if we make it a loan, a signed note, everything all neat and legal? Frankly, I don't see us losing any money. If we can nail Max on this, and the story is as powerful as I believe it will be, we'll be making plenty. I believe we'll get the money back and then some. I'm really not worried."

Tuck looked at Karen who, after a moment, indicated she was in agreement.

"Okay, but only on the condition that it's a legit loan—and you will get it back, one way or another. I promise."

Karen, who was quietly sipping her iced tea, finally spoke up, "I've been working around Max for a long time,

A Baby To Die For

and I know damned well he never sells a baby for the first amount he asks for. We can try to play games with him and kid ourselves, right? But in the end, it's not a matter of *if* he will ask for more, just *when*, and how much more he'll try to get. If we're not prepared for that, we can forget about the adoption and the story."

"Karen's right," Ken said. We need to find a way to access at least another $25,000, maybe more."

They sat quietly sipping their drinks. Finally, Tuck spoke.

"Okay, we need to find a way to line up more cash. But right now, we need to get back to Max with an answer. Are we agreed? Ken will call Max and tell him it's a deal at $75,000, okay?"

"But with a caveat," Karen added. "I don't think we should be that anxious to accept. If he thinks we're too eager, you can be sure he'll ask for more. I'd rather show him a bit of leg before we totally disrobe—something like 'yeah, we really want to go forward, but Mary isn't completely on board, et cetera, et cetera'—that sort of thing. Let him hear a yes, but with a few alarm bells going off on your part," Karen said.

Chapter 47

Gramercy Park, New York City

Even in winter, with its bare elm trees and some of the plantings dormant, the gated oasis in Gramercy Park was lovely compared to any concrete-paved alternative.

Max Garfield strolled the twenty-five blocks from his office in the Pan Am building to meet Ken Flower at his club for lunch. It was an invigorating walk, though damned cold. Max reasoned the exercise would do him good and, besides, it gave him time to figure out how and when to give Ken the bad news.

The two men enjoyed a long lunch at the historical Players Club and then decided to walk off the meal and wine with a stroll around Gramercy Park, which was across the street from the club. They walked close together like old friends and chatted casually, hunched against the bitter cold in the bright February sun. White puffs of condensation surrounded their words, which were simultaneously—albeit surreptitiously—captured by the tape recorder tucked in Ken's pocket. Its microphone, not much larger than the tip of a wooden match, peeked out from under his jacket collar. An occasional low growl came from the machine's barely audible little motor. Ken had become so accustomed to the sound during his meetings with Max Garfield that he no longer noticed it.

"Thanks for lunch, Ken. It's a lovely club," Max said.

Ken responded while looking straight ahead. "Look, Max, I know you're hot to have a firm answer, and believe me, you will get it. In the week since you told us about the baby, about its—you know—incredible background, Mary and I have discussed nothing else. We agree it's an opportunity of a lifetime. But Lord knows, it's not the easiest decision we've ever had to make."

"I understand. I really do," Max said, shivering and wishing he'd taken Ken's offer of a brandy after dessert.

"Good. It helps that you understand," Ken said.

The men fell silent. Finally, Ken continued.

"To be honest, Mary is the holdup. She's a tiny bit less convinced than I am. Don't get me wrong, Max. She's not against it, mind you, just a bit less convinced. I can't get her to put into words exactly what's bothering her. Obviously, the baby's background is beyond question. But Mary can be stubborn. Maybe it's her medical training, but she does tend to circle a problem until she's totally satisfied with the solution, you know. Anyway, it's been a struggle to get her final commitment. But I think I'll have a solid yes in a day or two."

Max placed a reassuring hand on Ken's arm.

"You can be honest with me, Ken, is it the money? I know you said from the very beginning that it wasn't, but let's face it, $75,000 is not small change."

A Baby To Die For

"No, no, that isn't it at all, Max. Really. Money has nothing to do with it."

"But Mary does have doubts, right? And there's always a chance—I mean, it's possible for her answer, when it does finally come, to be negative, am I correct?" Max asked, trying to sound concerned but not too anxious.

"I told you she has doubts, and yes, I guess a negative answer is a tiny possibility. But, I'm ninety-nine percent confident that by next week we'll be moving full steam ahead."

Max nodded, then raised his shoulders to get his neck as far down into his collar as he could and away from the cold.

Ken broke the silence. "You know what excites us, Max? Raising a baby fathered by someone so famous—and, therefore, the half-brother or sister to so many incredible and accomplished people. Their scholarship! Their accomplishments! Good lord, with antecedents like that, what an incredible child it will be!"

"Yes, it's quite a prospect, Ken—but, please—try not to get ahead of yourself. Certainly, there's an outstanding genealogy, to be sure, but try not to extrapolate too much. In the end, it is just a baby—special, to be sure—but in the end—" Max's voice trailed off.

"Are you kidding, Max? The baby will be...I don't have the words to express how lucky we would be to have it. I know Mary will come around. I just know it."

"You're right, but do yourself a favor and don't order any champagne just yet," Max said, chuckling.

Max was trying his best to manage Ken's expectations

down a bit since, albeit counterintuitive, experience had shown that in certain instances by doing that, a prospect does their own 'selling' rather than Max's having to do it.

Ken fell silent, thinking, shaking his head from side to side in wonderment. He placed his arm across Max's shoulder and spoke in a low, even tone.

"I'd say that baby is going to be a shade above the average, my friend—that's exactly why we want it so badly—way above average. Wouldn't you agree?"

Max had to smile at Ken Flower's enthusiasm.

Hell, my strategy is working.

Normally, it was Max pitching the adoptive parents on how wonderful the child was going to be, chatting up the bloodlines, talking about how great an athlete or scholar the father had been or some other such crap. Well, the turnaround was just fine as far as he was concerned. It would make what he needed to tell Ken now a bit more upsetting and, therefore, a lot more powerful.

"Yes, of course I agree with you, Ken. And I'm glad you and Mary are both so excited. It is a hell of a fine opportunity. But keep in mind, you two kids are pretty special, too, don't forget that. There are probably no more than a handful of couples in this whole country that would have the intelligence and foresight to appreciate this extraordinary opportunity. Yes," Max continued, "very few couples. But apropos of that, the call I made to the office after lunch? Well, there was a message. And I'm sort of in an awkward position here, Ken."

"An awkward position?"

"Yes. It seems another couple is interested in the baby."

A Baby To Die For

"What do you mean, another couple?"

Max stopped walking. Ken had taken several steps before the full impact of Max's words sank in. Then he wheeled to face Max and barely controlling his voice, demanded, "What the fuck are you talking about, another couple?"

Max, an experienced grifter, arranged his features to appear appropriately upset.

"Why didn't you tell me about this before?"

"God knows, I'm really sorry, Ken. But I didn't want to say anything because I never, in a million years, believed they were serious."

"Damn it, Max, who are *they*?"

"Who they are isn't really important. They're just a well off, young couple from Chicago, a referral from a lawyer out there. They came in to meet with me last week. You and Mary were still uncertain about any final decision. I couldn't stop seeing other couples, and frankly, I never thought I would hear from them again. The call today was a complete shocker. I'm sure we can get it all straightened out."

"What the hell is there to straighten out? I said we would take the baby," Ken shouted, showing great concern.

Ken knew he was being conned but even so, just the idea of another couple possibly getting the baby was, nevertheless, strangely upsetting, and he was actually feeling a real fear of loss—vicarious though it was—from this charade, through which Max Garfield had led so many couples.

A Baby To Die For

"I'm so embarrassed about this, and very, very sorry. I'm stuck in the middle between the biological mother and getting the very best home for the child. Please understand that the birth mother's welfare is important to me. On one hand, I need to make sure the baby gets a great home. At the same time, I've got to make sure the mother gets fair compensation for what she's going through. Believe me, I'm on your side. But for the baby to be yours, I need your commitment. The Chicago people are, like you and Mary, good, solid folks, and if they're serious—and it seems they are—all things being equal—I'm duty bound to deal with whoever is first with the cash. It's only fair. I really have no choice. This is Friday, so take the weekend and think it over, okay? I promise not to take any calls from them until I hear from you. I promise—and I really do hope the baby will be yours, Ken. I'm sorry. This took me by surprise, too."

Ken took a deep breath. He had to stay calm. It would be okay. The network was like a sticky spider's web, and he was getting as caught up in it as if he were really trying to adopt a child, not just writing an exposé about it. His stomach growled with the same low pitch as the pesky tape recorder tucked inside his jacket pocket.

"Shit, Max. Why didn't you just tell me about the other people when you got off the phone over at the club? I could have called Mary, and maybe gotten her on board, right then and there. I would go back and call her," Ken said checking his watch, "but she'll be going into the O. R. about now and won't be out for hours."

"I know, you're right. I should have told you. I don't mean to upset you, but it's my obligation to handle this situation—*especially* this situation—with total impartiality."

"I'm confident she'll come around, Max. This will be a done deal as early next week as possible," Ken said.

"Okay, Ken, your word is good enough. And don't forget, the way this works is the $75,000 needs to be in two parts: $20,000 by check and the rest in—cash. I hope I made that clear at one of our earlier meetings?"

"Yes, I'm clear on that. You want $55,000 in cash. But run me through it one more time, since you may have some tax angles that I could use," Ken said, knowing damned well he needed as much of this on tape as he could get.

"Well, it's more of a cash-flow issue than anything else. As you know, the birth mother isn't your run-of-the-mill young woman. She's accustomed to a relatively high standard of living, so we've put her up in a very respectable—not fancy, mind you, but very respectable—hotel down in Florida. She's provided with healthy, nutritionally balanced meals and excellent medical care. All this costs a great deal of money, and I'm paying for it all up front, including the doctor in California who has the sperm bank. He needs to be paid, as well," Max said.

The only number Max cared about was the final selling price for the baby. Of course, he would have expenses, but the bulk of the money received for the child would end up with Max Garfield, less, of course the half of the net profit that would be paid to Karen. Only a small portion would be declared as income on his tax returns, the rest would be cash hidden in one of his safe deposit boxes.

All Max had to do now was keep pumping up the price of the EC-9 baby. At the rate things were going, he didn't see how that would be a problem. The opening bid of $75,000 was just that—an opener. He felt sure that Ken and Mary, once committed, could be pushed higher. He could feel it in his bones.

"I understand all about the expenses," Ken said, gesturing his frustration with his hands. "But I'm still a bit fuzzy about your need to have so much paid in cash."

Ken stopped and faced Max. He wanted this part on the tape and wasn't taking any chances. Let Max freeze his ass off. He wasn't going to walk now. He moved in closer, inches away from the baby lawyer.

"Okay, look, Ken, let me be candid with you. Cash is the best for all concerned. I don't—*we* don't want to have to tell a judge how much money is passing between us. These judges are accustomed to very small, almost token amounts being charged when an adoption goes through one of the State agencies, which are—let's face it—not for profit operations subsidized in all kinds of ways, including funds from the government. That's not my fault it's just a fact. The court has no understanding of the real cost of an adoption like this. If they saw the numbers we're talking about, I think they would be a little upset, you know, maybe even hold up the adoption. That would give the mother a chance to change her mind, basically snatch the baby out of your arms. It could be a mess. I've seen it happen, believe me.

"Our prime concern here is to have a clean adoption. Cash is easier all the way round. We do our business and it stays our business, not the judge's. She sees canceled checks and a fee that is in keeping with her experience and comfort level. She's a happy camper, doesn't freak out and, God willing, everything goes smoothly. That's why cash."

"But it's not quite legal, is it?"

"Legal, illegal? Come on, Ken, don't be naïve. Cash is legal. Since when did cash become against the law?"

Max smiled, his eyes dead, as he used the lawyer's trick of ignoring the question.

"Okay, Max, let me get this straight. You intend to lie to the court about the amount of cash you are getting from Mary and me for the baby we're adopting. Really? I'm not trying to judge you. I just want to make sure I understand. Is that what you're saying?"

"I think *lie* is a rather pejorative word. I consider it *omission*, as opposed to *commission*. It doesn't hurt anyone. Really, who does it hurt? You get a super-baby—you said so yourself—and the whole thing is certified A-OK by the court. You, Mary, and the baby can get on with your lives. Whoever gets the baby is going to be very lucky. Do you think for a minute that when the kid graduates from Harvard or Yale, you'll give a damn about the piddling financial frippery? But don't get me wrong, please, Ken —if these arrangements bother you, if you feel you don't want to do this my way—we can end it here without hard feelings. The other couple was told about my cash requirement and, clearly, the issue doesn't bother them."

Max said all these words as matter-of-factly as possible, knowing the knife-edge he was walking had the potential of blowing the deal.

Ken started walking again. An attractive jogger

passed, bouncing like a middleweight in training. Ken watched her moving forward before finally replying.

"Okay, Max, you're right. I'm just a little shaken from this other couple raising the stakes, so I guess I'm being a bit paranoid. I'll talk to Mary, get her final buy-in, and arrange for the cash. It might take me a day or two, so figure I'll be in touch on Monday and, hopefully, we'll be ready to arrange all the final details."

Chapter 48

San Francisco

Kevin Tyler did the best he could. Applied all his skill and knowledge to the task for which he was being so handsomely rewarded. But still, in the end he failed—never able to manipulate Edmond Calendar's sperm to sufficient levels that would produce what his benefactor wanted most in life. So, the old man died without an heir. As a result, court battles over the disposition of his fortune started in earnest even before the body was cold. The legal haggling would go on, ad nauseam, providing income to generations of lawyers.

Curiously, it was the unimposing Dr. Tyler who came out smelling like the proverbial rose. Thanks to an ironclad contract with the dead billionaire, Kevin now possessed the basic accoutrements of the "good life"—a spacious, well-furnished Pacific Heights apartment, a steady, generous income, and a state-of-the-art laboratory. Only missing was someone to share it with. Not an heir—that held no interest. But a steady girlfriend—possibly a wife. Sadly, success with women had not been one of

A Baby To Die For

God's gifts to the scientist. At least not until Silvia Wilson plucked him off a bar stool at Sam's and proceeded to treat him as an object of value.

He liked Silvia. They had fun together. She was smart and funny, and the sex was fantastic—although he had little in his past to compare it with. But now he was among the few mature and financially comfortable adult males who find themselves in an adolescently erotic relationship.

And if Silvia Wilson wasn't enough, Kevin had met still another woman. Blessings, like trouble, seemed to arrive in bunches.

Ironically, it was the success with Silvia that gave him the confidence—for the first time in his life—to actually pick up a woman. The "new girl," as he thought of her, had been standing outside his apartment building, and—as she explained—had been wandering the neighborhood searching for a friend's apartment. Clearly the address she had been given did not exist.

Tyler, always the gentleman, offered the attractive woman the use of his phone to contact her friend. Before he knew it, they were having a drink, and not long after, a quiet dinner in a lovely little restaurant on Fisherman's Wharf.

It was a most pleasant evening. Robin Marche was a good listener. And Kevin, after the first drink, was more than willing to talk. Later, he escorted Robin back to her hotel and in a remote corner of the lobby, next to an overly large potted fern, was rewarded with a lingering kiss—a momentarily probing tongue away from being chaste. The following night, after an insanely expensive meal at the Blue Fox—an exclusive restaurant situated in an ally across

A Baby To Die For

from the city morgue—they returned to the hotel. This time to her room where Robin permitted several minutes of drive-in-level petting. Fortunately, Silvia Wilson was in Arizona on assignment. Had she not been out of town, Kevin would have had a few logistical problems keeping his newly acquired women apart.

Now Kevin stood by the big picture window of his living room sipping a single malt Scotch. He never tired of watching his spectacular view of San Francisco Bay—a pleasant way to wait for his latest "acquisition" to arrive.

By golly, at the rate things are going, this evening I just might be able to bed the wench. The silly expression made him laugh. *Imagine—me—actually juggling two women at the same time.*

Both Sylvia and Robin liked him—or so they said. Both materialized completely out of thin air, and both, in their way, were total knockouts.

Yes, Tyler felt quite good—taller than his five-foot-seven height would indicate and much handsomer than his mirror ever reciprocated.

Late blooming is doing good things for me. And it's about time. I think I'll have my teeth capped.

The doorbell interrupted his thoughts, and he quickly crossed the room, took the five steps along the front hall to the door, and yanked it open.

Robin stood encased in a stunning black trench coat—cinched tight at her waist. From the upturned collar it flowed seamlessly from shoulder length blonde hair, down, past the tops of her calf-high, black-leather boots. An oversized handbag of soft black leather with a gold Gucci buckle hung from her shoulder.

A Baby To Die For

Oh my God! Gestapo Barbie!

For a moment they just looked at each other. She seemed to be memorizing him with her moist, dark eyes, looking larger, and very sexy, thanks to her contact lenses.

He felt himself becoming aroused and boldly made no attempt to hide the fact.

Damn! I wish I hadn't promised to show her my laboratory.

There wasn't much to see—just a bunch of freezers and test tubes and other paraphernalia. But she was fascinated to know more about his work. She was, she said, a science groupie. He didn't make a habit of taking people to see his lab, but he found it difficult to say no to this woman.

What the hell, if it turns her on, that's all that really counts.

"Wow, Robin, you look great. Come in. Please."

Robin smiled and slowly squeezed past him into the apartment—like a cat rubbing close across its owner's leg. He followed her into the living room and she walked toward the bar.

"Could you turn off the lights, Kevin? The view is better without them," Robin said. "And I'm dying for a drink. A double, if you would? It was a long day."

Kevin did as asked. She took the glass and generous sip of the scotch. It was a clear night, and the moon along with the city lights gave the room a romantic illumination. Robin turned away from the view and with her back to the window, the outline of her silhouette glowed. She smiled and Tyler felt a surge of desire. He put down his drink and walked toward her.

"Here, let me help with that coat."

A Baby To Die For

She extended her drink toward him, and he took it from her hand, placing it on the low, glass coffee table.

"Come on. The coat. Take it off. You must be boiling."

Robin smiled coyly, slowly unbelting and unbuttoning the black coat, then holding both sides open away from her body. Kevin's eyes went round and his jaw dropped a fraction before a Cheshire smile cut across his face.

She was naked save for the high black boots and black lace bra and panties. A single choker of matched pearls encircled her long, slim neck. Her body was lovely framed against the rich, blood red silk lining of the coat and when, as the coat slid to the carpet, lovelier still, against the view of San Francisco and the bay.

"A special preview just for you, Kevin. I've a stunning little silk dress in my handbag so we must go somewhere fabulous for dinner. I'm absolutely famished. I hope seeing me like this will help your digestion."

Kevin just nodded, too gobsmacked to speak.

Does the sun set in the West?

"And after dinner, your laboratory. You promised, right? But I warn you labs make me horny. They have ever since my high school science teacher showed me some interesting experiments that he never assigned to the rest of the class. Then, if you're not too tired, we can go back to my place. I may even demonstrate a few of the marvelous things that dirty old professor taught me, okay?"

Kevin Tyler swallowed hard, grinning stupidly in anticipation. "Whatever you say, my dear."

Smiling broadly, Porter Gibbs hoped her itchy blonde wig would stay in place.

Chapter 49

"So then Max tells me another couple wants the baby. Well, shit! I just lost it—went nuts—you can imagine."

The four were at the Flowers' apartment for dinner—too nervous about being seen in public since there was always the sliver of a chance they'd cross paths with Garfield. Highly unlikely, but in the "small town" that is Manhattan, it was possible.

"But he didn't say they offered more money? I find that really strange," Tuck said.

"Yeah, I thought so, too."

Mary added more ice to her drink. "Another couple in the mix puts a lot of pressure on us—"

"Pressure to make a firm commitment, and quick," Ken completed his wife's thought.

"Remember, as far as Max knows, Mary is not a hundred percent on board. So, he's probably reluctant to throw up a higher price as an additional hurdle for us to jump. Pushing for more money too soon could make us bolt. I don't doubt he'll ask for more money. It's just a matter of when," Tuck said.

A Baby To Die For

Karen shifted in her chair trying, without success, to find a comfortable position.

"It's actually pretty damned brilliant," Ken said, splashing more Vodka into his glass. "Think about it. We're on the fence, so he sets the hook by producing a competitor. Now, all of a sudden we are forced to start thinking, *'Hey, wait a minute! That baby is ours!'* And he knows, when we start thinking that way, the cost becomes secondary—an afterthought."

"Psychologically, it makes perfect sense," Mary added, "I mean, good God, we know this is a setup, yet here we are, caught up in the whole idea of having a superbaby—of wanting it. And this so-called new couple has put us into a phony competition—one that Max is betting we're desperate to win! What's so crazy is, he's right, even though we're just competing with ourselves! Max's next logical step has to be—"

"Ask for more money," Ken says, completing his wife's sentence. "If he had upped the price when he brought in the other couple, it would simply be asking us to pay more—to *buy* the baby. But the new competition makes us think, *'Dammit, that baby is ours.'* Which puts him in a stronger position to jack up the price. At that point, the higher price will be seen as the cost for *keeping* our baby. The difference between paying more to 'buy' or paying more to 'keep' is a whole different ballgame."

"Paying to keep the baby is a much more powerful motivation," Karen said softly.

The four sat silently for some time contemplating the complex and diabolical box Max had maneuvered them into.

A Baby To Die For

Finally, "Either way," Ken lamented, "it brings us back to the same conundrum. When he does ask for more, where in hell are we going to get it?"

"Okay, look—let's take it one step at a time," Tuck said. "At least for the moment, we've got the $75,000 he's asking for."

"Yeah," Ken said. "But it took everything we had. Right now we're tapped out. Max asks for any more and we're basically screwed."

Ken got up, paced for a moment. "When you think about it, there's a certain irony in all this. If the story is half as good as I think, it will easily make back what we end up giving him. There's a story here—without question— maybe even a movie. Hell, there are millions and millions of adopted people in this country—their parents and grandparents—the birth moms and the doctors and lawyers involved. Hell, for all we know, there are fifty or sixty million people out there who are interested in some meaningful way in adoption. Maybe more. That, my friends, is what publishers call a built-in franchise. It's the kind of audience the media and movie studios lust after. Do you think I'd invest so much of my time in a totally futile idea?"

"Actually, now that you mention it," Mary said, smiling tolerantly at her husband, "I seem to recall your devoting a year's worth of work on what was to be your Pulitzer-winning fast-food exposé."

"And thank you for your continuing support, darling," Ken said, an acid smile on his face. "Seriously, this isn't like that at all. Selling customized überkinder to the highest bidder is way beyond that. Oh, it's going to work, you can bet on it," Ken said with a level of conviction, which the other three could only hope would prove to be true.

"What if you pitch the story to one of your publishers—maybe get an advance?" Tuck said.

Ken rolled the idea around for a moment then shook his head.

"Nah, I don't think I want to take the chance until we're finished and the story is locked up. I might be able to get some money that way, but I'd really be afraid it would leak prematurely. An idea like this is almost impossible to embargo."

"Well, my friend," Tuck said, patting the journalist on the shoulder. "I hope you're right, but waiting until it's over doesn't do us much good right now. I doubt Max will take an IOU."

Again, they sat in silence.

Finally Tuck shrugged. "Let's get our priorities straight. Right now our only job is to somehow get some more money. Without the cash we'll never bring Max down. After that, the courts and the IRS will take care of the rest."

"Once that happens Max's clients would have a pretty strong case for getting some of their money back—at least the cash part," Mary said.

"I can't picture any of them wanting to get involved. Max's clients may have been fleeced, but they were happy lambs. He delivered what they wanted, and they gladly paid for his services. I've worked in that office for a long time and never once heard a complaint from anyone,"

A Baby To Die For

Karen said, shifting her weight yet again as she felt the baby kick. "You saw his collection—the rattles—those are from very contented clients. So why would they take a chance with courts, lawyers, or judges? They'd be afraid of losing their baby. Remember, the right of a birth mother is very powerful and, given a legal conflict…well, who can say how it would turn out?" Karen paused to let what she'd said sink in. Then she continued. "But listen, I do have something I want to bring up. There is another option we've never discussed."

"Option?" Ken said.

"Yes. We can pull out now," Karen said. "Just end it. Ken tells Max that Mary won't budge and the deal is off. As for me, I have no problem telling him I've decided to keep the baby. We don't give him any money, and we just walk away. He wouldn't dare do anything about it. Actually, there's nothing he *can* do about it," Karen said, absently caressing her stomach as she felt the baby kicking again. "It's up to you guys. I'm happy and content with my baby," she said, and smiled at Tuck. "…sorry darling—our baby. And, to be honest, in the last few months my attitude toward Max has moved from anger to ambivalence. I could easily walk away from this whole thing." Karen looked around at the others, waiting for a reaction. "But I'll go along with whatever the rest of you decide," she quickly added. "I just needed to raise that—option—you know?"

"Stop now?" Ken exploded. "After the work we've put in? No fucking way!"

"I agree," Tuck quickly added. "For me, this is payback for Ellen—what Max did to Ellen. I could never walk away from that. Not without his getting nailed."

A Baby To Die For

Ken paused for a moment, looked slowly around the table, sensed an implied agreement—even from Karen—and continued.

"Okay, we move forward. Our first question—how do we raise more money?"

"Anybody got any bright ideas?" Tuck asked the table at large.

Silence.

"What about Uncle Saul?" Karen asked Tuck.

"Twosie? No way. Hell, if he had that kind of money, he would have given it to us when we were trying to adopt," Tuck said, sadly.

Awkward silence.

Finally, Tuck spoke, but with little conviction. "I guess I could give Pauline Shelby a call. She does have money. At least, her family is loaded."

"She sure as hell was affected by Max—at least indirectly," Karen commented, "From what you said, she'd still be married if her ex hadn't gotten involved with Garfield."

Tuck couldn't help but remember how hurt she'd been by Rick's intransigence and its part in ending her marriage. But when he was in Dallas, he also got the feeling she had more than a casual romantic interest in him. By calling now he'd be taking advantage of that. With difficulty, he forced the thought from his mind.

"Okay, look, I'm not completely comfortable calling her, but I'll give it a shot. The big question is how much are we looking for?"

"Max could easily jump to $100,000. And there's no

guarantee he'll stop there," Mary said. "I'd say we need another $25,000—minimum."

Silence all around seemed to indicate agreement with the number, so for the next fifteen or twenty minutes they concentrated on small talk and finished the meal Mary laid out on the large wooden coffee table. When the last of the Montrachet was poured, Ken opened another bottle. "Hell, if we're going to drown in total poverty, let's do it in style," he said.

Karen would have liked a glass of the excellent white wine but settled, reluctantly, for another ginger ale.

"What about your agent, Ken?" Mary said, bringing up the subjet of money once again. "Can't you call Gene and see what he can do? Maybe some discreet inquiries—shop the story? Test the waters? Who knows, he might turn up a book offer or a movie deal or something—maybe get an advance? He's done it before."

"I hate going outside our group—with this," Ken responded. "Let me think about it. Meanwhile, Tuck, you call the Shelby woman. If she can lend us the money, fine, if not, I can always try something with Gene. But let's wait and see what comes from your call to Dallas."

Pauline Shelby listened, her ear pressed to the receiver, as Tuck described the plan that he hoped would bring down Max Garfield and unlock his stranglehold on the adoption network. He held nothing back. He told her about Kevin Tyler, Edmond Calendar, the Library of Life, and how Max now believed that the baby Karen carried was fathered by a famous person's frozen sperm. Max believed he was selling the baby to a well-to-do couple looking for a very special child. What he didn't know was that the husband was a journalist who was helping us set a net to trap Max.

And most importantly, he explained the delicate financial position they found themselves in, having already promised Max $75,000, which represented all they were able to scrape together. It was certain he would ask for a lot more.

"Your plan is nothing short of brilliant. But I can't believe Garfield actually thinks he's selling a celebrity's offspring. From everything Rick told me about how Max operates—actually, the way the whole damned network operates—your fear that he'll ask for more seems well founded."

"Which is exactly why I'm turning to you, Pauline. I don't know anyone else I can trust enough to talk about what we're doing—and to ask for help. We're so damn close to nailing this bastard, but it won't happen without more money. And it's not as if the money would be gone. I'm confident we'll profit from selling the story—to papers, TV, probably a book, maybe even a movie. Naturally, we would pay you back first, regardless," Tuck said. He paused. "Honestly, Pauline, I'm embarrassed to even ask, but we really need your help."

There was silence, and Tuck could hear Pauline breathing across the fifteen hundred miles of telephone line—the soundtrack for her thought processes.

Finally, "You've nothing to be embarrassed about. There's little more I'd like to see than Max Garfield in prison. Give me a day or two to talk to my father. He's plenty pissed off at Rick and, by association, Max Garfield. I think there's a damned good chance he'd be happy to put up some money."

Two days later, true to her word, Pauline phoned Tuck and told him her father had agreed. Fortunately, Pauline's father's distaste for her ex-husband was almost as strong as the family's fortune. Other than a nuts-and-bolts promissory note, there were no other strings attached to the loan. They now had a $25,000 line of credit to draw upon.

Tuck and Pauline spent some time on the phone—she rummaging through her memory bank for any additional details about the network that she might have forgotten or neglected to tell Tuck when they were together in Dallas.

"By the way, has Karen mentioned Max's brother, Jake?

"Nothing really. Mentioned him once or twice. Said he was very troubled."

"According to Rick, he's certifiably nuts. Says he can be a very dangerous man. He had a bad time in the war—captured by the Vietcong. He was a gunner on a helicopter that was shot down and captured. He somehow managed to escape and spent a long stretch in some military medical facility. Karen told me that when he came back he was somewhat in control, thanks to a cocktail of heavy-duty medications, but without them.... The only reason he's on the street and not in an institution is thanks to the magic of pharmaceuticals. Rick was a phony and a liar about many things, but I believed him about Jake Garfield. Be careful if you happen to run into him. After all, he's going to be your brother in law."

The subject of his impending marriage injected a moment of awkwardness into the conversation.

Pauline broke the silence, "By the way, Tuck, I'm really happy that you two got together. I knew you'd hit it off."

"Well, thanks, I owe it all to you. Without your official imprimatur, she never would have agreed to see me in the first place."

"Have you set a date?"

"Not yet. But I hope you'll come back here for the wedding."

He could hear Pauline breathing.

"Wouldn't miss it," she said with a touch of sadness in her voice.

Chapter 50

Beneath a conservative, academic persona, there lurked within Kevin Tyler, a vivid, albeit dormant, imagination. Robin (aka Porter Gibbs) had inadvertently tapped into this side of the good doctor in her quest to learn as much as possible about the Edmond Calendar Library of Life.

Naturally, Porter knew that Max was involved with Kevin Tyler, and still had the faint residue of bruises on her face to prove it. What she didn't know—and was stunned when she heard—was that Karen Garfield Boyd was no more carrying a child fathered by one of Tyler's ultrafamous sperm donors than Porter Gibbs was a duck-billed platypus. The lying bitch was having a child fathered by an ex-cop named Tuck Handler. And that was only the half of it. A journalist and his wife were posing as the couple that would adopt the baby, in a sting designed to destroy Max Garfield. Kevin had revealed the whole story, one fragment at a time.

The revelation was as valuable as it was jaw-dropping. The challenge it presented for Porter was to figure out how to apply the information to advantage. The idea of using

Kevin Tyler's sperm bank as the source for a supply of superbabies—real or imagined—was brilliant. She would have little trouble getting him to give her bragging rights to designer sperm. All she had to do was play her hand properly to make a fortune.

And as for Max, she wouldn't need him much longer. Through the years, he had gotten terribly lazy and performed less and less of the actual work. He was like many founders of successful companies who were lucky enough to have a strong number two executive. In time, as more and more of the day-to-day responsibility was wicked away from the top, the business operations slowly ceased being in control of the employer, other than in a legal sense.

For all intents and purposes, Porter ran the network, pulled all the strings, kept up the contacts, maintained all the records. Contrary to what Max believed, she was the one with control over the sensitive area of supply and even the bulk of the referrals. And now, with Kevin Tyler under her thumb, she had the potential of access to a reproductive gold mine. If and when it ever came to a pissing match between her and Max over control, she felt certain she could count on Kevin Tyler's voting with his romantic fantasy.

Without Porter, Max would have to start over—if he wasn't in jail—and Porter doubted if Max had the energy or would even know where to begin. It was about time, Porter mused, for her to help Max Garfield fall on his hateful, sadistic ass. He had hit her for the last time. Now it was her turn to hurt him.

Porter calculated Max's role in the network could

easily be replaced by hiring another lawyer. So, instead of Porter working for a lawyer, a new lawyer would simply work for her. Someone like Rick Shelby down in Dallas would be ideal. He had the mentality of a good number two. And he liked Porter. On his last trip to New York, he had made it clear he would welcome a more intimate level to their relationship. Yes, Rick Shelby would do fine. Since his marriage fell apart, he no longer had ties to Dallas. She could move him up to New York, and Porter Gibbs would be in business.

Yes, sir, if Max went through with the adoption of Karen's special baby, he would be in deep trouble and probably finished as a lawyer. He'd be lucky to stay out of jail, let alone run the network.

She had always cautioned Max that there was no love lost between him and his sister, Karen. Now he was chest deep in his sister's plan to destroy him. Well, it served him right. Max's smug face would be smeared across every newspaper, magazine, and TV screen in the country. All the negative publicity would provide her with a convenient smoke screen to hide behind as she took over the operation. Once in charge, Porter was certain the network could become more profitable than ever.

Maybe women's lib was okay after all.

It was obvious to Porter that the only smart thing to do right now was absolutely nothing. Just let Max keep moving along his self-made track, stupidly thinking he was making the deal of his lifetime selling the most expensive baby ever adopted, when in reality, he was negotiating his own downfall.

Yes, that's what Porter would do—absolutely nothing.

Chapter 51

"For crying out loud, Max," Ken exploded, "we had a deal!"

"Believe me, Ken, I'm as upset as you are," Max replied, as he reached out to lower the volume control on his speakerphone, even as Ken checked to make sure his recording device was secure on his phone receiver.

"The hell you are! We're the ones getting jerked around. All it means for you is more money. I want to know what the fuck happened?"

Max never got used to his clients' reactions when he had to tell them the price for the baby they wanted was going to go higher than planned. Some were philosophical and quickly adapted. Some, having reached the limits of their resources, actually broke down and cried. Still others became quite pissed off. So, over time, he had steeled himself to be as calm as possible, regardless of the reaction.

"As best as I can piece it together, Ken, it seems another couple found out about the baby and upped your offer," Max said evenly, his office speakerphone lending a slightly detached quality to his voice.

A Baby To Die For

"What the fuck do you mean they upped my offer? We didn't talk about an offer. We had an understanding to go forward with the adoption. We gave you the check you asked for. You said we had the baby. What kind of last-minute horse shit is this?"

"I don't know what to say. I'm sorry, truly sorry."

"*Sorry* doesn't cut it, Max! How much more did they offer?" Ken asked, yelling into the phone's mouthpiece.

"Another $25,000," Max said, and waited for the explosion.

Ken was silent. The financial pressure he was expecting had finally hit. And damn it, Ken had to hand it to Garfield. He certainly was a master of timing. Karen was obviously due to deliver soon, and if the doctor's calculations were correct, the baby would be born in a week or so. Max had waited until the very last minute to spring the news, an optimal moment when the concept of having the baby would have imbedded itself as a reality in the minds of the adopting parents. And even though he and Mary knew that, in their case, the whole process was a sham, even *they* had been whipped into a frenzy of excitement about the arrival of the baby. Ken could only begin to imagine the panic and anguish an actual adoptive couple would experience when they suddenly found the price for "their" child had gone through the roof—just when they truly believed the transaction was a fait accompli.

Ken remained silent.

Finally, Max, uncomfortable with the lack of response, said, "You can't imagine how sorry I am, Ken, but the birth mother is insisting. She's very nervous. She's having all sorts of second thoughts about keeping her baby. I can't even picture what the poor girl must be going through, with her changing hormones and psychological pressures. Personally, between you and me, I think she's using the demand for money as an excuse."

"An excuse? What the hell does that even mean, Max?" Ken said, with as much disgust as he could muster.

"Well, I know this will sound strange, but it's possible she doesn't really want to give up the baby. In her current confused frame of mind, she might be hoping the higher price will force everyone to drop out, just walk away. In that way, the decision she can't make on her own would be made for her. Don't you see? If there are no buyers, then by default, she's forced to keep the baby. And maybe that's what she wanted all along."

Ken couldn't help but grudgingly admire the man on the other end of the conversation. Max was quite amazing. He possessed the heart of a black mamba snake, but without any of its empathy.

"Please, Max, spare me all the psychobabble. You told me the Chicago couple was out of the picture. You said that when we shook hands—and, as promised, I gave you the $20,000 check."

"No, no…I'm sorry…apparently, I didn't make myself clear. I'm not talking about the Chicago people. This new couple were a referral by the girl's doctor. They're from Scottsdale, apparently real estate money I think, lots of it. Clearly, the unique nature of this baby has distorted all the normal sensibilities in this adoption. The whole thing is just maddening," Max said, trying as best he could to sound flummoxed.

"First of all, Max, why the fuck would you even tell the doctor about where the sperm came from?" Ken said, incredulously.

"I didn't! I swear! The girl told him. I admit I'll have to take the blame. I never should have said a word to her about it. But, Ken, I had no choice. She was having nicotine fits and wanted to smoke—not just cigarettes—and have an occasional drink, as well. I couldn't let her do that stuff while she was pregnant. I had to say something to convince her how special the baby was, how important it was for her to have a healthy pregnancy. God knows why she mentioned it to the doctor. Now the greedy bastard smells some extra cash, so he found this couple," Max lied.

"But that means this baby is going to cost $100,000, Max, and how do we know it will stop there?"

"I sympathize, really I do, but there are no absolutes in life. That said, I think this is it. I've convinced the girl to give us right of first refusal, but it wasn't easy. Once she got a whiff of those extra dollars, she was suddenly gripped with delusions of grandeur. But now, I feel certain that if you can match their offer, the baby is yours."

"Damn, Max. It's not a matter of *can we*, it's more about *should we*? I just don't know. This just might be the last straw for Mary. And it's not just the money——she feels that she's being jerked around, manipulated, you know? You've got to give me a little more time so I can talk some sense into her."

"Oh, God, I'm not sure I can pull this off," Max said in as miserable a tone as he could muster. "Okay, look, maybe I can stretch out a decision to midweek. In my experience, these procedures tend to go slowly—at least, up to a point—and then it becomes like a fast slide down a greased pole. And we're just about at that point. Once you give me the word, I will do my best to put an end to any further negotiations. If the girl keeps her word, the price won't go any higher. There isn't any more time for her or her doctor to play games. It really is the moment of truth. As for the final cash settlement, it won't be needed until you pick up the baby. You hand over the cash, and you'll walk away with one extraordinary baby. You can trust me on this, Ken."

Ken held back a laugh. Max Garfield's name along with the word *trust* in the same sentence was a laughable oxymoron. Now Ken wondered if this was really it, if the pot in this human poker game they were playing would sit pat at $100,000? This last squeeze would wipe out the line of credit from Pauline's father, but if Max pushed the price any higher, they'd be out of luck. Tuck had been clear that he didn't think he could go back to Pauline again. Now Ken's mind was pumping hard, trying to think of how exactly to handle this current and, hopefully final, bit of extortion. He again checked the tiny, quivering red needle on his recorder to make sure he was picking up Garfield's conversation through the small rubber suction cup affixed to the telephone receiver. Max was still coming through, loud and clear.

"Look, Max, as I said, I'm going to have to talk to Mary. She's got to be on board or it's over."

"I understand. How soon can you get back to me?"

A Baby To Die For

"I don't know for sure. This throws a wrench into the deal. First, you ask for $75,000 and now another $25,000—all for a baby conceived from a very special donor's sperm."

Ken spoke dramatically for the recorder, which sat next to the phone, growling its usual growls.

"Give me your best guess, Ken," Max said.

"Mary is working in surgery all day. I should be back to you before the end of the day."

"We haven't much time. Please call as soon as you can. If the girl's OB is right, she's going to deliver soon—the timing's not an exact science. We've got to get this thing finalized," Max said, urgently. "I will stay late at the office, so please call me, either way."

Max heard a hint of genuine panic in his own voice, something he wasn't accustomed to experiencing. He would be in big trouble if Ken backed out of the deal now. If that happened, the chances were good that he'd end up getting a lot less for the baby. Once born, the value of a baby declined rapidly. A child handed over directly out of hospital was the gold standard.

"As soon as I speak with Mary I'll call, I promise. But to be honest, she's going to really be pissed."

Just maybe, if I imply the other people have greater financial resources, it would play to Ken's ego, applying a slightly different sort of pressure back on the Flowers. I'd better careful not to scare them with too strong a show of force. Shit! I hate this part of the negotiations more than anything.

Max cleared his throat, took the call off speakerphone, and addressed Ken in his most serious tone, "Ken, listen. You tell Mary—assure her for me—that I will completely understand if you decide not to go through with the adoption, especially since these other people apparently have deeper pockets. Worst case, you will get every penny of your money back. Less, a few incidental expenses—maybe a $1,000, probably less."

Ken's reaction was visceral, a surprising and uncontrolled spinal reflex for combat.

"Fuck them and their deep pockets! We have enough money to buy this baby regardless of the price. Getting a few bucks back doesn't mean shit, Max, you know that. It's that baby we want, and we intend to get it. I'll be back to you, Max, and you sure as hell owe us," Ken yelled, as he slammed down the receiver.

His hand was shaking. He had let Max get to him, and he could feel his journalistic objectivity slipping away—not a good sign. He needed to slow down and think. Garfield had no idea he was playing in a game with loaded dice, but even so, the plan, in order to work, had to be taken to its final conclusion. Max's demands, regardless of the amount, had to be met. Dropping out at this point made no sense. Ken couldn't be certain, but a day before, he would have made book that the final price for the baby would be an even $100,000. But now he wasn't so sure. It could easily go higher. If Tuck's instinct about $100,000 being the final price was too low, they were going to be hard-pressed to find more cash.

Ken shut off the tape recorder then sat staring into space, mentally sifting through a tissue-thin range of alternatives. After some time, he made a phone call, dressed, and left the apartment.

Clearly, he had only one choice.

A Baby To Die For

It was past seven o'clock when Ken breathlessly stormed back into the apartment.

"Where have you been? Ten more minutes and we were starting dinner without you," Mary said.

"You won't believe the fucking day I've had! I've got good news and bad news. Which do you want first?" he asked, as he quickly shrugged out of his overcoat and moved to the front of the fireplace to warm himself. "But first, I must catch my breath and get circulation back into my highly talented typing fingers."

Mary, Tuck, and Karen watched Ken and waited patiently. The smell from a roast cooking in the oven permeated the apartment. A log burned in the small fireplace. Vodka and a bucket of ice sat on the coffee table. Karen had forgone her usual ginger ale for a nonalcoholic Bloody Mary, which she laughingly referred to as a Bloody Shame.

Finally, Ken poured himself two inches of vodka over a single ice cube. "Okay, I'm ready."

"What's with the suit and tie? I thought your meeting today with Max was on the phone." Karen said.

"It was. That's the bad news. He asked for more money. He claims there's a new, higher offer."

"Oh, shit!"

"Damn it, I knew this would happen!"

"How much more?"

"As you predicted, Tuck. He wants $25,000 more."

No one spoke. They just remained frozen—seated, standing, holding drinks—as if they were trapped inside some sort of diorama of disappointment.

Ken took the next few minutes to fill them in on the gory details of his highly contentious phone conversation with Max.

"So how come the fancy outfit for a phone call?"

"That's the *good* news. After I spoke with Max, it was clear—to me, at least—that we must have access to more cash, just in case he ups the price again, which is certainly a possibility. So after Max's little bombshell, I called Gene Rubin."

"You said you wouldn't do that," Mary said.

"I know, but Max really shook me up. Anyway, I called him. It's done. I met him for drinks after he finished work. We met at his club, ergo the suit and tie. I just left, but not before we consumed several very dry martinis. I told him the whole story."

Karen responded, frowning, "But you were so positive that telling him was risky. Now, all of a sudden, you trust him?"

"Yes."

"How can you be so sure?" Tuck said, concerned.

"Because as of now, he's our partner."

The room went silent, the only sounds coming from the logs crackling in the tiny fireplace. A buzzer sounded from the kitchen announcing the roast was done, and Mary ran off to take it out of the oven.

"Listen, before everyone has a frigging fit," Ken said. "This is not a bad thing. Rubin was so excited about the story and the financial potential, he's committed to bankrolling us for any additional money—within reason, of course—that Garfield might demand."

A Baby To Die For

"So how much are we borrowing?" Tuck asked.

"That's the best part, we're not. It's not a loan, this is his own personal investment."

Mary, from the doorway of the tiny kitchen, immediately spoke up. "Wait a minute, Ken. You're telling me that Gene Rubin, the same Gene Rubin I know, is actually giving us money? Okay, now tell me about the strings, because I know the guy and when it comes to money, there will be a cat's cradle of strings."

"Believe me, this is a very good deal. He gets twenty percent commission on all income from the project until he gets back whatever amount he ends up investing."

"Twenty on top of his usual commission? That's crazy!" Mary shouted.

"No, no, Just an extra ten more than his normal commission. And after his initial investment is paid back, he agreed his commissions go back to his normal ten percent. It's a fair deal, and besides, I already said yes."

"What else? There has to be more. We're not getting money from him out of the goodness of his heart."

"One point on the movie, but only if he ends up giving us any money. No money, no points."

"I'll bet anything it's not on the net," Mary said, sarcastically.

"No, on the gross, but it's worth it," Ken added, defensively. "Look at it this way, we now have the money to go forward. If the price ends up at an even $100,000, fine! Then we don't need a penny from Rubin, and he gets nothing more than his usual commission on whatever I earn. But if Garfield pushes the price higher—say another

$25,000 more—we won't have to run around hunting for the cash. It's like an insurance policy. We know if this is to work, we've got to see it through to the end, regardless of how much Max asks for. The other benefit we get with Rubin on board is his enthusiasm for the plan. Even if he doesn't put in a dime, we have his undivided interest and attention."

Tuck rolled his drink between his palms and took a deep breath.

"I guess there's really nothing more to discuss. Ken's agreed to the deal, and it seems reasonable, so let's not waste time debating it. I guess the next step is to call Garfield and tell him Mary has agreed and we're okay for the additional $25,000. And if I'm right, he'll be happy for about twenty-four hours, after which time he will come up with another cockamamie excuse to push us for a bit more."

"Maybe we'll get lucky, and he'll stand at the even hundred?" Mary whispered, more to herself than to anyone else in the room.

"I told him I'd call before the end of the day. He's probably ready to open a vein by now, so let's give him the good news," Ken said, checking to make sure the tiny recorder had a fresh tape and the machine was attached properly to the back of the phone's receiver.

Then suddenly, he clamped the receiver back down on its cradle.

"Hey, I just had an idea. We know there's no other couple. This crap he's giving us about the mother needing more money and the girl maybe changing her mind about giving up the kid is very imaginative but pure baloney. I vote we call and tell him Mary refused to go forward. It will be much more authentic and shake him up a little."

Tuck thought for a moment then bobbed his head up and down in agreement.

"Yeah, let's let him sweat a bit. The transcript of the conversation should be fantastic. It will make for a strong chapter in the story," Tuck laughed. "Do you think he'll cave in? We can let him sweat for a while before we call back and agree."

Ken dialed the number and Max immediately answered. "Ken—it's getting late, I was starting to worry."

"Yeah, Max, look, I've been talking nonstop to Mary. She's livid about this new couple coming up out of left field, not to mention the additional money. She says the mother and the doctor are both ripping us off. She doesn't want to play. She's just plain fed up. I tried every which way I could to convince her. I'm sorry, Max. I guess the deal is off. You can send me the deposit whenever it's convenient. It doesn't make any difference. Christ, I'm crushed over this. We had a room all decorated…"

Ken let his voice drop off, trying to sound as despondent as he could.

The silence from Max's end of the phone was deafening. The lawyer felt a rush of acid rising into his throat. He was fucked! He had overplayed his hand and made the foolish mistake of pushing this deal too damn far.

"Uh, Ken—listen," Max said, while fighting mightily to regain composure. Then, finally under a modicum of control, continued, "I truly understand. This was so unprofessional on the doctor's part. He's acting atrociously, without question. But regardless, let's try to keep our eye on our objective and not the difficulties of the process. Are you absolutely sure you want to pull out now? This baby is very important to both of you. We've gotten to be, well, we've become friends. So I know how much this child means to you—to both of you. I would hate to have you, uh, miss out. This caliber of infant—doesn't come along like a bus, with another just minutes away. It's very special. Think about it, Ken, very, very special! A month or a year from now, you might regret this hasty, emotional decision."

Max's mind was snapping back and forth like a sail luffing in the wind, as he tried to adjust to this sudden and devastating turn of events. His fist was clenched and hammered the air, up and down, in utter frustration. He never dreamed that the Flowers would turn down the jacked-up price. He had calculated so carefully, played them the way an experienced fly fisherman tangles with a wily bonefish. Shit! Now he was truly stuck. He had to keep playing this as if there really was another couple and another offer. To cave in now would be to lose all credibility. He needed time to think.

"I'm sorry, Max. I really am. Take whatever expenses you think are appropriate out of the money we gave you. I'm really not in any condition to discuss those details now. You understand. We appreciate your effort. It just didn't work. I guess we'll just have to take a chance on catching the next bus. Goodbye, Max. Thanks for everything."

Ken hung up the receiver and rolled back on the sofa, laughing like a kid who had made his first ever crank call.

A Baby To Die For

"The old bastard was—devastated! His voice was actually quivering, for crying out loud. I could have sworn he was having a heart attack. I'll lay odds he calls back within a half hour. It'll take him that long to concoct another cock-and-bull story. Wait, you'll see."

Tuck wasn't laughing. Something about Ken's call was starting to bother him.

Karen wasn't laughing, either.

"What did we accomplish by pretending to pull out? First of all, he'll be forced to actually find another couple, and besides, we gain nothing by trying to keep Max's price down. If he goes higher, we have access to more cash from Rubin, right?"

Tuck nodded silently, agreeing with Karen's point.

"She's right," he said, finally. "We have the money so why not let him take us for the full $100,000? Hell, the more he takes, the more trouble he'll be in. Anyway, the $100,000 sounds stronger to me as a headline that says $97,500 or some other oddball number we might force him to settle for."

Ken's eyes fixed on Tuck for a moment, then stared at the fireplace as he weighed the various sides of the argument Tuck and Karen were posing.

Finally, with a grunt of agreement, Ken said, "Damn it, you're absolutely right. Now you know why all great writers need to be edited. He picked up the phone, and slowly dialed Max Garfield's number.

Max stood, head down, the dead phone in his hand. He felt as if he were going to throw up all over his desk.

A Baby To Die For

He was stunned, pole-axed. They had actually turned him down. The biggest sale in his career, and he lost it! Slipped through his fingers like mercury off a sheet of glass. He had no choice now but to call them back and make up some sort of story about the mother backing off her demands or the other couple reconsidering or something. Anything! He had to think. What could he do now? It was a disaster. The power to negotiate a price for the baby had shifted to the Flowers.

Infants, even a special one like this, have a decaying shelf life. The time it would take him to put together another deal could be months! And the chances were great that he would have to go through another lawyer, and that would mean splitting fees. Damn it, this was going to be a disaster, no matter how he did it. And then there was Karen.

Oh, God. What if it takes months to find another buyer, and Karen decides to keep the baby?

A few months was certainly enough time for her to bond with the child, and he knew how devastated she was giving up her first child.

"Shit!" Max said out loud, still holding the phone receiver.

Just then Max's other line rang. It was probably Jake and of all the people on earth, the last one he wanted to talk to was Jake. But maybe it was Porter.

He punched the flashing button, "Max Garfield," he said.

"Max, it's Ken Flower."

Max closed his eyes and said a little prayer to the profit gods, then, "Yes, Ken. I was just on the other line with the gentleman who is—with the other buyer, you know—for the baby."

Max's heart was pounding. Maybe the money wasn't lost after all.

"Max, you were right. As soon as I told her the deal was officially off—Christ, she just dissolved into tears. I've never seen her fall apart like this. She wants that baby. We'll commit now for sure, okay? It's final. You have my word on it."

"But, Ken, the other man is on the line and—" Max said, out of pure bargaining reflex.

"Fuck the other man, Max! This is our baby, shut this goddamn nonsense down now!" Ken screamed.

Max Garfield smiled. Well, that was that! Under any other circumstances, he would have tried for a few thousand more, but he sensed he'd pushed this one about as far as it could be pushed.

That one big jump from $75,000 to an even $100,000 was huge, and he had taken a big risk doing it. But he got away with the strategy, at least this time. In the future, he would take the people to the top of the financial mountain a little more slowly. That was for sure.

"Yes, Ken, you're right. I'm glad you called in time. After what you told me before, I was about to commit to the other couple. A minute more and I would have given this man my word—and you know, once I do that—well, let's just say I'm really glad you changed your minds. I think you and Mary are making a wise move. You'll be hearing from me very shortly. The girl is about to have your baby any day now. I'll get back to you with the information about the hospital, when and where to be for the pickup and, of course, there's the final cash payment."

"We can't wait to get the word, Max. This is very, very exciting," Ken said, slowly nesting the receiver.

Chapter 52

Karen instantly recognized it, even though the last time she felt the pain was almost a dozen years ago. Experiencing labor pain for the first time, according to many who have, is like other firsts: love, sex, funerals, and broken bones. One tends never to forget them.

Karen had stopped by the office to see Max. She was walking past the door to his office when the first little jab hit her. She grimaced.

Damn, these things usually come in the middle of the night.

She would call Tuck and tell him the good news.

Just then, Max's head poked out from his office.

"Hey, you're supposed to be staying at home," Max said, as he stepped out into the hallway. Then after a second look, he approached her, "Are you okay? You look pale. You really should be home."

"I had a few things that needed—Ow!"

Karen couldn't help grabbing at the edge of Isabel's desk for support and clutching at her stomach.

An alarm went off in Max's head, and he ran around the desk and grabbed Karen's arm. "Shit, you're not going into labor, are you?"

"I think so," she said. Moments later another stab of pain forced a guttural groan from Karen.

"Oh, my God, you are," Max said. "Isabel, call and have them bring the car! Tell them to be quick, it's an emergency. And call Jake. Have him meet us at the hospital. He knows where it is. Let's get you to a couch. Come into my office." Max, holding her by the arm, led her forward to the couch in his office.

She was going into labor, all right. But her water hadn't broken yet, and she felt no panic or nervousness. This was the event she had been so patiently waiting for and she was very happy.

"Max, honestly, I'm not going to have the baby this minute. The pain stopped. We'll have plenty of time to get to the hospital. Really."

"They're bringing the car up, so we should start down now. It will be at the ramp entrance. Think you can navigate the elevators if I help you?"

"Yes, Max, really. I'm just fine. I feel good. It's going to be an easy delivery. I can feel it. I'm very relaxed."

"Good, good. I'll call Dr. Ubell and have him meet us at the hospital."

"Now, let's get your coat and get you down to meet that car," Max said.

"Uh, fine, Max, but let me go to the bathroom. I've got to pee. It won't take a minute. Believe me, the baby won't drop out. I'll keep my knees together," Karen said, laughing.

With Max's help Karen struggled up off the couch trying not to show just how much discomfort she was really experiencing. She was starting to have difficulty thinking. The pain had stopped for now, but there was little time to waste. And she needed to quickly find a phone and let Tuck know. He couldn't be with her, but she wanted him to know.

Chapter 53

A New York City hospital

Five hours later, in a small private hospital at 106th Street and Fifth Avenue, Karen delivered a healthy, eight-pound boy.

The hospital catered to an exclusive clientele: corporate hotshots and coupon clippers and, of course, Max Garfield. It was an excellent facility and the staff seemed to know Max quite well. Few questions were asked when she checked in, and Karen could only presume that Max had taken care of the insurance or, at least, arranged to be billed in some other way. It was as simple as that. Obviously, this was a facility that had delivered many of the babies Max sold for adoption.

As for Tuck, Karen managed to get a call in to him while Max was taking care of the hospital admission, and naturally, he longed to be with her. He couldn't help thinking about Ellen and the restroom where she died. He fantasized about rushing into the hospital and taking Karen and the baby. He had to force himself to keep his mind focused on the objective, and why it was worth all the trouble they had gone through. So Tuck focused on missing Karen and looked forward to meeting his new baby.

Obviously, visiting the hospital was out of the question. Even phone calls to speak with Karen had been discussed and ruled out. Max was just too much at home in the tiny private hospital at 106th Street. The monitoring of Karen's calls was not out of the realm of possibility. This was no time to have Max become suspicious. Everything was going according to plan, and they were just too close to make any foolish mistakes.

Naturally, Max called Ken and Mary as soon as Karen was giving birth and then followed up after the delivery. In turn, they were able to pass the salient points to Tuck.

"It's healthy and it's a boy."

The adoptive parents were not permitted to see the baby. Their introduction would be made when they came to pick up their son. With an adoption, Max had carefully explained, it was very important that the adoptive family never meets or even sees the birth mother. Ever. All the adoption papers would eventually be sealed.

But the Flowers, along with Tuck and Karen, did derive some small satisfaction knowing that Max would probably have a hemorrhage if he even suspected that they'd all had dinner together less than a week before the delivery.

The charade was moving along on plan.

Max visited his sister's flower-filled room every day and dutifully reported back to Ken and Mary. He even brought them a Polaroid photo of the baby, which he said would be ready to be picked up and taken home in two or three days. He kept pointing out to Ken and Mary how he looked so much like them. He was serious, of course, and really believed what he was saying. They found it difficult not to laugh in his face. But Max was totally caught up in the process and called every day to report up-to-the-minute progress of things like feeding, weight gains, and the general health of the mother and child.

He also gave detailed instructions for the delivery of the remaining purchase price. Since the Flowers had already given Max certified checks in the amount of $20,000, as far as anyone was concerned—the courts and the IRS included—that was the licit payment for the baby.

The balance of $80,000 in cash would be handed over in exchange for the baby when it was handed into the arms of Ken and Mary Flower, bringing to an end that particular phase of the plan.

After that, there was little to do but wait for the next step—an appearance in court for the adoption's final decree. And where, if all went well, Max and the Flowers would swear to the details of the adoption, including its "total" cost of $20,000, thereby, officially committing perjury. After that, they would have to wait to see if he declared his windfall to the IRS. They wouldn't have to wait long since the calendar year was nearly over.

Their collective opinion: Fat chance he would ever declare the income to the IRS!

Chapter 54

Sunday dawned cold and turned colder still every minute. By seven o'clock the thermometer stood several notches below zero and the wind chill took it down another few painful degrees. The detritus-strewn streets were weekend deserted. This early on a weekend morning, New York does not bustle. An occasional blue-and-white police car crisscrossed, like a shoelace, from the East River to the Fifth Avenue border of Central Park and then worked its way back again.

Most honest working folks were still asleep or getting ready to attend church. Either way, Sunday represented a well-earned truce after a hectic New York week.

Tuck drove with Ken and Mary from the West Side across 110th Street, then south on Fifth Avenue to 106th Street, and onto the square of macadam that served as the hospital's parking lot. The open area was practically empty, save for two cars with MD license plates and now his red Volvo. A cold wind churned up tiny, frantic dirt devils that skipped across the parking lot's surface. Ken, Mary, and Tuck got out of the warm car to stand hunched and shivering.

A Baby To Die For

They had debated whether or not to have Tuck come along. But it made no difference now. Ken would simply introduce him as a close friend.

Ken had the bulging, blue Pan Am flight bag slung over his shoulder. It was filled with $80,000 in sixteen banded packs, each with fifty used one-hundred-dollar bills. Getting the money in cash was easier said than done. Luckily, Tuck was able to call in a favor from Ellen's old boss at the accounting firm, who was able to use his banking connections to get the cash in the form it was needed.

Tuck had his service pistol in its holster, comfortably resting under his arm beneath his heavy coat. He felt foolish bringing it, but habit prevailed. The three of them tensed against the biting cold as they walked to the side of the building and stood in its lee, where, absent the wind, it did seem less cold.

"Shit, here they come!" Tuck suddenly tensed and motioned with a move of his head toward the hospital's side door.

Two people emerged and walked toward them: Max Garfield clutching a cocoon of baby blue blankets, like a soldier holds a rifle at port arms, and next to him was Porter Gibbs, smiling.

It was the first time Tuck had ever laid eyes on the lawyer, and he marveled at how unremarkable looking was this object of his intense scorn.

Ken Flower stamped his feet and made applauding movements, trying to keep his hands warm.

"I feel like Rumpelstiltskin come to get the baby," he said, between chattering teeth.

A Baby To Die For

"I think you mean Rapunzel?" Tuck said, hoping the small talk would calm his nerves.

"No, Rapunzel is the one who let down her hair," Mary said, shivering, as much from nerves as the freezing temperature.

"Yeah, well, get ready guys—here he comes. My baby. I hope they have enough blankets around him," Tuck muttered, his stomach churning with a vertiginous mixture of fear, pride, and frantic anticipation.

Max and Porter were not yet in earshot.

Just then, a beat-up, four-door, black Buick rocketed into the parking lot, kicking up debris, as Max's brother, Jake, navigated the big sedan, sliding it expertly into the space next to the red Volvo. Obviously, Jake had taken in too many Clint Eastwood movies.

Max was pleased to see Jake had taken the interest to show up, albeit late. There may be hope for him yet, Max thought.

Porter's gloved hand tugged her mink more tightly against the wind. It only took Porter a moment to place Tuck as the man she'd glimpsed briefly in front of Sarah LaFrance's house on Rainbow Drive. She never forgot a handsome face.

Tuck instantly recognized Porter and could only pray she'd forgotten their eye-to-eye contact in Florida. But he really had no cause for alarm, since the last thing in the world she intended was to say or do anything that would screw up this adoption. She was just along for the ride, nothing more, and was enjoying her front-row seat at Max's financial and professional execution. The only thing missing was a priest and a final meal.

A Baby To Die For

Now, the five of them stood face-to-face, with the sixth, Jake, sidling up slowly from the parked Buick.

"And here is your lovely new baby boy, as promised," Max pronounced, in a stage whisper, to a broadly smiling Mary and Ken Flower. "And I might add, the little angel is sound asleep. I personally made sure the mother was released and into a cab just minutes ago," Max said. "She completed and signed all the necessary paperwork, and it's here in this envelope. You can examine it at your leisure. I'm sure you'll find everything in order."

It was all Tuck could do to keep from grabbing his baby. It took all his control to keep his emotions in check, his fists clenched so tight, he was sure his fingernails would cut into his palms and draw blood.

Ken slipped the airline bag containing the $80,000 from his shoulder. Mary reached out and gingerly took the baby from Max's arms. In exchange, Ken handed the bag to Max.

"The cash Max, as promised, $80,000 in circulated bills," Ken said, rather loudly, reflexively checking the tiny microphone that barely peeked from the top pocket of his heavy overcoat, his heart pounding.

Meanwhile, Mary Flower was holding the baby, while Ken hovered over them, genuine tears streaming down both their faces. They were totally caught up in the charade and greatly moved by the beautiful child that she held in her arms. It was taking some effort for the couple to remember that it wasn't actually their own.

"By the way, Max," Ken said, turning to Tuck, "this is my friend, Tuck Handler. He's going to drive us home."

A Baby To Die For

Tuck nodded curtly to Max. He wanted to study this man. He looked so ordinary: just a medium-size, slightly overweight lawyer. Somehow, he was having trouble feeling an appropriate degree of hate or rage or even a decent level of fury toward this man. He just wanted his baby and his wife—to hold them, kiss them and be a family. Soon he would be able to, and Max Garfield could get the punishment he deserved and go to hell, where he belonged.

Out of the corner of his eye, Tuck noticed a cab on Fifth Avenue glide slowly to the entrance of the parking lot and stop. Deep in the backseat, almost out of sight, was Karen, not daring to lose sight of her child.

Hurry, let's get this over with already, and get the hell out of here.

Jake glanced at the cab but obviously thought nothing of it, then drifted closer to his brother. He was hunched up inside his old, leather, Air Force flight jacket. His face was flushed from the bitter cold. An unlit cigar was clamped in his mouth. The engine of his automobile wasn't audible from where they stood, however, billows of smoke from the exhaust were visual proof that it was still running.

Max, with Jake so close, felt obliged to make an introduction.

"This is my brother, Jake, everybody."

Jake nodded and moved closer, toward the warmth of the other bodies. Tuck was now close enough to see the man's black pupils were dilated to the size of dimes.

The guy is totally whacked out.

Jake suddenly cocked his head to one side. "Hey! What's that?" he said, loudly.

A Baby To Die For

Five people turned toward him as his words cut the cold air, startled at the ferocious tone of the seemingly nonsense question.

"What's what, Jake? What are you talking about?" Max asked, confused and slightly irritated by the interruption.

With his hands, Jake motioned for silence. The six adults automatically froze in a wind-whipped tableau, the only sound being the faint wail of a far-off ambulance headed farther downtown.

And then, in horror, Ken realized the sound Jake heard was his damned tape recorder growling. He couldn't possibly reach the controls under all the clothing. Shit! Beads of sweat broke out across his half-frozen face.

Jake, using his ears like a hound dog uses its nose, inched around the group, then closer to Ken. Suddenly, his hand whipped out toward Ken's coat and grabbed the tiny microphone. A length of cord followed as Jake pulled violently at the wire.

Tuck, from instinct, unbuttoned his outer coat then the button on his sport coat. His clothing flapped in the wind, but he felt no chill.

"It's a fucking microphone!" Jake screamed. "This prick is wired, Max. This goddamn fucker is wired for sound. Holy shit!" Jake bellowed, as he spun around, looking in all directions for the danger he was sensing, knowing damned well that nothing good is ever at the other end of a wire.

And as he spun, Jake clawed into the pocket of his flight jacket. The hand emerged with a knife handle that, with a flick of his wrist, suddenly sprouted six inches of ugly blade.

A Baby To Die For

It happened so fast. Jake's hand coming out with the knife, Tuck's hand grabbing under his coat for his pistol, everyone else just standing there staring, frozen.

At the sight of Tuck's gun, Jake's already fragile mind simply blew away. He stupidly lunged at the ex-cop.

In an instant, Tuck realized the baby was only an arm's length away. He had no room to maneuver or to do anything but shoot. He aimed low.

The sound of the shot slammed back and forth between the buildings. The brittle, frozen air amplified the single shot into an explosive cannon roar.

The baby wailed out of its deep sleep.

Jake, leg shot, dropped to a knee, teeth clenched, and face contorted at the excruciating pain in his leg. His sanity oozed out in a primitive scream as blood colored the macadam.

Max, startled at first, was finally able to lunge to his brother's side, but in an instant, Jake hauled himself upright and spun Max around, pushing him violently into Tuck. In the next instant, he grabbed the bundled child from Mary's arms.

Tuck brushed Max aside but froze as he saw that Jake had his baby.

"Max, damn it! Get over here," Jake shouted. "Get your ass over to the car, and let's get out of here."

"No! You're crazy, Jake. Give back the baby. Don't do anything stupid. Where are you going?" Max's voice, high-pitched with fear, echoed off the buildings.

"Do what he says, damn you!" Tuck shouted, and pushed Max toward his brother. "He'll hurt the baby! Do what he says!"

A Baby To Die For

Tuck, Ken, and Mary stood helplessly as Jake pushed his protesting brother into his car and slipped behind the wheel, putting the baby on the seat, then accelerated hard, fish-tailing the Buick out of the parking lot. The big sedan took the left turn onto Fifth Avenue and shot downtown on the wide, nearly deserted thoroughfare.

Karen, frantic from the scene she had just witnessed, quickly left the cab and, walking as fast as her sore body would allow, headed toward the red Volvo. Tuck embraced her, kissed her, and hugged her to him.

"The baby, my baby..." was all she could sob.

"Get in," Tuck snapped at Ken and Mary.

The doors slammed, and the old Volvo engine took a few seconds in an attempt to turn over in the bitter cold.

The baby lay screaming on the seat between the two brothers. Jake, wild-eyed, pushed the Buick hard down Fifth Avenue. He pounded his fist against the steering wheel with uncontrolled frustration. Searing pain shot through his leg like fire.

"He was wearing a goddamned wire, You dumb bastard," he shouted at his brother. "The fucker shot my leg. I'll kill him, I swear to Christ, I'll kill the son-of-a-bitch!"

"Jake, please! Stop the car! What are you doing, for God's sake? He shot you because you pulled a knife, you asshole. Stop the car, Jake! Please."

The baby was screaming, a loud, red-in-the-face, high frequency, glass-shattering infant's wail. Max carefully picked up the bundle of blankets that held the baby and cradled it tenderly to his chest.

Jake snaked past the few cars that were moving down Fifth Avenue, his dangerous maneuvers were followed by honking horns. Joggers, braving the early morning cold, picked their way along the cobblestone sidewalk next to Central Park. One or two glanced up as the Buick sped by. Max, in a daze, looked over at the runners, seeing them, and at the same time, not seeing them.

At Forty-fourth Street, Jake nosed the car hard into a left turn, and Max was thrown against the passenger side door. As the Buick fish-tailed around the corner, Max, glancing back, thought he saw a speck of red behind them, far up Fifth Avenue.

"Jake—the red car—they're following us. Stop, please! Let me get out with the baby. Let me give them the baby. Jake! Damn it, this is kidnapping. Why are you doing this?" he screamed.

A moment later, on the Vanderbilt side of the Pan Am Building, Jake skidded the car to a stop, jumped out, and ran around to the passenger side. He yanked the door open, and grabbing his brother by the collar of his overcoat, dragged him out of the car. Max, still clutching the baby, was petrified, confused, not knowing what his insane brother would do next, terrified of what he *might* do next.

"Come on, move it, Max. Get your ass in gear. I don't want to bleed to death here."

The lobby of the building was deserted. The sleepy guard immediately recognized the brothers and scarcely looked up from behind the high, semicircle console that served as his office. The Sunday comics took up most of his attention. They headed for the elevators.

Arriving at their floor, high in the building, Jake shoved his brother out of the elevator ahead of him and down the hall toward Max's office.

"Unlock the door," Jake snapped.

"Jake—I'm begging you—"

Jake's hand shot out, palm open, and caught Max hard. His head snapped forward and hit the doorframe. He managed to hold onto the baby, but a line of blood appeared along the fresh opening in the lawyer's forehead.

Max's mouth started to form an outraged objection, but he thought better of it and, swallowing the words, fumbled with an unsteady free hand for his keys.

Jake quickly retrieved the small chrome pistol in Max's desk drawer just where he remembered Max kept it. He grabbed a towel out of Max's private bathroom, ripped off a long strip, and used it to tie the rest of towel tightly around his leg. The blood flow slowed a bit. At least, the shot hadn't hit the femoral artery.

In a moment, they were back out in the deserted hall, moving toward the bank of elevators.

Jake, his gun in hand, pushed Max toward the elevators, *heading where?* Max had no idea.

"Your leg, Jake. The blood—you're losing blood. Where are we going? Let me get you to a doctor—or a hospital. You need help."

"Max, just shut the fuck up and keep walking."

Suddenly, the center door of the three elevators slid open, and Tuck, crouching low, pistol in hand, was framed in the opening. Karen, Ken, and Mary were pressed up against the interior of the car, horrified.

Jake immediately tensed at the sound of the opening door and, seeing Tuck, squeezed off a wild shot. It imbedded in the elevator door as it began to close.

But before it did, Tuck fired, and the bullet tore through the flesh on Jake's forearm.

Karen was screaming, but the elevator door hissed shut, "Don't hurt my baby, *plea*—" and then it closed, and there was nothing but a muffled silence.

Max was crazed and frantic. His brother kicked and shoved him farther back down the hall past Max's office. Jake tried several doors, but they were locked. He randomly picked one and shot into the lock, and kicked opened the heavy door.

"We'll hide in here," Jake screamed at his brother, pushing him through the door.

Trying to shield the baby, Max did as he was told. Once inside, Jake struggled with a heavy reception desk, pushing it in front of the broken door. Then he shoved several more pieces of furniture behind the desk until the entry was heavily barricaded.

Jake was obviously in shock, but moving. His wounds, not yet fatal, were bleeding heavily. He grabbed scissors from the desk and cut two long swatches from one of the baby's blankets. He removed the blood-soaked towel from around his leg, then showed Max how to use the strips of blanket to tie tourniquets, a new one on his leg and one on his arm.

Max set the screaming baby on the desk and tended as best he could to his brother's gunshot wounds.

A Baby To Die For

The office Jake broke into belonged to a representative's showroom for companies selling outdoor camping, climbing gear, and backpacking equipment. It was a large, loft-like space. Basic office equipment and a few desks stood off to the side, obviously for use by the salespeople. The remainder of the room was jammed with the colorful gear.

At the far end of the office, opposite the door that Jake had barricaded, was a large picture window.

Nylon fabric backpacks hung all along one of the walls—big packs in various colors with multiple pockets, aluminum frames, and sturdy straps—each stuffed to appear fully packed.

Several tents in various sizes were erected and, along with other assorted gear, arranged in campsite dioramas, complete with mannequins dressed in camping gear.

Tuck, Ken, Mary, and Karen returned to the hallway, cautiously exited the elevator and followed the trail of Jake's blood to the office he'd broken into. One push and they realized it was barricaded. They quickly searched for something they could use to break down the door. At each end of the long hallway, they spotted large, heavy fire extinguishers.

Tuck yelled to Mary, instructing her to go to the lobby and have the guard call the police.

Inside the office Jake was still seeping blood, his strength clearly slipping away, began babbling, and Max quickly realized his brother was hallucinating, convinced he was back at his forward base in Vietnam. Suddenly loud pounding started, coming from Tuck and Ken as they attempted to smash the outer door using the fire extinguishers. Jake heard the sounds and thought they were bombs, their muffled explosions and heavy vibrations getting closer.

"I've been under attack like this before," Jake screamed, his mind wildly distorted. "The best thing to do is get up in the air, above it all. The bombs can't get us up there. But where's the pilot? The fucking pilot is late. Nothing worse than a raw butter bar lieutenant!"

Max didn't know what to say. His brother was going insane in front of his eyes and there was nothing he could do about it.

The violent pounding, pushing, and bashing of the barricaded door were to Jake's ears getting much too close for comfort.

Tuck was frantic. His baby was inside—his baby with two madmen.

Max, screaming now, tried to talk sense into his senseless brother. Finally, Jake, unable to bear the whining any longer, whipped the gun across Max's face.

"Shut up, you goddamn fag, and get the plane ready."

Silent, bleeding, and confused, Max moved into a corner with the child in his arms. His terror had reached a new and higher level. His brother, he now saw, was gone. All that remained was a maniac who would kill him and the baby if necessary. Jake was beyond help. There was no choice, Max had to help Tuck get into the showroom. It was, he realized, his only chance, the infant's only chance.

Jake began to shout at Max again, talking incoherently about Vietnam and the plane he flew in as a gunner. He started referring to Max as the fag lieutenant pilot.

A Baby To Die For

Max tried to reason with Jake.

"I'm not the pilot, Jake. I'm your brother. Look at me. It's me, your brother, Max. Stop with the lieutenant nonsense. You need help, Jake. Please, let me open the door," Max said, and started toward the desks that blocked his escape.

"Stop, you coward fucking pimp. You're not running out on me. We're gonna fly out of this mess. You're gonna get your ass up in that plane, mister. You're an officer, you shithead, so act like one—now move!"

"Jake, it's your last chance, stop it—give the baby back—let me just give them the baby. You don't want to hurt the little baby, do you? Please, Jake."

But Jake no longer heard Max. He was back over North Vietnam, and he was talking to the pilot over the imaginary intercom like a child playing war.

"*Gunner to pilot, gunner to pilot. Lieutenant, we're hit. I'm bleedin' like a stuck pig back here. Left engine is out,*" Jake shouted, his hand pressing his neck to activate his imaginary throat microphone.

"For Christ's sake, we're not in a plane, Jake! We're not hit! We're in the fucking Pan Am building!" Max screamed at his brother.

"Don't sweat it, Lieutenant, we'll get out," Jake said, confidently. "I'll take care of everything. Ol' Jake is coming up with the chutes," he said, as he limped over to the wall and pulled two large backpacks off the display.

He threw one to Max. Max just sat there staring at the big, paper-stuffed pack in his lap next to the baby, not comprehending what Jake meant for him to do. The

A Baby To Die For

screams of the baby were deafening. The pounding on the door was intensifying. Sounds of the wood finally starting to splinter were lost on Jake and Max.

"Put that fucking chute on, man. It's gonna save your life—*sir!*" Jake shouted, sarcastically.

"Please. Jake, you're sick. This is madness! Please—" Max pleaded weakly.

Tuck was now making some headway on the thick, barricaded door. He had succeeded in splintering some of the wood around the hinges with a few shots from his pistol. He and Ken now both pushed at it with their shoulders.

Jake limped to the blocked door and wrestled a heavy file and some other pieces of furniture on top of the desk.

He limped back to where his brother sat slumped, the baby in his arms, and speaking more gently to a terrified Max, said, "We're gonna get out of this mess, Lieutenant. You're gonna be okay. I'm gonna save you. Gonna get you a shiny new airplane. It's easy as shittin' in a hole. You just count to ten and pull the D-ring. It'll be okay, you'll see. Don't be a damned fucking pussy!"

Max could hardly breathe. His brother had scared him before. He'd seen him close to the edge. But now, Jake was maniacal and totally out of control. Max started to shout to Tuck, begging him to help, to save him, to save the baby.

"Stop it, Lieutenant!" Jake screamed, slapping Max again, hard, and thinking his superior a fool and a coward. "Be a fucking man! Stop whimpering like an asshole!"

Jake grabbed the baby from Max and laid it aside,

shrugging himself into one of the backpacks. Then he began to wrestle his brother into the other one.

The screams of the baby and the sounds of Tuck splintering the door piece by piece mixed with the sobs of the terrified lawyer, as Jake pushed and prodded Max into the harness of the bright red backpack.

Jake checked the straps and harness, pulling Max to his feet in the process. Satisfied that his "chute" was on properly, Jake grabbed an ice ax off the display and, using its pointed end, struck the ax into the center of the large picture window. The entire huge pane turned into a pebble-like spider web of cracks radiating from the point of Jake's blow. He smashed at the pane several more times until he was finally able, with the help of a chair, to clear the window of glass.

The showroom was near the top of the forty-nine-floor building, and the sound of the wind roared past the smashed window, and the cacophonous roar seemed only to heighten Jake's madness and Max's sheer terror.

The Manhattan skyline spread out beyond and below them. The very same view, Max realized through terrified eyes, that he viewed from his own office window.

Why can't I be back there? Why was this happening?

In total desperation, Max took one last lunge and ran to the barricaded door, trying to drag away the heavy furniture blocking it. But Jake, even wounded, was too quick, too strong, and he pulled and dragged the now-whimpering lawyer to the window, soothing him, reassuring him that the jump would be fine.

Jake carefully placed the baby back into Max's arms.

A Baby To Die For

"Hold it tight, Lieutenant, and we'll be okay. The engine's smoking now. We gotta jump before this fucker blows us to shit and gone."

Now with the certain knowledge that Jake was going to push him out the window, Max lost control of his bladder, and the bitter cold air rushing into the room caused steam to rise from his urine-soaked pants.

"Don't be scared, I've done it before, Sir. Once the chute opens, you'll love it. Just hang loose, Lieutenant— and hold onto that kid. You'll get a medal for this one."

Max desperately grabbed at the edges of the window with his free hand. The sharp edges of its frame and the remains of jagged glass ripped and tore into his hand. He gagged and retched from the certain knowledge that he was about to die.

With a explosive crash, the door broke off its hinges. Tuck and Ken pushed and forced the desks far enough into the room to squeeze through.

Tuck sprawled forward onto the floor and froze in horror as the bizarre scene snapped into focus.

"Oh, God," he moaned.

Jake and Max, still holding the baby, were silhouetted in a bizarre tableau against the skyline of downtown New York. Both men were strapped haphazardly into large backpacks. The wind had sucked the drapes out the window, and they waved and snapped frantically in the swirling air. The brothers' clothing was flapping wildly in all directions. The screams of the baby clutched in Max's arms combined with the harsh sound of wind rushing past the broken window.

A Baby To Die For

Max, now deeply in shock, pleaded and sobbed, and he would have collapsed if not for being held upright by the insane and bleeding Jake.

Tuck reflexively crouched to fire, screaming, "Jake!"

Max, seeing Tuck was going to shoot, threw the baby into the room just as Tuck's finger closed over the trigger.

Jake, mortally hit, used his last breath of life to hurl Max—his lieutenant—to what he thought was safety, then dying from the gunshot, followed him into the void.

Max's screams were lost in the sound of drapes whipped in the frigid wind around the gutted frame and snapping like colorful bunting inches from the safely swaddled, albeit screaming baby.

Chapter 55

EPILOGUE

The red Volvo, fully serviced, washed, and fitted with new tires, headed west on Interstate 80, a highway that lays across America like a limp 2,900-mile-long strand of fettuccini, running from Teaneck, New Jersey, to San Francisco, California.

The car's front windows were open wide, and the air blowing in from each side converged between Karen and Tuck, swirling around a balled-up Big Mac wrapper and causing it to gently levitate and hang suspended on the merged air currents.

They laughed, watching the change in the delicate balance as the air lifted the paper when Tuck accelerated and allowed it to drop as he slowed. They joked how great it would be if it continued all the way to California—maybe stay with them forever—a funny, anomalous mascot to accompany their new life.

Karen opened a large thermos and poured iced coffee into two cups. Then, reacting to a small noise, she shifted serving gears and removed a bottle from the cooler at her feet. She twisted and leaned over into the back of the car to feed Sidney, their beautiful, three-month-old son.

Much had transpired after the deaths of Max and Jake Garfield. The press had an orgy with the story. The media was smeared with the sensational details like blood after a grisly axe murder.

Ironically, it was Max who saved the baby's life, assigning his last few seconds of conscious thought to the welfare of someone other than Max Garfield. Totally out of character.

His brother Jake's passing went essentially unnoticed. He had no real friends, since at his best his erratic behavior was more than enough to alienate anyone who came within his orbit. In the end, Max may have been his only true ally.

Max—to no one's surprise—died a very rich man. A carefully drafted will directed all his wealth to be left to his sister, Karen. Jake was awarded a large trust to be controlled by Karen, which, because of Jake's death, reverted to her. The keys for opening Max's four safe deposit boxes had been given to Karen by his accountant, nevertheless, as soon as the story of the lawyer's involvement in black market adoption was made public, the IRS had frozen every asset that they could lay their hands on. Obviously, there was going to be one hell of an investigation.

A raft of hungry lawyers had already reached out to many of the parents who had adopted through Max and encouraged them to sue his estate. For reasons that ran the gamut from outright fear of losing their child to total disinterest, almost none of the adoptive parents wanted anything to do with legal action of any kind.

Karen made no move to fight any of the threatened litigation. She really didn't care. Max's life insurance alone had provided enough money for her and Tuck to lead a very comfortable, albeit not ostentatious, life.

As for the Flowers, Mary finished her internship and joined a surgical practice in New York City, and Ken was working with his agent, Gene Rubin, to produce the movie property, which had the working title of *A Baby to Die For*. They had every expectation it would shortly be green-lighted by a major studio.

Ironically, when the brothers took the baby from the hospital parking lot, the $80,000 in cash was left behind so Pauline, as promised, was paid back the $25,000 loan immediately. The only money Max actually got from them was the $20,000 check.

Tuck experienced a frisson of nostalgia when Pauline told him she'd met a man—"a wonderful fella," she had called him. "And *not* a lawyer," she had taken pains to add. They planned on getting married right away.

As for the adoption? there never was one. Nor was one needed. Karen had given birth to little Sidney and had the certificate of birth to prove it. Other than the terrifying time when Max and Jake kidnapped the boy, it was Karen and Tuck's baby, and that was really that.

Just outside Des Moines, Iowa, Tuck and Karen checked into a Holiday Inn, strapped the little plastic portable bassinet onto a chair in the dining room of the coffee shop, and proceeded to have a quiet family dinner. Little Sidney sucked contentedly on his bottle while Karen and Tuck cleared the road dust from their throats with a local beer.

Earlier that same day, moving east, at thirty-five thousand feet through an atmospheric groove as well traveled as Interstate 80, was a Boeing 747. On board drinking champagne, Porter Gibbs and her newest employee, lawyer Rick Shelby, were celebrating in spite of a disappointing meeting in San Francisco with Kevin Tyler.

After the death of Max Garfield, Kevin Tyler realized he wanted nothing more to do with the baby business— or Porter, for that matter. He'd only lent his name to Tuck's and Karen's plan for the thrill it had given him. He was now living with Silvia Wilson and running the Edmond Calendar Library of Life for its original purpose: to be the genetic benchmark for the future security of the species. Although his intentions were altruistic, there had been some unintended consequences from the publicity generated by Ken Flower's story. Tyler, having been named prominently in the subsequent media firestorm, was flooded with requests, both from potential adoptive parents as well as some very famous people, including several Nobel laureates, each wanting their "essence" filed away, along with the great and near great. Ego, it seemed, had few boundaries.

Porter had been disappointed by Tyler's decision but not deterred and quickly realized she no more needed the sperm bank than she needed Max Garfield. She and Rick

A Baby To Die For

Shelby were headed back to New York and would pick up the network just about where Max had left off.

Even with the tsunami of publicity—more likely, *because* of it—the black market, far from dying along with Max, would survive, becoming larger, stronger, and more profitable than ever. All Porter required were a pregnant girl, a file folder, and someone wanting a child.

Max's death had taught her a valuable lesson: "special" babies don't have to be special.

Just the suggestion, the mere hint of specialness to a young couple dying for a baby was enough to make them secure in the belief that they were, in fact, getting a special one.

Because, above all, they wanted to believe, *had* to believe, and always would believe.

Photo by J. E. Cohn

ABOUT THE AUTHOR

Mike Slosberg lives with his wife in New York City. Both are theatre-lovers, they feed that passion in New York as well as in London.

CPSIA information can be obtained at www.ICGtesting.com
Printed in the USA
LVOW04s1458010615

440721LV00018B/996/P